The Lost Soldier

DINEY COSTELOE is the author of seventeen novels, several short stories, and many articles and poems. She has three children and seven grandchildren, so when she isn't writing, she's busy with family. She and her husband divide their time between Somerset and West Cork.

Also by Diney Costeloe

The Girl With No Name
The Runaway Family
The Sisters of St Croix
The Throwaway Children

DINEY COSTELOE

The Lost Soldier

HEAD of ZEUS

First published in the UK as *The Ashgrove* in 2004
by Castlehaven Books

This edition first published in 2016 by Head of Zeus Ltd

9 7 5 3 1 2 4 6 8

A catalogue record for this book
is available from the British Library.

ISBN (HB) 9781784972578
ISBN (TPB) 9781784972950
ISBN (E) 9781784972561

Typeset by Adrian McLaughlin

Printed in Germany
by GGP Media GmbH, Pössneck

Head of Zeus Ltd
Clerkenwell House
45–47 Clerkenwell Green
London EC1R 0HT

WWW.HEADOFZEUS.COM

The
Lost
Soldier

The night air was chilly, clinging as a misty drizzle fell steadily. The child clung to her mother's skirt, afraid of the dark, afraid of the night sounds, cold and miserable. She began to whimper, her quiet tears escalating into wails.

At once her mother turned and hushed her with such unaccustomed sharpness that she gulped a rising wail and stuffed one small fist into her mouth, while the other closed more tightly on the rough wool of the skirt.

"Be quiet, like a good girl," hissed her mother again, "and stay here." She tried to move away, but the child's grasp on her skirt held her back.

"Let go," the mother whispered harshly, and with some force uncurled the little girl's fingers from the skirt. She knelt down so her face was level with her daughter's, though neither could see more than the outline of the other in the darkness. "I need you to stay here, pet," she said, more gently. "I'm just going to fetch something. I'll be back in a moment, I promise. Just stand still here. I won't leave you." She leant forward and touched her lips to the child's damp cheek and smoothed her wet hair comfortingly, before moving off into the night.

Terrified, the little girl stood rooted to the spot, her wide eyes staring into the black emptiness where her mother had been. She strained her ears to listen for her mother coming back, but all she could hear was the sound of the rain dripping off the nearby trees and a quiet rustling in the grass near her feet. The hoot of an owl above her startled her into a cry, but she stayed where she was. She was afraid of the dark night and what it might hide, but she was even more afraid that her mother wouldn't find her if she moved. Another sound made her jump, but this time it was her mother creeping through the dark night towards her, carrying something.

"Rosemary, are you there, girl?" came the quiet whisper.

"Here I am, Mam." Her reedy voice cracked with fear and relief.

"Good girl. Stay put."

There were more sounds then, a shovel breaking the earth, grunting and panting as the metal bit into the ground.

"What are you doing, Mam?" whispered the little girl.

"Just be quiet, there's a love," replied her mother softly, "and I'll show you in a minute."

The digging sounds went on for several moments and then the little girl felt her mother's hand on hers. "Come over here." She followed the pull of the hand until she was standing at her mother's side, safely within the circle of her arm. It was still raining, but there was the faintest moonlight breaking through the ragged clouds, and with her night vision now well established, she could see a small hole had been dug in the wet ground. Beside it stood a tiny tree, ready for planting.

"Now, Rosemary," said her mother, "we're going to plant a tree for your dad, just like the other ladies and gentlemen did this afternoon. Remember?"

Rosemary nodded in the darkness. She had seen the group

of grown ups standing round one end of the village green earlier in the day, planting trees.

"Those are for the poor soldiers who didn't come home from the war," her nan had told her as they stood at a distance and watched the ceremony. "Each tree's got a name beside it, see, so that everyone remembers."

"Well, they didn't know to plant one for your dad," murmured her mother, now, "so we're doing it ourselves, just you and me." She reached for the little tree and carefully placed it into the hole she had dug. Holding it steady she whispered, "Push some of the earth back into the hole, Rosy."

The little girl knelt down and pushed some of the wet, muddy earth into the hole. It stuck to her fingers, thick and gluey, and smelt of damp leaves. She didn't like the feel of it and pulled her hands away, holding them out, but instead of wiping them as she would normally have done, her mother ignored them and whispered, "That's it, good girl, just a bit more." Looking across her daughter's head, she scanned the darkness nervously. Reluctantly the child pushed more of the heaped earth in round the tree roots, until her mother said softly, "That'll do." She picked up the spade and quickly filled the rest of the hole, smoothing away the extra earth so that the heap disappeared. Scraping together some leaf mould, she spread it round the base of the tree, so that the new tree was no more conspicuous than the other eight ash saplings that had been planted earlier in the day.

She put down the spade and reached for the big, black handbag, which she had discarded when they'd arrived and pulled from it a small photo frame attached to a wooden spike. Behind the glass, written in neat, black capitals on a piece of card, were the words *FOR THE UNKNOWN SOLDIER*. She put it into her daughter's hands. "The writing

3

on this is for your dad," she explained, "so we'll put it in the ground beside the tree." She placed her hands over the child's and together they pushed the long wooden prong on the base of the frame, into the ground beside the little ash tree's trunk.

"God bless you," she murmured, "we'll never forget you." She pulled her daughter, and his, into her arms, and their tears mingled in the darkness with the falling rain. For a moment they stayed together, kneeling on the wet ground, and then the mother got to her feet. She bent and kissed her daughter's wet cheek. "This is our secret, pet," she said gently. "You mustn't tell anyone about us planting this tree for Dad. It's our secret."

"Not even Nan and Gramp?" asked the little girl. She was not surprised at this prohibition, Mam never talked to her about her dad when Nan or Gramp was there.

"Not even Nan and Gramp," replied her mother. "Only you and me in the whole world will ever know who this tree is for, and who planted it. Promise?"

"Promise," answered the little girl solemnly. "In the whole world...ever!"

The moon sailed out from behind the bank of cloud, and the two hurried away, anxious not to be seen by any curious eyes, but that night the mother went to bed with a quieter mind than she had known for nearly four years.

The ninth tree stood peacefully in the moonlight, an extra tree in a new-made grove of remembrance.

2001

"**O**ver my dead body," Cecily Strong declared roun. "That's the Ashgrove!"

"The Ashgrove?" Mike Bradley, managing director Brigstock Jones the developers, for once in his life was at a loss. "I'm sorry, madam, if you could...I mean of course I..."

"The trees at the end of the green," Cecily said patiently. "You can't fell those trees to make a road! That's the Ashgrove."

"Madam, I do assure you..." Mike Bradley began, wondering who the hell this weird old bird was, and angry at being attacked like that by an old dear who was ninety if she was a day, "that if there was any other..."

"And do you know what the Ashgrove is, my good man?" Cecily continued calmly, as if he hadn't spoken. "No, of course you don't. You haven't a clue."

"Well, it's, um..." began Bradley who indeed hadn't a clue.

Cecily interrupted him again. "It's a memorial," she said. "That's what it is."

All through the meeting there had been shuffling and muttering, even while the main speakers were on their feet, but now you could have heard the proverbial pin drop, all eyes were on Cecily.

"The grove was planted eighty years ago, in 1921," Cecily "as a memorial to those from our village who their king and country in the Great War. For our s who didn't come home. Each tree was planted for a man o died, and one of them was my brother, Will." Cecily's es were fixed firmly on Mike Bradley as she spoke. "I'm ninety-three next June. My brother, Will Strong, was just seventeen when he went, and he was dead before he was eighteen, blown to bits by a shell. All that's left of him now is that tree planted in his memory, all that's left of him and the other boys who went. If the only way you can put your road in, is by cutting down those trees, destroying the memorial to those boys, then I tell you this, Mr Bradley or whoever you are," she glared up at the platform, "you'll do it over my dead body!"

Mike Bradley had been hard at work all evening trying to sell Charlton Ambrose the proposed development of its allotment site, hard at work as the village was divided over the proposed development of the old allotments. When Cecily Strong had finished speaking, the meeting, which had been rumbling ominously all evening, finally erupted. The momentary silence that greeted her words was shattered as everyone started to talk at once. Ignoring the stir she had caused and with great dignity, the old lady grasped her zimmer, walked slowly through the hall and out into the night.

Mike Bradley was on his feet at once, and with the very force of his personality quelled the uproar in the room.

"Ladies and gentlemen," he cried, "ladies and gentlemen, I can assure you that the memory of the war dead will not be dishonoured. My company will, of course, erect a stone monument in their memory, a permanent memorial to their courage and sacrifice."

8

"They've got a permanent memorial now," called out someone angrily, "till you go and cut it down, that is."

The noise erupted again, people calling out, trying to make themselves, and their views about this latest development, heard. Mike Bradley sat down again, his face red with anger, furious that he had been ambushed like this. Why hadn't he been told about these memorial trees? Someone at the office hadn't done his homework properly and whoever that was, his head would roll. Mike Bradley did not like being in situations he could not control.

Access across the village green to the site was critical to the whole project, otherwise he'd never have agreed to replace this tatty village hall as an essential part of the deal. Bradley glowered round the room, but he was forgotten in the uproar.

It was quite clear to Paula Sharp, chair of the parish council, that the meeting would go no further this evening and she banged again with her gavel, trying to bring some order.

"Ladies and gentlemen, Miss Strong has brought up a matter which will concern several families in the village, and I am sure must be discussed in some other forum than this. I thank Mr Bradley for his offer to replace the memorial trees, but clearly we can proceed no further this evening, and so I declare the meeting closed."

Rachel Elliott from the local newspaper, the *Belcaster Chronicle*, had been sent by her editor to cover the meeting. The brief note Drew had left her simply said, *"Public meeting, Charlton Ambrose village hall. 7.30. Proposed housing development."* When she had arrived, it was to find the little village hall humming with expectation and Rachel felt with a tingle that there must be more to this public meeting than she had anticipated.

As the evening had progressed, the split in the village over the proposed "Charlton Ambrose Enhancement Scheme" had polarised into two distinct camps and, despite an occasional voice of reason, feelings were running high.

Rachel had never met Mike Bradley before, but his reputation as a hard-headed business man preceded him and she had watched with interest when he rose to his feet. An impressive man in his late forties with thinning sandy hair and a florid complexion, there was a sharpness in his pale hazel eyes, an underlying ruthlessness, which Rachel recognised had brought him to his present position. She felt those eyes rest on her for a moment, taking in her reason for being there, as she waited, pen poised for him to speak.

Confidently and rather patronisingly, Rachel thought, Mike Bradley explained his planned development of the old allotment patch that he had bought from the parish council. Deftly he fielded questions about the number of starter homes, the size of the other, executive homes and the proposed new village hall. As she made notes on what he said, Rachel had to hand it to him, it was a thoroughly professional performance from a man who knew what he wanted and was determined to get it. He remained calm and unruffled in the face of a fair amount of acrimony from the anti-development lobby, and it wasn't until Cecily Strong dropped her bombshell that Rachel saw him lose his cool. Then the flush of red creeping over his collar and the gleam of anger in his eyes would have warned all the staff in his office to keep their heads down; nor were these signs lost on Rachel. She watched with interest as, entirely forgotten by those talking excitedly around him, Mike Bradley rammed his papers into his briefcase and prepared to make a swift exit. Clearly, all he wanted to do now was to get out of this dreary hall and find out who had cocked things up.

Rachel intercepted him as he stepped off the platform. He scowled at her as she barred his way, but she'd been in her job long enough not to be intimidated by his bully-boy tactics.

"Mr Bradley," she smiled up at him. "I'm Rachel Elliott, from the *Belcaster Chronicle*, and I wondered if I might ask you a few questions..."

He forced his face into the semblance of a smile and said, "Certainly, Miss Elliott, any time. Just give my secretary a call." He reached into his inside pocket and extracted a card, which he handed to Rachel. "I shall look forward to seeing you. Now if you'll excuse me..." He didn't exactly push her out of his way, but as she later told Drew Scott, her editor, "He just barged past me and headed for the door."

She had stowed the card into her pocket and glanced at the platform where Paula Sharp was still deep in conversation with David Andrews, the planning officer. Rachel knew where to find each of them when she wanted to, so she turned back to the body of the hall to talk to one or two of the Charlton Ambrose residents. It was beginning to empty now, but she saw that one of the more vociferous of the "anti" lobby, who had identified himself to the meeting as Peter Davies, was still chatting to a tall man in his early thirties, and she went over to him.

"Excuse me, Mr Davies?"

Peter Davies looked up and said gruffly, "Yes. Who might you be?" He was a short, stout man, probably in his fifties, but looking older, with a round face and untidily cut grey hair hanging over the collar of his old tweed jacket. He scowled at Rachel, the lines round his eyes and mouth indicating that this was an habitual expression, not that he was particularly annoyed with her.

"Rachel Elliott, *Belcaster Chronicle*. I just wondered

how you felt about this proposed development...in principle I mean. I gathered from your comments this evening that you have reservations."

"Reservations!" Peter Davies gave a harsh laugh. "I'll say I have, and what I want to know is how that bloke Mike Bradley's got as far as he has with it. How's he managed to get his hands on our allotments, for a start? How come the parish council can sell them from under us?"

"I imagine because they belonged to the parish council," replied Rachel lightly, "but I shall be asking about that, don't you worry." She smiled at him and said, "Can you tell me any more about those trees? About the Ashgrove...is it called?"

"That's right, the Ashgrove. Well, them was planted after the first war, see. In memory, like. Two of them is for two of my great uncles, Uncle John and Uncle Dan, my grandfather's brothers."

"Are they?" Rachel was fascinated. Peter Davies had made no mention of the trees himself whilst expressing his opposition to the development and, Rachel thought wryly, he probably hadn't given them a thought until Cecily had spoken of them. "So you won't be keen on those trees being cut down."

"I will not," Peter Davies said firmly. "We have to show respect for our dead. Them trees has been there for nigh on eighty years, and no developer," his tongue rolled round the word, "no developer is going to march in here and cut them down."

"How many trees are there?" asked Rachel with interest.

"Eight," answered Peter Davies, "or nine."

"Who are the other ones for...I mean, in memory of?"

Peter Davies shrugged. "I can't remember," he said. "One of them's for old Cecily Strong's brother, that's for sure. You'll have to ask about, though I shouldn't think there's many left what knew any of them now. Except Cecily, of course. Cecily'd probably remember. She's a bit queer in her attic these days, but she does remember stuff from when she were a girl."

"I'll ask her," said Rachel. "Can you tell me where she lives?"

"Yew Tree Cottage, next to the church."

"Thank you very much, Mr Davies, you've been a great help."

She turned to the other man, smiling. "I'm afraid I don't know your name," she said, "but I'd be very interested to hear what you think of the village enhancement scheme."

"Nick Potter," said the man. He held out his hand and his grip was firm. He was tall, well over six foot, with broad shoulders, and as Rachel shook his hand she was aware of a controlled strength. He had a thatch of fair hair, worn a little too long, and his eyes, smiling at Rachel now, were a deep-set blue.

"Mr Potter," she said easily, "I remember, you spoke at the meeting..." her mind raced as she tried to hear again in her head the words that voice had spoken earlier "...about how much of the village green might be lost."

"That's right, I did."

"And how do you feel about the proposed development?"

Nick Potter replied, "I am actually in favour of it, in principle. We do need more housing in the village, especially more affordable homes for young couples, but it needs to be considered carefully, and to be done in the right way."

"And what about the Ashgrove?" asked Rachel.

"Well, I knew nothing about the trees until this evening. I'm a relative newcomer to Charlton Ambrose..."

"Blow-in," muttered Peter Davies, who was still standing beside them.

Nick Potter glanced across at him and grinned. "Yes, Peter, a blow-in. But it is my home nonetheless and I don't want it ruined with over-development, or development badly planned."

"And you think this plan would be over-development?" Rachel asked.

"I'm not sure," Nick Potter replied. "Clearly Brigstock Jones have to build enough houses to make it worth their while at all, especially if they also have to put in the road and build a new village hall. But a housing estate of that size could well change the character of the village, and must be given serious consideration before it's approved. I shall be writing to the planning authority with some questions that I think should be taken into account."

"Including the trees?" asked Rachel quietly.

Nick Potter shrugged: "Well, if I don't, others will. Clearly they are going to be extremely important to some people."

The lights began to go off in the hall and Rachel looked round to find that the three of them were the only ones left and that the caretaker was hovering at the door.

"I think that's a hint we should go," said Nick Potter with a grin.

"I think you're right," agreed Rachel. "Thank you for your time." She handed them each one of her cards and added, "If you think of anything more about all this, please do give me a call."

They left the hall then, the two men heading off together into the darkness of the village, Rachel to her car.

When she got home, Rachel drew the curtains against the cold damp of the night and poured herself a glass of wine before she switched on her computer.

What an evening it turned out to be, she thought. I was expecting a very dull meeting and it was fireworks all the way.

It was exactly such unpredictability that Rachel loved about her job. On the *Belcaster Chronicle*, no day was like another; no day boring. Though many of the jobs were routine, mundane even, Rachel loved talking to people, and learning their perception of the world. Hearing what was important to them, fascinated her. If she had the sniff of a story, she was like a terrier, worrying at it until she had discovered all and made it her own.

"And there is a good story here, I know it," she muttered as she waited for her screen to come up, and looking through her notes she began to consider how she would tackle it.

There were several aspects to be considered, and she soon realised that there was enough here for more than one article. She needed far more information, but if she could get it, she knew the story would continue to run. She certainly needed to talk to Cecily Strong, but there had been no point in chasing out after her this evening.

I need to see her in her own home if I can, Rachel thought. I want her to be at ease when we talk. She's the one who'll know about the Ashgrove and the men it commemorates.

Rachel spent most of that night working at her computer. Her piece on the meeting in Charlton Ambrose was the easy part. She settled for a factual account, offering each side of the "development" argument as it had been presented, before that was, everything had been complicated by the Ashgrove. Of course Cecily's revelation was the high spot of the evening, and Rachel explained the problem posed by the trees, but she decided she wanted to research the Ashgrove and its history in depth before following that part of the story any further. Here was a chance to build a story on her own, to develop it and follow it through. It was a chance she intended to seize. There were plenty of angles that needed following up, and Rachel wanted to get them mapped out in some detail before she put them to Drew Scott.

So, she worked all night, listing the things which had caught her attention, small things needing further exploration; expanding the notes she'd made, both at the meeting and afterwards, when talking to Peter Davies and Nick Potter. Determined to put everything down while it was still fresh in her mind, Rachel finally crawled into bed as the red figures of her clock radio flicked to four-forty-five.

Two

When she arrived at the offices of the *Belcaster Chronicle* next morning, Rachel headed straight for Drew's office, and found the editor behind his desk, a mug of thick black coffee at his elbow and his eyes glued to his computer screen. He glanced up as Rachel came in.

"Morning, Rach. Good meeting?" He grinned. He knew she hadn't particularly wanted to go, but that was tough.

"I've e-mailed it in," she told him, "but I've brought a hard copy for you to look at as well as I want your OK for some investigation." She handed him her copy with the headline:

DISCORD IN CHARLTON AMBROSE

"Some life to it then," he grinned as he glanced through the piece. "Mike Bradley not having it all his own way this time?"

"No," Rachel agreed. "Do you know him?"

Drew laughed. "Oh yes. He's been trying to ride roughshod over people in this town for years. Same last night was it?"

"Pretty much," Rachel agreed, "at first anyway. Then something unexpected came up and he was all red face and bluster."

Drew laughed. "Sounds familiar. What went wrong?"

Rachel outlined briefly the problem of the Ashgrove. "The thing is," she went on, "I'd like to follow up on this one,

Drew. There's more to this than meets the eye. There are two main aspects as I see it. One is the proposed development and the other is the history of the Ashgrove. I want to sound out local feelings on the housing scheme and to interview Mike Bradley about the project. That's one story, but then there's the Ashgrove itself. I think there's a real human interest story about those memorial trees. Perhaps I could discover descendants other than Cecily Strong—she's the one who brought the matter up at the meeting—and Peter Davies who still lives in the village. A bit of investigating. But there's no time for this week's edition."

Drew looked thoughtful. "OK," he said. "It's an interesting enough story. Get as much background on it as you can, and then if it comes up to scratch we'll run it as a spread. Jon can take some pictures." He tapped at his keyboard for a moment or two studying the layout of various pages of the paper, and then nodded. "We'll run your account of the actual meeting this week and if it all stacks up, follow it up with your article next week. Right, get on with it," then, as an elated Rachel turned away, he added, "Don't forget to pick up today's list from Cherry on your way out."

Cherry, in the outer office, handed her a list of jobs Drew wanted covered, the magistrates' court, Belstone St Mary's primary school nativity play, Christmas bazaar at St Joseph's. All pretty run of the mill, but Rachel didn't care. Now she also had something worth getting her teeth into, and she was determined to give it her best shot. She fished Mike Bradley's card out of her bag, rang his secretary and made an appointment to see him at five o'clock that afternoon.

When Rachel came out from the school nativity play, she found there was a missed call on her mobile. Checking her messages she found one from Mike Bradley's secretary cancelling her meeting at five and suggesting another for the same time next day. Rachel was annoyed, but she was also suspicious. What was Mike Bradley up to? Why had he changed his mind about talking to her? Was he trying to avoid her, or was he simply playing for time? She looked at her watch. It was nearly half-past four. Should she, she wondered, go to his office and confront him? After some thought, she decided against it. It would probably be counter-productive. If she antagonised him now, she'd never get anything from him, and she was very interested to hear how the whole deal had been put together. Better, she decided reluctantly, to wait and go when she was invited. Anyway, by then she might well have come up with more questions that she wanted answered.

She thought about Cecily Strong. Perhaps now would be a good time to go and see her. It was worth a try and she was sure the old lady would be extremely interesting to talk to. She picked up her mobile again and after a quick reference to the phone directory which she always carried in the car, she punched in the number for C Strong, Yew Tree Cottage, Charlton Ambrose.

"Yes?" The voice was elderly but firm. "Who is it?"

"Miss Strong?"

"Yes. Who is that?"

"You don't know me, Miss Strong," began Rachel, "but my name is Rachel Elliott. I work for the *Belcaster Chronicle*, you know the local newspaper? I was at the parish meeting last night and I wondered if I could come and have a chat with you."

"With me?" Suspicion crept into the old lady's voice. "Why do you want to talk to me?"

"About the Ashgrove, Miss Strong. I'd love to hear the history of the Ashgrove."

"I don't know you," came the reply. "I don't want to talk about it. Goodbye."

"Please don't ring off," cried Rachel hastily. "Miss Strong? Are you there?"

There was silence the other end of the line, and Rachel, certain that the old lady was still listening, hurried on. "I want to try and save your Ashgrove, Miss Strong. I want to write all about it in my paper, so that everyone will know what is happening, and the trees won't be cut down. May I come and see you? I'll come whenever you say. You could invite a friend to be there with you all the time, if you're worried."

The silence continued for a minute or two and Rachel let it lengthen before she said, "Well, thank you for your time. If you change your mind please ring me at the *Chronicle...* Rachel Elliott."

"Wait." The voice crackled in her ear. "Come this evening. My niece will be here. Come at about six."

"Thank you, Miss Strong. I'll be there then, and look forward to meeting you."

Rachel drove to Charlton Ambrose and parked beside the village hall. It was an old timber building with the paint peeling off and a rusting corrugated iron roof.

It really is past its sell-by date, she thought as she looked at it. They could certainly do with a new village hall.

She got out of the car and, in the cold dusk, walked across the green to the clump of trees at the further end. They were all ash trees, tall and well grown, their leafless branches making a dark tracery against the darkening December sky. They stood, moving restlessly in the winter wind, and as Rachel entered the little grove she felt as if they had closed in round her. She counted them. Eight, Peter Davies had said, or nine. There were nine. Rachel counted them again to be sure.

Definitely nine. She walked over to one of them and rested her hand on its smooth cold bark.

"Who do you belong to, I wonder?" she asked aloud. There was nothing to indicate whom each tree commemorated...or that the place was a memorial at all. She moved from tree to tree until she had rested her hand on each trunk, and thought of all the young, fresh-faced men who had gone so jauntily to war, never to return to their homes here in Charlton Ambrose. Such high hopes they must have had. The adventure of fighting in a war, seeing a bit of the world, before settling down to their humdrum lives here in the country. Rachel thought of the pictures she had seen of the trenches in Flanders, the mud and the squalor, the cold and the rats. She shuddered, and drawing her coat more closely around her, walked out on the far side of the grove where the allotment hedge barred her way. She peered over it, and through the gloom could just make out the strips of tilled ground, bleak with only the odd line of winter cabbages. Small sheds dotted the area and well-trodden paths criss-crossed between the plots. It was quite a large area, but even so, she found it hard to imagine twenty-five houses crammed in there. The right-hand side was edged by a grey stone wall. She couldn't make out what was immediately on the other side, but a little further over was the church, its squat tower faintly illuminated by the lights from the pub across the road. There was no way that the new road could come round that side of the green into the allotments unless it went through the Ashgrove; Rachel could see that. Turning back towards the village, now sprinkled with lighted windows, she realised how dark it had become and headed back to her car. As she passed through the Ashgrove once more she shivered. It was an eerie place to be in alone in the dark.

She still had some time to kill before she could visit Cecily

Strong, and it was too cold to wait in the car, so she went into the pub.

The bar of the King Arthur was very warm, with a huge log fire burning at one end and the cheerfully lit bar at the other. There were only two people already in there, leaning on the bar with their pints in front of them. They looked up as she came in and Rachel immediately recognised one of them as Peter Davies.

"Oh, it's you," he said with a sniff. "What are you back here for then?"

"Hallo, Mr Davies," Rachel said cheerfully. "It's cold, isn't it?" She turned her attention to the barman, a young lad of about twenty. "Half of lager shandy, please." As the lad poured her shandy, Rachel hoisted herself up on to a bar stool and looked across at Peter Davies.

"I came over to have a look at the Ashgrove in the daylight," she said in answer to his question. "They're beautiful trees, aren't they?"

Peter Davies took a pull at his pint and nodded, but said nothing.

"It's a pity there's nothing to show it's a memorial," Rachel remarked.

"Used to be," Peter Davies said laconically. "Little nameplates stuck in the ground."

"Really? What happened to them?"

Peter Davies shrugged. "Don't rightly know," he said. "There were still one or two there when I was a lad. There was some talk, I remember, of having the names put on stones, you know, by a stonemason. But it weren't never done."

"So now no one knows which tree is which," said Rachel, taking a sip of her shandy. "Which tree is for which man, I mean."

"I can tell you which were for my uncles," Peter Davies said. "They're side by side, on the left. One for John near the allotment hedge, and the other for Daniel next to it." He scratched his head. "Can't tell you which the others were. Maybe Cecily'll know. You'd better ask her."

Rachel smiled at him. "Thanks, I will."

The other man at the bar was about the same age as Peter Davies, short, with a small head and features, and a scruffy beard so that he looked like nothing so much as a gnome. He had made no contribution to the conversation, and Rachel addressed him now. "Good evening. I'm Rachel Elliott, from the *Belcaster Chronicle.*"

"Oh yes." The answer was disinterested.

"I'm hoping to write a piece about the Ashgrove and the new houses," she said cheerfully. "How do you feel about the scheme?"

"Taking away our allotments," he said. "My father used to work that allotment. Grew veg he did, all through the war. Digging for victory!"

"And have you worked it ever since?" asked Rachel.

"I have."

"You must be very upset that they've been sold off."

The man shrugged. "Parish council told us they was going to sell," he said resignedly. "We was lucky to have them through last summer. Always knew they'd build on them some day."

"So you weren't surprised by the housing scheme?"

"Had to happen sometime. We're getting a new village hall out of it, which is something, I suppose."

"So you're in favour of the idea?" Rachel smiled at him.

He took a pull at his beer. "Not agin it," he said.

"What about the Ashgrove?" asked Rachel.

"What about it?"

"Well, the plan is to cut it down to make way for the access road, isn't it? How do you feel about that?"

"Better if they didn't," replied the man. "But I expect they will. Money talks, don't it?" He finished his drink and, nodding goodnight to them, he left the bar without speaking again.

"Are you going to fight against them cutting the Ashgrove down, Mr Davies?" Rachel asked.

Peter Davies shrugged. "Doubt there's much we can do," he said. "Tom's right, money talks." He, too, got to his feet and downing the last of his drink said goodnight, leaving Rachel alone in the bar.

Rachel looked at her watch. It was nearly six, so she finished her shandy and paid up. Having tidied her hair and retouched her make-up in the ladies, she called goodnight to the barman and left the pub. As she opened the door, she almost collided with someone coming in. It was Nick Potter.

"Oh, hallo," he grinned as he recognised her. "We met last night. Still chasing your story?"

"Just having a look at the village," Rachel said casually. "I was over at the Ashgrove earlier. Mr Davies said there were eight trees, or nine. It's nine. There must have been nine men remembered."

"I suppose so." Nick looked interested. "I wonder who they were. Have you found out?"

"No, not yet," Rachel replied, "but I'm hoping to."

She made to move past him and he said, "Are you leaving, or have you time for a drink?"

"No, sorry," Rachel said, "I've an appointment," then realising she'd sounded rather abrupt, she smiled and added, "Thanks for the thought, but I'm going over to see Miss Strong."

"Another time," said Nick, standing aside and holding the

door for her. "Good luck with the investigations."

"Thanks," replied Rachel. "Goodnight." She found she was smiling as she stepped out into the darkness and the door swung closed behind her.

It was bitterly cold, and the canopy of the night sky was clear, its myriad stars sharp and bright above her as she walked across the road to the church. In the row of cottages beyond it Yew Tree Cottage was the second. There was a lamp in the porch spilling light out along the path, and, as Rachel walked up to the front door, a security light came on as well. She rang the bell, and the door was opened by a woman in her forties. She looked hard at Rachel, who smiled brightly and said, "Good evening. I'm Rachel Elliott from the *Belcaster Chronicle*. I've an appointment to see Miss Strong."

The woman gave a brief nod and said, "Have you any ID?"

Rachel produced her press card and once the woman had scrutinised it, she was admitted.

"I'm Harriet Strong," the woman now introduced herself. "Cecily's great-niece. I'm sure you'll understand we have to be careful."

"Of course," Rachel agreed.

Harriet led her into a small sitting room where the heavy curtains were drawn against the winter night and a fire burned in the grate. It was a snug little room, filled with ornaments on every available surface. Ensconced in a chair by the fire, her zimmer parked within easy reach, was Cecily herself, watching a television, on the top of which were a family of plaster cats. The real thing was asleep on her lap. Cecily looked up as they came in.

"Hallo, Miss Strong," Rachel smiled, "I'm Rachel Elliott."

"How do you do? Come in and sit down. Harriet, pull up the other armchair for Miss Elliott." Cecily tipped the cat off her lap and zapped the television into silence. "Will you have a cup of tea or coffee, Miss Elliott?"

Rachel saw that among the clutter on the table at the old lady's side was an old silver teapot and three cups. Two were already filled.

"Thank you," she said. "Tea would be very nice."

Rachel sat down and looked across at the old lady as she poured milk into the third cup and then filled it from the ornate silver pot. Old, Cecily Strong certainly was, her face crazed with wrinkles and her grey hair wispy round her face, but there was clearly nothing wrong with her brain. The pale blue eyes which gleamed at Rachel from under the pale brows were shrewd and probing. Passing Rachel the cup, Cecily studied her carefully, and Rachel instinctively let her do so without saying anything until the old lady herself spoke.

"Well, Miss Elliott, here you are. What did you want to see me for?"

"It's very good of you to see me at such short notice," Rachel said. "As I told you, I work for the *Belcaster Chronicle*, and I was at the meeting in the village hall last night." She paused for a moment and looked across at Harriet. "Were you there as well?"

"No." Harriet spoke wryly. "I would have been, if I'd known Cecily was going to go."

"I don't have to tell you everything I do," Cecily said serenely to her niece. "It was no concern of yours, you don't live in the village."

"It turned out to be a concern of mine," Harriet pointed out. "After all, those trees are in memory of one of my relations as well, you know."

"I know, as it turned out," agreed Cecily. "But let's hear what Miss Elliott has to say."

"Please call me Rachel, it's so much easier."

"Well then, Rachel, go on."

"I was at the meeting, and I was very interested in what you told us about the Ashgrove, on the village green. I don't know if you are in favour of the new housing scheme..."

Rachel let the sentence hang in the air for a moment, and Cecily considered before she said, "I've nothing against it in principle, though I would have preferred more lower-cost housing to encourage young married couples back into the village. My only real quarrel with Mr Bradley...though I must say I didn't warm to the man, did you?" She broke off, her eyebrows raised in query, and Rachel admitted she hadn't liked him either.

"Well, my only real quarrel with him is the question of the trees, and on that I will not back down. Those trees were planted as a solemn memorial and that's the way they should stay until they've lived their natural span. Ash trees live to a good age, and by the time they start to die of natural causes, we'll all be long under the ground and it won't matter."

"Can you tell me who they were all planted for?" Rachel asked.

"Of course," Cecily replied. "One for my brother Will, two for the Davies boys, John and Dan, Alfie Chapman, that's four." She thought for a minute, her face screwed up with concentration. "Will, John, Dan and Alfie," she muttered. "Oh, and Harry Cook, five. Oh, this is stupid, of course I know."

"Don't worry about them, Cecily," Harriet said quietly, "the others'll come back to you."

"But it's so stupid, I know perfectly well who the others were," Cecily snapped. "I grew up with them. Everyone round here joined up together—most of our local lads went into the

Belshires. There was this bit in the paper asking for volunteers and they all went."

"In the *Chronicle*?" asked Rachel.

"That's right," Cecily agreed. "My mother was so proud of Will in his uniform! She cut the picture out of the paper and kept it in her bible."

"Will was in the paper?"

"They all were. In a group," Cecily explained. "Just before they went off to France. The lads from Charlton Ambrose with Freddie Hurst in the middle. Freddie Hurst," she repeated triumphantly, "from the Manor. He's another. He was an officer of course." Suddenly her shoulders sagged. "Went off in such high style, they did. So few of them came back. All blown away."

"Which tree was dedicated to your Will?" Rachel asked gently as the old lady lapsed into silence.

"The one on the extreme right, next to the wall," Cecily replied.

Rachel tried to visualise the grove as she had seen it earlier. As far as she could remember, the tree on the right was in the direct line that any road would have to take.

"Were the trees marked in any way?" she asked. "With the men's names?"

"Well, the idea was that eventually there should be stones set in the ground beside each one, with the name carved into it, but in the meantime they put little metal plaques, stuck into the ground. Not big, but they were only meant to be temporary, like, till the stones were done."

It confirmed what Peter Davies had said earlier. Rachel nodded. "So what happened?"

"Well, the stones weren't ever made, and over time the little plaques got pulled up and lost. Will's disappeared once and I found it later tossed into the hedge. After that I brought it home. I know which his tree is, and I didn't want to lose his name-plate." She looked across at her niece. "Harriet, go up to the bedroom and in the tin box under my bed you'll find it. Will's name-plate. Can you get it for me please?"

Harriet nodded and disappeared upstairs.

"Do you know why the memorial stones were never made?" asked Rachel, interested.

"Probably because the squire died," Cecily said after some thought. "It was Squire Hurst's idea to have the trees planted. Freddie was his only son and he was killed on the Somme. Squire arranged the planting in 1921, but he died himself that same year. He paid for the trees and the name-plates, and I expect he'd have paid for the stones as well."

Harriet came back down, bringing a small metal plaque with her. It was about six inches square attached to a metal spike. She handed it to Rachel who looked at it with interest, running her fingers over the raised lettering.

PTE WILLIAM ARTHUR STRONG
1899–1916
1ST BELSHIRE LIGHT INFANTRY
KILLED IN ACTION

"They were all the same," Cecily said. "Name, dates, rank and regiment, and how they died. Harry Cook died of wounds. I remember it said so on his. Squire had them all made."

Rachel handed the plaque to Cecily. "Do the Hursts still live at the manor?" she asked, though without much hope.

The old lady held the plate in her hands for a moment, her finger tracing the letters of the name, then she put it down beside her. She shook her head. "No, bless you. Squire Hurst was the last. His wife died in childbirth when Freddie was a boy, and Freddie's wife never lived there."

"He was married?"

"Yes, to a girl from London. They had a child...a girl, I think, but I'm not sure. Anyway, when Freddie didn't come home his wife went to live with her parents. We heard in the village that she married again, but I don't know if it was true."

"Can you remember her name?"

Cecily shook her head. "It was something flowery," she said dismissively. "Violet or Pansy or some such. She never came back to see poor Squire."

"What happened when the trees were planted?" asked Rachel. She glanced up at Cecily and added, "Do you mind if I make a few notes?"

"No, that's all right. You write down what you want."

Rachel felt in her bag for her notebook and pen, and hastily scribbled the names Cecily had come up with so far.

"Your tea's getting cold," Cecily remarked, picking up her own cup and refilling it from the pot. "More tea, Harriet?"

"No thanks, Cecily," replied Harriet. "I'm just going out to have a look at the supper, if you'll excuse me."

Rachel wondered if that was a hint that she should leave, but she was very reluctant to do so. She found what Cecily had to say fascinating and she didn't want her to stop talking.

"You were going to tell me about the planting," she said encouragingly.

"Oh, yes. Well, Squire had the holes dug on the edge of the village green in a sort of group, so that they'd look natural. Then they were planted, and the rector said some prayers. Oh, and I remember, as each tree was put in the ground, the family came and threw earth into the hole, to be part of the planting of that particular tree, you know?"

Cecily sighed. "I remember Mother was very upset, but she wouldn't cry. Mother never cried, even when the telegram came. She stood by the tree, very stiff and straight, and pushed the first shovelful of earth, then my father, then me and then Joe, that's Harriet's granddad. We thanked the good Lord that he was too young to go." She paused. "He wanted to, mind you, when the telegram came, but he was only thirteen, and even the army didn't take them that young."

Harriet came back into the room and said, "Supper's ready when you are, Cecily." She looked meaningfully at Rachel, who reluctantly got to her feet.

"I really am very grateful to you for talking to me," she said. "I think it would be wrong to let your Ashgrove be cut down. I shall say so in my article. Perhaps we can get public opinion on our side." She reached over to shake Cecily's hand, and though the skin was dry and papery against her own, Rachel felt Cecily's grip firm and strong in the clasp.

"Come and see me again," instructed the old lady. "I like having visitors." She glanced across at Harriet and added with a wry smile, "As long as I know who they are."

"Thank you, Miss Strong. I'll probably take you up on that," smiled Rachel. "It has been lovely to talk to you...and I'll keep you in touch with anything I hear about the trees."

Harriet showed her to the front door. "If you are going to come and see her again, do ring first," she said. "I'm always telling her not to open the front door unless she's expecting someone."

"Don't worry, I will," Rachel promised.

Rachel spent the evening sorting out what she had discovered about the Ashgrove and those it commemorated. Cecily had mentioned the Hurst family and someone called Harry Cook and another, Alfie Chapman, as well as the Davieses.

31

They would give her a starting place for her research. The obvious place to begin, Rachel decided, was in the archives of the *Belcaster Chronicle*, and the first thing she would look for would be the photograph Cecily had mentioned, the picture of Will Strong and the rest of the men from Charlton Ambrose leaving for the front in such high spirits. She longed to put names to faces. It occurred to her that the paper might also have reported the planting of the Ashgrove. Something else to check. With all these things in her mind, Rachel finally drifted off to sleep.

Three

When Rachel reached the office next morning, she slipped unnoticed into the archive room in the basement of the building and began work. Unfortunately not all the back numbers of the paper had been computerised, and Rachel found that she had to look at actual copies of the earlier papers.

She pulled out the binder for the first quarter of 1915 and began with the first paper of the year, Friday, 1st January. She was looking for the photograph Cecily had mentioned. There were not many pictures in the paper, and she was quickly on to the second paper and then the third. She found what she was looking for in the middle of March. There, on the front page of the 19th March edition was a grainy photograph of a group men in uniform under the headline

OUR BRAVE LADS

The article was short and patriotic, but none of the young men in the photo was named. The only one Rachel could be sure of was the officer in the middle, Freddie Hurst. The paper was old and the picture poor. It was impossible to distinguish the features of any of them, but they were all young and laughing and Rachel found herself blinking away unexpected tears.

"Come on, Rach," she said aloud, "what is the matter with you?" She closed the archive and replaced it on the shelf. What she was really interested in, she reminded herself, was the planting of the Ashgrove. Cecily had told her that the trees had been planted and dedicated in 1921, but couldn't remember exactly when.

"It was cold," Cecily had recalled, "so it was probably January or February. I'm sure it was the early part of the year."

Rachel decided to start with the first issue of 1921 and work her way forward. She heaved the bound volume from the shelf and setting it on a table opened it and stared down at the yellowing pages. As she worked her way through she was surprised how many references there were to such a small place as Charlton Ambrose. Her eyes skimmed the faded print and she soon found that the name leapt out at her, but most items were of little interest reporting only rummage sales, lost cats and a sheep escaping into the rectory garden. One or two articles were longer and there was more detail of what was affecting those who lived in Charlton Ambrose eighty years ago. A flu epidemic struck with some severity, leaving several dead in its wake. A new rector, Henry Smalley, was installed by the Bishop of Belcaster. There was a short biography of the new rector who, it appeared had served at the front in the Great War, and had been offered the living by Sir George Hurst, whose son Frederick had been lost on the Somme.

That's Freddie, thought Rachel, the chap Cecily told me about. The Lieutenant Hurst in the picture. She put down the paper and thought about him; Freddie Hurst, killed so young all those years ago. Each time she heard of him he became more real to Rachel. First learning of him from Cecily and now reading about him in the paper made him something more than a name, and Rachel found herself wishing that the photo in the earlier paper had been clearer, so that she really knew what he looked like. No picture of him here of course, but there was a faded picture of the Rev Smalley. Again, it was difficult to distinguish his features in the old newsprint, just a youngish man, light-haired and bespectacled, wearing a dog collar. Had Cecily mentioned him too? Yes, but not by name, simply as the rector, who dedicated the trees. Rachel turned back to the paper.

The Reverend Henry Smalley was a bachelor, and thus most welcome in a village where so many young men had not returned from the war. There was a brief description of his institution and the small welcoming reception afterwards, arranged by the parish in the village hall.

"The same one still in use today?" wondered Rachel as she read on. Mention was made by name of the ladies who had made the cakes and prepared the tea, Mrs Day and her daughter, Miss Molly Day. Perhaps, thought Rachel, one of those young ladies who was so pleased that the new rector was unmarried. Mrs Davies...was she the mother of John and Dan? Mrs Cook, Mrs Crown, Mrs Swan, Mrs Strong... Cecily's mother? All ladies doing their best to make the new young rector feel welcome in the village. She noted the date of the article for future reference and moved on to scan the next paper.

It was three papers later, three weeks later, that she found what she was looking for.

MEMORIAL TREES FOR CHARLTON AMBROSE

On Wednesday eight young ash trees were planted on the village green at Charlton Ambrose. These trees were planted as a memorial to those who made the ultimate sacrifice in the Great War. A tree dedicated to each man from the village who did not return from Flanders Field was planted in an attractive grove at the end of the village green. A short ceremony of dedication was conducted by the new rector, the Reverend Henry Smalley. The families of the fallen were all there to assist at the planting, and there were many tears among the onlookers as some of the younger brothers and sisters came sorrowfully forward to place a shovelful of earth around the roots of the tree in memory of a lost loved one. The final tree was planted by Sir George Hurst, for his son Captain Frederick Hurst of the 1st Belshire Light Infantry. It was through the generosity of Sir George that the trees were bought and planted as a permanent memorial to the glorious dead, the heroes from Charlton Ambrose. Each tree has a temporary name plate beside it, but it is Sir George's intention that small stones shall be carved with the names of the fallen...Captain Frederick Charles Hurst, Pte Alfred Chapman, Pte Harry Cook, Sgt Daniel Davies, Pte John Davies, Sgt George Hapgood, Pte William Strong and Cpl Gerald Winters, and placed at the foot of each tree. May they rest in peace!

Rachel smiled a little wryly at the florid style of the article. Clearly in his element, the writer had given full rein to his prose, wringing every ounce of emotion from the scene.

She read through the names again and wrote them in her notebook. Now at least, she thought, I know who all the trees are for. The names Davies and Cook caught her eye and she recognised them as the names of some of the village ladies who had made the refreshments for the rector's welcome party. Were they the same families, or part of extended families? Two of Peter Davies' great uncles were commemorated there, and even though, of course, Peter could not have known his uncles, as Cecily had known her brother, the direct link was there; an unbroken line of history in the village.

Wondering if there might be any further references to the Ashgrove in the subsequent weeks, Rachel decided to skim through the next few issues before photocopying the tree-planting article. What she found amazed her. In the edition of the *Chronicle* that came out two weeks later, Charlton Ambrose made the front page with the headline

PUBLIC OUTRAGE IN CHARLTON AMBROSE!

Clearly the work of the same reporter as before, Rachel thought with a smile as she began to read.

There was great public outcry in the village of Charlton Ambrose this week when it was noticed that the small plantation of ash trees dedicated to the glorious dead of the village has been desecrated. Someone, since the day of dedication a mere two weeks ago, has planted a ninth tree among the others. Also an ash tree and of similar size to the others, the extra tree went unnoticed at first. It is not known who might dare to perpetrate such an outrage! Sir George Hurst, whose idea the memorial Ashgrove was, and whose generosity made it possible, has no knowledge of whence the tree came. Though this ninth tree has not yet been uprooted, it is, according to many in the village, almost certainly only a matter of time before it is. When interviewed, Sir George said that he would be considering the matter. The rector, the Reverend Henry Smalley, said it was a decision entirely for Sir George, but added he was sure that no hasty decision would be taken in such a serious matter. Our reporter has spoken with all the families of those already commemorated for their sacrifice, and none of them has any idea where the tree came from, and most of them think it should be removed forthwith.

A ninth tree! Rachel stared at the article. Yes, of course, there are nine trees, she thought excitedly, I counted them yesterday.

She checked the names she had just written in her notebook; definitely only eight men commemorated by name.

Sir George must have been persuaded to leave the ninth tree with the others, but who had planted it and to whom was it dedicated?

Rachel moved on to the next edition of the paper to see if there was any more about the trees, or mention of who the ninth was for. At first she could find nothing, but then in the paper several weeks on, she found a small paragraph tucked in a corner of an inside page.

THE ASHGROVE, CHARLTON AMBROSE

A small service was held on Charlton Ambrose village green on Wednesday, when the Reverend Henry Smalley dedicated a ninth tree in the Memorial Ashgrove to 'The Unknown Soldier'. To the surprise of those concerned, Sir George Hurst has forbidden the uprooting of the tree. 'We do not know who put it there, or for whom, but it is clearly in memory of a fallen soldier,' he told our reporter. 'He may be unknown but he gave his life as surely as did the others, and it would be wrong to remove the tree.'

Investigations have failed to uncover who planted the tree and for whom, but its formal dedication has now included it in the village memorial.

So, thought Rachel reading and re-reading the piece, the ninth tree was left and is still there with the others.

Fascinated by the affairs of Charlton Ambrose, Rachel continued to search the back numbers for 1921. She wanted to read more about Sir George Hurst. Cecily said he had died that same year, and Rachel was anxious to see if there was any mention of his death, and if there were, whether there was any more information about his daughter-in-law and her child. She found the squire's death in the second week of September. There was formal notice of his death and also a short article about his life.

Sir George Hurst Bt died of pneumonia at his home, The Manor, Charlton Ambrose, on Tuesday last; Sir George had been unwell for several weeks. A Justice of the Peace, Sir George sat regularly in Belcaster court until just before his illness. For many years he represented Belcaster in Parliament, only resigning his seat in 1918. With him the family name and title die out as his only son Frederick, a Captain in the 1st Belshire Light Infantry, was killed on the Somme in 1916. He is survived by a granddaughter, Adelaide, born posthumously to his son, and living with her mother and stepfather in London. The funeral will be held on Monday next at 2 p.m.

So, thought Rachel excitedly, Freddie did have descendants, or one anyway. Poor Freddie. How sad that he never even saw his daughter.

She turned to the next issue of the paper and found the account of Sir George's funeral.

The funeral of Sir George Hurst Bt took place at the Church of St Peter, Charlton Ambrose, on Monday at 2 p.m. The service was conducted by the rector, the Reverend Henry Smalley, who paid tribute to Sir George's life and work as a landowner, Justice of the Peace and sometime Member of Parliament. His loss to the village would be sadly felt, particularly as the Hurst family had been squires at the manor for more than five generations, and now there would be no more. The whole of Charlton Ambrose would mourn his death, the rector said.

The coffin, with a single wreath of white roses, was followed by Sir George's daughter-in-law, Mrs Richard Anson-Gravetty, accompanied by her husband and daughter, Adelaide. The pallbearers were John Dickson, Francis Peters, Thomas Davies and Gordon Smith. Sir George was buried in the family vault alongside his wife, Charlotte.

After the service, tea was served by the parish in the village hall.

A book of condolence was opened and there were fifty-one signatures recorded in it.

I wonder what happened to that book of condolence, thought Rachel. Taken away by his daughter-in-law I suppose. Mrs Richard Anson-Gravetty. Cecily was right when she thought that Freddie's widow had remarried.

Rachel photocopied all the articles she had found and added them to the research folder she was compiling for her own article. Each piece of information had made her more and more determined to find out all she could about everyone with any connection with the Charlton Ambrose Ashgrove. The more she discovered, the more she felt involved. She wanted to know about these people who had lived there eighty or more years ago. Cecily was the link. Cecily could surely give her some more information about the village during the Great War and after. Rachel decided to go and pay her another visit as soon as she could and then write her article in defence of the Ashgrove. In the meantime, she had an appointment with Mike Bradley, and she wanted to press him on what he intended to do to preserve the trees.

Five o'clock found her at the offices of Brigstock Jones for her appointment. She was asked to wait and sat impatiently on an uncomfortable chair in a small, orange waiting area. After ten minutes she was about to return to the reception desk when a man appeared and greeted her with a smile.

"Miss Elliott? So sorry to have kept you. My name's Tim Cartwright." He gripped Rachel in a strong handshake and went on, "Would you like to come through to my office?"

"Thank you," replied Rachel, "but my appointment was with Mr Bradley. Is he not here?"

Leading her into his office, Tim Cartwright treated her to his widest smile, which she instantly mistrusted, and said, "I am so sorry, I'm afraid he's unavailable this afternoon. Won't you sit down? Tea?"

Rachel declined the tea and sat in the indicated chair. Putting her bag at her feet, she drew out her notebook and pen. "He cancelled our appointment yesterday, Mr Cartwright," she said crisply. "It really is most unfortunate that he's had to do it again today."

"I haven't got time to talk to the woman," Mike had snapped half an hour earlier. "I told you yesterday. You talk to her, Tim. Impress upon her we're looking into the problem of the trees. Great sympathy. Propose a new memorial with names, et cetera. Make sure she knows we aren't riding roughshod over the concerns of the people. We need her to write sympathetically."

Tim Cartwright was used to doing Mike Bradley's dirty work for him. He sighed inwardly. "She was at the public meeting, Mike," he pointed out. "It's you she wants to talk to."

"Tell her I'm held up in a meeting. For Christ's sake, Tim," Mike glowered at him, "you know what to do. And, by the way have you got hold of the Sharp woman yet?"

Tim nodded. "Yes," he said, "I'm seeing her this evening."

"Good. Well, I want to see you first thing on Monday, so we can prepare for my meeting with the planners."

Tim had spent the previous day looking into the problem of the Charlton Ambrose trees. He already knew there was no tree preservation order on them, but he also knew that to fell them, now they had been acknowledged as a war memorial, would cause outrage in the community. He had been out to look at the site again, to see if there was any possibility of looping the access road round the trees through the adjoining ground which was an extension to the churchyard. That would mean buying the strip from the Church Commissioners, and it was unlikely they would sell, but approaching them would be Mike's job, thank God. Tim had also been into the church and found the names of all the men on a brass plaque. He was about to begin the process of tracing their descendants. Mike Bradley had some idea of individual compensation for each family...to buy them off.

"They've already got a memorial in the church," Tim pointed out, handing Mike the leaflet on the church's history he had bought.

"So they have," Mike had agreed, "but we have to find the best way to resolve this mess. We need this project, Tim. It's a bloody good deal if we can pull it off. So, sort it...and keep this *Chronicle* woman on our side and off our backs."

Now Tim looked across the desk at Rachel. She was a good-looking woman, he had to admit, even if not his usual type. Tim preferred blondes, but she had an interesting face with broad cheeks and a wide mouth. He liked the way her full lips had an almost sculptured edge to them; the glint of anger in her eyes gave them a sparkle which brightened their hazel intensity and a sharp, determined chin warned him that she was no push-over. Tight dark curls, cut short to her head, showed off its neat shape, and from what he could see whilst she was seated, her figure was as attractive as her face. She faced him squarely across his desk and he recognised at once that she was definitely not a lady to be trifled with.

"I know," Tim said sympathetically. "But something came up and he was called to another meeting this morning and he isn't back yet. Rather than put you off again, he called and asked me to help you in any way I can." He grinned ruefully, "So I'm afraid you're stuck with me."

Rachel eyed him, in no way disarmed by this act, and said, "Well, I suppose I'll have to make do with you, then."

"Where would you like to start?" asked Tim, meekly.

"Background first. Can you outline exactly what the plans for the Charlton Ambrose development are?"

Tim picked up a glossy brochure from his desk and passed it across to her. Flipping through it she saw that it showed a plan of the site, the floor plans and artist's impressions of the proposed houses...three different models...and of the new village hall. She opened it at the site plan and turned back to Tim.

"I see that the proposed access is along the edge of the green as far as the churchyard wall and then across the end of the green into the allotment patch."

"That's right. The idea was to use as little of the actual green itself as possible. You see there's a footpath along that side already," Tim pointed to the site plan, "with a small gate into the allotments. By widening that path slightly, we can bring the access road round to the end of the green and into the site."

"But the Ashgrove covers the width of the green at that end," Rachel pointed out. "Some of those trees at least will have to come down."

"As things are at present they will," agreed Tim. "The problem is that we had no idea of the significance of those trees. There was no preservation order on them, you know, and as far as we knew there was no reason why at least some of them should not be felled." He gave her his sincere look and went on, "We never fell mature trees unless we absolutely have to, Miss Elliott. Mature trees *make* a new development. New modern houses, yes, but in a mature, well-grown setting. Gives a feeling of permanence. People don't feel they're moving on to a building site."

"Is there no other way into the allotment patch?" asked Rachel.

Tim shook his head. "Not at the moment. It is bounded on this, western side," he pointed to the plan, "by Scotts Road which has a row of houses along it, and on this, the east, by the churchyard." No point, he thought, in mentioning the possible access through that until Mike had approached the Church Commissioners. "Beyond it," he went on, "the ground drops away steeply down to the stream." He indicated the blue line on the plan. "Of course we are looking into all the possibilities. We don't want to cut down those trees if we don't have to. They are clearly important to people...it's just that we didn't know that before."

"Does the planning permission rest on this?" Rachel asked.

"Mr Bradley is seeing the planners again next week to try and sort something out," Tim said, "but the whole development may depend on the access. If we can't get it, we can't build there, and that's it." He shrugged and added, "It would be a pity for the village as a whole, though, because this is a pretty good deal for them. They've been trying to raise money for sometime to replace their village hall. This way it's done for them...and of course gives them some affordable housing right in the middle of the village."

"Not all starter homes though," pointed out Rachel.

"No," agreed Tim, "but we have to have some more expensive housing to make the whole proposition viable from our point of view. Until the question of the trees was raised, all parties concerned were getting what they wanted from the plan."

"Not everyone in the village is in favour of it anyway," Rachel said. "There were other voices of dissension at the meeting you know, before the trees were mentioned."

"There always are," sighed Tim. "However good a scheme is, someone won't like it and kick up a fuss."

"Well, it is their village."

"It's everyone's village, everyone who lives there I mean. The parish council is representing everyone in cases like this, and it is the parish council that we deal with." Tim spoke firmly. "The parish council did not mention the trees."

"What will you do?"

"We have to make further enquiries," Tim replied. "We'll find out who the trees were planted for and approach their families...if they're still around. We are very happy to build a new memorial to the men commemorated there. None of those trees has got a name on it, you know. No one can tell, if they just walk over there, that they are memorial trees at all. There's no sign, no name-plates, nothing. We shall offer to build a new memorial, perhaps a fountain beside the new village hall, with the names beside, and perhaps the names from the Second World War as well."

"Is that a definite offer?" Rachel asked as she scribbled his words down in her notebook.

"It is certainly the sort of offer Mike Bradley has in mind," replied Tim. "Obviously it hasn't been made yet as the question has only just arisen, but I have no doubt that the parish council will be approached with something of that order." He smiled at her reassuringly.

Rachel looked at him consideringly. She had spoken to Paula Sharp herself earlier in the day and realised she knew something that Tim Cartwright did not.

"We are going to have a problem," Paula Sharp had told her that morning when Rachel had called on her. "The parish council owns the land, all of it...the village green and the allotments, all that land was left to the parish by Sir George in his will, but not the actual trees in the Ashgrove. They were given to the families of the men they commemorate by Sir

George Hurst, in perpetuity. Each tree is owned by a different family. If they need to fell them all, they will have to get permission from each family, and," she smiled wryly, "we already know what Cecily Strong will say, I think."

"Do you know where all the other families are?" Rachel asked her.

Paula shrugged. "Some of them. A search will have to be made for the others, or the descendants of the others."

"And if they can't be found?"

"An interesting point," acknowledged Mrs Sharp. "We shall have to take advice on that."

"Do they need to fell all the trees?" Rachel wondered. "It might not be necessary to cut all of them down."

"No," agreed Mrs Sharp, "but consider the dreadfully bad feeling there will be if some are felled and some are left."

Rachel knew that she was right. As she looked across at Tim Cartwright she wondered briefly whether to tell him who owned the trees, but decided against it. He'd find out soon enough, and if her paper were going to do battle with his company, it was better to keep some cards hidden. Rachel had every intention of trying to trace the descendants of each family, and she wanted a head start. She wanted to know what each family really thought, not what they might be bribed or coerced into thinking by Mike Bradley and Tim Cartwright, with offers of compensation and new memorial fountains. Of course Tim Cartwright hadn't mentioned compensation yet, indeed Brigstock Jones must be hoping that the memorial would be enough, but she was sure that the wisdom expressed in the pub had been right, it was almost certainly only a matter of time until it all came down to money.

"I see," she said returning his smile. "Well I suppose it can't be helped. But it looks as if you'll have a battle on your hands. As you already know there will be opposition from some of the families. For instance, Miss Strong spoke out against it very firmly at the meeting. One of the trees is in memory of her brother."

"Yes, William Strong," Tim Cartwright said, and seeing her surprise that he was able to come up with the name so quickly, added, "There is another memorial to them in the church. Even if the trees went, they wouldn't be without memorial, you know. They're all named in there."

Rachel didn't know, but she kept further surprise from her face and said, "Even so, that doesn't have the emotional appeal of a living memorial, does it?"

"I agree," Tim said smoothly, "but that's not our fault. We want to be as sensitive about this as possible, but the bottom line is that if this development is to go ahead for the benefit of everyone, we may have no alternative but to fell the trees."

Rachel stood up. "Well, thank you very much for your time, Mr Cartwright. Please tell Mr Bradley that I am sorry he wasn't able to see me, but I think I have all I need now."

Tim Cartwright held out his hand again. "Well, if I can be of any further assistance, please don't hesitate to give me a call." He took a card from his desk and gave it to her. "This is my direct line and my mobile, just give me a call, any time."

Rachel went home to put the notes she had made into her computer and as she sorted them she considered exactly what she had learned. The ownership of the trees had not been the only thing of interest Paula Sharp had told her. It was the question of the actual land involved.

"The village green used to be part of the Manor estate," Paula had said. "Though the village people had various rights over it. When Sir George died he left the green and the piece of land beyond it to the parish council, to be used for the public benefit of the village. The village green was left as it was, but the extra piece of land was fenced off and offered as individual allotments to residents of Charlton Ambrose at peppercorn rents. They were all taken up and worked by local people, though the ownership of the land still rested with the parish council."

"And now the council has sold that land to Brigstock Jones," said Rachel.

"Yes, subject to planning permission."

"Didn't the wording of the will prohibit that?" asked Rachel, surprised.

"We took legal advice on that," said Paula Sharp. "It was considered that new housing and a new village hall *was* for the public benefit of the village, the village as it is today. In 1918 there was no question of there being no pub or shop or school in Charlton Ambrose, but now there is a very real danger of all three disappearing. We have to move with the times, and help provide the sort of housing needed now. By using the money from the sale of the allotments, we are able to fund the new hall. Part of our deal with Mr Bradley is that he will build the hall at cost. We already own the land, so it is just the building costs we have to find. The sale of the allotments covers those."

"Let me get this straight," said Rachel. "You mean building the hall is the price Mike Bradley has paid for the allotments?"

"Not exactly in those terms," Paula Sharp replied, "but I suppose that's what it boils down to, yes. As far as the parish council is concerned, it really is a deal beneficial to the whole community. We need a new hall, but more than that, we need those new houses. We must attract young families to Charlton Ambrose. At the meeting Mike Bradley said that it would bring our village back to life and he was quite right."

"But you must have known about the trees," pointed out Rachel. "You must have known that the developers would have to cut down the trees to get access to the site. It's clear from the plans."

"We did," admitted Paula. Her face was pale and strained as she spoke. "We did, but none of us knew why they were there. Of course there are families still in the village who have been here for generations, and presumably they knew all about them, but many of us have moved here more recently and didn't. There is no one from one of the older village families on the parish council at present, you know. None of us knew the significance of those trees." She looked across at Rachel earnestly. "Have you been to look at them?" Rachel nodded. "Well, there's nothing to identify them as a memorial now, is there? And none of us knew that's what they were. It is extremely embarrassing. I went to the public record office yesterday and found the document recording the donation of the trees to the families. It's quite explicit; the trees are theirs. We'd only checked Sir George's will when we wanted to sell the land, and the trees were planted when the land still belonged to him. They weren't mentioned in the will."

Rachel mapped out her article. She needed to speak to the planning office, but there would be no one there now until Monday. In the meantime she would begin her research on the families.

Four

Saturday morning found Rachel on the road to Charlton Ambrose on her way to visit Cecily Strong again.

She had phoned first thing, to see if she might call and Cecily, pleased to hear from her, had invited her to come round for coffee. Rachel readily accepted. Since her research in the *Chronicle* archive she had some more, specific, questions she hoped the old lady could answer. With luck, Cecily would be able to put Rachel on the trail of some of the other families still living in the village.

Over her breakfast coffee, she had looked up the surnames from her list in the phone book. Several of the names were listed, but whether they were actually the same families, only time would tell.

Rachel parked outside Cecily's cottage, but before she called there she went to the church to look for the memorial Tim had mentioned. The church was old, its golden sandstone smooth and mellow. Huddled all round it, like chicks about their mother, were the gravestones of the people of Charlton Ambrose, a higgledy-piggledy mixture of stones and crosses and two large sarcophagus tombs, one on each side of the path. The winter grasses straggled between the stones and grassy mounds. There were one or two graves with fresh flowers, an occasional Christmas wreath, but several were marked only by withered stems standing spikily in jam jars, or long-dead, skeletal pot plants.

The old oak door was open and when Rachel pushed it wider, she found two women inside, cleaning the church. They were chatting to each other as they worked and took little notice of Rachel as she wandered round the church looking at the various memorial tablets and plaques.

She found what she was looking for at the back, beneath the large west window. The first was a brass plate which said:

TO THE GLORY OF GOD

AND IN LOVING MEMORY OF THOSE BRAVE MEN FROM

CHARLTON AMBROSE

WHO GAVE THEIR LIVES FOR KING AND COUNTRY

IN THE GREAT WAR 1914–1918

CAPTAIN FREDERICK CHARLES HURST

PTE ALFRED JOHN CHAPMAN

SGT DANIEL DAVIES

PTE HARRY COOK

SGT GEORGE HAPGOOD

PTE JOHN DAVIES

CPL GERALD WINTERS

PTE WILLIAM ARTHUR STRONG

THEY LIVE ON IN THE HEARTS OF THOSE WHO ARE LEFT.

Underneath on a different plaque, almost as if it had been wedged in as an after-thought, was a second plate on which was inscribed:

ALSO THOSE MEN WHO DIED FOR KING AND COUNTRY
IN THE SECOND WORLD WAR
1939–1945

SIMON BRADWELL	GORDON DAVID BLUNT
PAUL ANDREW CARR	HAROLD CHAPMAN
STEPHEN DREW	CHARLES FINCHAM
DONALD STEWART	THOMAS SWINFORD
JACK TURNER	GEORGE JOHN WEST

LEST WE FORGET

Rachel read through the names on both tablets, before taking out her camera and photographing them. The flash drew her to the attention of the cleaning ladies and one called to her, "There's a postcard of the west window in the stand by the door."

Rachel turned round. "The west window?"

"Yes," the woman pointed to the window above the memorial tablets. "There's a postcard of that if you want to buy one, and a history of the church too."

"Oh, thank you," Rachel replied. "It was actually the war memorial I was looking at, not the window. Though," she added hastily, "it's very beautiful." She raised her eyes to look properly at the stained glass and found that it was indeed a beautiful window. Even without benefit of sunshine to illuminate it, the colours were rich and strong, depicting the story of the Good Samaritan; the man lying injured at the side of the road and the Samaritan tending him, holding a cup to his lips, while the donkey the Samaritan had been riding waited patiently on a windswept road.

Underneath the picture were the words:

And when he saw him, he had compassion on him

Below the quotation was an unfurled banner with the words:

RUFUS HURST
Captain 1st Belshire Light Infantry
Died of wounds 5th November 1854
after the Battle of Inkerman

Reading its inscription for the first time, Rachel realised that the window too, was a war memorial, in memory of another Hurst, an earlier Hurst than Freddie; killed in an earlier war. The Hursts had given up more than one son for their queen, or king, and country.

The woman had left her polishing and crossed to stand by Rachel. She looked up at the window too and said, "It's a dreadful waste, isn't it...war? All those young men never having proper lives, never seeing their children grow up...never *having* children."

Rachel nodded and then remarked, "There are several names the same here...they must have been brothers. How dreadful to lose two sons or two brothers." She stared at the lists again and then said, "Look, there was a Chapman killed in each war, I wonder if they were father and son."

"I don't know. Probably relatives of some sort anyway." The woman smiled: "I'm afraid we're comparatively new to the village, so I don't know much about its history." She thought for a minute and went on, "The rector might know I suppose and of course, he'll have all the parish records. He might let you see them if you're interested; you could always ask him. The rectory is across the road."

"Thank you," Rachel said. "I might just do that."

"His name's Adam Skinner."

Rachel thanked her again and the woman went back to her duster. As she left the church Rachel bought a postcard of the west window and the history of the church. Glancing through this she found the paragraph that dealt with the window.

> The west window depicts the story of the Good Samaritan, with the Samaritan tending the wounded traveller at the side of the road.
>
> This example of Sir Howard Morgan's work was placed in the church by Sir Frederick Hurst as a memorial for his son, Rufus, killed in the Battle of Inkerman in 1854.
>
> Beneath this memorial window are tablets commemorating the dead of the two world wars, naming all those lost from the parish. It is interesting to note that there is also a memorial of nine ash trees on the village green to commemorate those who fell between 1914 and 1918. These were presented by Sir George Hurst, whose son Frederick was killed on the Somme 1916. They were dedicated by the rector, Henry Smalley, in 1921 to the memory of all who fell.

So, Rachel thought ruefully, the information about the Ashgrove was there for anyone to find if they simply read the little church history, but nothing to tell me about any of the men concerned.

She decided that she would certainly call on the rector to see if he could help her with the construction of the family trees that interested her. However, before that she had a date with Cecily Strong.

When she reached Cecily's cottage she found the old lady waiting for her, with scones on the table and a pot of coffee already made. They sat down in the crowded sitting room, surrounded by ornaments and souvenirs, each a memory in Cecily's long life, and Cecily poured the coffee.

As they drank their coffee, Cecily said, "I've got a photo you might like to see. It's of Will. It was taken in France. He sent it back to us." She picked up an ornate picture frame from the table beside her and held it out to Rachel. There, smiling cheerfully up at her, was a sepia Will Strong. Rachel studied him for a moment and almost without thinking she murmured, "He looks so young!"

"Seventeen," Cecily said softly. "Only seventeen."

Rachel handed the picture back and Cecily, setting it back on the table, said, "Now then, tell me what you want to know."

"Well," Rachel set her cup aside, "I need to trace the families who had people commemorated in the Ashgrove. I want to write a proper article on the Ashgrove; about what it meant to people when it was planted, and what it means to people today. It seems to me it would be dreadful if it were simply cut down as a convenience to the developers. I know that's what you think too, so I was wondering if you could help me trace the living relatives of the men who are commemorated there."

"I can try," Cecily said doubtfully, "but most of them have moved away. Why do you need to find them?"

"Well, I reckon that Mike Bradley and his firm will be looking for them too, and I wanted to try and get there first. I want to know what they really think and feel, before they are offered a bribe not to make waves."

"A bribe?" Cecily sounded shocked.

"Well, an inducement anyway," said Rachel. "They'll call it compensation. The thing is that Brigstock Jones have got too much to lose if this deal is called off, and planning permission could well rest on the consent of the relatives being obtained to remove the trees. It will be well worth their while to pay off the relatives, with the promise of another memorial in place of the Ashgrove, and cash in hand."

"Well, they won't get my consent," Cecily said stoutly, "whatever money they offer."

"No, but that may not be enough to save the trees. The whole point of the Ashgrove is that it is a communal memorial, all the men remembered together, irrespective of rank and family. It may be possible to do what they want by removing just some of the trees, but the memorial will still be destroyed as a whole."

Cecily nodded glumly. "I see, so I can't stop them."

"Probably not on your own," Rachel agreed, "but I've made a list here of all the men named." She pulled out a paper from her bag and looked at it. "Captain Frederick Hurst. Well, you told me a bit about him last time I was here, and I've found out some more. He had a daughter, Adelaide, born posthumously, and his wife was married again to a man called Richard Anson-Gravetty. I read a report of Sir George's funeral in 1921, and it said they were there. Do you remember that funeral? Did you go?"

"Everyone in the village went," Cecily replied. "I was only a child still, of course, but I remember the school closed as a mark of respect, and we all stood alongside the road when the coffin was carried from the manor to the church."

"Do you remember his daughter-in-law being there? Or the little girl? She'd have been about five."

"I suppose I knew they were there," Cecily said doubtfully, "but I can't say I remember actually seeing them."

"Not even at the tea in the village hall afterwards?"

"Us kids weren't asked to the tea," Cecily said. "We were packed off outside to play. All the grown-ups went into the village hall and there were some speeches and that, but we weren't interested in any of that, we were just pleased to have the extra holiday from school."

"So you don't know where the Anson-Gravetty family lived in London?"

"No, love you, I haven't a clue. I didn't even know it was London."

"It was in the report in the paper."

"Then it must be right," Cecily said. "All I know is that Freddie's wife seldom came back here after Freddie died, and certainly not after Sir George did."

"Well," sighed Rachel, "it's going to be difficult to trace Adelaide Hurst now. She may well have taken her stepfather's name as she never knew her real father, she probably married and so had yet another name and on top of that, it's quite possible she's already dead. If not, she's in her eighties and could be living anywhere."

She glanced down at her paper again only to look up with a start when Cecily said, "And of course Miss Sarah never came home again either."

"Miss Sarah? Who's Miss Sarah?"

"Miss Sarah? She was Sir George's daughter, Freddie's sister. Went nursing, she did, in the war, though Sir George thought she ought to stay at home and look after him."

"But I didn't know Freddie had a sister. There was no mention of her at the funeral." Rachel was amazed.

"No," agreed Cecily, "I said she didn't come home from France. I think she was killed there when the Germans shelled a field hospital."

"Shelled a hospital?" cried Rachel.

"They did that kind of thing," Cecily asserted.

"But on purpose? Surely not on purpose."

"Who knows?" Cecily shrugged. "I'm sure she was killed. She didn't come home, anyhow."

"She isn't mentioned on the war memorial," said Rachel

thoughtfully. "I wonder why? I mean, she was Sir George's daughter and he arranged for the memorial. He must have wanted her commemorated too."

"She wasn't fighting," pointed out Cecily.

"Maybe not," Rachel agreed incredulously, "but she died for her country just the same!"

"Most people wouldn't have looked at it like that," Cecily said, and Rachel had the feeling that Cecily was one of them. Although she didn't say so, Rachel got the feeling that Cecily didn't approve of Squire's daughter gallivanting off to France to nurse wounded soldiers and she wondered why.

"I still can't believe he wouldn't commemorate his daughter in some way." Rachel was baffled and then she suddenly said, "Of course! The ninth tree! He must have planted the ninth tree for her. You know, there are eight men and nine trees."

Cecily looked doubtful. "I never heard it was for her," she said.

"Well if it wasn't, who was it for?" demanded Rachel.

"I don't know," said Cecily, leaning forward to top up their coffee cups. "I'd forgotten that there was an extra tree, to tell truth, but I doubt it was for Miss Sarah, because it never had a name on it."

Realising Cecily had nothing more to tell her about the squire's daughter, Rachel made a quick note to try and find out exactly what had happened to Sarah and turned back to her list to ask, "What about Private Alfred John Chapman?"

"Jane Chapman," said Cecily. "She was his daughter. We were at the village school together. She had an older brother. What was his name now?" She wrinkled her brow in concentration, trying to remember.

"Harold?" suggested Rachel, glancing again at her list.

"That's right," cried Cecily, delighted. "That's right. Harold. Went into the RAF," Cecily pronounced it "raf", "in the second war and was killed in the Battle of Britain. Flew fighters he did, and got shot down. Poor Jane. Lost her dad in the first war and her only brother in the second."

"What happened to her?" prompted Rachel. "Jane Chapman?"

Cecily shrugged. "She married a chap from Belmouth way. Can't remember his name, but she got married in the village here, and Harold, he gave her away. Ever so handsome he was in his RAF uniform."

"So she got married during the war," Rachel said, making another note on her pad and thinking that she must check the marriage register to find the married name.

Gradually she went down her list of people, and was continually surprised at what Cecily could remember. Once she said so, and the old lady laughed. "I can remember things like these," she said, "it's what happened yesterday that gets me confused."

Not trusting her own memory with such gems, Rachel made detailed notes about each family.

"Cooks? Yes, they are still about. Mary Bryson was a Cook. She lives in a home in Belmouth now; her son David Bryson lives in Belcaster somewhere and his daughter, Gail, is married to Sean Milton and runs the post office."

"The post office? You mean here in Charlton Ambrose?" Rachel couldn't believe her luck. They were right here in the village.

"Yes," confirmed Cecily. "Round the corner from the pub."

Peter Davies, she told Cecily she had met already, after the public meeting. "I think he said he was a great nephew or something, of two of them."

"That's right," Cecily said. "Still lives in the same house where they've always lived. Just him and his wife now, both their girls married and gone."

Rachel asked about George Hapgood, but Cecily knew very little about him. His parents had lived in the village after the war, but had moved away before the second war and she didn't know what had happened to them. "There was another boy, can't remember his name, a younger lad, too young to fight in the first war. He got married, I think. Yes, to that Sheila."

"Sheila?"

"Yes, what was her name? Sheila. Her parents had the other pub."

"Other pub?" queried Rachel, scribbling furiously on her notepad to keep up with the little snippets Cecily was giving her so casually.

"The Bell," replied Cecily. "It was at the other end of the village by the bridge. It's a private house now. Can't remember their name, but they were there up until the beginning of the next war." She screwed up her face again as she searched her memory.

"Don't worry," Rachel smiled at her, "I can always find that out."

"I don't know if they had any children," sighed Cecily. "I'm not much help to you, am I?"

"You've been tremendous," Rachel assured her. "You've told me lots of things it might have taken me ages to discover." She paused and then said, "You realise other people will probably come and ask you the same things. The developers are sure to want to trace the families as well."

"Yes," agreed Cecily serenely, "but I doubt if I shall be able to remember it all so clearly another time."

Rachel laughed. "They'll find out in the end you know," she warned. "They'll get the information from somewhere."

"I expect so," Cecily said. "But not from me."

The only other family was the Winters, and Cecily knew nothing whatever about them.

"I don't remember them at all," she said. "Maybe they moved straight after the war. I was still only a child, remember."

When Rachel finally took her leave she took both Cecily's hands in hers. "Thank you for being so patient," she said. "You really have been most helpful."

Cecily Strong returned her grasp. "I don't want the Ashgrove cut down," she said simply. "Those trees were planted as a solemn memorial, they're part of the history of our village, and they belong to the families that still live here. I don't want to see them go, just so they can build a few houses."

"Nor do I," Rachel said firmly, "and I will do all I can to protect them."

"If enough people say no, they won't be able to cut them down, will they?" asked Cecily, suddenly sounding querulous.

"I hope not." Rachel tried to sound more confident than she felt. Developers like Mike Bradley didn't allow much to stand in their way, and they had far bigger guns in their arsenal than a few elderly folk in a quietly dozing village. Too much money was at stake for Mike Bradley to take defeat easily, and as far as Rachel could see there was no other way of developing that particular site than by chopping down the trees of the Ashgrove to provide the access. She didn't hold out much hope for those trees.

As she reached the front door Rachel turned back to Cecily. "Have you met a man called Nicholas Potter?" she asked.

"No, who's he?" Cecily had come to the door to see her out, and looked out across the road to the pub.

"He was at the meeting the other night, said he was new to the village. He sounded fairly objective about it all, so I thought he might be worth talking to. I just wondered where he lived."

"Gail in the post office might know," suggested Cecily. She put her hand on Rachel's arm. "Let me know how you get on," she said. "It's important to me."

Rachel promised she would and as the door closed behind her, crossed the road to the pub. She settled herself at a corner table and checked her phone for messages. There were several but none of them important enough to deal with immediately, and she turned her attention to her lunch.

Over half a pint of shandy and a ploughman's she considered what she had learnt that morning, and made notes on the lines of enquiry she could follow up easily. Gail Milton, who ran the post office, would be easy. She needed to look at the marriage register and see whom Jane Chapman had married. She wanted to find out more about Sarah Hurst. Imagine not being commemorated simply because she was a woman! That's what it boils down to, thought Rachel furiously. Her father didn't consider her sacrifice as important as that of her brother.

And yet Rachel's mind wouldn't allow her to accept that. No father would think like that. He had lost his children in the service of their country and, surely, even in 1918, that must mean an equal loss, even if one of them was a girl, perhaps even more so. She remembered Cecily's words, "Squire didn't want her to go, he wanted her to stay at home and look after him." Maybe he did, but surely he would love her as much if she didn't. Then she thought about what she had read in Vera Brittain's *Testament of Youth* and remembered how Vera's parents had reacted to her going to nurse the wounded, both in London and France; how they had expected her to drop everything and come home and look after them, run their home while her mother was ill. Parents of that generation believed that their daughters' first duty was to be at home for them. Girls of her sort didn't go out to work, or if they did it was a little genteel voluntary work.

I'm looking at this through twenty-first century eyes, Rachel decided, that's the problem.

She started as her musings were interrupted by a voice saying, "If you're on your own, may I join you?" and looking up found Nick Potter standing beside her, holding a pint and a plate of food. She was surprised by his approach, but gestured to the bench seat opposite.

"Feel free," she said, and, glancing round the room, found that the bar had filled up considerably since she had come in, and there was little space elsewhere for him to sit.

"Thanks." Nick set his plate and glass down on the table before saying with a nod at her half-empty glass, "Can I get you a top-up for that?"

Rachel smiled back at him. "No thanks," she said. "Only one at lunch time or I go to sleep."

She tucked her notebook back into her bag and took a pull at her shandy, thinking as she did so that this would be a good chance to do a little probing into village affairs, even if Nick were a self-confessed blow-in. "It's getting crowded in here," she remarked as an opening. "Is it always as full as this on a Saturday lunch-time?"

"It has a good reputation for bar food," Nick said. "People come out from Belcaster for a pub lunch."

"It is an attractive villagey sort of pub," Rachel agreed, spreading the crusty brown bread roll with some delicious looking chutney. "This is supposed to be home-made," she indicated the chutney with her knife and Nick said, "I believe it is. Mandy is an excellent cook, and everything is home-made."

"I heard today," Rachel said conversationally as she watched him begin to eat his curry, "that there used to be another pub in the village. The Bell?"

Nick looked interested. "Was there? I didn't know that. Where was it?"

"Not sure, but I understand it's a private house now. I suppose a village this small can only support one pub."

"Probably," agreed Nick, "but it's sad don't you think, that such places should have to close? It would certainly be the beginning of a lingering death to this village if the Post Office Stores closed. The school would probably go too."

"So you're in favour of these new houses then?" Rachel asked.

"As I said the other night, in principle I am, but it depends how things are done."

"What about the Ashgrove?" Rachel watched him over the rim of her glass as he considered his reply.

"That's a difficult one," he conceded. "A memorial like that shouldn't be destroyed, especially when there are still people alive who remember the men who are commemorated there."

"But there is already a memorial in the church," Rachel pointed out, playing devil's advocate. "They are all commem-orated there." She nearly said "all but one", but something held her back. She wanted to do a lot more research on Sarah Hurst. She felt there was another human interest story there in its own right, and decided to say nothing about it until she had discovered more.

"Is there?" Nick looked surprised. "I didn't know, but I

have to admit I've never been into the church. So, they wouldn't be without any memorial." He laughed. "That'll please Mike Bradley."

"Yes," Rachel agreed bleakly. "And he knows about it too. It was one of his blokes, Tim Cartwright, who told me it was there."

They both turned their attention to their food and ate in companionable silence until Rachel said casually, "Whereabouts do you live? Right in the middle of the village?"

"More or less," Nick replied. "I'm living in a house on the main road into the village. It's very small, and only temporary, while I look for something else."

"In Charlton Ambrose?"

"Probably. My firm has relocated to Belcaster, so I want to find something permanent in one of the outlying villages. I like it here."

"Perhaps you could buy one of Mike Bradley's executive homes," suggested Rachel, watching Nick Potter out of the corner of her eye to judge his reaction.

He looked at her quizzically and then laughed, "No, no I don't think so. Not my scene."

"What is your scene?" asked Rachel.

"Something a bit older, with character."

"You mean with mullioned windows and roses round the door?"

"More like needing a new roof, re-wiring and re-plumbing," he replied.

"Have you found somewhere?"

"All these questions," Nick said lightly. "Anyone could tell you're a journalist."

"So, have you?" Rachel persisted.

"Nothing definite," he answered, "I'm still looking round.

I can take my time till the right thing comes up. How are you getting on with your piece about the trees?"

Now it was Rachel's turn to be evasive.

"Oh, I've just been chatting to people, you know. Testing village opinion."

"And?"

"And, you'll have to read my article in next week's *Chronicle*." She picked up her bag and slinging it over her shoulder got to her feet. "I must make tracks," she said. "Nice to see you again."

"Are you busy this evening?" Nick asked suddenly, and when she paused and looked surprised he went on, "It's just that I've heard there's a rather good night-club opened up recently in Belcaster."

"The Grasshopper?"

"Yes that's the one. Have you been there? Is it good?"

"No," Rachel replied, "I haven't. It is supposed to be good."

"I wondered if you'd like to go this evening." Nick watched her face as she considered the invitation, and he wondered what had actually made him issue it. He had had no thought of going to the Grasshopper when he'd come into the pub, but there was something about this girl opposite him. He had only met her three times, two of them very briefly, but each time she lingered in his mind, and he wanted to get to know her better. He liked the way her dark curls framed her face and the way her eyes crinkled when she laughed, and the laugh when it came, delighted him. Nick thought as he watched her that he enjoyed making her laugh.

"No, I don't think so, thank you very much." Rachel sounded apologetic. "It's kind of you to ask, but I think not."

"Me, or the club or both?" enquired Nick cheerfully.

That made Rachel laugh. "Neither," she said. "It's just I've got stuff to do before Monday and I'm spending tomorrow with my grandmother. Thank you all the same."

"I won't be discouraged then," Nick grinned, finding he meant what he was saying. "I'll ask you again. Shall I ring you at the office?"

"If you like," Rachel agreed. "But I must warn you that I often work anti-social hours."

"Fine," Nick nodded. "I can be anti-social too, no trouble. Give my love to your grandmother."

"I will," promised Rachel still smiling. "She'll be delighted. Goodbye, now," and turning away she left the pub without looking back.

She spent the rest of the afternoon in the village, and her first stop was the Post Office Stores. The post office part was shut, but the shop was open.

"Excuse me, are you Mrs Gail Milton?" she asked the woman sitting reading her book behind the counter. The woman who was about the same age as Rachel, looked at her a little suspiciously and said that she was.

Rachel handed over her card. "I was at the meeting in the village hall on Wednesday," she explained, "and I wondered how you felt about the proposed housing development."

"All in favour of it," replied Gail. "We need more people to keep the village alive, 'specially the younger ones. This place is fast becoming a dormitory for Belcaster."

"Don't you think the executive houses proposed for most of the site would only make that worse?" suggested Rachel. "I understand that there aren't many starter homes planned."

"No," agreed Gail, "but any are better than none. I'd welcome anything that would boost our trade." She indicated the book she'd been reading. "If I was in a supermarket on a

Saturday afternoon, there'd be no time for reading at the cash desk, would there? We stay open for the few customers who drop in, but if we had to pay someone to do it, it wouldn't be economic."

"What about the Ashgrove?" asked Rachel.

"What about it?"

"Well, I understand from Cecily Strong that your grandmother's brother, Harry Cook, is commemorated by one of the trees."

"So?" Gail's tone was more guarded.

"So, would it matter to you if they had to be cut down before the development could go on?"

"I expect my gran wouldn't like it," Gail conceded. "It doesn't matter so much to me. It was all so long ago."

"So you wouldn't fight to save them?"

"I didn't say that." Gail was quickly defensive. There was a moment's silence before she went on. "Thing is you have to weigh it up, don't you? I mean my kids go to the village school, at least two of them do, but every year the intake gets smaller, and by the time my Janie is five the school could be gone and she'd have to go Stone Winton or somewhere like that. I don't want that. It isn't just the business."

"Were you at the meeting?" Rachel asked. Gail nodded.

"Mike Bradley has offered to put up a stone memorial on the village green," Rachel said. "Perhaps that is as good a memorial as the trees."

Gail considered for a moment and then said, "Not as good, no. Not for the people who remember why the trees are there. But those men who died wouldn't want the village to die as well, would they? Uncle Harry went to the school here, the old one that is, but I'm sure he'd want there to be a school in the village, and homes for people, and that."

"Perhaps you're right," Rachel acknowledged. "Does your grandmother know what they want to do yet?"

Gail shook her head. "No. At least I haven't told her. Dad may have heard and told her." She thought for a minute and then added, "People are saying that Mike Bradley bloke might offer compensation to the families concerned. Gran could certainly do with the money...and my parents, for that matter."

"I am sure you'll hear if that's what they plan to do," said Rachel. She picked up a box of chocolates. "I'll take these, if I may," she went on. "I'm going to see my grandmother tomorrow."

Her next stop was the vicarage. Having checked the vicar's name on the church notice board, Rachel walked through the vicarage garden and knocked on the front door. Adam Skinner answered it and when she explained who she was and what she wanted, he invited her in and led her through to his study.

"Sorry about the mess," he said, gathering up a pile of papers from a chair and pulling it up towards the gas fire, "but this is the warmest room in the house. Do sit down."

Rachel saw that the desk lamp was on and there were two books open on the desk with a notebook and pen laid beside them. "I'm sorry to interrupt you," she began, "I can see you are busy."

She looked up at him. With the light on his face she discovered he was far younger than she had first thought, not much more than thirty, with shrewd grey eyes that looked out at her from under an untidy thatch of dark hair. He sat down at the desk, and leaned forward, resting his arms on the sprawl of papers.

"Saturday is usually quite busy," Adam Skinner agreed. "I have to prepare for Sunday, but that doesn't mean I don't have time for visitors. How can I help you?"

"I want to see if there is some way that the Brigstock Jones development can go ahead without destroying the Ashgrove," Rachel replied. "I've done some research on its history. There are accounts of its planting in the *Belcaster Chronicle* in 1921. I know that was a long time ago, but there are still people who remember it." She explained how she was going to try and find all the descendants of the men commemorated. "I wondered about looking in the parish records. A lady in the church said you had them."

"You can, of course," Adam agreed, "but they're not here in the parish any more, at least not the old ones, before 1945. They are in the record office in Belcaster. You'd have to go there to see those. I'm comparatively new to the parish, so I'm afraid I don't know the history of many of the families in the village."

"How do you feel about the proposed development?" Rachel asked.

"Probably as most people do, if they're honest. They don't like it, but recognise that without it the village will continue to dwindle away."

"And the Ashgrove?"

"If there is some way it can be preserved, then it should be. It was designed as a living memorial to those men, but it hasn't been maintained as such. The families concerned haven't made sure it is recognised as a memorial, and many people in the village had no idea of the significance of those trees. I wouldn't have known myself if it hadn't been for the history of the parish written by one of my predecessors."

"Is that the booklet in the church?" Rachel said, thinking that the Ashgrove had had only a passing reference in that.

"No, another little history which was left here in the vicarage. Written by a man called Smalley soon after the first war."

Rachel felt a surge of excitement. Henry Smalley was the

rector who had dedicated the trees. "I don't suppose I could see it, could I?" she asked casually. "It sounds most interesting."

The rector reached on to a shelf behind him and took down a slim volume bound in linen covers. "Here it is," he said, and passed it across to her. Rachel took it and opened it at the first page. On the flyleaf, written in faded brown ink, was a name she didn't recognise. Underneath was the title *A History of the Parish of Charlton Ambrose*, by Henry Smalley. Flicking through it quickly Rachel could see that for anyone interested in the parish it would make fascinating reading.

"Perhaps I could borrow this?" she asked.

Adam Skinner looked a little doubtful and said, "I've only this copy. I've never seen another and I wouldn't want to lose it." Then he smiled at her, shaking his head at his own reluctance. "Of course you can borrow it. I know you'll take care of it, and it isn't as if I don't know where it is."

"Don't worry," Rachel beamed at him, "I quite understand. Are you really sure? I promise I'll look after it and return it to you in the next few days."

"Yes, that's fine," Adam Skinner agreed.

"Thank you," she said softly, stowing the little book in her bag. "I'm sure it will be most helpful."

The rector got to his feet to show her out. "Do come back and tell me how you are getting on," he said. "If there is some way we can preserve the memorial without losing the houses, that would be perfect."

The December evening had closed in and it was almost dark as Rachel made her way back to her car. She tossed her bag on to the passenger seat and climbed in behind the wheel. Suddenly she'd had enough for one day and she longed to be back at home and soaking in a hot bath, after which she planned to spend the evening curled up in her big armchair reading *A*

History of the Parish of Charlton Ambrose, by Henry Smalley.

Later, as she did just that, she found herself immersed in the history of the little village. She read the whole book. It wasn't very long, but the part that fascinated her most were the years immediately after the first war when Henry lived and worked in the village himself. He told of the struggle to readjust after the war, of the flu epidemic, of how much the men who had not returned were really missed, of the planting and dedication of the eight trees, and then mentioned the unexpected arrival of the ninth.

> There was great uproar in the village when the extra tree was noticed. Many people wanted the tree uprooted, but stuck into the ground beneath it was a small frame containing a card on which were printed the words "To the unknown soldier". The Rector was much moved by this small memorial and discussed it at length with the squire. He was finally able to convince the squire that the tree did not detract from the memorial, but rather enhanced it with the addition of yet another man who had made the ultimate sacrifice. The squire allowed him to perform an additional service to dedicate the last tree. Thus the Ashgrove Memorial has since had nine trees. It is unfortunate that the carved stones that Sir George intended to have placed under each tree had not been commissioned when he died and his heirs did nothing about them. The small metal plaques originally naming each man disappeared over the years, and most of the trees are now unmarked, including the ninth tree, the man unidentified to this day. It is fortunate that the eight men are also remembered in the church on a separate memorial, so that it shall not be forgotten that they laid down their lives for their country and for their fellow men.

At last as she lay in the quiet darkness of her room, Rachel's thoughts drifted to Nick Potter and his invitation for this evening. In the circumstances it was a good thing she had refused, but she hadn't known that at the time. Why had she refused it, she wondered? She hadn't been out on the town for ages and it might have been fun. She had no regular boyfriend—several embryo relationships had bitten the dust when Rachel had put either her work or her independent life-style ahead of the man concerned. As a result she was sometimes lonely and missed having someone special to do things with; perhaps, if Nick did ask her again, she would go. After all, he was an attractive man and, more important to Rachel, he was interesting to talk to. But it would be strictly no strings. Rachel valued her independence too much.

1915

Belcaster Chronicle
Friday, 19th March 1915

OUR BRAVE LADS!

Nurses from the cottage hospital were among the families and friends who crowded Belcaster Station last Wednesday to wave farewell to our brave lads. Any tears shed by those left behind were tears of pride as our boys set off to France at last, to do battle with the Hun. The 1st Belshire Light Infantry are newly trained and ready for action and they will soon be joining their comrades at the front holding the lines against the German aggressor. A group of pals from Charlton Ambrose (pictured below), with their officer Lieutenant Frederick Hurst, were in high spirits as they set off with their mates to fight for king and country. Look out Kaiser Bill! Our lads are on their way and there are plenty more where they come from!

Five

The post lay on the brass plate in the front hall when Sarah came down for breakfast, and, seeing the letter with the French stamp addressed to her in a familiar, sloping hand, she caught it up and ran back upstairs to the privacy of her own room. Sitting on the window seat, she held the letter unopened in her hand for a moment, almost afraid to open it. She looked out over the dear, familiar garden, bright with the autumn morning. Sunlight struck fire from the beech trees that lined the outer edge of the paddock, and chrysanthemums in the bed against the southern wall of the vegetable garden glowed golden, orange and rust against the mellow stonework. As always, she thought of Freddie and wondered if he would ever see the garden again.

"None of that, Sarah," she admonished herself, and drawing a deep breath, she slit the envelope and drew out the letter.

My dear Sarah,

Thank you for your letter. It was lovely to hear from you after so long. I am glad your father remains in good health and that so far Freddie is safe.

You ask if you may come and work with us here, but though you tell me you have done your Red Cross nurse's training and have been helping at your local hospital I am not sure it equips you to work in our hospital here in France. I am sure you have had some useful experience there, but here would be quite different. We have been flooded with wounded from the front and working with such badly injured men is most distressing and stressful. It would probably be better if you joined up as a VAD and came over here after some experience with the wounded in a hospital in England.

However, as you asked me, I have spoken to Reverend Mother and she says if you are determined to come and nurse in France she will have you in our hospital here as we could do with all the help we can get. Obviously you would live in the convent with us, and be bound by the convent discipline that governs all our lay helpers, but this offer is entirely conditional on written consent from your father. If he forbids you to come there is no place for you here.

My dear child, I would love to see you after all these years, but am anxious about you leaving home at your age to come into such a dreadful business. The work here is never-ending and extremely hard. The sights we see are indescribable, the pain and the despair harrowing, but if you have the heart for it, your hands will be most welcome.

I wait to hear from you again, and in the meantime send my love,

Aunt Anne

Sarah read the letter through several times, her heart beat quickening.

I can go! she thought. I can go to France! All I have to do, she continued more ruefully, is to convince Father.

She thought of the letters they had received from Freddie, telling of the hideous casualties his regiment was suffering and how, despite all the work of the doctors and nurses in the army hospitals and casualty stations, there was never enough medical care.

"The dressing stations and casualty clearing stations can't cope with the number of wounded," he had written, "and the base hospitals are swamped. Everyone does his best, but men are dying from relatively small wounds simply because they aren't being treated in time and their wounds become infected."

Immediately she had read this letter, Sarah had written to Aunt Anne, her mother's sister, who was a nun in a nursing order in France asking if they would let her come to them and help nurse the wounded.

Sarah's mother, Caroline was Roman Catholic, and it had been considered most unusual for someone like her father to have married into a Catholic family. Certainly his mother had never approved, especially as he had had to agree that the children should be brought up as Catholics, but the marriage had been very happy, and when Caroline had died having her third child, and the child with her, George had stuck by his promise and continued to have Freddie and Sarah taught the Catholic faith. He, however, remained the patron of St Peter's Church in the village, and the children often accompanied him to the Manor pew where they seemed as comfortable as in Our Lady of Sorrows Church in Belcaster.

Aunt Anne had shocked even her own family years ago by joining a nursing order in France and becoming a nun. She had kept in touch with her sister's children by letter since Caroline had died, and it was to her Sarah had turned when she had been told by the authorities that she was too young to go and nurse the wounded in France.

"It's not fair!" she railed at her father when she had been turned down. "Freddie's out there fighting for his country, and so are thousands of men, much younger than I am, but they won't let me go to do my bit."

"You're doing good work here," soothed Sir George. "Look at the hours you put in at the cottage hospital."

"But it's not a hospital for the wounded!" cried Sarah in frustration. "I want to help nurse *them*."

"You are in a way," her father pointed out. "By giving your time here, you're releasing fully trained nurses to go to France, or to help in the big London hospitals."

But Sarah continued to brood, and one hot afternoon she let her frustration flow over again as she and Molly, the housemaid, were turning out the linen cupboard to find extra sheets for use in the cottage hospital.

"But don't your auntie nurse in France?" asked Molly as she folded the sheets they had found. "Can't you go to her hospital?"

Sarah stared at her. "I...well, I don't know," she said uncertainly. She got to her feet and, pushing a pile of towels towards the maid, said, "Fold these too, please Molly, and then pack them into that trunk on the landing. I'll get Peters to take them down to the hospital later."

Molly's idea took hold, and Sarah thought of it day and night for a week. Why not, she asked herself? Why not ask Aunt Anne? They must need help over there. The convent hospital had started as a couple of large rooms in one wing of the convent building, well away from those nuns who led a more contemplative life, but it had grown gradually over the years, and now, like all the hospitals in the northern parts of France, it was struggling to help with the ever-increasing convoys of wounded that straggled back from the front.

Without telling her father, Sarah had written to her aunt asking to be allowed to come and help with the nursing. Now, with Aunt Anne's answer in her hand, she not only had to break it to her father that she wanted to go, but had to persuade him to give his permission in writing.

She stared out over the garden again. It looked so peaceful

in the morning sunshine, it was hard to imagine the desolation of the battlefields just across the channel. Freddie had been home on leave some weeks earlier, and it had been several days before he had spoken to them of his life in the trenches; before he had opened up enough to give them just a glimpse of the misery he, and thousands of others like him, were sharing in the front line.

On two successive nights he had woken up shouting, and Sarah had rushed into his room to find him sitting up in bed, a cold sweat breaking on his forehead as he forced himself awake to escape from the nightmare. Gradually he told Sarah a little of what it was like, keeping most of the horrors from his father, who, though guessing much, asked nothing. Sir George was the sort of man who coped with his son being at the front and in constant danger by refusing to let his imagination run free. Freddie was there to serve king and country, and it was his duty, but his father didn't want or need to know the details of that service.

When Freddie returned to the front at the end of his leave, they had not accompanied him to the station as they had when he and his battalion had first left for France. The razzmatazz of that day was long gone and the cold reality of what he was going back to invaded their hearts with icy fingers. Freddie had taken his leave of them at home in the library, with the evening sun streaming in through its long windows.

"Easier not at the station," he had said. Sir George had, in a rare demonstration of affection, gripped his son in a bear-like hug, and then turned away to stare into the garden as Sarah hugged Freddie tightly in her own farewell. He was still alive, thank God, and kept in constant touch by letter, but they had not seen him since.

Sarah looked down at her aunt's letter again. There was little in it to recommend the idea to her father, except the fact that it was clear that any help would be welcomed, was indeed desperately needed. That was the way she must try and persuade her father; she must convince him somehow that she was needed.

There was a light tap on the door and Molly came in.

"Excuse me, Miss Sarah, but Squire says are you coming to breakfast today?"

Sarah jumped to her feet saying, "Yes, yes of course." She slipped the letter into the pocket of her skirt, and followed Molly downstairs to the dining room.

Sir George looked up from *The Times* when she came in and said rather irritably, "You're very late this morning, Sarah." He looked across at Molly who hovered by the door. "Off you go, Molly. Miss Sarah will serve herself."

"Sorry, Father." Sarah slid into her seat and reaching for the coffee pot, topped up his cup before filling her own.

"So, why are you so late?" he asked, putting down the paper and regarding her over his reading glasses.

Sarah felt the letter, stiff in her pocket, and deciding he had given her the opening she needed, plunged in.

"I had a letter this morning," she said, taking a sip of her coffee and looking at her father across the rim of the cup.

"Did you? Who from?"

"Aunt Anne."

"How is she?" Sir George enquired, about to retire behind the paper once more.

"Exhausted. The convent have opened their hospital to the allied wounded and they are completely swamped." She had his interest now and she drew a deep breath and went on, "She says Reverend Mother says I can go out and help with the nursing. I can stay at the convent, so I'd be quite safe, and..."

"No, Sarah, I'm sorry. You can't possibly go. You're needed here."

"No, Father, I'm not. The cottage hospital can manage perfectly well without me..."

"But I cannot," interrupted her father. "I need you here, to run this house. It's your duty to look after your family at home."

"You wouldn't say that if I were a boy," said Sarah, trying to sound reasonable. She knew that it would be disastrous for her to lose her temper. Once her father had taken a decision he seldom changed it; she needed time to work on him, to persuade him that going to nurse in France was the right thing for her to do.

"No, I wouldn't," he agreed. "But you're not, and the duties of men and women are different. Yours, as my daughter, is to remain at home and keep that home running smoothly for your brother to return to."

But supposing he doesn't come home, she wanted to cry out. Supposing he gets wounded and doesn't make it home because there aren't enough people to tend the wounded? But she fought down that cry, knowing it was far too dramatic for her father and would simply anger him. Very calmly she said, "Our home would run very smoothly without me, Father. Mrs Norton is an excellent housekeeper, and already it is she who sees to everything. She only consults me as a matter of form, you know." This was not quite true, and Sarah knew it. Mrs Norton could certainly run the house without aid from Sarah, but the housekeeper considered it a matter of great importance that Miss Sarah should be consulted in all things.

Miss Sarah would have her own house to run some day soon, Mrs Norton reasoned. She had no mother to teach her how and it was important she should know what went on below so that she could keep a firm hand on the helm, and take no nonsense from lazy servants.

Sir George grunted and turned back to his paper as if the matter were already closed.

"So, will you think about it, Father? Can we discuss it again at dinner?"

"My dear girl, there's nothing to discuss. You can hardly imagine that I'd let a daughter of mine traipse off all alone to France." He folded the newspaper and getting to his feet rested his hand lightly on her shoulder. "I'm out for lunch today, but will be home in time for dinner. Are you at the hospital?"

"Yes, I'll be there all afternoon," replied Sarah. She sighed as he left the room, then helped herself to a piece of toast and buttering it thoughtfully, she planned her campaign.

Molly came into the dining room in answer to the bell a few minutes later, and was surprised when Sarah pointed to a chair pulled clear of the table, facing her.

"Sit down, Molly," Sarah said. "I want to talk to you."

Molly perched awkwardly on the edge of the chair, and wondered what this was all about. "Yes, Miss Sarah?"

Sarah looked at her, taking in the pale face and the strands of dark hair which had escaped from Molly's cap, the rather skinny childish body, but the strong arms. She smiled at her and said, "How would you like to go to France, Molly?"

Molly looked startled: "Beg pardon, miss?"

"I said, how would you like to go to France? Remember the other day I told you I wanted to go and help nurse the wounded soldiers in France? Well, I have contacted my aunt and she has told me I can go and work in the hospital run by her convent."

Molly stared at Sarah, but said nothing, and Sarah went on, "They really are short of nurses out there, there are so many men wounded who need looking after, and I thought if I went, you might like to come with me."

Molly looked alarmed. "But I don't know nothing about nursing, Miss Sarah. I ain't done them exams what you have."

"I don't think you have to worry about that too much, Molly," Sarah said reassuringly. " I doubt if I'll be doing very much actual nursing either, but what they need are extra hands to do the cleaning and scrubbing. You know in a hospital everything has to be kept scrupulously clean so that there's no infection."

Molly nodded dumbly, and Sarah laughed. "Let's face it, Molly," she said, "you'd be far better at that than I am, you've been taught how to do it."

"I dunno, Miss Sarah," Molly said dubiously shaking her head. "I dunno."

"Are you worried about what your parents will say?" asked Sarah. "Do you think they'll say you can't go?"

Molly's lips tightened a little and she said, "It ain't got nothing to do with them."

"Well, it might do, you know. You aren't twenty-one yet, are you? How old are you?"

"Twenty, but my dad won't say nothing if Squire says I can go. If Squire says I can go, my dad won't complain."

"Just think, Molly what an adventure it would be! We'd go across the channel in a ship and then my aunt has arranged for us to live in the convent and work in the hospital there."

"In a convent, miss? With nuns?" Molly looked scandalised. "I don't know about that."

"You don't have to be afraid of nuns, Molly," Sarah said gently. "They are just women who've decided to work for God, and these ones do it by nursing."

But Molly was highly suspicious. She didn't like the sound of Catholics in general, and nuns...well. She said nothing and looked uncomfortable, suddenly remembering that Miss Sarah herself was a Catholic.

"I dunno, Miss Sarah," she mumbled, and her eyes slipped away to her hands twisting in her lap.

Sarah looked at her and considered what to say next. She needed Molly to be willing to go with her to have any chance of her father allowing her to go. If Molly were with her, she would not be traipsing all over France on her own. It would be perfectly respectable for her to travel with her maid.

She leant forward and took Molly's twisting hand in her own. Molly looked up startled, to find Sarah's face close to hers.

"Molly, I need you to come with me. My father certainly won't let me go on my own, and I know I have to go. Will you come with me? Will you come with me as a friend and companion? Molly, we've known each other all our lives, and you've been with us in the house for six years. Shall we go on this great adventure? If we were men, not women, we'd be there already, wouldn't we? We'd be doing our bit like everyone else. Think about it, Molly. Think about it and tell me later on. But I have to have your answer before dinner this evening, when I talk to my father again. All right?"

Molly nodded dumbly, and getting up from the chair, bolted from the room.

Oh dear, thought Sarah with a sigh as she watched her go, I didn't handle that very well. She left the table and whistling the dogs, set out for a walk to clear her mind and to decide exactly what she was going to do.

She spent the afternoon at the hospital, moving round the peaceful ward and following the quietly given instructions of the sister, and as she did so, she tried to imagine what it must be like in a hospital behind the lines, where there was no peace and quiet and where, it seemed, the wounded and dying lay side by side in rows on the floor.

Molly was waiting for her when she got home. As Sarah removed her hat the girl touched her arm shyly and said, "I'd like to go to France with you, Miss Sarah, if Squire says we can go."

Sarah's face broke into a dazzling smile as she said, "Molly, you're wonderful! Are you sure?"

Molly nodded and answered with quiet determination, "Yes, Miss Sarah, I'm sure."

"Have you mentioned the idea to anyone else?" Sarah asked anxiously.

"No, I haven't."

"Well don't, not for the moment anyway. I have to talk to my father again this evening. If he sends for you, what will you say?"

"I'll say I want to go with you to France to help look after the wounded Tommies," replied Molly.

"He can be a bit fierce," Sarah warned her. "You won't let him frighten you, will you?"

Molly shook her head. "No, Miss Sarah. The worst he can do is sack me, and then I can go anyway, can't I?"

Sarah had never seen Molly looking so determined, so positive, quite unlike the timid girl who had answered her this morning, and she wondered what had caused the change of heart. Still, that didn't matter now, and Molly's attitude to being sacked which was most unexpected, actually fitted in with Sarah's own plans if her father still refused her permission to go.

"I'm going up to dress for dinner now," Sarah said. "Don't worry about anything. I'll talk him round, it may just take a little time, that's all."

Sarah took extra care as she dressed for dinner. She knew her father liked her to look attractive, and though there were no guests coming that evening, he would appreciate the care she had taken, and she wanted him in a good mood.

She had decided to say nothing until they had eaten the pheasants she had instructed Mrs Norton to have braised with baby carrots and onions from the garden. It was one of Sir George's favourite dishes.

"Father," she began, "Pop, dear..."

At the use of her childish name for him, Sir George looked up and said wryly, "No, Sarah, I shouldn't think so for a minute!"

Sarah laughed and he did too. "I know that wheedling tone of old," he went on, "and I'm sure the answer is no."

"Well," agreed Sarah, "I know it was this morning, but we didn't really get a chance to talk things through, to discuss things properly."

Sir George put down his knife and fork and pushing his empty plate aside, looked at her across the table. Candles shone from the candelabrum in the centre, twinkling on the silver and glasses, and playing on the planes of his daughter's face as she gazed at him earnestly. Flashes of red glinted in her smooth dark hair, and her dark eyes glowed in the candlelight, giving life and warmth to her face. He felt a surge of love shake him as he looked at her. She was so like her mother had been at the same age, the age when he, one of the most eligible bachelors in the area, had seen her in the County Hotel in Belcaster having tea with her mother, and instantly and irretrievably lost his heart.

"There's nothing to discuss," he said now. "You are not going to go to France alone to nurse in a convent hospital."

Sarah gave him one of Caroline's dazzling smiles. "No, indeed, Pop," she agreed serenely, "Molly is going with me. So we shall be perfectly respectable, you see?"

"Molly?" repeated Sir George incredulously. "Molly is? Molly, my housemaid?"

Sarah nodded. "We will travel together to St Croix, and then we shall live in the convent and help in the hospital."

"But Molly doesn't know anything about nursing," began Sir George.

"I know, but she won't be doing any real nursing. Nor will I probably. We shall be another pair of hands to do what we can, to do what's needed." Sarah looked earnestly at her father. "They're desperate out there, Pop," she said quietly. "Read Aunt Anne's letter." She withdrew the letter from her bag and passed it across the table. Sir George took it and perused it in silence, then he looked up at her with pursed lips.

"This makes me less inclined than ever to let you go," he said. "It would be no place for a girl, gently brought up like you."

"Freddie was brought up in exactly the same way," pointed out Sarah, "and he's out there. Pop, just think what we should feel if Freddie were wounded and there was no one there to look after him; if everyone said, 'It's no place for a nice girl!' Men are dying out in France. They're dying because they need more nurses."

Her father sighed. "I know," he said flatly, "but it doesn't have to be you. Suppose something happened to you? Have you thought of that? Suppose you were injured, or caught some awful disease and died? Freddie is there, doing his duty. It is your duty to stay here and look after his home." He got to his feet and as he reached the door turned and cried out in anguish, "I don't want to lose both of you."

"If I were a man I'd have to be there and the risk would be the same." Sarah said levelly, trying not to hear his anguish.

"But you're not," her father said firmly and left the room.

Sarah sat at the table staring at the door he had closed softly behind him, the very gentleness of its closing emphasising to her his restraint despite his anger, and for a moment or two she was tempted to give in and stay. Perhaps her place was with him. If she went, who would look after him? She looked up at the portrait of her mother looking serenely down from the wall, painted when she was little older than Sarah was now. Sarah's memories of her mother were blurred at the edges. She had been young when her mother died trying to give birth to her younger brother, but she had always liked this picture of her, she seemed so calm, and despite the ghost of a smile playing at the corner of her mouth, there was strength in her eyes and determination in the tilt of her chin.

"I think I have to go, Mummy," she said aloud. Sarah had never progressed to calling her mother anything but Mummy, a little girl's name for a mother trapped in time, forever young. "Aunt Anne says they could do with all the help they can get. We can't just leave this war to the men." The final part of her plan slipped quietly into place in her mind, and with a quiet sigh, she followed her father to his armchair in the library.

Six

Molly Day had been planning to spend her precious afternoon off with her mother as she usually did. Her father would be working, and she and Mam could have a quiet time by the kitchen range with a pot of tea and a pile of griddle scones, dripping with butter. She only had one afternoon off a month, and she and her mother looked forward to it with eager anticipation. Today she finished clearing the lunch table and the washing-up in the kitchen in record time and then pulled on her coat and set out into the bright autumn afternoon.

Her mind was still buzzing with the idea that Miss Sarah had put to her that morning, indeed she had thought of little else as she had spent the morning polishing the furniture in the drawing room. Her mind swung from one reaction to another. One moment she was terrified at the thought of travelling so far and with no other companion than Miss Sarah, and the next she allowed herself a sudden shiver of anticipation at the adventure of it all, to go to France! How would they ever manage, working in a hospital there?

I don't speak a word of French, she thought. I don't know how to be a nurse! I've never been further than Belcaster, not even to London. I couldn't possibly go.

Then her thoughts swung the other way. I might be able to

do something real for the war effort. I might help our brave men win the war.

Her thoughts continued to tumble over each other, churning in her mind, excitement one minute, alarm the next, so that Mrs Norton had to scold her for not giving attention to the preparations for luncheon.

As she walked home, Molly wondered if she should mention it to her mother; certainly not if her father was there, but Mam...? No, she decided gloomily, Mam would tell her father anyway, and it wasn't worth a scene. Even so, as soon as she was in the lane which led out of Charlton Ambrose from the manor gate she felt better, almost light-hearted. She was away from the manor and work for a few precious hours. The amazing and completely unexpected suggestion Miss Sarah had made that morning could wait for its answer until later.

The sun flashed fire from the turning leaves, and those already fallen rustled and crunched under her feet as, child-like, she kicked her way along the path. Climbing over the old stone stile, she took the footpath across the fields and up the hill towards Valley Farm where she had been born and brought up. As she crested the rise and looked down into the valley that gave the farm its name, she saw there was a thin column of smoke rising steadily from the kitchen chimney. The farm was grey stone, long and low, its tiny windows peering out from under deeply overhanging eaves, the slate of its roof mellowed with lichens and moss. It looked from here, Molly always thought, as if it were nestling into the fold in the hill, like a hen fluffing out her feathers and settling on to her eggs. To the right of the farmhouse was the yard, on two sides of which were the hay barn and the milking shed. Beyond, in the fields that crept up the other side of the valley, the cows munched contentedly on the last of the summer grass. A cart track emerged from the farmyard and wound its way along the valley floor towards the road that led from Charlton Ambrose to Belcaster. It dipped down through the hedgerows in places only to reappear further on, the only link for a horse and cart between Valley Farm and civilisation. Often in the winter a fall of snow, driven by the wind, could cut them off for days at a time, and digging their way out the length of the track was the work of a week or more. Now however, the track, curving its way, muddy and rutted but reasonably dry, provided easy, if bumpy, access to the main road, and Molly knew the hedges that lined it would be heavy with blackberries, just ripe for the picking.

Molly wondered where her father was this afternoon. Sometimes from this vantage point she could see him working in one of the fields, but today there was no sign of him. She looked down at the house again and hoped he wasn't indoors. He always came in for his supper before Molly set off back to the manor, but that was all she saw of him, and if she were honest, all she wanted to. It was Mam she came to see.

She climbed the last stile and hurried down to the farm, where she was given an ecstatic welcome by Daisy and Ben, the two collies, as she entered the yard. She returned their boisterous greeting with hugs and cries of "Good dog, Ben! Hallo, Daisy pet! Good dogs! Good dogs!"

At the sound of their welcome the back door opened and her mother came out. As always she was dressed in a wraparound overall over her skirt and blouse, with a scarf tied up round her hair, but Molly, not having seen her for four weeks, noticed that she looked different...tired, well even more tired than usual, her face pale and drawn, her lips slow to curve into a smile of welcome.

Molly reached out to her, and they hugged briefly, a little awkwardly. Mam had never been one to demonstrate affection, though Molly never doubted that she loved her.

"Mam," she said now, "Mam, are you all right?"

"All right? Course I'm all right, why wouldn't I be?"

"No reason," Molly said hurriedly. "You just look a bit tired, that's all. You work too hard."

"And who's to do it if I don't?" enquired her mother. "Quiet, you dogs." At the sharpness in her voice, the two dogs stopped barking and wandered back to their kennels at the farmyard gate.

"Come on in," Mam said, and turning she led the way into the warm kitchen.

Molly loved the kitchen. It was always warm, and the comforting smell of baking ever-present, part of the atmosphere even if it were not a baking day. The huge deal table stood foursquare in the middle, and there were rag rugs on the flagged floor adding splashes of colour and warmth. Windows looked out on two sides and through one the afternoon sun poured in, beaming on the polished case of the grandfather clock that ticked solemnly in the corner. The range was always alight, and on their afternoons together, Molly's mother would open its door and they would sit before the open fire, enjoying its direct heat. Today the front was open already, the chairs drawn close for gossip, but sitting in one of them was her father.

"Hallo, Dad," Molly said a little uncertainly, taking off her coat and hanging it on the back of the door. "Why're you here?"

Her father looked up and glowered at her. "Why shouldn't I be in my own kitchen?" he growled, and taking his pipe from his pocket began to fill it from tobacco in a twist of paper.

"Oh, no reason," Molly replied hurriedly, "I—I well I wondered if you was ill or something...not working I mean."

"Ill?" repeated her father. "No, I'm not ill. Your mam told me you was coming this afternoon, and I wanted a word with you that's all."

Keeping the big table between herself and him, Molly said, "With me? Why what have I done?" and then was angry with herself. Why did she instantly assume she must have done something wrong when her father wanted to speak to her, and why did she allow him to see that he could still alarm her?

"Nothing," he replied, striking a match on the mantelpiece and applying it to his pipe. He drew hard, and said no more until the tobacco was well alight and glowing. In the silence, Molly looked anxiously across at her mother, but Jane Day was studiously making the tea, as if she had heard nothing of the exchange. She set out cups on the table and said casually, "Will you have a cup of tea, too, Edwin?"

Edwin continued to draw on his pipe, blowing smoke out of the corner of his mouth, but he nodded and waited while his wife poured tea for all three of them. Molly pulled out a stool from under the table and perched on it, still keeping the table between her and her father. Her mother took a plate of griddle scones out of the oven where they had been keeping hot and set them on the table.

"I thought we might go blackberrying in the lane this afternoon, Molly," she said evenly. "I want to make some more blackberry jelly this year. It is so good for colds in the winter." She put plates and knives on the table and a pot of last year's jam, but neither her daughter nor her husband took a scone.

"What did you want to say to me, Dad?" Molly asked, trying to keep her voice firm and strong.

Her father finally looked at her and said abruptly, "You're to give your notice in at the manor, and come back here." He blew a plume of smoke across the table. "You can go and work in the munitions factory at Belmouth. The money there is far better, you can make as much as five shillings a day there."

Molly stared at him in horror. "But I don't want to work in the munitions factory," she stammered. "I want to stay working at the manor. I like it there."

"Can't always have what we want in this life," her father said grimly. "You should know that by now. We need your wages to keep things going here."

"But Dad," protested Molly. "You already have half my wages every week."

"So, this way we'll all have a bit more," he said. "You're to give your notice in to the squire when you get back this evening, and move back home at the end of the month."

"Mam." Molly turned in appeal to her mother. "Mam, I don't want to work in a factory. I don't want to come back and live at home. I'm happy at the manor, I like being in service."

"You heard what I said, Molly," said Edwin Day implacably. "You should be doing your bit for the war effort, my girl, not running round after gentry what sit in their houses and do nothing."

"Mr Freddie's at the front..." began Molly, but Edwin cut across her.

"It's decided. You'll come home here and work in the factory. You tell Squire." He put his pipe in his pocket and downing the cup of tea in one swallow, he got to his feet and headed to the door. As he passed her, Molly instinctively shrunk away from him, but he made no move to touch her, simply picked up his cap from a chair by the door, and cramming it on his head went out into the farmyard, where he could be heard calling to the dogs.

"He speaks to the dogs far better than he does to you or me," Molly muttered, picking up her teacup. "Mam, I don't want to leave Squire and Miss Sarah. I like working at the manor."

Her mother shrugged slightly and said, "You'd better do what your dad tells you, Molly. He knows what's best."

"Mam," Molly looked beseechingly at her mother, "you know why I don't want to come home."

Her mother's face went suddenly rigid. "Now, Molly, let's have no more of that nonsense! I won't have you say things like that about your father, and if you so much as hint at such a wicked, wicked thing again, I'll take a stick to you myself." She banged her teacup down in her agitation, slopping the contents on to the kitchen table. "You give your notice in, like your dad says, and let's have no more of this. Now, pick up that pail over there and let's get out to those blackberries." She turned away from her daughter, and taking a basket from a cupboard, headed for the door, calling over her shoulder, "Come along, now, there's a good girl. It's a lovely crop this year, and with two of us we'll have plenty in no time."

Molly set her own cup down with a sigh of resignation, and picking up the indicated bucket, followed her mother out into the yard. There was no sign of her father, but the brilliance of the day had gone. As her own horizons loomed grey and ominous, so the sun had slid behind heavy clouds which scurried in on a rising west wind, and the day became overcast and chill. What would have been, on any other September day a pleasant afternoon's occupation, seemed now to be a chore. The thought of coming back to live at Valley Farm permanently filled Molly with dread.

Ever since she had turned nine, she had had to fend off her father's attentions, and as the months had turned into years her childhood love for him had turned into fear. He had not been unkind to her at first, but his cuddles altered in some way that she didn't understand, and gradually Molly grew to dread them. She began to withdraw from him, slipping from his grasp when they were alone together in the house. Often her mother went over to Granny Cook's house to help her. Granny was her mother's mother, and very old so that, although she stayed in her own cottage, refusing to move, she needed Mam to come in each evening after tea to help her get ready for bed. It was then that Dad would sit Molly on his knee and stroke her hair. Then one day he asked her to stroke him. At first she laughed awkwardly, and said she couldn't stroke someone big like him, it was silly.

"But you stroke Pusskins," he pointed out, leaning down and picking up the cat by the scruff of its neck. He dumped it in Molly's lap and almost automatically Molly began to stroke the cat so that he set up a steady rumbling purr.

"See? See how much he likes that, you stroking his tummy?"

Molly giggled nervously and said, "But I can't stroke your tummy, Daddy!" She pushed the cat down and scrimmaged her way off Dad's knee. He had let her go that time, but his strange attentions didn't cease. By the time she was twelve, he had taken to coming to her room when she had gone to bed and her mother was out. There he had made a game of saying goodnight, tucking her in; but he touched her in places that Molly didn't like, private places, patting her bottom and slipping his hand under her nightie. He told her she was growing into a lovely girl, and placing his huge hands on the budding breasts that stood out through the woollen night-dress, he stroked them with his thumb.

"Lovely little bubbies, you've got, Moll," he muttered.

She would push him away and say, "Go on, Dad! Get away with you." But he had not been so easily put off and he said, "All dads like to see their daughters growing into lovely girls, it's only natural," but his voice was gruff and he sounded funny. Sometimes he leaned over and lifted her out of the bed as if she were no more than a doll, sitting her on his lap and bouncing her up and down so that her little round bottom bumped against him. "Dad, you're hurting," Molly cried, but he laughed and bounced her all the more, his breath hot and ragged on her face. Other times he lay on the bed beside her, holding her against him in a bear-like hug, rubbing himself against her and saying, "See, I'm like Pusskins!" Molly pushed him half-heartedly away, saying "Dad! Give over! It's too hot. Get off!"

He'd laugh then and roll off the bed. "Give your old Dad a kiss goodnight then," he'd say, and, reaching down to put his hands round her face, would kiss her full on the lips. "And don't tell your mam you was up so late, or we'll both be in trouble. Our little secret, eh pet?"

When he left the room, Molly often found she was shaking. She could still feel his hands on her body and his lips on her mouth. He had always kissed her goodnight when she was little, but it had never been hugs and kisses like this, and for some reason she found she didn't like it. She had said nothing to her mother because really there was nothing to say. She didn't understand what was happening, all she knew was that if Dad was playing a game, she didn't want to play any more.

One evening when he had finally left her to sleep, she gave long thought about what she should do. The idea, when it came to her seemed remarkably simple, and she decided to act on it. The next evening, when her mother was at home and they were all in the kitchen, Molly got up to go to bed. She said goodnight to her parents, but made no move to kiss either of them as she had always done before, just moved towards the door.

"Don't we get a goodnight kiss, then?" asked her mother looking up from her mending with a smile.

"I reckon I've got a bit old for that now," Molly said nervously. "That's only for little'uns. I'm nearly grown up now."

"Never heard such rubbish," puffed her father. "Come here and say goodnight properly like." He reached out his hand to her, but she evaded him and slipped round the table.

"No, Dad," Molly said warily. "I don't want kisses any more, not like last night."

"Like last night?" queried her mother with a frown. "What are you talking about, Molly?"

"Daddy kissed me last night at bedtime, but I'm too big for that now," Molly said firmly. "Grown-ups shake hands when they say goodnight." She proffered her hand to her mother who took it with a rueful shrug and said, "Well you *are* a funny girl."

Dad had taken her hand too, but his grip had been so hard that she almost cried out with pain. "Goodnight, then, Molly," he said. "I hadn't told Mam that I let you stay up late last night before I came to tuck you in, but it is clear that we mustn't have secrets from her." It was indeed clear. There was no doubting the message in that grip. It was clear that there would always be that secret from Mam, and Molly's anxiety burgeoned into full-blown fear from that evening on.

She kept well clear of her father from then, and it became so obvious that her mother said to her, "I don't know what's the matter with you, Molly. Have you and your dad had a row or something? You hardly speak to him these days. What's the matter? Tell me and perhaps I can put it right."

So Molly tried to tell her, but it came out all wrong and her mother exploded with fury.

"How dare you say such things about your father!" she cried. "He loves you and wants you to love him too, that's all. You're a very wicked girl to say such things, and if I hear anything like it again I shall tell your dad what you say about him."

Her mother must have done just that, because Dad came roaring at Molly for making up stories to upset her mam, and threatened to take his belt to her if she ever did such a thing again. In her innocence Molly had no idea what her parents thought she was saying about her father. She knew how lambs and calves were born, she had grown up with that, but she knew nothing about human intercourse; her reaction against her father had been entirely instinctive. She was accusing him of nothing, but his reaction to her perceived accusation was violence, and it was not forgotten. Whenever she did wrong in his eyes from then on, he would lash out at her with hand or belt, and Molly lived in fear of his anger. Mam had tried to make up for it all by being the buffer between them, but she soon realised that it was time for Molly to leave home and as soon as she was old enough to go into service Jane Day went to see Mrs Norton, the squire's housekeeper and arranged for Molly to be taken on at the manor as a maid-of-all-work.

Life at the manor was strange at first and Molly had to learn fast to avoid Mrs Norton's sharp tongue, but there were no beatings there and she soon got used to how the house ran and was comparatively happy. Half her wages were paid to her father, which left her with very little, but with no living expenses she had enough and it was worth it to be out of Valley Farm. She and her mother seemed closer now that they no longer shared a roof, and with her father there was a sort of armed neutrality.

Today was the first real confrontation they had had since she had left, nearly five years ago, and Molly was shaken that he could still frighten her. As she followed her mother down the track and began to pick the blackberries, Molly thought about her father's ultimatum.

"I'm not going back to live there," she told herself fiercely. "I'll never live under his roof again." Now that she was old enough and less naïve, Molly had some idea of what her father had been doing. She realised too, that her mother probably had believed her, but had been in no position to protect her. She, too, was afraid of Edwin, and though Molly had never seen any actual bruises on her mother's face, she never saw the rest of her body unclothed, and didn't know if it carried bruises like her own or not.

Today Molly had felt the usual fear when confronting her father, but there had also been something else, something extra which made her feel different. She had felt anger, and this anger had lessened her fear. Why should he treat me like this? she thought crossly as she stripped the ripe berries from their brambles, hardly noticing the thorns which ripped at her fingers. How dare he tell me what I can and can't do, where I must work? He may be my father but he don't own me. She said this several times under her breath, "He may be my father, but he don't own me!"

Hearing her voice her mother called across and said, "What did you say, Molly?"

Feeling suddenly brave, Molly called out, "He may be my father, but he don't own me, and I'm not going to work in no munitions factory, neither. I'm going nursing, to France, with Miss Sarah." As she shouted it out, Molly knew that her decision was taken. She put down the bucket and went over to her mother, who was staring at her open-mouthed.

"I'm sorry, Mam. I was going to talk to you about it this afternoon, but well, things was different today." She took her mother's basket from her and set it on the ground, then she looked up at her. "Mam," she said softly, "Mam, I'm sorry, but I'm going to go with Miss Sarah. She asked me this morning if I'd go to France with her to help nurse our wounded soldiers. I said I'd think about it, and I have. I can do more good in a hospital in France than I can in any munitions factory. Still doing my bit for the war, even Dad will see that. I'm not coming home to live. I'm going to France."

"Your dad won't let you," her mother said flatly. "He won't let you go, a girl of your age."

"He won't be able to stop me," Molly said firmly. "Not unless he locks me in the barn and throws away the key." She took her mother's hand and gripped it tightly. "I could go without telling him," she said softly. "He wouldn't know I was going if I didn't tell him…and you didn't."

Jane Day stared at her daughter, her mouth working with agitation. Molly seemed different today, suddenly adult and positive, and Jane feared for her. She knew only too well what happened if you crossed Edwin, and she could see the same obstinacy in Molly's eyes now, that she had seen so often in Edwin's.

"I don't know anything about your weird ideas, Molly," she said indifferently, pulling her hand free and turning away. "I expect you to go back to Squire and give in your notice and then we'll see you in a month's time. I doubt if we'll see you before." She picked up her basket and set off back to the farmhouse. For a moment Molly stared after her, wondering if this time Mam actually meant she wasn't going to tell her dad what she planned. Had she just been offered the breathing space of a month, or did Mam really mean that she expected her to come home when the month was up? She picked up her bucket and followed, and when they reached the farm, her mother led the way into the farmhouse, made more tea and set Molly to sorting the blackberries, just as if the conversation had never taken place, and Molly left early, before her father came in for his evening meal.

2001

Seven

R achel arrived at her grandmother Rose Carson's home just before lunch, and made the short dash up the path to the front door through the driving rain. Her grandmother, who was as fiercely independent as Rachel, lived in a ground floor flat in a block of sheltered housing on the edge of the town. She had given up her old home when Rachel had moved out and was now comfortably settled in Cotswold Court, where she could have as much independence as she liked, but where there was a warden on hand if necessary. There was a tiny kitchen where she could prepare food if she wanted to, but a main meal was provided at midday in the communal area every day. It suited Rose Carson very well.

Rachel had her own key and to save Gran from having to come to the door she used it now, calling out, "Hallo, Gran, it's only me."

Her grandmother was in the sitting room, her wheelchair pushed up beside the window that looked out over the dank, winter garden. Her tapestry was on her knees, but there was no thread in the needle that lay on the table beside her, and the local paper was folded tidily, apparently unread. Her face lit up with a smile as Rachel came into the room and crossed over to give her a hug and the chocolates she had bought the day before in Charlton Ambrose village shop.

"Hallo, darling! How lovely. Black Magic, my favourite!" Gone was the lethargy that had seemed to hold her and she spun her chair away from the window. "What a dreadful day out there! Lunch will be ready in about half an hour. Why don't you pour us both a drink?"

"Yes, all right. Gosh, Gran, it's cold in here," Rachel scolded. "You should keep the fire on." She went to the fireplace and pressed the starter. The gas ignited with a whumpf and immediately the room looked more cheerful.

"I usually do," Gran said equably. She was used to Rachel ticking her off for being frugal, but to her it was a way of life. All her life she'd had to watch every penny and she couldn't bring herself to waste money on gas when a blanket over her knees and a shawl round her shoulders kept her as warm. Rachel looked across at her affectionately and switched on the standard lamp as well, suffusing the room with warm light and making the aspect from the window even bleaker.

A drink to Gran meant a glass of sweet sherry, and Rachel went to the cabinet in the corner and poured two glasses. "How've you been this week?" she asked as she handed Gran one glass and sat down with the other on the opposite side of the fire. They chatted easily for a while before Rachel dished up the casserole Gran had in the oven.

"By the way," Rachel said, "I've got a message for you. A man called Nick Potter sent you his love."

Gran looked amused. "Did he now? Isn't he a wizard?"

Rachel laughed. "No," she said firmly. "That's Harry Potter! This one's a very ordinary man."

"Is he indeed? And why did this very ordinary man send me his love?"

"I told him I was coming to see you today, and well, he just did."

"How very kind of him," said Gran with a speculative smile. "Do give him mine back."

"I will if I see him," Rachel said casually.

It was as they ate their meal Rachel began to tell Gran about the Ashgrove.

"Yes, I saw your piece in the *Chronicle*," Gran said, "all about Charlton Ambrose. It was very interesting. You know I lived there when I was a little girl." It was a statement, not a question and Rachel looked up, startled.

"No, I didn't. I didn't know that. When did you live there?"

"My grandparents lived there," Rose said. "When I was born my mother went home to them. My father had been killed in the war, in France. I never knew him."

Rachel stared at her grandmother in amazement. "I never knew that!" she said. "I mean, I know your father was killed in the first war, but I never knew you lived in Charlton Ambrose, I thought you'd always lived in Belcaster. Where did you live? How long were you there?"

"On and off till I was about fourteen, I suppose," answered Gran.

"Fourteen!" Rachel shook her head. "So you were living there when they planted the Ashgrove."

"I suppose so," Gran agreed.

"Do you remember it?"

"I have a vague memory of people standing about on the village green and planting trees," said Gran, "but I didn't really know what it was all about."

"But Gran, that's amazing. You were actually there! Can you remember any of the people from the village...any of the families?"

Gran laughed. "Darling, I was only four."

"But you said you lived there till you were fourteen."

"So I did, most of the time, but I can't remember many of the people. We kept very much to ourselves."

"So you don't know anyone who lives there now?"

Gran shook her head. "No, no one."

It's strange, Rachel thought as she looked across at Gran, dear Gran, who had taken her in so readily when her parents had been killed in a motorway pile up. I've lived with her for years, but I know so little about her early life. She never talks about it, and, Rachel thought ruefully, I've never asked.

She said as much now and Gran gave a sad smile.

"All so long ago," she replied. "I don't talk about it because I've tried to put it out of my mind. It wasn't a particularly happy childhood."

"But you spent it all in Charlton Ambrose? I never knew that," Rachel said again.

"Not all of it. My mother and I moved away for a while, but when she died I had to go back and live with my grandparents. They took me in out of duty and I left as soon as I left school."

"Out of duty?"

"Oh yes. They didn't approve of me, you see," Gran's eyes twinkled, "I was a scandal. My parents weren't married! My father was killed before he could make an honest woman of my mother."

"That was hardly your fault," retorted Rachel.

"Ah, but it was a different world then," Gran reminded her. "Nice girls didn't get pregnant. She may have been only the daughter of a small farmer, but my mother had been very strictly brought up. I was her child of shame. To begin with I think they tried to pretend my mother had been married and widowed almost immediately, but the truth came out after the war, and though they stuck to the story for a while, no one believed them and of course there was no marriage certificate to wave in the faces of the gossip-mongers."

"Oh Gran, how awful," cried Rachel. "Your poor mother, and poor you."

"It's why we moved into the town," Gran said. "I must have been about five or six when we left. My mother worked in a pub as a barmaid and a room went with the job. They let her bring me, but I was expected to help with the chores as soon as I was able."

"What, at five years old?" exclaimed Rachel.

"I could dust and polish brasses, and I learnt to iron very early on." She smiled, "Stood me in good stead when I wanted to leave home later. I managed to get work in a big house as an under-housemaid."

"But what happened to your mother?"

Gran's face hardened. "She got ill and died. No one would tell me what happened and I still don't know for sure. In retrospect I imagine part of her job was being nice to the landlord, you know? I hated him and I was afraid of him too. He was fat and greasy and smelly. I hated him near me. He used to poke his finger at me. It was just like a grubby sausage."

Rachel had an instant visual image of the landlord and it made her shudder.

"I was very young," Gran went on, "but I shall never forget his hands . . . fat pudgy hands with black round the fingernails. The memory still makes me shudder." For a moment she paused, her eyes resting in the middle distance, then she smiled at Rachel. "Anyway, one evening my mother came upstairs groaning. We only had one bed, which we shared, and I was already in it, but she lay down beside me. I remember I was very scared, but she said she'd be all right soon. Of course she wasn't, and I realised there was blood seeping into the bed covers. I started to scream and eventually the landlord's wife came in to tell me to shut up. When she saw my mother and the blood and the mess, she started shrieking and fetched her husband. They carried me out of the room and I never saw my mother again. Nobody ever told me what had happened to her, all I knew was that she was dead. I can only assume she'd been to a back-street abortionist."

Rachel reached out her hands to take her grandmother's, her plate pushed away, unfinished, forgotten. "And you went back to your grandparents again?"

"My grandmother came and fetched me," Gran said. "I know she didn't want me in the first place, but this latest must have been an added scandal. My mother was buried in the churchyard at Charlton, and after that she was never mentioned again."

"Gran, how awful!" Rachel was horrified. "Their own daughter!"

"I think they had long ceased to think of her as that," Gran said quietly. "They took me in and fed me until I was old enough to go into service, and that's what I did, without a backward glance."

"Where?" asked Rachel. "Where did you work?"

"In Belstone St Mary," said Gran, "at The Grange. It was a relief to get away, particularly from my grandfather...and I expect they were relieved to see me go."

"Why from your grandfather?" asked Rachel, but even as she asked she realised she already knew the answer. "He didn't...?"

"Not in the way you mean," Gran replied. "Nothing specific, just touching and, well, I was always uncomfortable when I was left alone with him, and so I tried not to be."

"Did your grandmother know? Surely she knew. Didn't she realise what was going on?"

Gran smiled ruefully. "I'm sure she did, but she turned a blind eye. Things like that were never admitted, you know. Certainly not in a respectable household. Most men were masters in their own homes, and their wives seldom went against them." She sighed. "I've often wondered if that was really why my mother moved away again; whether he had abused her as well. Perhaps she was afraid for me. It's only a guess, we shall never know. Suffice it to say that I was delighted to escape into service in the relative safety of The Grange."

"Dear, dear Gran. How awful for you." Rachel felt the tears in her eyes. How different from the way Gran had taken her in; had loved her and made her feel precious. Gran had tried in every way to be father and mother to Rachel. She had encouraged her in everything she did, in school and out. She had run side lines on cold winter afternoons watching Rachel play hockey, turned out for parents' evenings, sat through school plays and concerts and she had continued to work long after she should have retired so that Rachel could go to university. What a contrast, Rachel thought to the grudging home provided for Gran by *her* grandparents.

"But Gran, why are you telling me all this now, after all this time? I mean, well what's brought all this on?"

Gran shrugged. "I don't know, really," she said. "Maybe your article."

"My article? About Charlton Ambrose? Why?"

"Well, reading all about the village and its problems made me look back." She smiled ruefully: "When you get to my age there's nowhere much else to look. Anyway, your article decided me. There's something I've been considering giving you for quite a while, and I think perhaps now is the time for you to have it. I want to give it to you myself, not leave it for you to find after I'm dead, because I want you to understand where it comes from. If you go into my bedroom you'll find an old biscuit tin in the cupboard by my bed. Please could you get it for me?"

Rachel went to fetch the tin, thinking as she went of Cecily and her biscuit tin, and smiling, wondered if all old ladies kept their treasures in biscuit tins. She found the tin, tied up carefully with tape, and carrying it back into the sitting room, put it in Gran's lap. Gran's arthritic fingers struggled for a moment with the tape and then she passed it back to Rachel. "You open it," she said.

"These knots are tight," said Rachel, struggling as well. "When did you last have this open?"

"I don't know, about fifty years ago, I suppose."

"Fifty years!" Rachel echoed, amazed. She had been about to suggest that they cut the tape, but now decided to persevere with the knots. Eventually she began to work them loose and at last the tape fell away and she could open the tin. Before she did so, she looked across at her grandmother and asked quietly, "What's in here, Gran?"

"Letters and a diary. I used to think that when I was gone and you were another generation away from those concerned, you could publish them as a book. Telling people how it really was, but I think perhaps they will be more use to you now, while you're trying to save the Ashgrove."

"The Ashgrove?" Rachel was intrigued.

"I don't know. Have a look. I may be quite wrong. I haven't read everything in there, none of the letters. I felt they were too private, but I did read the diary, that didn't seem so much of an intrusion."

"But won't I be intruding too?"

"Perhaps, and if you feel you are, then you can stop, but I think you may well find the answer to the Ashgrove in them, and saving it may be a justification for the intrusion."

Rachel opened the old tin and carefully lifted out the contents. There were several packets of letters and an old exercise book bound with hard covers. She opened the book and looked at the first page. There in faded pencil it said, *This is the diary of Molly Day. Extremely Private.*

Rachel closed it again and looked at the letters. Each packet was tied up with the same sort of tape that had secured the tin. The letter on the top of the first packet was addressed to *Miss Molly Day* at a convent in France, and the one on the top of a second packet to *Pte Thomas Carter.*

"Was Molly Day your mother?"

Gran nodded

"But how did you get these, Gran?" Rachel asked. "I mean, if your mother was disowned...?"

"I found them when my grandmother died, during the second war. I was the only one left and I went down to clear the house. My grandfather had been dead for years and the farm gone long since, but my grandmother lived in a cottage on the estate and it had to be cleared immediately when she died. This tin was in the attic. She must have found it after my mother died and kept it hidden, her last link with her daughter." Gran gave a sad little laugh. "I nearly threw it away unopened," she said, "there was so much junk up in that attic, but something made me look inside. When I realised what was there, I just closed the tin up again and took it home with me. It was days before I could bring myself to open it again."

"But why?" Rachel was fascinated. "Didn't you want to find out about your mother and father? I mean I assume Private Tom Carter was your father."

"I wasn't sure," admitted Gran. "I had my own life by then. I'd changed my name when I went into service, broken with my past life, and I wasn't at all sure I wanted to look back again." She sighed. "I knew there was something wrong about my parents, but I didn't know what. I was twenty-six, newly married, and at last somewhat established in the world. I had struggled for all those twenty-six years in one way or another, and I was afraid that these voices from the past would rock the boat. I didn't tell John about them. I was so afraid there might be something that would make him think less of me. He'd already taken the bold step of marrying a girl who was illegitimate, a brave thing to do even in 1941."

"So, if you couldn't tell Grandpa about finding the tin, what did you do with it?"

"I hid it as well. When he went away to sea, and I was left on my own in London, I finally got it out again, and that's when I read the diary."

Rachel picked up the exercise book again and looked at it. The writing inside was rather childish, a pencilled scrawl.

"Don't read it now," Gran said quickly. "You need to take your time."

Rachel replaced the diary in the box. "And the letters? Did you never read them...any of them?"

"No. They were not mine to read."

"And are they mine?" Rachel scanned her grandmother's face to try and discover her true thoughts about the letters, knowing if the choice had been hers she would probably have been consumed by curiosity and read them.

"That's for you to decide. They are your inheritance, part of your history. For me they were too close, even though I'd never known my father and scarcely remembered my mother, but for you, eighty years on...well, they are a piece of social history. Feel free to read them, there's no one who'll be hurt by them now, whatever they say."

Rachel said, "I'll think about it." She placed everything back in the tin and carefully re-tying the tape set it aside.

"The rector of Charlton Ambrose lent me a book yesterday," Rachel went on, "a history of the parish, by another rector, called Henry Smalley. He seems to have been rector for quite some time. Do you remember him?"

Her grandmother thought for a moment and said, "Well, there certainly was a rector, he could have been called Smalley. I don't remember going to church much, until after my mother died. After that I had to go every week with Grandma. I remember the rector always seemed a very sad man, but he was always kind to me, he probably was to all the children. I don't think he had any of his own. Sorry, Rachel, but I really can't remember his name.

"Probably the same man," Rachel said. "He wrote the book in about 1930, so I assume he was still there then. It doesn't matter, I just wondered, that's all."

When she left Cotswold Court later that afternoon, Rachel went straight home, poured herself a proper drink and curled up on the sofa. The biscuit tin sat on the table, still tied with tape, waiting for her. Even as she reached for it, her mobile buzzed beside her to announce the arrival of a text message. She flicked the switch. *Hope you gave the grandmother my love.*

Rachel stared. A message from Nick. How on earth had he got her mobile number? She had switched her phone off while she was at Gran's, she usually did, and only put it back on again when she reached home. However, she had too much seething in her brain to think about Nick Potter now, so she ignored the message and switched the phone off again, tossing it back into her bag. Then she took hold of the waiting biscuit tin and untied the tape.

1915

This is the diary of Molly Day

Monday, 4th October 1915

Today we set off on our adventure, Miss Sarah and me and I have decided to keep a journal of how we go on, to tell our adventures to the village when we get home. Squire came with us to the station and as we left he put a guinea in my hand...a whole guinea...and he said, "Look after Miss Sarah for me, Molly, and make sure she doesn't get into mischief." And I said, "Lord, sir, I can't tell Miss Sarah what to do!" And he smiled and said, "No, nor can anyone, but look after her all the same."

We went by train to London. It was a cold day, and London was very big and dirty. When we were on the train it was as if we were in London long before we got to Paddington station. I've never seen nothing like London with all its traffic. There were motors everywhere as well as trams, and people, hundreds of people. Some officers helped us find a cab, and we went to Carver Square near the British Museum where Miss Sarah's auntie, Squire's sister lives. There's trees there in a sort of garden in the middle. I didn't know there'd be trees in London, I thought it was just houses. We are to stay here for a few days before we go to France. Her auntie, Lady Horner is a very nice lady. They've given me a room to myself on the servants' floor, and I eat in the servants' hall. There's lots of food and it is very good. They talk different here, even the servants, so I am going to try to talk posh like them so's not to disgrace Miss Sarah. I have nothing to do but look after Miss Sarah, and at present that takes no time at all. We were very tired so we went to bed early, but it took me ages to get to sleep I was that excited to be here. That's when I wrote this, about the first day of my adventure.

Tuesday, 5th October 1915

Don't I feel a country fool in this great big town! When we walk down the street, there I am gawking at the buildings, and there's Miss Sarah saying, "Come along, Molly, do! Don't dawdle." We have done lots of shopping. Miss Sarah bought new clothes to take. She says her auntie, the one that's a nun, says we must have grey skirts and white blouses and lots of warm underwear. I've never had so many new clothes, and boots too, and a new winter coat. I really am spoilt. It wasn't just clothes either, but all sorts of other things. Mam's eyes would stare if she could know how much money Miss Sarah paid out for me today. I thought she might take it out of my wages, but she says no, it's because of her I need the clothes and she'll pay. I'm not saying no to that!

Tomorrow we are going by train to the boat to cross the channel. I've never been on the sea before.

Eight

They left for France four days before Molly was due for her next visit home. She had seen neither of her parents since she had left the farm on that last occasion, and as far as she knew her father had no knowledge she was going away. Had Mam managed to keep the secret after all, she wondered? Or had she not really believed that Molly would go? Had she simply assumed, as no doubt her father had, that Molly would obey his dictates and come home docilely after working her month's notice? Whichever it was, Molly was relieved that her father had not arrived breathing fire at the manor to button-hole the squire and announce that his daughter was leaving the manor and going to work in the munitions factory. If Dad had heard about nursing in France, he would have dragged her home on the spot, notice or no notice.

Sarah had had a battle with her own father. The evening she had followed him into the library, the squire had remained adamant that she could not go, but as she finally pointed out to him, "You can't stop me, Father. I shall use mother's money and Molly and I will travel together quite safely."

"Your aunt says that the Reverend Mother, or whatever the woman is called..."

"You know perfectly well what she is called, Father," put in Sarah patiently.

"Your aunt says that she must have my permission in writing to allow you to go, and I shan't give it!"

"Then I shall go without it," Sarah returned quietly. "They are crying out for nurses, and I doubt if they will actually turn me away if I turn up, even without a letter from you."

"I shall write and say you are not coming," her father said firmly.

"And I shall go just the same," Sarah said, equally firmly. "If they turn me away, I shall find another hospital that will have me." She smiled seraphically at her father. "Of course that would mean wandering about France on our own with no particular place to go, but I expect we could find somewhere in the end."

Her father looked at her and saw, on his daughter's face, the steely expression of determination her mother had worn when she had announced to her parents that she was marrying George Hurst, not of the Roman Church. It was an expression with which he had grown familiar, and seeing it again on Sarah's face now, he knew when he was beaten.

"You can't drag young Molly Day round the battlefields!" Sir George continued to sound outraged. "What does her father say to all this nonsense?"

"He says that provided we are travelling together to a relative of mine, he has no objection to Molly going. After all, maids travel with their mistresses every day. Why should this be any different?"

Molly had taken a risk. When Sarah had asked her if her parents had any objection to her going to France, she had said, with a perfectly straight face, "None at all, Miss Sarah. I work for Squire now, miss, and if he says I should go then that's all right with them. They know I'll be quite safe with you, miss." Sarah had been so pleased that Molly had agreed to go that she didn't query this easy acceptance of the situation from Molly's parents. She made no effort to check that they had given their approval, and with her acceptance, Molly was relying on the fact that the squire would accept it too. Once they had gone, and her father discovered they had, he would be over to the manor in a towering rage, but with luck he wouldn't discover immediately and by then it would be too late.

As she had left the farm that last afternoon, Molly had hugged her mother tightly, taking a silent farewell. Her mother had returned the hug and then they parted, neither of them speaking another word. Molly, turning away, strode out of the farmyard without a backward glance. Her father, returning through the autumn twilight for his tea, had seen her tramping up the footpath to the hilltop, and knew that she had left early to avoid him. He was not surprised, but he certainly expected her to be moving back home in a month's time.

Once he had given in, Sir George had been generous in his defeat. He gave Sarah a three-month advance on her allowance, and promised to arrange for her to continue to receive it whilst she was in France.

"You'll have to pay young Molly her wages as usual," he told her, "so I've added them to what I'll be sending." He looked resignedly at his daughter and said, "Oh Sarah, I do hope you know what you're doing."

Sarah's answering hug confused him, he was not a demonstrative man, and he turned away to hide his emotion.

Sir George drove them to the station in his motor. Molly felt very grand sitting in the dickey seat, their luggage piled round her. Her one fear was that her father might see them on the road or be in Belcaster that day, but as they followed the road past the end of the Valley Farm track there was no sign of him, and even if he were in Belcaster, Molly thought, he was most unlikely to be at the station.

They reached the station in plenty of time and when the London train chuffed in, blowing steam and smoke up into the glass roof above the platform, the porter Sir George had found put their luggage into an empty first-class carriage compartment. They stood on the platform, surrounded by crowds of men in uniform saying goodbye to their loved ones, packs and kitbags heaped beside them. The noise and the bustle were exciting, and Molly felt the hollow feeling she had had in her stomach all morning, give way to the contagious excitement around her. Her eyes roved the platform, but returned hastily to their own little group as she saw several women bravely fighting tears as they said their farewells.

While they were waiting for the guard to whistle them aboard, the squire looked down at Molly and said genially, "Your parents not coming to see you off, young Molly?"

Molly flushed but offered her prepared lie smoothly, "No, sir. We didn't want to say goodbye at the station, like. We said our goodbyes at home."

Sir George nodded approvingly and slipping a guinea into her hand said, "Something to keep by you on the journey, Molly, just in case."

Molly looked at the coin in her hand. She had never had so much money at one time. "Oh, sir, thank you, sir." She managed a flustered bob and then as she scrambled up into the carriage, Sir George added, "Look after Miss Sarah for me, Molly, and make sure she doesn't get into mischief."

Molly looked down at him, startled, and said, "Lord, sir, I can't tell Miss Sarah what to do!"

The squire smiled and said, "No, nor can anyone, but look after her all the same."

The train stopped at several stations on the way, and at the first three officers clambered up into the compartment. Seeing Sarah and Molly seated there already they apologised. One of them introduced himself as Captain James Shiner and said, "So sorry to disturb you ladies, but may we share your compartment? The train is devilish full today."

"Certainly, please do," Sarah replied, and for the rest of the journey, she, at least, was supplied with interesting and congenial conversation. Molly, of course, took no part in this conversation, but spent the journey looking out at the countryside through which they sped. She was fascinated by the glimpses of the country she saw. Villages, nameless in the distance, crouched round their parish churches, factory chimneys stood out against the sky belching out smoke into its autumn paleness; wagons drawn ploddingly along the lanes and the occasional gleaming motor, speeding along at anything up to forty miles an hour, a policeman on his bicycle and a woman pushing someone in a Bath chair; it seemed to Molly an endless tapestry of other people's lives. Workers in the fields paid no attention to the passing train, but children on bridges and beside level crossing gates jumped up and down and waved vigorously, and Molly, after one quick glance over her shoulder at Sarah, laughing with the officers, waved back.

I can't believe we're really on our way, she thought with a surge of excitement. We're really going to France. It will be the adventure of my life and I must never forget a minute of it. I'm going to keep a diary, a journal, and write down everything that happens to me.

Molly had been made to read diaries at school, but though she liked the idea of recording her doings she had always considered her own life too ordinary and boring to write about;

the parts that were not dull, she would never have dared to record. How her father treated her and her mother, she could never have put down. There was nowhere safe in the house to hide that sort of diary. But now, on the train rushing her, unknowing, into the future, she tried to clasp to herself all that had happened so far that day, so that she wouldn't forget it. Suddenly, clearly, a diary was the answer. At the first opportunity, she promised herself, she would buy a notebook and several pencils and she would begin.

At each stop more and more servicemen poured into the carriages, so that when the train finally approached London, it was crammed to capacity. It lumbered slowly through the outskirts, and the scenes through the window changed. Fields and woodland gave way to built-up areas, villages to sprawling suburbs. Molly was amazed at the views she got of terraced houses in endless rows, their small rectangular gardens running to the edge of the track. Bustling streets, lined with houses or rows of shops, and the occasional church on a street corner towering over it all. How could so many people live so close together she wondered?

At Paddington, Captain Shiner helped them to find a porter and then a taxi to take them to Carver Square in Bloomsbury, where Sir George's widowed sister, Lady Horner, lived. He asked if he might call on Miss Hurst there, but Sarah felt that meeting on a train hardly constituted being introduced, and regretted that they would be on their way to France in a couple of days, and preparing for the journey would allow them no time to receive social calls. Captain Shiner appeared to accept this refusal and wished them the very best of luck in France.

Sarah wished him the same, and when he had handed her into the cab he added, "All of England will be grateful to you, ma'am," and saluting smartly, turned away and was swallowed into the crowds on the station.

Looking out of the taxi window, Molly exclaimed, "Oh Miss Sarah, I've never seen anything like this. When we was on the train I thought we was in London long before we got here, what with all them houses and all! Look at this traffic! There's motors everywhere as well as trams, and people, hundreds of people."

Sarah laughed. "It is the capital, you know," she said. "It's the biggest city in the world." But even she had not expected such a crush at the station. Last time she had ventured up to London, it had been with Freddie and her father, before the war. The trains had been half empty, and the station concourse had not been a mass of khaki. She had been very grateful to Captain Shiner for helping them with luggage and cab, and was looking forward to their safe arrival at her aunt's house in Carver Square.

Carver Square proved to be a quiet little square near the British Museum, with a fenced garden in its centre, shaded by tall trees. There was a sharp wind as they alighted from the taxi, and leaves whirled down from the garden trees, scurrying across the road in swirling eddies.

Sarah shivered and said briskly, "Now Molly, run up and pull the bell, it's too cold to stand out here." She paid off the cab and turned to find that Molly had done her bidding and there was a manservant coming down the red and white brick steps to collect their luggage. He picked up Sarah's valise and left Molly to struggle with the dressing case and her own suitcase.

"Follow me, Miss Hurst," he said leading the way up the steps again. "Madam is expecting you."

At the door another man was waiting to greet them, older

and far more imposing, whom Sarah recognised from previous visits as Roberts, the butler.

"Please come in, Miss Hurst, Madam is in the drawing room. May I take your coat?" He entirely ignored Molly, but Sarah said straightaway, "Thank you, Roberts. How are you? This is my maid, Molly Day. I'm sure you'll look after her." She turned round to Molly and said in a lofty tone Molly had never heard her use before, "Molly, go with Mr Roberts and when you have seen where you are to sleep, you can unpack for me. I'll send for you when I need you." She turned away again and walked towards the door that Roberts was opening for her. Molly watched as she disappeared into the fire-lit room beyond and then, picking up the cases once more, followed the footman, who was called John, through the heavy oak door that led below stairs.

The next day was spent in a whirl of shopping. Sarah had written to Freddie to tell him of her plans, and though he, too, was doubtful of the propriety of her expedition, he knew her too well to think he could dissuade her from it, and answered in detail with a list of things which she should bring with her, most for her own comfort, a few things for his.

> I hope to be able to get some leave before very long, he wrote, not Blighty leave, but at least a few days' local leave so that I can come and see you at Aunt Anne's convent. We are not allowed to name places in our letters as you know, but I am not far from there.

They spent an eye-opening morning in large London stores buying almost everything on the list including socks and shirts to take out to Freddie.

"He says it's almost impossible to stay dry in the trenches," Sarah told her aunt. "These are not all for him."

It would be difficult to carry very much with them, but Sarah packed all their purchases into parcels and addressed them to herself care of the convent. There were bandages and aspirins, thread and needles, chocolate, paper and pencils, soap, towels and some fine-tooth combs. Freddie had said that one of the problems they all faced was lice. Sarah shuddered at the thought of lice in her long hair and not for the first time hoped that she was not too squeamish for the task she had set herself. At the last minute she added some feminine requirements for herself and Molly. These had not been mentioned by Freddie, but had been suggested delicately by Lady Horner.

"It's not the sort of thing a gentleman would think of, but you will need them nonetheless and they may be difficult to acquire in a military hospital."

No less embarrassed than her aunt, a red-faced Sarah agreed and discreetly sent Molly to buy the required sanitary towels and added them to one of the parcels.

They sailed from Newhaven on the *Sussex*, a small civilian boat that still carried passengers across the channel. Although it was an entirely civilian boat and held firmly to the international agreement that no military supplies should be carried, the captain was a cautious man and the journey took twice as long as in peace time as he zigzagged his way to France for fear of German submarines.

Molly was terrified they would be torpedoed and sunk by one of these, but Sarah, though also afraid, tried to reassure her.

"We're quite safe, Molly," she said cheerfully. "This is not a military ship, you know. It's just the steam packet. We've no supplies for the army on board or anything like that. Even the Germans wouldn't sink a ship full of civilian passengers." She lowered her voice and nodded in the direction of a middle-aged couple standing at the rail and gazing out towards France. "Those people are called Mr and Mrs Hodges. They've been called to the hospital in Etaples to see their son. He's so badly wounded that they can't even get him home to England."

Molly flicked her eyes in the direction of the couple where the man stood with his arm round the woman and she gripped his hand in one of hers, an unusual display of affection in such a public place. "How do you know, Miss Sarah?"

"I heard Mrs Hodges ask one of the crew when we would dock. She said her son was dying."

Molly stared at her for a moment and then murmured, "Oh, Miss Sarah, I don't think I'm going to be any good at this, boys dying round me and that."

Sarah put her hand on Molly's arm and said, "Of course you will, Molly. Better than me probably. But we'll both just have to do our best. At least we'll have somewhere safe to live, and will be able to get cleaned up when we go off duty. My aunt says they have set aside a room for us in the guest wing of the convent."

"Both of us together, miss, sharing?" Molly sounded startled.

"Certainly sharing," Sarah said firmly. "And we're lucky to have that. There's no space for separate rooms. Some of the building has been turned over to make more wards, and I believe there are huts outside as well." Sarah paused, gazing out over the steel grey sea that heaved gently as they chugged their way across. Might there indeed be a submarine lurking under the water? Might they unknowingly be minutes away from death in the cold English Channel? It put life into perspective; things that had seemed so important only recently now seemed of little consequence, and other things, other people, suddenly became much more significant. She glanced across at Molly, brave Molly, who had followed her to France because she thought she ought to, not from any real conviction of her own about nursing the wounded; who had left home and family and ventured out into a world from which she would have shrunk only weeks before.

"Molly," she began, and then hesitated, wanting to say something of her thoughts, but unsure of exactly what.

"Yes, Miss Sarah?" Molly, clutching her overcoat about her thin shoulders against the wind, turned her gaze from the sea and looked expectantly at her.

"I think," began Sarah and paused again before saying in a rush, "I think while we are out here in France together, you should simply call me Sarah. Drop the 'miss'."

Molly looked horrified. "Oh, Miss Sarah, I couldn't!"

Her horrified expression made Sarah laugh and she took Molly's hand. "Yes, you could. We're in this together, Molly. I dragged you here, and while we face the same difficulties and dangers," her eyes returned for a moment to the grey water, "it seems to me that we should be friends, each helping the other, not mistress and servant. Don't you think?"

Molly looked extremely doubtful. "Oh, Miss Sarah, I don't know. What will your auntie think of such a thing?"

Sarah laughed. "I'm sure she'll approve. After all there are no servants and mistresses in a convent. All the nuns have their own jobs to do, but they are all equal under the Reverend Mother."

"That's another thing, Miss Sarah…"

"Sarah."

Molly flushed, "Sarah. I don't know nothing about convents and nuns and the like. What do I call them? Do I have to cross myself and that? I don't do that in church."

"Molly, you don't have to do anything like that. All the nuns you call 'Sister', except the Reverend Mother and you call her 'Mother'. If it turns out to be any different they'll tell us when we get there." She smiled reassuringly, and then exclaimed, "Oh, look I can see the coast of France." Both girls ran to the rail and peered into the distance where, eerily floating on the horizon the low hills of the French coast drifted into view.

They made the journey to St Croix by train. Crammed into a compartment in a small civilian train, with their luggage at their feet, Sarah and Molly spent several hours in uncomfortable confinement. Their travelling companions were a succession of local French country people, who climbed in and out of the train at the small stations along the way. Most of them chatted volubly in French to each other, ignoring the two English girls once they had subjected them to short but intense scrutiny. The train was cold, but the crush of bodies produced enough heat to warm them although the rank odour was almost overpowering. Sarah listened to their talk, and was dismayed to find that, while she had thought she spoke reasonable French, she found their harsh accents and their speed of speech made them almost impossible to understand. She could only pick out occasional words and phrases, but had no hope of following the conversations.

Oh dear, she sighed inwardly, at least I thought I would be able get along in French.

At the station in Dieppe she had successfully bought them two tickets for Albert, the nearest large town to the village of St Croix, where the convent of the order of Our Lady of Mercy was situated. She had discovered which platform they should find and at what time the train was supposed to leave. There were no porters to be had, but the two of them had managed to manhandle their cases on to the train themselves, and Sarah was quite proud of the way she had made herself understood and of the way they had coped without the assistance to which she, at least, was used. However, now as they were pressed about with local French peasantry carrying everything with them from a basket of apples to a small crate containing a vociferous cockerel, she knew a gnawing anxiety. Were they on the right train? This train seemed to stop everywhere and perhaps it was just a local train and not going to Albert at all.

As they drew into yet another tiny station she said to Molly, "I'm just going to get out and check we are on the right train."

Molly grabbed her by the hand. "Oh, no, Miss Sarah, don't get off. The train might go without you and then what should I do?"

"You'd stay on it and go to Albert," Sarah replied briskly, not correcting her for using 'miss' again. This was a time to be in charge, even if she was apprehensive herself. "You have the name and address of the convent written down, just in case we get split up, and I gave you some money, so you'd be perfectly all right." However, Molly had added to her anxiety. Sarah didn't want them to get separated either, so she contented herself with leaning out of the window, and calling out to some sort of official, he was wearing a uniform anyway, on the platform. "Monsieur, Monsieur. C'est le train pour Albert?" The man glanced up. "Quoi?"

Sarah tried again: "C'est le train pour Albert? Ce train vient a Albert?"

He still seemed puzzled, but on recognising the word Albert he nodded vigorously and answered in a torrent of words, none of which Sarah understood. However, her mind eased a little by the nod she smiled at him and said, "Merci, monsieur," Drawing her head back inside, she regained her seat, about to be invaded by a huge countrywoman with a large wicker basket containing something live.

"We're all right, Molly," she said. "It is the right train. I suppose most of the express trains are used for the troops." Even as she spoke another train chugged past them as they waited in the station, its carriages packed with men in khaki and two covered wagons on the end carrying horses.

Time and again their little train stopped, sometimes for an hour or more, without apparent reason, but often shunted into a siding as another train rumbled its way back from the front. These were often hospital trains with huge red crosses painted on their sides and roofs. From what the two women could see as these trains trundled slowly by was that they were crammed to capacity with men.

Sarah stared in horror as one of these trains stopped for a few moments alongside them. "My God," she whispered. "Do you think all those men are wounded?"

Molly followed her gaze, taking in the sight of the crushed humanity heaped into the train before it jerked suddenly and then chuffed slowly away. Even as it did so, she caught the eye of a soldier with a bandaged head whose face was pressed against the dirty window. For a moment their eyes met and held. There was such patient sadness in his eyes, that Molly instinctively raised her hand, and as he slid away from view, she saw the flutter of his hand in a return salute.

"There were hundreds of them," was all she said, before leaning back into her seat and closing her eyes to cut out the sight of the still passing hospital train.

There were trains going the other way as well; trains filled with men in khaki, far more important than the little local train which civilians might use. Their train would wait in its siding until the line was clear again and then jolt on once more, slowly crossing the dull flat countryside towards Albert. Both girls were very hungry and thirsty. They had had no idea that the journey would take so long and had not thought to buy more food at Dieppe. It hadn't looked far on the map, and they had hoped to arrive in Albert in time to reach the convent that evening. The small packet of sandwiches they had brought with them did little to assuage their hunger, and the bar of chocolate that Sarah produced from her bag and shared with Molly, was fixed upon by eight other pairs of eyes. It made uncomfortable eating. Night came on and still the train rumbled slowly along, stopping, starting, stopping again, until at last they reached the outskirts of a town.

"I think we might be there," breathed Sarah, peering out of the window. "It certainly looks more like a big town." Molly too, pressed her nose to the window. There was not much to see, but occasional pinpricks of light suggested houses, and darker shapes, presumably large buildings, loomed in the darkness beside the track. Once again the train wheezed to a halt, and this time they realised with tremendous relief that they had arrived as they heard the strident cry of a porter, "Albert, Albert. Terminé. Albert." It was indeed Albert at last. It was also, apparently, the end of the line, and the train disgorged its passengers on to the platform, where all was noise and confusion in the semi-darkness.

Sarah and Molly got their luggage out on to the platform, and Sarah said, "Stay here with the luggage. I will go and find out how we get to St Croix." She had instructions from Aunt Anne in her pocket, but she hadn't bargained for arriving in the middle of the night to a blacked out town. As she headed for the entrance she was hustled and bumped in the bustling crowd, but at last she found a ticket office and in her careful, schoolroom French made the man understand that she had to get to St Croix. He shrugged energetically and regretted that mademoiselle would not be able to continue her journey this evening. She must go to an hotel and wait until the morning when one might perhaps engage a horse and cart to take her to St Croix. He, himself, was unable to assist mademoiselle further as he could not leave his position, but he suggested that she went to the Hotel de la Reine which was just two hundred metres from the station, where she could be accommodated very moderately.

Sarah understood at least two-thirds of this, when he had said it all twice, and thanking him she went back to Molly, whom she found standing exactly where she had left her, but surrounded by a group of soldiers offering their assistance. Flushed and determined, Molly was guarding the cases and facing them down with short sharp answers. But at least they spoke English, and at least she could understand them. Naïve though Molly was, she had held her own against footmen and stable boys before, and these were, after all, only footmen and stable boys in uniform. However, she looked extremely relieved when she saw Sarah pushing her way back through the crowds.

"We can't go any further tonight," Sarah told her. "We have to go to an hotel."

"Where you trying to get to, miss?" asked one of the soldiers.

Sarah turned, and in him she saw an answer to their immediate problems. "We are going to St Croix in the morning, but for tonight we have to get to the Hotel de la Reine. I believe it's not far."

"No, miss, just across the square. 'Ere, Charlie, grab them bags and we'll show the ladies the way."

"How kind of you," Sarah beamed, at her most gracious. "Would you really? Thank you so much."

To her delight, Charlie and his friend hefted the cases under their arms and forged a way through the undiminished crowds on the platform and out of the station into the night. Sarah and Molly followed and as they emerged they heard dull thuds and thumps in the distance.

"What's that?" Molly whispered to Sarah. "Are those guns?"

"Artillery further up the line," the soldier said. "Not too close tonight, miss."

He led them to the hotel where the manager offered them a small room on the top floor, and with their thanks in his ears the soldier smiled and said it was quite all right, before he and Charlie, his mate, disappeared into the darkness.

The hotel was able to supply them with soup and bread and cheese and this they devoured greedily before repairing to their garret on the top floor. The guns continued to boom intermittently in the background, and the night sky flickered with light, like distant sheet lightning, but after a moment of staring out over the strange town below them, resolutely they closed the wooden shutters on these reminders that the war was suddenly closer and went to bed. Exhausted from their hours of travelling and despite the uncomfortably narrow bed that they had to share, both of them slept like the dead.

Next morning, much refreshed from their sleep and a breakfast of hot chocolate and bread with ham and cheese, they held a council of war to decide what to do next.

"We must find some sort of transport to St Croix," Sarah said. "I will ask at the desk. Perhaps they can find someone to take us, or at least set us on the right road. If we have to walk, we'll leave our luggage here and send for it later."

"There must be somewhere we can hire a wagon, or a dog cart," Molly said and then added hopefully, "or maybe there is a train."

"No train," Sarah said consulting her instructions from Aunt Anne. "Anyway, I've had quite enough of trains for the time being, haven't you?"

Molly agreed that she had, and then Sarah looked again at the directions she'd received.

"My aunt says, there are usually people coming and going between the village and Albert, and if we send her a message when we get here, she'll try and send someone for us. That seems a waste of time to me. If we can find someone to take a message, we can travel with that someone. I'll go and see what I can find out."

The manager of the hotel was desolated that he had no transport of his own in which he could send mademoiselle to St Croix, but his horses had been taken by the military, and even his donkey would have been if it had not been too old for active service. However, he said he would make some enquiries if mademoiselle would care to wait in the salon.

Mademoiselle treated him to her most dazzling smile and said she would be enchanted to wait, and that she had the utmost trust in him.

This trust turned out not to have been misplaced, for within the hour, Sarah and Molly found themselves ensconced with their luggage on the back of a wagon that had brought vegetables into the town at dawn that morning and was now returning to St Croix.

A steady drizzle fell from the leaden sky above them, but it did little to dampen their spirits. They were nearly there, the worst was over, and what was a little rain compared with what the men in the trenches must be suffering? As they looked back towards the town, they saw the towering steeple of the church in its centre, the golden Madonna which topped it leaning perilously at an angle of ninety degrees, testament to the closeness of the front line and the artillery fire which had been poured, from time to time, into the town.

An hour in the creaking cart brought them at last to the village of St Croix. The wagoner drove through the village square or *place* and along a twisting lane leading to the tall grey convent building that dominated the whole village. Its stone walls towered to four stories, and there was a stubby turret on one corner. The wagon trundled up to the main entrance, a huge oak door bound with iron hinges, above which was a large statue of the Virgin Mary, reaching with outstretched arms to the world at her feet. Molly and Sarah clambered stiffly off the back of the cart and dragged their luggage to the ground. Sarah handed the wagoner the agreed money and with a wave of his hand he drove off, leaving the two women standing outside the great door. They stared round.

"It's a pretty grim-looking place," said Sarah, looking up at the grey walls towering above them. "Still, I expect it's better inside than it looks from out."

Molly could only hope she was right. She was horrified by the formidable building, and the thought that they were going to live there for the foreseeable future made her shiver.

Sarah was at once concerned. "Poor Molly, you're cold. We'll go in at once." But even as she turned towards the door her eye stayed on the view spread out before them. Below, between the convent and the village, was a field covered with what looked like huge marquees.

"Do you think that is part of the hospital too," Sarah asked Molly, "or perhaps a camp of some sort?"

Shivering again, this time truly from cold, Molly spoke. "Sarah," Molly used the unadorned Christian name for the first time unprompted, "it's pouring with rain. Let's get inside."

The stab of surprise at being addressed in such firm tones by her maid, passed immediately, and Sarah grinned at her. "You're right. We've made it. Ready?"

Molly nodded, and together they approached the front door and Sarah pulled hard on the iron bell pull. At once a grill in the door opened and a small face looked out at them.

"Can I help you?" asked the face in French.

"Our names are Sarah Hurst and Molly Day," Sarah announced clearly, in her best French. "Reverend Mother is expecting us."

There was the sound of bolts being drawn and the door swung open to reveal a diminutive nun standing inside, her hands folded tidily into the long sleeves of her grey habit, her head encased in a starched, white fly-away headdress.

"Welcome to the convent of Our Lady of Mercy," she said. "My name is Sister Marie-Bernard. Please come in."

She led them into a small room furnished with a table, two upright chairs and a prie-dieu in the corner. The floor was stone and the walls were without adornment except for a large crucifix over the prie-dieu. She asked them to wait and then disappeared, closing the door softly behind her. Molly looked round apprehensively. The inside of the building seemed to be living up to its grim exterior.

It was almost ten minutes before the door opened again and a tall, handsome nun, dressed as the other had been, came in.

"Sarah?" she looked uncertainly from one to the other and Sarah stepped forward, her hands held out and said, "Aunt Anne!"

They embraced awkwardly and then Sarah introduced

Molly. Aunt Anne shook her hand and said, "I am delighted to meet you, Molly. I am Sister St Bruno, Miss Sarah's aunt. You are most welcome here."

"We've dispensed with the 'miss', Aunt Anne," Sarah said quickly. "We are here as friends, both ready to work in whatever way you need us."

"That's splendid," cried her aunt. "Now first I will show you where you will be, and then I'll leave you to unpack and get yourselves sorted out. Later, when you've changed, I will come and find you and introduce you to Reverend Mother. I'm afraid the midday meal was at twelve, but we'll find something in the kitchen for you, don't worry."

She led them out into the main part of the convent and then up a winding staircase to a stone corridor that seemed to stretch the length of the building. Stopping at the first door, she opened it and ushered them into a cell-like room. Two single beds had been crammed in side by side, in a space meant only for one. A chest of drawers, topped with a large water jug and bowl, took up almost the rest of the space, but the inevitable prie-dieu was tucked in a corner behind the door, its crucifix on the wall above it. Aunt Anne pointed to some hooks on the door and said, "You can hang your coats there. I'm afraid it's a bit cramped, but I doubt you'll be in here much except to go to bed."

Sarah looked at the tiny room and smiled at her aunt. "Don't worry, Aunt, we shall be fine in here."

Aunt Anne looked relieved and said, "Well, you get unpacked and settled and I'll come back for you in half an hour. I expect you'll want to wash and change. There's water in the jug today, but from now on you'll have to fetch your own from the tap at the end of the passage."

Left alone the two girls looked at each other and began to

laugh. "It's a good thing neither of us is very big," Sarah said, dumping her case on one of the beds. These beds are so close together I can't get between them!" She edged round to the other side, squeezing past the chest of drawers.

Molly looked round the room doubtfully. "Are you sure you don't mind me being in here with you, Miss Sarah?"

"Sarah," Sarah corrected her. "No, of course not, Molly. We're in this together." She looked round and said, "Nowhere much to put our things, just these drawers. I'll take the top two, you have the bottom two." She pulled off her coat and put it on the bed ready to hang on the door as she went out. Molly picked it up and put it on one of the hooks, and then hung her own beside it. She opened her case and took out the dark grey skirt and the white blouse Sarah had bought her in England and laid them on the bed. Sarah was looking out of the tiny window on her side of the bed.

"Come and look here, Molly," she said craning her neck to peer down at the ground below. "There are some huts out here below us. Do you think they're part of the hospital, or some other camp?"

Molly joined her at the window and Sarah moved aside so that the other girl could see. Molly stared down at the scene below. There were several wooden huts crammed into a sort of courtyard. They looked ramshackle affairs, each with a tin roof and a bent chimney threading smoke into the cold autumn air. The windows, symmetrically set into the wooden walls, seemed to be closed, but the door at the end of each hut stood open. Even as she looked a nun hurried out through one of these and disappeared from view, presumably into the main convent building.

A high, stone wall, apparently the boundary wall of the convent garden, encircled the huts, and set in this Molly could see an old wooden door. Beyond the wall, and some way off, the tops of the big tents they'd seen earlier were visible.

"There's that camp we saw, set up beyond the wall," she said to Sarah, and in her turn moved aside so that Sarah could look out again.

"So there is. Well, I suppose it is all part of the hospital," Sarah said. "It must be too big to fit into the convent grounds. We'll ask Aunt Anne." She turned back to the case on her bed and flinging it open, pulled everything out on to the bed.

"Oh Lord," she said ruefully, looking at her belongings. "I'm never going to get all that into two drawers!"

Molly, who was carefully folding her own few clothes ready to put into her own two drawers, laughed. "Most of them will fit if you fold them properly," she said. "The rest will have to stay in your case and go under the bed."

The beds were metal framed on high legs, and apart from one chamber pot tucked underneath, there was nothing using the space.

"Oh, Molly, of course," Sarah said, and began to fold her clothes. She made a poor fist of it and with another laugh Molly reached over and took a blouse from her.

"Here, like this." She laid the blouse on the bed and showed Sarah how to tuck its sleeves in neatly before folding it on itself and tweaking the collar into position. Sarah had another go, and though her folding was nothing like as quick and as careful as Molly's, she managed to fold her clothes tidily enough to fit most of them into the drawers.

"You see," she remarked as she struggled with a particularly recalcitrant jacket, "I told you you'd be far better at this sort of thing than I am. You've been trained up to be useful, whereas I have no training for anything!" She stowed the last few bits and pieces, her bible, a book of poetry into the case and pushed it under her bed. A framed picture of Freddie and her father, taken when Freddie came home on leave, she stood on the top of the chest.

Molly, her own unpacking finished quickly and efficiently was pouring water from the jug into the bowl. She sponged her face and hands, and ran the cooling flannel round the back of her neck. Then she looked in horror at Sarah.

"Oh, Miss Sarah, I'm sorry. There's nowhere to tip this dirty water so you can have clean." Colour had flooded her face, and she stared down at the cold soapy water in the single bowl. "You should have gone first, and then I could have used the same water."

"Oh." Sarah looked at the uninviting water for a moment too, and then giggled. "We could put it in the chamber," she suggested, nodding at that receptacle, still showing from beneath the bed.

"But we don't know where to empty that either," pointed out Molly, still flushed with embarrassment.

"We'll ask my aunt when she comes back," Sarah said airily. "Now, just pour that into this," she proffered the chamber pot from under the bed, "and we can get on."

By the time Sister St Bruno came back to fetch them, both women were neatly attired in their dark grey skirts and white blouses. Each had a large white apron tied over her clothes, and her hair confined under a white cap.

Sister St Bruno looked at them critically. "You'll do for now," she said, "if you make sure those last wisps of hair are tucked securely under your cap, Sarah." Her eyes took in their black boots and she said, "I hope those are comfortable. You'll be on your feet for sixteen hours a day."

"We'll be fine, Aunt Anne," Sarah assured her, and then added, "Do I still call you Aunt Anne, or would Sister be better?"

"Sister, I think, when you're working, anyway," replied her aunt. "Ready?"

"Just one thing, Aunt...I mean, Sister," Sarah said in response to urgent hand signals from Molly, "could you tell us, I mean...?" Molly's embarrassment resurrected itself in Sarah and she too turned red.

"Well?" Sister St Bruno said encouragingly.

"Where do we empty that?" She pointed to the chamber pot now back under the bed, but full of dirty water.

"I'll show you on the way past," said the nun with a faint smile. "There's a lavatory at the end of the corridor."

They followed Sister St Bruno along the stone passage. She pointed to a door at the end and said, "There is a lavatory and a basin in there, where you can collect water for yourselves and empty your chamber. In the daytime it can be used in the normal way, but at night no one leaves her cell except to go to chapel to say office, or to go on duty on the wards." She waited patiently for a moment or two while the girls made use of the facilities and then continued on along the passage and down another set of stairs, not the ones they had mounted to reach their room, to a different hallway.

"I hope we can find our way back," murmured Sarah to Molly, as they were led across this hall and along yet another corridor.

Sister St Bruno heard her and said over her shoulder, "Don't worry, Sarah, you'll soon find your way about." She stopped outside a heavy wooden door and knocked. A bell jingled from inside the room and Sister St Bruno turned the heavy handle to swing the door open into Reverend Mother's office.

Standing in the doorway, Aunt Anne spoke in French, "My niece, Sarah Hurst, Mother, and her friend, Molly Day."

"Come in, Sister, come in."

Sister St Bruno stepped inside and gestured to the two girls to follow her.

The room was comfortably furnished with a sofa and some chairs, a desk behind which the Reverend Mother sat, and a prie-dieu in a corner. There was a crucifix above this and a picture of Christ displaying His bleeding heart on the wall behind the desk. A small fire burned in the grate, but it did little to dispel the chill of the room, which had stone walls and a stone floor.

"Perhaps you would wait outside, Sister," Reverend Mother said, rising to her feet as Sarah and Molly slipped into the room. Sister St Bruno inclined her head in acquiescence and stepped out of the room without another word, closing the door behind her.

"Come in and sit down," Reverend Mother said. She spoke in fluent but heavily accented English. She stood and came out from behind her desk holding out her hand. "How do you do, Miss Hurst? Miss Day?" They shook hands and Sarah said, "How do you do, Mother?" while Molly, rather unnerved by the picture that hung behind the desk, murmured something unintelligible. Sarah moved to the sofa that Reverend Mother indicated, and seeing that Molly was at a loss, took her arm, pulling her gently behind her. Reverend Mother seated herself on an upright chair opposite them. She looked them up and down as she might a horse she was considering buying.

"Your aunt has convinced me that you will be able to help us in our work here, nursing the wounded." Reverend Mother did not sound very convinced. Sarah looked back at her with steady gaze, but Molly, feeling entirely out of her depth, kept her eyes fixed on the flagstones of the floor.

"Your letter said you had Red Cross nursing experience." Reverend Mother's eyes bored into them. They were dark blue and deep set, penetrating, it seemed to Sarah, her very mind to read her thoughts. The nun was a tiny woman with small hands and feet; she would hardly have reached Sarah's shoulder without her fly-away headdress, but she had a presence which made one forget her small stature and remember only her authority.

"I have, Mother," replied Sarah, "though no real nursing training. I took the Red Cross certificate." She faced the nun across the room and added, "My friend Molly has no Red Cross training, but in most ways I am sure she will be more use to you than I am. Her training has been in household duties, and as I am under no illusions that we shall be doing any real nursing for the foreseeable future, I imagine she will have the skills you need more than I have."

Reverend Mother nodded at this and addressing herself to Molly said, "Miss Day, it will be up to you to instruct Miss Hurst in the most efficient,"—Mother drew out the word into four syllables—"way to do the tasks which you will be asked to do." She fell silent for a moment, looking at them with unblinking eyes, then she went on, "You are now living in a convent. It is a sisterhood of God. All the sisters here have devoted themselves to Christ and his work. At present that work is looking after the wounded men who come to us from the front. All men—" She paused and then repeated, "All men, no matter which side of the battle. You understand?"

"Soldiers, whether they are French, Canadian or English," Sarah reiterated.

Reverend Mother's eyes never left their faces, "French, English, Canadian...or German. They are all God's children." Neither Molly nor Sarah offered any comment after this statement, and the nun went on. "We work for Our Lord Jesus Christ and we live as a sisterhood. There are rules by which we live. The religious ones do not affect you; you are not part of our sisterhood, but our house rules are yours whilst you are with us. You may not leave the convent without permission. You take orders from any sister who is set in authority over you. You keep your heads covered at all times." She paused again, her eyes intent. "Is this understood?"

Sarah nodded. "Understood, Reverend Mother."

The tiny nun allowed herself to smile at them, then and said, "Then I welcome you here, into our home, and thank you for your offers of help in our task. I must remind you that your life here will not be an easy one. You will see sights that no woman should have to see, perform tasks that should need no performance, but if you succeed in seeing and doing these things, you will ease the pain and suffering of many a poor man, the death of many another, and you will ease our work here in Christ Jesus."

Molly looked much more uncomfortable at these final words than at any time so far. She had been brought up low Church of England, and all this talk of "Our Lord" and "Christ Jesus", unnerved and unsettled her. People she knew did not bring Jesus into their conversation, He stayed firmly in the church to be spoken of on Sunday, and then only by the vicar.

"Now, I will call Sister St Bruno and she will take you to the kitchen for some food. Then someone will show you the wards and introduce you to the sisters with whom you will be working. I have news that we are to receive some more wounded this afternoon, so your work will start at once." She got to her feet to indicate that the interview was over, reaching for the little bell that would summon Sister St Bruno back into the room, but paused as Molly took her courage into her hands and spoke.

"Please, Mother—" Molly hesitated over this form of

address, but Reverend Mother smiled encouragingly at her and she stumbled on. "I don't know nothing about nursing, I'm better at cleaning and the like..." Her voice trailed away and the nun said, "We shall use whatever talents you have to the full, Miss Day, never fear. And as to the nursing, I have no doubt you will learn fast as we've all had to."

"Yes, Mother, I will try." Molly paused again and then emboldened by nun's kind manner, added, "And please could I just be called Molly? Miss Day doesn't feel like me."

This brought a real smile to Reverend Mother's face and she said, "Indeed you may, Molly," and turning to Sarah she said, "And you shall be called Sarah, it is so much easier for all concerned." She picked up the small brass bell from the desk and gave it a shake. Immediately Sister St Bruno came in and stood waiting by the door.

"Please take Sarah and Molly to the kitchen and make sure Sister Marie-Marc gives them something hot to eat." She smiled across at the two girls. "I'm sure you're hungry after your journey. Then one of the novices will show you round, help you get your bearings. If the convoy comes this afternoon, I am sure you will be needed at once, if not you'll start work on the wards tomorrow at six. Go with God."

Friday, 8th October

After our long journey we have at last reached the convent at St Croix. It is all very strange to me and I am not sure I like it at all. Miss Sarah and I share a tiny room, like a cell with stone walls and floor. It is very cold in it. We have a bed each and there is a chair and a chest of drawers, but no other furniture. It will be very strange to share a room with Miss Sarah. She says she doesn't mind, but getting undressed and such…using the chamber in the night, I'm sure she won't like it. We have met the Reverend Mother, who is very small but has eyes like a bird of prey. She is in charge of the convent, and all the nuns, who I must call "sister", do what she tells them. Sister Marie-Paul is a novice. Miss Sarah says that means she is learning to be a nun. Her headdress is different to Miss Sarah's auntie Anne, Sister St Bruno. Sister M-P showed us the chapel. It is covered in gold and smells of incense, and I don't like it.

We have to eat with the nuns in the refectory. The meal is taken in silence and one of the sisters reads while we eat. The reading is in French. I don't understand, except that I know it is from the Bible. I would hate to be here on my own. I'm to call Miss Sarah "Sarah". It will be most peculiar, though I tried it out a couple of times on the train. Even though she'd told me to, I think she was surprised when I did.

Nine

The silence in the refectory was only broken by the voice of Sister Lucie, reading from the gospel of St Matthew, and the sound of spoon on bowl as the sisters ate their evening meal of soup, bread and cheese. Sarah and Molly were seated at the end of a long table with Sister Marie-Paul and the other novices. By listening carefully, Sarah found she could follow the reading, but Molly had no idea what it was about, and she let her eyes rove over the austere room and its occupants as she ate her soup. The sisters fascinated her. She had never seen a nun at close quarters before today, and she was intrigued by everything about them; the way they moved everywhere without haste, coasting along smoothly in their flowing habits as if they ran on oiled castors; the way they tucked their hands, when not needed, into their wide sleeves; the way they held their heads high and steady to accommodate their fly-away headdresses.

Had they, Molly wondered, donned this measured way of moving when they had donned their habits? Or did some of them, the younger ones anyway, still have to quell the urge to run or skip or dance, as Molly often found herself doing, simply for the joy of the sun on her face and being alive. She could not imagine turning away from the world with all its richness, and walling herself up to live such a tightly ordered, strictly disciplined life. Even as she watched them, Molly knew that boring and humdrum as her life had been so far, she could never turn away from it. Eternally the optimist, she was sure there was something better or more exciting just over the horizon; after all, only a month ago, she would never have thought to find herself in France, indeed she could hardly believe it now.

The nuns had all filed silently into the refectory and waited, each standing behind a chair, until Reverend Mother came in. She said grace and they all sat down. The sister at the head of each table ladled soup from a tureen into bowls and when everyone was served, Mother picked up her spoon and at this signal, they all began to eat. Even the way they ate their food seemed alien to Molly as she watched them spoon soup into their mouths, and each breaking a piece from one of the long loaves, before passing it to the sister next to her. A dish of cheese was passed from hand to hand without a word and everyone had a glass of water at her place. Molly drinking from her own, discovered it immediately refilled by the novice on her right. No request was necessary, while eating her own food, each sister looked after the needs of those beside her.

In the meantime, the voice of the nun who read droned on in French, and Molly decided she must at least learn the basics of the language. She caught Sarah's eye and they exchanged smiles of encouragement. Sarah might be a Catholic, but the convent environment was as strange to her as it was to Molly and it was comforting to both to have the other one there.

The only place where Sarah had felt instantly at home was in the chapel. During their tour of the convent that afternoon, Sister Marie-Paul had taken them into it. It was a lofty building, its high roof supported by elegantly arching beams. Most of the chapel was shadowed, but its east end glowed with

candlelight. A statue of the Virgin, arms reaching out in sup-
plication, stood to one side of the altar; and before this were
rows of tiny votive candles, their flames, disturbed by the
opening of the door, flickering and flaring. The altar, dressed
in richly embroidered cloth gleamed and glinted as the flickering light danced across it and the heavily gilded reredos
behind it reflected the moving flames in a golden glow. Above
the altar hung a single red sanctuary light, and kneeling
before it was a single nun, her hands clasped together, her
head bowed in prayer.

Molly drew back uncomfortably from the scene. She
thought the gilding garish, so different was it from the sim-
plicity of the parish church in Charlton Ambrose, and she
found the smell of incense that hung in the air unpleasantly
sickly and sweet. The kneeling nun seemed entirely unaware
of their presence at the back of the chapel, but even so Molly
felt like some sort of voyeur, watching as she prayed, so intimate seemed her prayer.

Sarah, on the other hand, had felt a jolt of recognition. As
she entered the place, she was moved by the aura of sanctity
that filled it, loving the richness of its decoration, and inhal-
ing the fragrance of the incense as the fragrance of prayer
itself. This was the sort of church she loved, the house of
prayer made as beautiful for God as man knew how, and the
peace of it reached out to her, soothing her and calming the
fears so near the surface of her life. The scent of the incense
and the dancing light of the candles carried her back to
another church, the church of her early childhood, where she
attended Mass with her mother. They had walked into church
one day and Sarah had asked what the smell was. Her mother
had smiled and answered that it was the scent of prayers
rising in an endless stream to God in heaven. Sarah

remembered little of her mother, but she had never forgotten this answer, and found the idea of prayers rising steadily like a column of smoke extremely comforting.

Sister Marie-Paul indicated the sanctuary light and whispered, "The sacrament is always reserved and never left unattended. Someone is always with Our Lord."

This murmured confidence made Molly feel more uncomfortable still, and she backed out of the door to wait outside, leaving Sarah and the novice to kneel for a moment in prayer, before coming away and softly closing the door behind them.

"Mother said to remind you that you are welcome to any of our offices, or to the daily Mass if you are not on duty in the wards. Father Jean comes twice a day most days as we cannot all attend Mass at the same time."

Sarah had thanked her, already deciding she would go when she could; but Molly said nothing, looking away so as to avoid the sister's eye. She had no intention of going into the chapel again unless she absolutely had to, she did not believe in worshipping the Virgin Mary, and the idea of Mass, chanted in Latin, with smells and bells, made her Protestant soul shudder.

As they moved away from the chapel and back towards the hospital area, Sarah squeezed Molly's hand and murmured, "Don't worry. You don't have to go if you don't want to."

Molly had given her a faint smile and whispered firmly, "No."

Sarah was surprised at the firmness with which Molly answered her; she would never have presumed to speak to Sarah that way even a day ago.

In the refectory, they had only been seated for five minutes when a nun, swathed in a huge white apron, scurried into the room and made her way to Reverend Mother's side, whispering hastily into her ear. Mother set down her spoon, and all the other nuns did so too.

"Sisters," said Mother, "the convoy of wounded has reached St Croix. They will be with us at once. Please finish your meal as quickly as possible. We will all be needed. Please go to your usual stations as soon as you are ready."

Sarah made a brief translation for Molly in the flurry of noise and activity as the meal was finished quickly and the nuns left the tables. Clearly everyone knew where she should be except the two English girls, and Sarah caught hold of Sister Marie-Paul's arm as she prepared to leave her place.

"Where should we go?" she asked in French. "What should Molly and I do to help?"

"You must ask Sister St Bruno," the novice replied. "She will tell you."

At that moment Sister St Bruno appeared at their side. "It would be of most help today if you were to take the name and regiment of each man as he arrives. We have to keep detailed records of our patients, names are not really enough, but they are a start." She spoke in English to be sure that Molly could understand her. "Come with me and I will give you the notebooks."

She took them through the cavernous entrance hall to a small room on the side where she produced the pads and pencils they would need for their task and then gave them their instructions.

"Rule the pages into columns," she instructed. "Name, number, regiment." She looked at them seriously. "Some of these men will be in a bad way," she said, "and you will have to rely on their friends to give you what information they can." She led them to the great front door which now stood open, and said, "Wait outside here and as the ambulances unload, write everything down. The drivers should have the names of those who can't answer for themselves, but they don't always. Each man will be assessed by Sister Magdalene and then taken round to the wards. Note down which ward."

Sister St Bruno had taken them to meet Sister Magdalene before the evening meal.

"She is the matron here," Sister St Bruno told them, "with overall responsibility for the running of the hospital. Of course she refers to Mother, but in practice her word is law, like any other matron."

Sister Magdalene had welcomed them, promised them plenty of exhausting work, and handed them back to Sister St Bruno.

Sister St Bruno bustled off round the side of the building, leaving Sarah and Molly standing by the door, looking down the hill towards the village. It felt perfectly normal to Molly to be wearing a cap, but as Sarah waited by the door for the men to arrive she kept fiddling with hers trying to settle it comfortably on her head.

"This cap is very uncomfortable," she murmured to Molly who smiled and replied, "You'll get used to it!"

Darkness was slipping across the cold autumn sky, but in the dusk they could make out some sort of vehicle lumbering up the hill, a lantern on its front, pulled by a huge cart horse. It bounced and jolted on its iron-rimmed wheels, jarring to further agony the injured men who were lying inside it. Behind it came several more, the sound of their wheels sharp and rattling against the stony track that led to the convent gate.

Someone had switched on an outside light, and several lanterns were lit and hanging from wall hooks along the outside wall, but the eerie flickering of these made it difficult to see anything not in an immediate pool of light. As the first vehicle pulled up in front of the door, Sarah moved forwards to speak to the driver, but he sprang down from his seat and went round to the back of the wagon. She stared in horror as the door was dragged open and she saw the state of those inside it. Two other men had jumped down from the front and run round to the back to begin heaving out the stretchers and the soldiers who lay moaning upon them. As she approached, Sarah was assailed by a hideous stench that wafted in an almost tangible cloud from the ambulance. Her recoil was instinctive, and it took all her strength of will for Sarah not to cover her nose and turn away coughing, her revulsion clear to see. But this was her first day, and she was conscious of the nuns and felt they were watching her for signs of weakness, though in fact none had time for any such thing. Every one of them had her job to do, and no time to be checking on whether the English girls had the stomach for the work. Gripping her notepad and pencil tightly in her hand, Sarah stood by the emerging stretcher.

"I must have his name," Sarah said urgently to one of the men, "and his regiment." The man shook his head, exhaustion showing in his own bloodshot eyes. "Don't know, miss," he said, wearily. "There's a list somewhere, but I can't tell you which is which." He turned back to the task in hand, and he and his mate pulled the first casualty clear of the cart. The man was lying on his back, a makeshift bandage round his head, the blanket covering him, caked with blood. A sour smell hung about him that Sarah later came to recognise as a combination of urine, faeces, blood and putrid flesh. For now it was just an almost overpowering stench and once again she had to fight the urge to turn away, retching. His hands plucked at the blanket and his whole body seemed to be shaking. As the stretcher-bearers took a better grip on the stretcher to carry it round to the waiting wards at the back, Sarah reached out and touched the twisting hands. "Tell me your name," she said gently. "Tell me who you are."

"Hodgson. Charlie Hodgson," came the muttered reply, and the hand broke free to continue pulling at the blood-soaked blanket. "Charlie Hodgson. Charlie Hodgson." The man continued to mumble his name as he was carried away.

"Ward three." A sharp voice called to the stretcher-bearers. After one look at Charlie Hodgson, in the light of the lantern that hung above her head, Sister Magdalene had directed the men to the ward where few of the casualties were expected to live.

As the stretchers were unloaded from the ambulances, Molly and Sarah wrote names and details as far as they could, always adding which ward as Sister Magdalene directed the bearers. But the ambulances were not the end of things. A column of men toiled up the hill from the village, following the ambulances in a seemingly never-ending line. Some struggled on makeshift crutches, leaned on sticks or were supported by their less seriously injured companions.

Sarah stared at them as they plodded wearily in through the gate towards her, to wait patiently to be dealt with in turn.

"Where have they come from?" she whispered in French to Sister Marie-Paul who was also helping with lists.

The novice shrugged. "From Albert." she replied. "The train brings them to Albert." She hurried forward to help another sister with a man who had simply pitched forward on to the ground in front of them.

"From Albert?" Sarah repeated incredulously, thinking of how long it had taken them that morning on the carrier's cart. "These men have walked all the way from Albert?"

"They have indeed," agreed a sharp voice behind her. "And

I've no doubt they'd be grateful if you would stop staring at them and get on with taking their names so that they can be looked after."

Sarah flushed with mortification as she turned to see a nun she did not yet know at her shoulder. "I'm sorry," she muttered and went forward again to speak to the men who still toiled in through the gate.

Despite their exhaustion, many of these walking wounded were resolutely cheerful and grinned back at her tiredly as she fixed a smile on her face to greet them. They gave their names and details and then sat down on the ground to wait to be told what to do. A novice appeared from somewhere carrying a huge tureen of soup that she set up on the step. Ladling soup into bowls, she gave them to Molly who carried them to the weary men sitting patiently on the ground. There were no spoons, but the men tilted the bowls to their mouths, drinking the warm soup greedily, the first hot food they had received in days.

As the last of the men were accounted for, Sarah set aside her notebook and went to help with the distribution of the food, tearing long loaves into pieces and handing each man his share.

Sister St Bruno appeared at Molly's side and said, "We need you in the ward now. Sarah can stay and help Sister Marie-Marc with the food."

Surprised to be the one chosen as she had no pretence of nursing skills, Molly followed Sarah's aunt round the building to the courtyard. She was led into one of the wards where wounded men lay, some still on stretchers, some on the floor.

"We're having to move some of the convalescent men out to make room," Sister St Bruno said quickly. "There're clean sheets on that table at the far end. Please strip and remake the beds as they empty. You can start with that one there." The nun indicated a bed at the end of a row where a man, still in pyjamas, was standing, his few possessions already gathered into a bag. He had a stick beside him.

"Where are they going to go?" asked Molly as she started to strip a bed.

"They go to a ward in the main building," replied Sister St Bruno. "We call it the restoration ward. It's the sort of halfway house before they move on to the convalescent camp in the meadow." She glanced round the ward and added, "As quick as you can now, Molly."

This was work Molly was used to. She stood at the end of the bed, stripping the soiled sheets towards her and tossing them aside, folding the thin blankets into a tidy pile. Then with practised ease she flipped the clean sheets on to the bed, letting them float upwards to billow out before they settled flat and straight on the bed ready to be tucked in neatly at the corners. The blankets followed with a shake and an arch. It took her less than two minutes to strip and remake each bed with the sheets from the table. The dirty linen she put in a heap at one end of the ward, and saw it being heaved away by one of the novices.

Sister St Bruno watched her approvingly for a moment before leaving her to it, confident that the job was being done as quickly and efficiently as possible, and thinking that at least Molly would be of use to them; she wasn't so sure about her niece, only time would tell.

The patients vacating the beds disappeared into the main part of the building, led by Sister St Bruno, and men brought in and allocated a bed immediately took their places. Many of these collapsed fully dressed and exhausted on to the clean sheets Molly had prepared for them, only to be pulled up by Sister Eloise, who ran this particular ward.

All modesty flew out of the door as the nuns, under her guidance, helped the men strip and wash away, as far as possible, the filth that had coated them in the trenches and on the battlefield, and the lice which were their constant companions. Often the only way to remove the caked and stinking garments was to slice through them with a huge pair of scissors, and peel them away from the dank and grimy body underneath. Under instruction from Sister Eloise, Molly stood by bedside after bedside, holding a washing bowl of warm water, her eyes averted from the revealed bodies, trying to allow them some semblance of privacy and the dignity it might bring, but most of the men were beyond dignity. The fact that it was a young nun or any young woman who gave them a blanket bath and then eased them into clean pyjamas and lowered them on to the thin mattress of a clean bed, ceased to impinge upon them. Tattered and filthy bandages were left in place until the overworked doctors had had a chance to look at each man. Many then had to face the agony of having the blood-soaked field dressings removed, the bandages pulling viciously at early scabbing and revealing oozing pus and the putrid flesh that exuded it.

For the next five hours Molly did nothing but fetch and carry bowls of hot water from the kitchen; tipping the foul water away into the outside drain before refilling the bowl from one of the cauldrons which stood on the kitchen range. The three nuns who were nursing in that ward moved methodically from bed to bed, until every man was washed, his filthy, lice ridden clothes taken away to be cleaned if possible, to be burned if not, along with the soiled bandages, none of which could ever be re-used.

Sarah, left out in the driveway with the walking wounded, finished distributing the food and followed Sister Marie-Paul round with a large pitcher of water and a glass, giving each man a drink before moving on to the next. As each man was assigned to a ward, Sarah noted the number against his name. Gradually the line of men grew shorter. Despite the cold, some of the men had fallen asleep where they sat, finally over-come by their exhaustion.

It was the early hours of the morning before the two girls crawled into bed with the promise from Sister St Bruno that she would wake them for their shift at six.

"That's only three hours," groaned Sarah as she stripped off her now soiled apron and crumpled cap, threw her clothes over the chair and eased her aching body on to the bed.

"Well, make the most of it," Molly said and turned out the light. Each lay in the darkness, thinking about the day, but it was only moments before she slid into the deepest sleep, and only moments more before Sister St Bruno was shaking them awake again, to start another day.

Saturday, 9th October

We hardly had any sleep last night as a convoy of wounded men came in and we didn't get to bed until nearly three in the morning! When we went on duty soon after six I thought I wouldn't be able to keep my eyes open. We have quite a lot of work to do before we are released to go to the kitchen for some breakfast. Miss Sarah and I are in different wards, so we had a lot to talk about. Don't think she likes her ward much, she's got that Sister Bernadette who shouted at her last night. I'm lucky, I'm so used to making beds and doing general cleaning I don't find the work difficult, though we could do with a new scrubbing brush, and a broom too! Some of the men are very bad, but others are quite cheerful and chirpy. They have all been asking who I am and where I come from. One asked me if I was going to become a nun and I said not likely and he laughed and said good, because they'd need lots of pretty girls to come home to at the end of the war. I didn't know where to look when he said this, but he laughed and winked and said that I must know that I'm a pretty girl. I said go on with you, and we both laughed, but then Sister Eloise, who's the sister in charge of my ward told me off for wasting time. Lucky she don't speak much English!

Ten

Next morning the two girls were at work in the wards from just after six, in fresh aprons and caps, and continued there until they had a short break for some breakfast. For those working on the wards the breakfast was served in shifts in the kitchen, and by the time Sarah and Molly were called they were both very hungry and ready for the hot chocolate and fresh bread and jam that constituted the meal. They were not working in the same ward so they had experiences to exchange as they ate. The silence at meals rule did not appear to operate in the kitchen, for although the other nuns who were eating with them did not converse, it was more likely habit that kept them silent than a hard and fast rule. It seemed they had no objection to the girls chatting away in English.

Sarah was working in ward four which was run by Sister Bernadette. Her heart had sunk when she reported for duty that morning and discovered that Sister Bernadette was the sharp-voiced nun who had chided her the previous evening for wasting time.

Sister Bernadette spoke no English, but greeted her briskly in French and set her to work sweeping out the ward and then scrubbing the floor with an elderly scrubbing brush, carbolic soap and a pail of cold water. The floor was covered in tough linoleum, but was constantly made dirty by tramping feet coming in from the courtyard. This morning there were also traces of mud and blood from the arrival of the new wounded the previous night, and these stains must be scrubbed away and the clean floor washed through with disinfectant. Sarah had thought she was prepared for such hard work, but it proved to be much harder than she expected and she was soon scolded for taking so long. Wiping down surfaces was easier, though Sister Bernadette kept an eagle eye on her to be sure she was thorough and missed nothing. She was then set to carrying heavy pails of hot water from the kitchen so that the round of washing could begin before the men were given their breakfast.

When at last she was sent to have her own, she met Molly in the kitchen and slumped on to a chair with a groan.

"Oh Molly!" she cried pushing the hated cap from her head. "I'm exhausted and it isn't even eight o'clock yet. How will I ever last all day?" She looked ruefully at her hands that were red from the cold water and the carbolic soap.

Molly, who had had much the same to do, smiled at her and said cheerfully, "You'll get used to it!"

"I'm to make all the beds when I get back," Sarah groaned. "I can make a bed of course," she said, "but certainly not fast enough or neatly enough to please Sister Bernadette. She's shown me what to do, but most of the time she thinks it would be quicker if she gave it to someone else." She sighed. "Trouble is, Molly, that she's right! I don't think I'm an asset to ward four!"

"Of course you are." Molly was reassuring. "You may not be as fast at the work as other people are, but if you weren't doing it, someone else would have to be taken off another job."

"I suppose so." Sarah didn't sound convinced, but as they washed up their plates and cups before going back to the wards she made an effort to cheer up. It was only the first morning of the first day, for heaven's sake, she told herself fiercely, she couldn't admit defeat yet, and Molly seemed to be coping. When Sarah had asked her what it was like in ward one, she had replied, "Not too bad. Sister Eloise speaks a little English, and with sign language we seem to communicate all right. Mostly it's very clear what has to be done. Sister Marie-Paul is there too, so between them they make me understand."

They left the kitchen to return to their wards so that the next set of nuns could go for their breakfast, and as they parted in the yard outside, Molly grinned impishly at Sarah and said, "As for the bed-making, I can teach you to do that properly and you can practise in our room." She giggled and added, "You can make my bed every morning until you can do it as quickly as I can!"

Both girls laughed, and it was still with a smile on her lips that Sarah returned to ward four and the eagle eye of Sister Bernadette.

She spent the rest of the morning helping with the beds, taking trolleys round, distributing food, collecting rubbish and emptying ashtrays that seemed to refill themselves as quickly as she emptied them.

During the morning Sister Magdalene, the matron, made her rounds and Sarah and Molly soon learnt that this was an unvarying routine. She would sweep into the ward and immediately the nuns ceased whatever they were doing and stood silently ranged round the room while she completed her inspection. Occasionally she snapped out a question, which was answered by the sister in charge of the ward, occasionally she reprimanded someone for some error or neglect. Molly and Sarah soon learned to make sure there was not a thing out of place; one blanket untidily tucked in, one scrap on the floor, and the person responsible would get the rough side of

Sister Magdalene's tongue. She seldom spoke to any of the patients as she had no English and few of them spoke French, but they would pull wry faces behind her back and send sympathetic smiles to Sarah or Molly if her sharp comments were addressed to them. Doctors' rounds were a far more relaxed affair, though the men greeted the doctor with a mixture of hope and fear. Dr Gergaud, the French surgeon or one of the medical officers from the convalescent camp, Major Jackson, or Captain Dale, were the men who attended to all the patients. It was they who decided when a man should be sent home to England for treatment; who was too ill to travel, who should remain to make his recovery here, ready to return to the lines. These men moved quietly from bed to bed, escorted by the sister in charge, inspecting wounds, ordering treatments and dressings, and the men watched them, hoping desperately to be marked for home. Sarah could see the hope die in their eyes as they were told it would be the restoration ward and then the convalescent camp, or relief burst on their faces when they heard theirs was a "Blighty one" and they were going home.

Most of Sarah's time was spent in the most menial tasks in the ward, but there were occasions she had to help feed men who were unable to feed themselves. One, a young Scots private, had lost his right arm completely, leaving only a stump at the shoulder; his left arm ended in a bandaged stump at the wrist, his hand shot away by a German machine gunner. Sarah could see he was in great pain, and exhausted from having the dressings changed. She sat beside his bed with a bowl of soup in her hand and spooned it into his mouth. She tried not to look at the bandaged stump and the empty pyjama sleeve, but Private Iain Macdonald was not one to accept pity, nor slip into self-pity either for that matter. He managed a grin and said to her, "Good thing I'm left handed, aye? When I get back to Blighty they're going to fix me up with a new hand, right and tight." He winked at her and added softly, "Pity in some ways. I shan't get a pretty young lady like you to sit by my side once I don't need the feeding!"

Sarah was both touched and saddened by his courage, but over the following days and weeks she saw courage like it time and time again. Private Macdonald was typical of the men who came through the wards, brave and stoical about their wounds, and relieved to have them classed as "Blighty ones" and to know they were going home; thankful their war was over, even though their struggling civilian lives were only about to begin.

Long years after Private Macdonald had been shipped home to England, Sarah could still hear his slightly mocking voice as he walked out to the wagon that was to take him to the train in Albert and home saying, "I'm off to found a dynasty. There must be some poor girl desperate enough to settle for a wreck of a man with no hands." Still no self-pity in the tone, just statement of fact with a hint of mockery, a touch of bitterness, in the smile that accompanied it. She would have grasped his hands in hers, but he had none, so impulsively she reached up and kissed his cheek. He looked taken aback, but his smile was transformed into a genuine one, lighting his eyes and making him look even younger than his nineteen years.

"If she can't see past your hands she's not worth having," Sarah told him. "Good luck, Private Macdonald."

Her display of emotion cost her a huge dressing down from Sister Bernadette who had witnessed it through the window of the ward and come sailing out, habit flying behind her, head-dress flapping round her ears.

"Mademoiselle Hurst! You must not become involved with

the men in the ward!" she expostulated. "It is unkind to raise their hopes in this way and not at all *comme il faut*."

"Raise their hopes?" Sarah ventured to defend herself. "I was simply saying goodbye and wishing him luck. I could hardly shake him by the hand, could I?" she added imprudently.

It was a mistake. Sister Bernadette bristled with indignation, her face mottling with anger.

"You will not answer me back, young lady. In this place you will be obedient to your superiors and if they need to correct you in anything, you will listen in silence and learn from what they say. Do you understand?" She fixed Sarah with a steely glare and Sarah had the wit to say no more than, "Yes, Sister."

"I hope you do," said the nun. "Now, there is a stack of bedpans in the ward scullery which need scouring. Please make sure they are all done before you go to have your lunch. We shall need them before afternoon rounds."

Sarah knew that there would be plenty of time to do this job, one she hated, and one that Sister Bernadette knew she hated, after the midday meal, but she did not argue. She had already discovered to her cost that arguing with Sister Bernadette got her precisely nowhere except into the realm of even more unpleasant work. Sister Bernadette, she was sure, did not approve of her being there at all, and never missed an opportunity to find fault. Sarah was quite prepared to carry out the most menial tasks in the ward, thus releasing the nuns with nursing experience to do the actual nursing, but she did resent the way in which such orders were issued. She turned her attention to the offending bedpans, but she never forgot Private Macdonald. He had been her first real patient, the first man she had actually helped, and he continued in her prayers long after he had left.

Gradually she and Molly got into the routine of life at St Croix. Their few hours off did not always coincide, but when they did Reverend Mother allowed the girls to walk to the village, to the post office and the village shop, provided they always stayed together. Sometimes they went across to the tented village of the convalescent camp to see how any of their erstwhile patients were doing; and though it would not have been allowed had it been known, they occasionally had a piece of cake and a glass of wine in the estaminet run by Madame Juliette in the village.

Madame Juliette's was no more than the large front room of her tiny house, with extra tables standing outside when the weather allowed. The first time they went there was when they were looking for somewhere to buy some cake or biscuits to supplement their rather meagre fare at the convent. It wasn't that they were ever really hungry, the food served in the refectory was plentiful enough, but it was dull and unimaginative in the extreme, consisting of thin stews or casseroles, with vegetables and small pieces of meat floating about in grey gravy and nondescript fish, also grey, on a Friday. Both Molly and Sarah found that they were craving for something sweet. Madame Juliette had a sign outside her establishment advertising beer, wine and "gateaux".

Eagerly the girls went in through the open door and found themselves in a café bar. There were a few people in there, but Madame Juliette bustled forward, looking vaguely disapproving, to ask what they were doing there.

Sarah explained they wanted to eat some gateaux, and Madame Juliette, hearing the accent, relaxed a little.

"You're English," she said in a voice that explained everything. "You are the young ladies working at the convent, yes?"

Sarah agreed that they were and asked again if they could buy some gateaux.

"Of course," Madame said. "Please sit here at this table." She indicated a small round table crammed into a corner by the window, where they could view the rest of the room and see into the "Place" outside. She had produced some flat-looking biscuits made with oatmeal and a jar of honey to spread on them. The girls were enchanted. This was exactly what they needed, something filling and sweet.

"Have you any tea?" Sarah ventured to ask, though she thought it most unlikely, "And even if she has," she murmured to Molly as it was being fetched, "it'll probably be undrinkable!"

Madame Juliette produced tea; it was much as Sarah had feared, though they managed to drink one cup each so as not to upset their hostess, but she also brought a carafe of wine.

"You will be tired from working in the hospital," she told them. "This will refresh you."

To please her they each drank a mouthful from the glasses she poured, and found that though it was not like any wine Sarah had tasted before, it was not unpleasant. Molly had never tasted wine, so to her the whole thing was a new experience. Afraid it would go straight to her head she only sipped from her glass, but she found she liked the taste once she got used to it.

On fine afternoons they walked beside the river that wound its way through the village and out into the water meadows, where a few cattle still grazed and tenacious willows clung to the bank. They would sit for a while in the autumn sunshine, glad to be away from the wards and the smell of disinfectant, and watch the dark brown water slide by. Sometimes they took their gateaux with them as a picnic. They had found an old stone barn, and as the weather grew colder and the ground became hard and chill, they would sit in the barn, eating their picnic among the hay bales. Then November was upon them and on most days it was too cold to linger, and after a brisk walk along the bank they would return to the snug stuffiness of the estaminet for their oatcakes and honey.

Neither of them thought it necessary to mention these visits to the sisters. They allowed the nuns to think that they walked for exercise in the strange way of "les Anglais" and as they had no wish to find they were banned from leaving the convent, they could only hope no word of their patronage of the estaminet would leak back from the village. Molly, particularly, found the convent buildings almost suffocating. When she was working she never gave the place a thought, but the minute she left the ward and went to the refectory, or up to their room, she felt the walls crowding in on her and she longed to run out through the front door and draw great gulps of fresh air into her lungs so that she didn't suffocate.

Occasionally Sarah went to Mass in the convent chapel. She found the remembered words and rituals soothing after the hard work and bitter reality of the ward. The soft, golden light in the chapel and the fragrance of the incense calmed her anger at so much wasted humanity and took the edge off her despair at her inability to do anything about it.

However, despite gentle suggestions from Sister Marie-Paul that she, too, might like to attend, Molly steadfastly refused to go. She never went into the chapel, simply saying her prayers at her bedside as she had always done. Until that was, she started talking to Robert Kingston. He was the English padre, attached to the convalescent camp, who came almost every day to the convent hospital to visit the men. He was a cheerful young man who worked hard with the men in his care, doing his best to keep their spirits up, with a strong belief that, by bringing them spiritual strength, he could help to rebuild their physical strength.

His approach was practical. He joked with them, helped them write letters, brought them cigarettes, papers and chocolate that he received regularly from his family in England. Sometimes he prayed with them, sometimes he sat quietly listening to them talk of their families and home, and all too often he was at their bedsides as they slipped away from their agony into eternal peace. It was then his care to see them carried to the ever-growing cemetery beyond the convalescent camp and bury them, under a new white wooden cross, beside their comrades already lying there.

The nuns treated him with distant politeness, particularly Sister Marie-Paul, who felt, in the zeal of her noviciate, that he ran an extremely poor second to Father Gaston who visited the French wounded; but they could see that he was a comfort to many a dying man, and gave him a cautious welcome.

Molly was always pleased to see him, and once she had overcome her initial shyness, chatted with him cheerfully whenever he came into her ward. One day he mentioned the chapel he had made at the camp, converting a tent into a small place of worship each Sunday. He suggested that she might like to come through to the camp one Sunday to attend a service.

"There is one every Sunday, morning and evening," he told her. "We should be delighted if you could come and join us."

Molly looked doubtful. "I'd have to ask Reverend Mother," she said. "She might not let me come on my own."

"Well, do ask her," the padre said, "and if there is a problem I will speak to her myself. I can't see any reason why she should object. It's not as if you were going down to the village alone, you'd simply have to walk out through the garden gate and into the camp. I will arrange to have someone escort you if necessary."

So Molly took her courage in her hands and sought out Reverend Mother. To her surprise, Reverend Mother agreed readily enough. She had seen how uncomfortable Molly was with the spiritual side of the convent, and, unlike Sister Marie-Paul, had not pressed her to join in.

"You may go when you are not needed in the ward," she said. "It would be best if you go in the evening, then you will be able to work in the morning when the sisters want to go to Mass. It will suit everybody, *hein*? Father Robert will provide you with an escort from the gate, yes?"

After that, each Sunday evening that she could be spared, Molly would slip away through the convent garden gate into the camp. She let the padre know when she was able to attend and a soldier would always be waiting to escort her through the camp to the makeshift church. There, she was made welcome, and though she was sometimes the only woman in the congregation, Molly never felt ill at ease or embarrassed among the men. They were only too pleased to see her and soon she knew many of them by name, not only those she had seen in the wards, but others who had come from elsewhere. It was another escape from the confines of the convent, and Molly came to look forward to her Sunday evenings outside its walls.

The letters came as a bolt from the blue. Sarah had been writing dutifully every week to her father as she had promised, and she had received occasional replies written in his scrawling hand. Mostly they contained brief news of the household and the people she knew, but Sir George was no great letter-writer and they tended to be short and matter of fact. This one, however, was angry and as she read it Sarah could almost feel his fury in the paper, and his handwriting, always an impatient scribble, was worse than ever as his anger outstripped his hand.

My dear Sarah,

What on earth have you done, persuading that silly girl Molly to go with you to France without her father's permission? How could you do such a thing? I met him in town the other day and he told me she was to leave our employ at once and come back to live with him and her mother on the farm. He wants her to get a job in the munitions factory at Belmouth. He said he had told her to give in her notice weeks ago, and since then they had seen neither hide nor hair of her and when was she coming home? He had no idea she had gone to France and had certainly never given her leave to go. As you can imagine he is extremely angry, as I am myself. How could you allow such a thing to occur? Whatever made you take the girl without the knowledge and consent of her parents? They have been wondering why she had not been home and now they are worried out of their minds for her safety. He is even muttering something about kidnap, though that is surely a piece of fudge. I am in an extremely awkward position now and think that Molly should come home immediately. She is still under age and though she works for us she is still under the guardianship of her father.

Please ensure that she returns here as soon as can be arranged. I enclose a money order to pay for her fare. In my opinion you should both come home. You have been there long enough to have done your duty, and it now lies here. Your brother may be home again on leave soon and you should be here to look after him after his time in the trenches.

Your affectionate Father

Sarah stared at the letter. Had Molly really left home without telling them where she was going? Sarah could hardly believe it. She thrust the letter into the pocket of her skirt and went back to her ward. She would not see Molly until they fell exhausted into their beds that night, but then she would have to tackle her about it. It was strange, but she had got so used to Molly as a friend that she seldom thought of her in the capacity of housemaid as she had been for so long. She knew almost nothing about Molly's family life, and certainly Molly never referred to her parents. Thinking about that now, Sarah realised that it was odd that Molly never even mentioned them in passing.

When they were both safely back in the sanctuary of their room, Sarah handed Molly the letter.

"This came in the post, today," she said matter-of-factly. "You'd better read it."

"But it's from your father," said Molly, recognising Sir George's hand. "Why should I read it?"

"Just do," Sarah said, and something in her tone made Molly unfold the letter and scan its contents. Her expression changed and she read the letter again, more carefully this time. Then, she re-folded it and handed it back.

"Well?" said Sarah.

"Well what?"

"Why didn't you tell them you were coming to France? Why didn't you tell me that they didn't know?"

"None of their business," growled Molly, and climbed into bed.

"Molly! Be reasonable. They're your parents. They're worried about you."

"Worried about my wages, more like."

"Your wages?"

"They take half what I earn. That's all right, but they ain't going to tell me where and how to earn them."

Sarah said nothing for a moment, she didn't know what to say, and even as she was listening to Molly's words one part of her brain registered that, in her anger, Molly's carefully learned language had slipped back to her more natural country speech. Molly went on, "He wanted me to leave you and squire and go an' work in the munitions in Belmouth. Well I ain't going to, not then, not now."

"But why didn't you tell him you were coming with me?"

"Cos if I had, he'd have told your dad I couldn't go, and your dad would've stopped me. That's why!" Molly added even more vehemently, "And I ain't going back whatever either of them say. Even if they come and get me, I won't go."

Sarah looked at her thoughtfully. "You know what he'll do, my father I mean? He'll write to Reverend Mother and ask her to send you back."

"Let him. If he does that I shall speak to Reverend Mother. She won't send me home." Molly spoke with such certainty that Sarah stared at her.

"How can you be so certain?"

"She won't," was all Molly would say.

"So what do you want me to say to my father?" asked Sarah. "I have to answer his letter."

"Send back the money. Thank him for thinking of me and say that I will be staying here where I am needed. Tell him the sisters have been training me to nurse and that I'm going to work here until the war is over."

Sarah was shocked. "I'm not sure I can write that to him," she admitted. "He will be furious."

"Then I will write," Molly said simply. And that is what she did.

Sarah would not let her return the money. "We might need that for some reason," she said. "I will write as well and explain that I am keeping the money for emergencies." Despite her determination not to be beholden to anyone, Molly couldn't help but feel that a contingency fund might prove useful, so she made no objection to this idea.

When the expected letter to Reverend Mother came from Sir George, Molly was immediately sent for. She was called straight into Mother's office and as soon as she closed the door behind her, Mother said, "I have received a letter from Sarah's father. He is very angry and says I must send you home at once." She spoke her careful English with its strong accent, but Molly had no trouble in understanding her. She made no reply, however, simply stood in front of the little nun and looked back steadily at her.

"What do you say to me, Molly? You should not be here. Your father has not permitted it. You must go home."

"I'm not going home, Mother," Molly said then. "If you insist I leave here then I will, of course. But I will not go home. I will offer my services to some other hospital in France. No one will know where I am then, so no one will send me home."

"Sister Eloise tells me that you have become a good nurse. She says you have a natural flare. You have a steady hand and good common sense. She will not want to lose you. So give me the reason why I will not send you home."

Molly had expected this summons and she had rehearsed in her mind exactly what she would say, but, faced with the sharp blue eyes of Reverend Mother across the desk, her words deserted her. She could feel the hot colour creep up her neck and cheeks, and found it impossible tell this woman she hardly knew and a nun no less, why she would not return home.

Seeing her embarrassment, Reverend Mother waved to the only other chair in the room and said, "Sit down, Molly."

Molly sat on the edge of the chair, her back rigid, her

hands clasped in her lap, still tongue tied as she tried to find the words she needed.

"You are very determined not to go," Reverend Mother remarked, giving her time to collect herself. "I am sure your reasons must be good, but unless you explain them to me, I can do nothing to help you." She smiled suddenly. "Is it a young man? I have not always been a nun, *hein*? I shall not be shocked."

When Molly still remained silent she added, "So, an affair of the heart, *hein*?"

"No." Molly's voice was scarcely above a whisper.

"Then tell me what it is. Give me the reason." Her voice was soft but insistent, and so, at last, Molly gave it to her. Mother heard her in attentive silence and when she had finished speaking Reverend Mother simply nodded her head. She steepled her fingers and looked at Molly across the top of them.

"I see," she said. "And all this is true?"

"Yes, but you don't believe me?"

Mother looked her straight in the eye and Molly held her gaze levelly. "Yes, I believe you. These things happen, *malheureusement*."

Mother thought for a moment, gazing into the middle-distance and drumming her fingers absentmindedly on her desk. Then she looked back at Molly.

"Have you told Sarah all this?"

Molly shook her head. "No."

"Are you going to?"

"No. This is family."

"But she is your friend."

"She is not really my friend," Molly said slowly. "Circumstances have made her so, but though she may find the friendship easy, it does not come as easily to me. She is...was my employer. We come from different worlds when we are at home. She is my mistress and I am her maid. That is still the case even out here. She would not have brought me with her if her father had allowed her to come alone. It would not have crossed her mind."

"Do you resent that?" Mother asked.

"No, it is how things are, that's all."

Reverend Mother appeared to accept this, for she nodded and then said, "As far as I am concerned you may stay. I will not send a girl back to such a father. I will say that you are needed here, and that at least is true; you are a conscientious worker and have the makings of an excellent nurse. There is no need to explain any other reason to Sir George. He is not your guardian, *hein*?" She paused again and then added, "However, I think you should write to your parents, to your mother perhaps, and tell her where you are and explain the important work you are doing. You owe her that, I think. If you will write this letter, I will write to Sir George. You agree?"

Molly agreed.

Sarah was amazed at the outcome of Molly's interview with Reverend Mother.

"How did you persuade her to let you stay?" she marvelled.

"I told her what I told you," Molly said, "that I would not go home. I would just leave here and work somewhere else in France. She didn't want to waste the training Sister Eloise had given me, so she said if I wrote to my parents she would write to Sir George."

Years later, when going through her father's papers, Sarah found both the letter from Molly and the later letter from Reverend Mother.

Molly had written simply to Sir George.

Dear Sir George,

I am sorry I am not able to come home at present as I am needed here in the hospital. The wounded come all the time and
we are hard pressed to keep up with them. I will write to my
parents and I am sure they will understand.

    Thank you for sending money for my fare. I have given that
back to Miss Sarah.

Yours respectfully, Molly Day

Reverend Mother's letter was equally simple though perhaps more straightforward.

Dear Sir George,

Thank you for your letter. I am afraid I am not in a position to
send Molly Day home if she does not wish to go. I understand
your concern for her, especially if her parents do not approve
of her being here. However, she a great asset to our work here
with the wounded, and if she wishes to remain, I am more than
happy for her to do so.

    I have instructed her to write to her parents explaining the
situation, which she has promised to do, but more than that
is not within my power. If I sent her away from here she still
would not return home, but would move on to some other
hospital where she is unknown and we should lose her in the
confusion that is now France. I am sure you will agree it is better she remains here under our watchful eye.

Yours sincerely
Marie-Georges
Reverend Mother—Sisters of Our Lady of Mercy

Molly had stayed.

Sarah's other letter had come from Freddie. She recognised
his untidy writing, so like his father's and she opened the
letter eagerly as he had promised to come and visit her on his
next local leave, and she was longing to know when this

would be. On this matter, however, his letter was a disappointment. His plans had changed.

Dear Sarah,

As you know, I had hoped to come and visit you in your convent, but instead of the three days leave I had expected, I have been given ten days, and best of all it is over Christmas and New Year. This gives me time to go home, so I will be off to London first and then down to see the governor. Any chance of you coming too so we could all spend Christmas together? I will be going with John Driver, a brother officer who I've mentioned before I am sure, to stay with his family in London for two days on each end of the leave. If you came too we could all go out on the town…we need to have a few days' fun before we come back to this hell-hole. Write to me what you think, after all you are not a VAD or one of the official army nurses that have to apply for leave as we do. I am sure if you wanted to come you could.

If you can make it we could all cross together. Let me know.

Love from Freddie

Sarah read and re-read the letter. Part of her wanted to go home and spend Christmas back in the manor at Charlton Ambrose; to spend the festive season as they always did, the house swathed in holly and ivy, a Christmas tree decked and shining in the entrance hall. She longed for the encompassing warmth from the huge log fire in the drawing room and the wonderful smells of baking and roasting that emanated from the big kitchen, but she knew that if she once went home she would not come back to France. She was certain her father would find some way of persuading her to stay in England, and she was equally certain that here at the convent was where she should be.

Sarah had slipped with ease into the life she lived, and though it was strenuous work in the wards and most nights she fell into bed asleep almost before she undressed, she never went up to the room she shared so amicably with Molly without spending half an hour in the quiet of the chapel. Gradually she had become convinced that this was where God wanted her to be, and she was afraid if she once went back home, the green shoots of this conviction, so new as they were, might not survive the cold blast of common sense to which her father would subject them. She did not reply to Freddie's letter for several days as her decision wavered, swinging from determination to stay, to the possibility of going…it was just for Christmas after all, but at last she took the plunge and wrote saying that she could not be spared.

You know how bad the situation is here in France, the dreadful state of the wounded when they reach us is indescribable. The sisters are more than overstretched and though most of my tasks are fairly menial, I know I am useful and if I left everyone here would have to work that little bit harder. We had a convoy in last night, and there was no room for half the men. We have cleared the refectory and some of the men were lying on the tables, but others were left on the floor. It took all night just to log who everyone was. That is usually my job, and at least that is something I can do, leaving the more experienced to do the nursing. You know the filth that comes with them from the trenches, the untreated wounds, and those which have had rough first aid at the casualty posts. You will understand why I cannot just come home for Christmas, and I hope you will be able to convince my father, as he certainly doesn't believe me. Dearest Freddie, I am relying on you.

Come and see me on your next local leave.

With much love from your menial sister
Sarah

Wednesday, 3rd November 1915

Today they brought in Harry, my cousin, Harry Cook. I could hardly believe my eyes when I looked up from helping Sister Eloise and recognised him waiting on a stretcher. It was Harry. He was plastered in so much mud and filth, that at first I wasn't sure that it was really him. I haven't seen him since well before the war began, but once I had stared through the dirt to his poor pale face, there was no mistaking him.

Sister Eloise ticked me off for not paying attention, but when I told her who it was she was kind.

I spoke to Harry, but he was beyond recognising me. Though I don't think he was unconscious, his eyes were closed and he was unaware of his surroundings.

There was another man with him who said he was his friend. He was not so badly wounded as Harry, whose leg was shattered, surely beyond repair. The other man was wounded in the arm, and clearly in pain, but I don't think he will lose it. He was more concerned about Harry than himself, so they must be very good friends, though we've all noticed how much these wounded Tommies look out for each other. Is there anything good coming from this dreadful war, I wonder? Maybe the unselfishness we see among the men who come here to us...

Eleven

The days merged into each other. Gradually both girls were given a little more to do than simply scrubbing the wards clean, taking trolleys round and emptying bedpans. Sister Eloise had long since spotted Molly's natural ability to nurse. An able and dedicated nurse herself, she recognised the same concern for her patients in Molly, the simple efficiency with which she treated them; the easy way she talked to the men and the response she drew from them. She was always calm in a crisis, and there were enough of those, both when more wounded arrived and in the routine caring. Though Molly had not even had the basic Red Cross training that Sarah had, she seemed instinctively to know what to do or say. Because Sister Eloise had very little English, when Sister Marie-Paul was not there she had to rely on Molly to talk to the English patients for her. Molly's French had been non-existent, but she was picking up the words and phrases she needed with increasing rapidity, and though she could not hold a conversation in French, nor even follow one between the nuns, she could now make herself understood about matters in the ward.

Gradually, and under careful supervision at first, Sister Eloise taught her to change some of the dressings on the minor wounds, letting her gain experience in how it should be done, the careful cleansing and packing of wounds, the neat, firm bandaging afterwards. Molly was quick to learn and deft in her movements, and all the time she was able to keep up a cheerful flow of chatter with her patient, trying to keep his attention off the painful task she was performing. This was something that the other nursing sisters, most of them French, were not able to do with the English patients, and Molly worked more and more with them, leaving the few French wounded who arrived to their compatriots.

It was while helping with a new influx of men that Molly saw Harry. At first she thought she must be seeing things. She was helping Sister Eloise, who was swathed as always in a huge white apron over her habit, clean the wound of a man newly arrived from the front. Molly was holding the bowl of warm water, when her eyes slipped down to a new stretcher case that lay just inside the door of the ward. On it, lying motionless, she saw her cousin, Harry Cook, from Charlton Ambrose. She stared down at him, peering in the gloom of the late afternoon to be sure that it was indeed Harry who lay there, his familiar face gaunt under several days' growth of beard overlaid with dust and dirt. Sister Eloise had to call her attention sharply back to the job in hand as the bowl she held began to tip.

"I'm sorry, Sister," Molly stammered in her halting French, "but this man is—" she hesitated not knowing the word for cousin and finished, "—from my home."

Sister Eloise understood enough of her fractured French and said, nodding at the patient whom they had been washing, "We have nearly finished with this man. Ask Pierre to lift your friend on to the table, next."

Their patient, now cleaner than he had been for weeks, was moved gently by Pierre, the ward orderly, to an empty bed. Pierre then knelt by the unmoving figure on the stretcher and lifted him up on to the table where each man was cleaned up as far as possible before he was put to bed to await the doctor. Another man, also still dressed in dirty service tunic with the sleeve cut away and with a grubby bandage around his arm that had been sitting on the floor by the door, got to his feet at once.

"That's my mate, Harry," he said. "Harry Cook. He got it in the leg, and now it's going rotten." His own face was grey with pain or exhaustion, his eyes red-rimmed hollows above his gaunt cheeks. He half put out a hand as if to help Pierre, but dropped it again as the big orderly swung Harry easily up on to the table.

"What is he saying?" asked Sister Eloise.

"He says it is his friend, *son ami*," replied Molly. She turned to the second man. "Don't worry," she told him gently. "Harry is in good hands now. The doctor will be in here in a minute, and before that we'll do all we can to make him comfortable." She smiled at him and added, "What about you? Is your arm bad?"

The soldier shook his head wearily, "No, I'll live. Harry's the one who needs you now. I'll just wait here." He slumped down on the floor again, and Molly saw him close his eyes as he leaned back against the wall, instantly asleep.

Harry Cook was in a bad way. Whatever had hit him in the leg had ripped away much of the thigh muscle and smashed the bone to splinters. As they removed the remains of his trousers and makeshift bandage some overworked doctor had put on it at a casualty clearing station, a sickening stench of rotting flesh exploded among them, making both Molly and Pierre take an involuntary step backwards. Sister Eloise seemed not to notice the rank smell, but continued slowly and

steadily cutting away the dirty clothing until the man's shattered body lay exposed for them to wash and warm and put
into bed to await the doctor.

One look at the leg had told Sister Eloise that it must come
off, and immediately, if there were to be any chance of Harry
Cook surviving. She looked sharply at Molly to see how she
was coping with tending a man she actually knew, but after the
one moment of involuntary recoil, Molly had straightened her
shoulders and was standing ready with another bowl of hot
water and dry warm towels. With an approving look, Sister
Eloise gave Harry a shot of morphine and set to work to do
what she could for this latest piece of flotsam from the front.

As they worked, washing away the grime and the mud,
Molly looked down at Harry's exposed body and the thought
flew through her mind that the last time she had seen Harry
Cook naked was when they were both about six years old and
they had played in the river at home. She had had a beating
from her mother, not for getting her clothes wet, but for taking
them off to play in the water as naked as the village boys.

How long ago that was, she thought now, and how far away.

When Dr Gergaud appeared, Sister Eloise directed him to
Harry Cook first, explaining the wound, now marginally
cleaner and covered with a light sheet. Sister Eloise had seen
no point in putting the poor man through the agony of re-
bandaging a leg that must be removed within the hour.

"The poor man will have enough to go through if he sur-
vives," she murmured to Molly. Gently she took Molly's hand.
"Your friend is very bad," she said. "They will operate, but it
may be too late. There is gangrene."

Molly nodded, understanding what she was being told as
she recognised the words "bad", "operate" and "gangrene".

Dr Gergaud had Harry taken to the operating theatre in

the main convent building, and having watched him carried out of the ward on a stretcher, Molly forced her attention back to the other men who needed it. Harry's friend was still slumped against the wall. As he was asleep, they had dealt with the others first. Now, at last it was his turn, and Molly shook him gently awake. At her touch he was immediately alert, looking round him to remember where he was.

"It's your turn now," Molly said, and held out her hand to help him to his feet. He ignored it, however, and pulled himself up alone. Understanding his need for independence, she lowered her hand and turned her head to look down the ward, so that she shouldn't see him struggle, until he was standing beside her.

"What's your name?" Molly asked, smiling as she faced him again.

"Tom Carter," he replied. "Where's Harry? Is he all right?"

"He's in the operating theatre," answered Molly. "I'm afraid they have to take off his leg. They have no choice if he's to survive, you know."

Tom nodded wearily. "Yes, I know."

Molly smiled at him. "Now, what about you? Let's get you cleaned up and have a look at that arm." She helped him out of his tunic and as gently as possible cut away the bandage. It was soaked with blood, now dried, and peeling it away pulled at the scabs that had formed, allowing fresh red blood to ooze through the dirt that surrounded it. Tom Carter sucked in his breath as the bandage came away, but made no other sound, gritting his teeth against the pain. Sister Eloise was at once at their side, and sent Molly off for more hot water as she dealt with the wound herself. It looked much worse than it was and though it would take some time for Tom to regain the use of his arm, it did not appear to be life-threatening. She cleaned and dressed it and gave him a shot for the pain, before handing him over to Sister Marie-Paul to blanket bath and put to bed.

"Time and rest and he will be well," she instructed the novice to tell him, as she moved to another bedside.

As soon as he saw her again, Tom called Molly over and asked again about Harry Cook.

"He's not out of the theatre yet," Molly told him, "and when he is I doubt if he will come to this ward. I am surprised he was sent here in the first place. Usually the men we have in here are not so badly wounded." She smiled at him. "Try not to worry about Harry, he's always been tough, he'll pull through."

Tom looked at her in surprise. "What do you mean, 'always been tough'? You don't know anything about him."

"Oh, but I do," laughed Molly. "I've known him all my life. He's my cousin. We live in the same village, Charlton Ambrose. His mother is my auntie; they have the farm up the valley a ways from ours. I've known him and Tony always." Then she added, "Do you know his brother Tony as well?"

Tom nodded. "Yes, we're in the same unit. The 1st Belshires. We all joined up together."

"Did you? Do you come from Belcaster, then?"

"No, London born and bred. Harry and me worked in the docks at Belmouth, and as we signed up together we was put into the same platoon. We did our training and that, and we was really good mates, see. We've stuck together ever since."

"Well, as soon as I can find out anything about him, I'll let you know. How do you feel yourself?"

Tom Carter shrugged, "I'm all right. That nun, the one with the smaller headgear..." he nodded at Sister Marie-Paul, "she said I'll be out of here in no time."

Molly smiled at his description of Sister Marie-Paul. "Well, she's probably right...once we're sure there's no infection and you're starting to heal. You won't have to stay in bed long anyway."

"Will I be able to go and see Harry in whatever ward he is in, miss?" asked Tom. "I want to know he's going to be all right."

"I expect you can. I mean, I don't see why not." Molly said a little doubtfully. "But it's not up to me. I'll ask Sister Eloise, if you like...she's the one in charge in here, but I doubt if it'll be till tomorrow at the earliest."

"If you would ask, please, miss."

He looked so tired and worried, his face still grey with fatigue and the pain of his arm. Leaning back against the white pillow he looked much older than his twenty or so years, and yet vulnerable, like a little boy ill in bed. Impulsively Molly reached out her hand to him and said, "I will, I promise, if *you* promise me to try and get some sleep now. Next time I come on duty, I'll tell you her answer. Will you be good and try and rest now?"

He managed a tired grin and said dutifully. "Yes, miss, I will."

"My name is Molly," Molly said gently. "I'm going off duty now...Tom, isn't it?" He nodded. "So, Tom, I'll come and see you as soon as I'm back in the ward, and I'll bring you news of Harry."

Tom nodded again and closed his eyes. Even as Molly watched, his face relaxed and he was instantly asleep.

At the end of her shift she went into Ward Three where she expected to find Harry Cook. He was there, recently returned from the operating theatre. Sister Jeanne-Marie was not best pleased to see her, but when she finally understood that Harry was a friend from home she grudgingly let her go to his bedside.

He lay still in the bed, his face the colour of putty, the sheet pulled up to his chin, his hands lying motionless on the outside of the covers. If it hadn't been for the faintest rise and fall of the blankets with the sighs of his breathing, Molly would have thought that he was already dead. The small shape in the bed was lopsided, where the left leg had been removed, and Molly was as certain as she could be that death hovered over the fragile figure.

Softly she touched his right hand with her own. It was cold, and without thinking she tucked it gently in under the covers, and then did the same with his left. Watching her, Sister Jeanne-Marie made no comment, noticing only the gentleness with which Molly touched the young man.

"He is an old friend?" she asked.

Not quite sure of what she had been asked, Molly replied in her fractured French. "Family," she said, "from children. He is my friend age four."

Sister Jeanne-Marie nodded and reaching out her own hand to Molly said softly, "Unless he is very strong, and God gives him life, he will not live. Pray for him, my child."

Molly nodded. "May I sit with him for a while?" she asked, and then repeated her request as best she could in French.

Sister Jeanne-Marie smiled wearily. "Pull a chair to his bedside," she said, "but don't stay too long. You need your rest as well."

Molly found a wooden chair and placed it beside Harry, close enough to be able to touch him if he stirred, but his eyes remained closed and his breathing was swift and shallow, and she simply rested her hands on the smooth coverlet and watched him, willing him to hold on to his life, willing him to fight with all his strength.

When at last she stumbled wearily upstairs, she found

Sarah was already in bed. Molly tried to move into the room quietly, but the lamp was still burning and Sarah heaved herself up on one elbow and said, "Molly, where on earth have you been? It's very late."

Molly flopped on to her bed and said quietly. "Harry Cook was brought into our ward this afternoon. He's had to have his leg off."

"Harry Cook?" For a moment Sarah was puzzled then she said, "Harry Cook. Not Harry Cook from High Meadow Farm?"

"That's him. He's my cousin. I'm an only child so I used to play with him when I was a nipper, him and his brother Tony."

"Oh, Molly, I'm so sorry! How dreadful for you. I remember him. He had red hair."

Molly slowly began to get undressed. "No, that's Tony, his older brother. Harry's a sort of mousy colour. He's in ward three. I've been sitting with him."

"Is he really bad?" asked Sarah softly.

For a moment Molly didn't answer. From habit she folded her blouse and skirt over the chair and put her dirty apron to one side, laying out a clean one for the morning, then as she climbed into bed she said, "Sister Jeanne-Marie said to pray for him. You'd better do that, Sarah, I'm not very good at praying."

"Of course I will," Sarah said. "Do you think he'll get better?"

Molly gave a watery sniff and said simply, "He's in ward three, Sarah. What do you think? It'll take a miracle."

"Then I'll pray for one," Sarah replied, and closed her eyes.

When she opened them again, Molly was still sitting up in bed, her knees bent up to serve as a desk, scribbling in her diary.

"You should try and get some sleep, Molly," Sarah said gently. "Write your diary tomorrow."

"I must write it now," Molly answered without her pencil losing its flow across the page, "I must write it while I know what I think. I try to capture what I feel. By tomorrow the sharpness of it will be gone and I'll only write of shadows."

Next morning Molly spoke to Sister Eloise about Tom visiting his friend in ward three.

"It is his friend...l'ami de ce soldat," she explained. "His wound is bad...très blessé, ma soeur. He wants to see him...dans la salle trois."

Sister Eloise understood well enough, but she was not happy that one of her patients, who was weak enough himself, should wander off into another ward to visit a friend, even if that friend was probably dying. She told Molly to get on with her work and said she would discuss the matter with Sister Jeanne-Marie later in the morning.

As the ward came to life, Molly went round to each bed taking temperatures. Tom Carter was still lying flat when she reached him, his eyes closed, but something about him told her he wasn't asleep and she spoke softly.

"Tom. Are you awake, Tom?"

At the sound of her voice his eyes flew open and he tried to sit up. Gently she pushed him down again. "I've come to take your temperature," she said, putting the thermometer under his tongue. "I have been to see Harry. He's had his leg off, I'm afraid, but we knew he was going to, didn't we? He was very weak last night, and the sister in charge of his ward, Sister Jeanne-Marie, said that sleep was the best possible thing. I've asked Sister Eloise if you can go and visit him later today and she says she will discuss it with Sister Jeanne-Marie. I think it depends on how you are yourself. She doesn't want you to tire yourself either. She is still afraid that your arm may become infected. It's so difficult to guard against cross-infection in a place where there are so many putrid wounds."

Tom watched her as she explained the situation to him, his eyes intent upon her face, unable to speak with the thermometer in his mouth.

Molly went on: "If you've got a temperature, and I'm afraid you have," she laid a cool hand on his forehead and felt the heat of fever under her fingers, "I don't think she'll let you go, but I'll keep asking for you." She took the thermometer from his mouth and saw it read 102°. Too high, she thought, much too high. "Why don't you ask her yourself when she comes round? She doesn't really speak any English, but she will know what you are asking and will get Sister Marie-Paul, you know the one in the small headgear? She'll translate for you if I'm not here." She smiled down at him and, noting his temperature on his chart she moved away before he could ask her what it was.

In her breakfast break, before she went to the kitchen to join Sarah for their chocolate and bread, she slipped into ward three to have a look at Harry. Sister Jeanne-Marie was busy behind curtains around another bed at the end of the ward, and Molly was able to stand for a moment at Harry's bedside. He looked very much as he had the night before, his face ashen, his breathing quick and ragged. His hands were again outside the covers, and Molly reached down and covered his right hand with hers. At the touch of her hand, his eyes flew open and he looked up at her. For a moment he simply gazed at the woman who stood beside him, then slowly recognition slid into his eyes, recognition followed by incredulity.

"Molly? Molly Day?" His voice came as a croak, and she had to lean down to make out his words. "Molly, is it really you or am I dreaming? Where am I, Molly? Am I at home? Am I back in Blighty?" The ghost of a smile curved his lips as he said, "I'm back in Blighty! Thank God, I'm back in Blighty!"

Molly perched on the edge of the bed and squeezed his hand gently. "Yes, it's me, Harry. I'm here." She smiled, taking his hand in both of hers, "But I'm afraid you haven't reached Blighty yet. You're in a hospital in France, but as soon as you're a little bit stronger you'll be off home."

Harry looked confused. "But why are you here? Did Ma send you?"

Molly laughed. "No, Harry, I'm here with Miss Sarah from the Manor. We're helping in this hospital, you know, to nurse the wounded, like you."

"Miss Sarah is?" He seemed about to say more when a spasm of pain shot through him, making his body arch and sweat break out on his brow. An involuntary cry escaped his lips and immediately Sister Jeanne-Marie appeared from behind the curtained bed. When she saw Molly her face darkened.

"What are you doing here, upsetting one of my patients?" she demanded. Molly understood the look and the tone, if not the words. She stood at once and said carefully, "Ce soldat est Harry Cook. Il est mon *coos-san*." She had asked Sarah the word for cousin last night and produced it now with a flourish, adding with sudden inspiration, "Nous...prier. Vous me dire...prier."

The idea that they had been in prayer together rather took the wind out of Sister Jeanne-Marie's sails. She had, after all, told Molly only the night before that she must pray for her friend. She retreated into her position as sister in charge of ward three and said briskly, "Well, please ask before you come into my ward again, Molly. This man needs complete rest, so please leave at once." She waved Molly towards the door and her meaning was clear to both Harry and Molly.

Molly said demurely, "Oui, ma soeur," adding softly in English as she turned away, "I'll come back and see you again, Harry," and had the enormous satisfaction of seeing Harry's left eye droop in a wink.

Back in her own ward later that morning Molly saw that Tom was sitting up propped with pillows, his bandaged arm resting on two more. He had been washed and shaved, and though he still looked pale and ill, his eyes were alert. As she moved around the ward, making beds, sponging faces and helping the more experienced nurses with dressing changes, Molly was aware of those eyes following her, but she had no real chance to go and talk to him until it was lunchtime and she was sent to help him with his food.

"Have you seen Harry?" were his opening words. "Is he all right?"

Molly smiled at him. "Yes, I've been to see him. He's awake. He recognised me, which is a very good sign."

"Will I be able to go and see him?"

"I don't know. I've asked Sister Eloise, we'll have to wait and see what she decides. You've still got a temperature, you know, and I'm pretty sure she won't let you go until that's down. The best thing you can do is to eat up," she offered him a forkful of food which he dutifully ate, "and get all the rest you can. You were exhausted when you came in. Sleep is a great healer, you know, so the more you rest the quicker you'll be better."

Tom grinned and said, "Yes, miss," just as he had used to say to the teacher at school, except the teacher hadn't been anything like as pretty as this Molly who, amazingly, was

Harry's cousin. After several more mouthfuls Tom said, "I asked that nun, that Sister Louise…"

"Sister Eloise?"

"That's her. I asked her, when she came round, if I could go and see Harry."

"What did she say?"

"She said 'Tonday'. What's that mean?"

"Tonday?" Molly wrinkled her nose, as she considered. "Did she say 'attendez', do you think?"

Tom shrugged, and winced at the movement. "Maybe. Sounded like Tonday Der Man."

"Demain means tomorrow," Molly said. "So I expect she said you could go and see him tomorrow." She finished helping him with his meal and then pausing by the bed said, "Is there anyone you want to write to? I sometimes write letters for the men who can't write because of their wounds."

Tom shook his head. "No, thanks," he said. "I ain't got no one to write to."

"Not even your mother?" suggested Molly.

"No mother," he replied briefly. "I'm an orphanage kid. I've only got my mates in the platoon, and I ain't going to write to them, am I? They know where I am!"

The next few days Molly watched Tom grow stronger and Harry grow weaker. When his temperature was finally down to normal, Sister Eloise and Sister Jeanne-Marie agreed to let Tom visit ward three. Molly did not go with him, but she saw Tom's face when he came back and flopped on to his own bed. She left the washing-up she was doing in the ward kitchen and, braving Sister Eloise's displeasure, went and perched on the edge of Tom's bed.

"How was he?" she asked softly. She, herself, had not been in to see Harry that day.

"He looks bloody awful, begging your pardon, miss. Looks like he's dying. Didn't know who I was. His eyes was open, but they didn't seem to look at me, like. They was sort of staring, up at the ceiling, but not looking at nothing. When I spoke to him he didn't even turn his head, like he didn't hear me. I touched his hand, so's he'd look at me, and it was burning hot. I said, 'Harry, mate, it's me, Tom. You're going to be all right, mate,' I said to him. And then he started mumbling, something about the wire and his bayonet, all jumbled like..." Tom's voice trailed off and he looked up at Molly his eyes stricken. "He ain't going to be all right, is he? He's going to die."

Impulsively Molly took his hand and said, "We don't know that, Tom."

"Yes we do," he replied dully. "There's no hope."

"There's always hope," Molly told him firmly, "as long as he's fighting and we're fighting for him."

Tom said wearily, "But he ain't fighting, no more." He closed his eyes and Molly thought she saw a tear squeeze from the corner of one. Her heart went out to him, but the men she knew never cried and she turned away so that she should not see his tears.

Before she went for her breakfast next morning, Molly crept into ward three to look at Harry. Sister Jeanne-Marie wasn't there, and another sister, whose name Molly didn't know, gestured her to Harry's bedside and went back to her round with the medicine trolley.

Harry was lying still as death in his bed, his grey face shrivelled and drawn, his hands, claw-like resting as always on the outside of the covers. His eyes were shut and even when Molly took his hand he didn't open them. She felt for the pulse in his wrist, and it was some time before she could find the feeble flutter that told her his heart was still beating. As she looked down at him she knew Tom was right. Harry wasn't fighting any more. His exhausted body had given up the battle, his weary spirit no longer urged it on.

She felt someone beside her and turned to find Sister Jeanne-Marie at her elbow.

"He has not long, now," she said softly. "Will you fetch the padre from the camp?"

Molly nodded dumbly, and hurried out across the courtyard, through the gate and over to the camp beyond.

"I must see the padre," she told the sentry. "I must find Mr Kingston, it's urgent."

The padre often received summonses like these, and the sentry let her through, saying he thought that the padre would be in the mess just now.

Molly could not go into the mess, but a message sent in soon brought Robert Kingston out to her, and together they hurried back to ward three.

"He's just slipping away, padre," she told him despairingly as they went. "We can't save him."

The padre heard the choke in her voice and said, "Try not to be too upset, Molly, you've all done all you could. It's up to the Lord now. All we can do is pray for him."

"Well I don't think the Lord is listening," Molly said bitterly, "if he's there at all. How could this war be going on at all if there was a God? If God was real he wouldn't let Harry die." Tears ran down her face now and she dashed them away with her hand. "He's only my age, padre, he hasn't had a life yet."

Robert Kingston took her hand awkwardly. "Molly, if it's the Lord's will," he began, but Molly interrupted him, pulling her hand free: "If it's the Lord's will, then I don't think much of the Lord," she said angrily, and striding ahead, she led the way back into the hopelessness of ward three.

Sister Jeanne-Marie had drawn the curtains around Harry's bed, so that the padre could be private with the dying man. She held the curtain aside to let the priest in, allowing it to fall behind him.

Molly turned to the nun. "I am going to fetch his friend," she said. "He should not be allowed to die without his friends round him."

Sister Jeanne-Marie started to say something, but Molly had already walked out of the ward and was heading across the courtyard to her own ward. Sister Eloise saw her come back in, and read the determination in her face.

"Well, Molly, what is it?"

"I've come to fetch Tom Carter," Molly said in English, indicating Tom who was sitting out in a chair. "His friend is dying, he must come at once. Son ami, mort. He must venez, ma soeur, venez à la salle trois."

Sister Eloise disentangled the words and nodded, but Molly had already turned away and was approaching Tom, who sat at a table at the end of the ward smoking a cigarette.

A smile broke across his face as he saw her coming, only to fade as he saw the sadness and compassion in her eyes. She crouched down beside him and took his hand in hers.

"Harry's dying," she said gently. "Will you come to him?"

For a long moment Tom stared sat her unseeingly and then his eyes seemed to snap back into focus and leaning heavily on the table, he stood up. Without a word he followed her out of the ward and across to ward three. He walked in quietly and on reaching the bed pulled the curtain aside and looked in. The padre was sitting by the bed, speaking softly to Harry, but as soon as he saw Tom and Molly, he moved aside to let them approach the figure on the bed. They stood one each side and looked down at Harry, so small against his pillows, and Molly took his hand.

"Harry," she said gently. "Harry, can you hear me, Harry?"

There was the slightest movement of his head and then his eyes opened and he looked up, first at Molly and then at Tom. They closed again for a moment and then opened, this time with concentration, as if trying to see clearly who was there.

"It's me, Molly," Molly said. "Me and Tom. Can you hear me Harry?"

This time she felt the slightest pressure on her fingers and she said to Tom, "Take his other hand, Tom. Let him feel you're there."

Tom did as she asked and he too felt the faintest pressure on his fingers.

"Harry, mate," he said gruffly, and then fell silent, not knowing what to say.

"Tom." The word came as scarcely a breath. For a moment the eyes shut, but they opened again and he said, so quietly that Molly had to lean close to his mouth to hear his words, "Molly, tell Ma I tried. I did my best. I'm too tired to go home."

"I'll tell her," Molly promised. "You're so brave, Harry, a hero. I'll tell her you were a hero."

"So tired," Harry breathed, and then with a shuddering sigh his eyes closed, his face relaxed and his pain was over.

Molly found the tears were streaming silently down her cheeks as she looked down at the worn-out husk of a man, the cousin who had shared her childhood. Very gently, for the last time, she tucked his hand in under the bedclothes, as if to keep him warm.

Tom dropped the lifeless hand he was holding, and without a word to anyone, turned on his heel and strode out of the ward. The padre was murmuring prayers and Sister Jeanne-Marie crossed herself, fingering the rosary that hung on her girdle. Ignoring both of them, Molly blew her nose violently, took a deep breath to calm herself, and ran after Tom.

Tuesday, 9th November

Harry died today. Poor dear Harry! He was in such pain, but he never complained. His face got greyer and more drawn, he just seemed to shrivel away. In the end I think he wanted to die, to be done with it all, but I didn't want him to die. He had his whole life ahead of him. Now his children will never be born, and his line becomes extinct. What a dreadful and final word that is. Extinct. He was too young to have to leave the world before he had experienced it. Perhaps he had experienced too much already, but I ache for him that he won't fish the Belle any more, that he won't go into the Arthur for a pint of bitter. He has been snuffed out like a candle which can never be re-lit. His poor mam and dad! At least they still have Mary at home with them, but Tony's still in the trenches. How much life does he have left? Maybe he's dead too and we just don't know yet. I hate this war!

Tom took it very bad. I've never seen a man cry before, it's not what men do. He told me about his friendship with Harry, almost like brothers, he said, and with me and Harry close as nippers, it's made me and Tom friends as well. Now I have to write to Auntie Vi and Uncle Charlie. It will be the most difficult letter I've ever had to write.

Twelve

Harry Cook was buried on the day he died; a bleak day in November with dampness, a fine mist, hanging in the air, and cold grey skies. Tom and Molly followed the padre into the little cemetery and stood at the newly dug grave. His coffin was carried by four men from the convalescent camp and they ranged themselves, bareheaded, on the further side of the grave. Behind them, stretching away in neat rows were white wooden crosses each bearing the name of the man, buried beneath it, who had given his all for his country. Now Harry was the latest, but soon his grave with its own white cross would be swallowed up, engulfed in the steady and unending regiment of crosses to come.

Tom stood to attention, his injured arm in a sling, his cap in his hand. He looked paler than ever, his eyes two dark holes circled with grey. Molly, watching him, thought he looked younger and more vulnerable than ever, his short-cropped hair brushed smooth on his head so that his ears stuck out like a little boy's, but there was a firm set to his jaw and a look of determination in his tired eyes which made it clear he was not going to break down again.

When he had left the ward that morning in obvious distress, Molly had followed him, diffidently at first, not wishing to intrude her own grief on his. The feelings of loss and emptiness which hit her later had only just begun to invade her mind. They had not been particularly close in recent years, but Harry was part of her childhood, and although she had seen so much death lately, Molly felt an almost overwhelming surge of bitterness and anger at Harry's life snuffed out, for the loss of his life, for the waste of his youth; for the Harry who'd taught her to swim and to fish in the Belle, but who'd never again stand in the chuckling waters of the river with a fly rod in his hand. Part of her childhood had died when he had closed his eyes for the last time, the pain finally smoothed from his face, and with the tears slipping down her cheeks she too had hurried from the ward, leaving the padre to his prayers and Sister Jeanne-Marie to her rosary.

Molly found Tom in the courtyard, leaning against the wall, his head pillowed on his arm. For a moment she paused, looking at him unnoticed, his grief making him unaware of her. She could see his shoulders shaking with sobs and she hesitated still. Molly had never seen a grown man cry before and it unnerved her. She knew too, that he would hate to be seen weeping, but he seemed so alone. Instinct came to her aid. She crossed the yard to him and taking his hand led him quickly into Reverend Mother's garden. It was a private place, designed for peace and contemplation; a tiny walled garden with a rose bed in the centre and a carved stone seat on the southern wall. No sister entered it uninvited, and nor should Molly have done, but she gave no thought to that now.

Once safely hidden from inquisitive eyes, Molly put her arms round Tom, saying as she did so, "Don't grieve so, Tom. Don't cry, dear Tom. His pain is over now and he's with God."

"Is he?" demanded Tom bitterly. "Is he?" And then, echoing Molly's demand made of the padre earlier, "Is there a God? Where is he in this bloody war?"

Molly didn't answer, she simply held Tom gently in her arms as she might a small child, her cheek against his, and gradually his sobs diminished. As she stood there, feeling his tears on her face, she thought: What am I doing here, holding a man I scarcely know? And yet somehow it felt the most natural thing in the world, and as she gave comfort to Tom, she felt some of her earlier emptiness seep away, and this man's need for her take its place.

As Tom regained his composure, Molly led him to the seat and they sat down facing each other, their cheeks tear-stained, their eyes red.

"Sorry," Tom said, his gaze sliding away from hers. "Sorry. Thing is, he was more than a mate to me, more like a brother. The brother I never had, you know? We joined up together, come through our training together, and well, we always looked out for each other. Tony, his brother—you know his brother?"

Molly nodded.

"Yes, of course, he's your cousin too. Well, Tony, he never seemed to look out for Harry. Different sort of bloke. Had his own mates."

"Tony's much older," pointed out Molly. " I don't think they were ever close at home."

"Well, Harry and me was close. He saved my life. It was when he was getting me back to the lines that he got hit." Tom's eyes closed for a moment and Molly realised he was re-living whatever nightmare had happened.

"Tell me," she said gently. "Tell me what happened."

For a long moment Tom didn't reply, and Molly thought he wasn't going to say any more. Then he started to speak in a low, tired voice.

"We was out on a raid, on the German trenches, you know.

We was to crawl across no-man's-land and listen to what was going on there. Lieutenant Holt was leading, he could talk German a bit. Then there was me and Harry, and two other blokes from our company, Jim Hawkes and Bill Jarvis. We'd all been out before, knew the drill and that. We was to capture someone if we could so's he could be interrogated. It was night, of course, no moon, so very dark, but there was a sap out into no man's land..."

"A sap?"

"Yes, you know, a bit of shallow trench jutting out in front of the lines to be used as a listening post, or for observation. Anyhow, we went under cover along the sap and then crawled out into no-man's-land. We was all blacked up..."

"Blacked up? What do you mean?"

"Faces done with boot polish, nothing shiny on your uniform, nothing to chink or catch the light. Nothing to warn Jerry we was coming.

"There was still wire round us when we got out, but it had been cut to make a way through. We went in a V formation, Lieutenant Holt in front, me and Harry on the right, Hawkesy and Jarvis on the left. We took it very slowly because we didn't want to make no noise. Them Jerries was bloody close..." He broke off in embarrassment at the profanity he'd used, but Molly simply said, "Go on."

"Like I said, they was hoping we'd capture some Jerry from one of the forward trenches and bring him back for questioning, so me and Harry was armed with knobkerries, Hawkesy and Jarvis had hatchets, we all had bayonets... all ready for the quiet kill, see. In and out fast. We had mills bombs as well, to chuck into the trench once we was clear again, but crawling quiet like wasn't that easy. Someone, Jarvis or Hawkes out on the left, hit something, knocked into something, don't know what, but it made a..." he caught himself in time, "a dreadful noise and a Jerry sentry called out. Next thing we know is some machine gunner is opening fire right across where we was lying, frozen still like corpses. Several bursts into the dark. Then they put up a flare and it was like day. The raid was off. No point in lying there for their target practice.

"Lieutenant Holt ordered us back to the sap. Him and me and Harry started to crawl, very slowly, hoping when the light faded they might not catch the movement, but Jarvis and Hawkes made a dash for it. Mown down they was, poor bastards."

This time, caught up in his story, transported back to that dreadful night, Tom didn't correct his language, or even appear to notice his lapse.

"The gunner knew roughly where we was then of course, so Mr Holt said, 'Up to you which way you go, lads. Get back as best you can.' Then he stood up, tall as you please and hurled a grenade towards the machine gun nest. It exploded well short, but it stopped the gunner for a moment or two. He threw another, but while he was doing that another gun opened up from the other side and he was hit. Me and Harry had made it to the sap in the confusion of the grenade, and leapt down into it, but when we looked back over the top we saw that Mr Holt had been hit. Harry called to him and he answered, saying he was hit in the leg. Then Harry said to me, 'You take the left gun, I'll take the right.' We couldn't knock them out with grenades from there, but we hoped the explosions would blind them for a moment and we could go out for Lieutenant Holt."

"Back out of the trench, you mean?" gasped Molly.

"Well we couldn't leave him lying there, could we?"

"So what did you do?"

"We crawled out of the sap and hurled two grenades each in the direction of the machine guns, then we ran to where Mr Holt was lying. Harry grabbed one arm and me the other, and together we began to drag him back to the sap. The gunner opened up again and we all crashed flat, but I fell into a twist of wire. A bullet ripped through my arm—" he indicated his injured arm in its sling "—and I couldn't untangle myself. When the gunner stopped, Harry pulled Lieutenant Holt into the sap and then came back for me. I was well and truly caught in the wire, but lucky for me he was the man carting the wire clippers. It wasn't easy in the dark and I was no help to him with my right arm useless. They must have heard us, because as he pulled me free, that bloody gunner opened up again. Harry caught it in his leg... well you saw. We both lay flat, but when it was quiet again I found Harry was out cold. I managed to drag him the last few yards to the sap, but as we both fell in I must have hit my head because the next thing I knew was that it was daylight, and we was trapped there until it was dark again and we could get back to the lines."

"Couldn't you crawl back along the sap?" asked Molly who was both fascinated and horrified by the story.

"Not deep enough for cover in daylight," Tom replied. "It was only a few feet deep with a deeper hollow at the end. That's where we had to wait all day, in that hollow with our heads down. Lieutenant Holt died during the night, so that when I came round in the early morning I found myself with one dead body and a badly wounded man."

"And you were wounded yourself," Molly pointed out.

"Oh, my arm wasn't so bad," Tom said. "Not compared with Harry's leg. I did my best to get a field dressing on to that, but dragging him across the ground hadn't done him no good. He was conscious, and in great pain, but there was nothing I could do for that. We had water but nothing else. When you go on a raid you take as little as possible, so you can move more easily. Anyhow, we waited all day. It was cold, and we huddled together trying to keep warm. When it got dark we decided to risk it. We had to stand up. Harry couldn't crawl and I couldn't carry him. Either the gunners weren't keeping a proper watch, or they decided to let us get back. Which ever, we made it without being shot at, even though I was yelling ahead, 'Coming in! Cook and Carter coming in.'"

Tom smiled a bleak smile and continued, "The rest you know, really. We was sent back down the line to a dressing station, and then back to casualty clearing and ended up here."

Somewhere during the telling of his tale, Tom had taken Molly's hand, and he looked down at it now, as if surprised to find it in his. She squeezed his hand gently as if to reassure him she didn't mind.

He said, "So you see, Harry, well Harry saved my life out there. I'd never have got out of the wire without him. I'd have been stuck there until it was daylight and the Jerry gunners could use me for target practice."

"Sounds to me as if you saved his too," Molly said quietly. "He couldn't have got back to the lines without you. He probably wouldn't have got as far as here without you."

"But he wouldn't have been wounded at all if he hadn't come back for me. Don't you see?"

"Tom, you can't beat yourself with this," Molly said. "This dreadful war is not your fault. You both went back for Lieutenant Holt. Harry would never have left you any more than you left him."

Tom gave her a weak smile. "You're very kind, Molly...you don't mind me calling you Molly, do you?"

Molly returned his smile. "No," she said shyly. "I like it. And anyway I've been calling you Tom."

They sat on the stone seat for a while longer, not speaking, completely comfortable in their silence. At last Molly stood up, shook out her skirt and said, "I must go. I'm supposed to be on duty. Sister Eloise will be furious." She looked down at Tom. "I expect they'll bury him today," she said gently. "They usually do. I'll come across to the cemetery."

Tom stood up and reached for her hand again, raising her fingers to his lips. It was a far more intimate gesture than any other between them, even though they had stood with her arms around him while he wept. For a brief moment their eyes met and held, and Molly felt the colour flood her cheeks. She pulled her hand away in confusion.

Tom stepped back, his face reddening as well. "I'm sorry," he stammered, "I shouldn't have done that."

"No, no it's all right," Molly said. "It's just...I...no one's... I must go!" Suddenly she returned to being his nurse, "And so must you," she said firmly. "You shouldn't be out here in the cold. Sister Eloise would have a fit if she knew. Your temperature will be soaring!" With that she took his arm and led him back through the gate and across the courtyard to the ward and Sister Eloise.

Sister Eloise was not there when they slipped in and by the time the nun came back, Molly was going quietly about her tasks and Tom was fast asleep on his bed. She called Molly over and said that Reverend Mother wanted to see her before she went to her lunch.

Sister Eloise said briskly, "I shan't need you any more today, Molly. It's been a difficult day for you. When you have seen Mother, you need not return until tomorrow morning. You will attend the funeral, no?"

Uncertain that she had understood correctly, Molly checked with Sister Marie-Paul who was standing beside her, but she agreed that Sister Eloise had given her the rest of the day off, and she had leave to go over to the convalescent camp to the cemetery for Harry's funeral.

Reverend Mother was, as always, sitting behind her desk when she called to Molly to come in. She did not ask Molly to sit down, and from the look on her face, Molly could tell she was in some sort of trouble.

"Ah, Molly," was her only greeting, before she continued in her accented English. "Look out of the window, Molly and tell me what you see."

Molly went obediently to the window and looked down into the winter garden below. For a moment she was at a loss, then she recognised the stone seat carved in the wall and the little circular flower bed, and it came to her in a rush that Mother had been able to see her and Tom in the garden that morning. Colour crept up into her cheeks as she gazed down into the garden, not turning again to meet Reverend Mother's gaze. But the nun had seen the blush and said sharply, "Well may you blush, Miss Day. You were in my garden this morning." Silence. "With a patient." More silence. "That is not *comme il faut*."

Molly still said nothing and Reverend Mother said, "Have you nothing to say, Miss Day?"

Molly turned round from the window and lifting her chin said, "He was upset, Mother. His best friend had just died and I was trying to comfort him."

"So I understand from Sister Eloise. He was your friend too, *hein*? The man who died."

"My cousin. We live, lived, in the same village. We were brought up together as children."

"It is understandable that you were upset, but you must not become involved with the patients. How long were you in my garden, Molly?"

While she was relieved that she was again Molly and not Miss Day, Molly wondered if this question was asked to trap her. How long had Reverend Mother been watching her? Had she seen her with her arms around Tom? Has she seen them sitting together on the bench talking? Had she seen Tom kiss her hand? What had she seen and how damning was it? She drew in a breath as she decided to take a risk.

"Only a moment or two, Mother, while he composed himself."

Reverend Mother seemed to accept this for she nodded. Then she said, "It is not appropriate that you should be nursing this man now. He will be moved to the restoration ward this afternoon."

"But surely he is not ready to go there yet, Mother," cried Molly. "His arm is not healed yet and he still runs temperatures at night. The doctor hasn't said..."

"Nevertheless," Mother interrupted her, "he will move there this afternoon. Sister Eloise says that he would have moved in the next few days anyway for his restoration before going over to the camp."

Molly was horrified. The restoration ward was in the main body of the convent, where the men went to regain their strength before moving on to the convalescent camp outside the walls, but they were seldom sent there if they were still feverish. That only happened if there was a sudden influx of men as there had been on Molly and Sarah's first night at St Croix.

"We must protect your reputation, Molly," explained Reverend Mother. "Your reputation and not raise his expectations."

"Expectations!" cried Molly, her eyes blazing with sudden anger. "What expectation can he possibly have except to go back to those vile trenches and die? I gave him no expectations, I simply tried to comfort him for the death of his friend...our friend, Harry. Isn't that Christian charity, Mother? Isn't that what we are supposed to do as Christians?"

"Molly! That is no way to speak. You forget yourself, child. You are upset, I will forgive you for your outburst, but please do not let it occur again. You may go to your cousin's funeral, God rest his soul, and no doubt this young man will be there, but after that you will not see him, you understand? You will not visit him in the restoration ward. You will attend to your duties. I would not wish to have to send you home after all."

Molly held her tongue and said nothing, standing mutinously in front of the little nun.

"You understand, Molly? I will not have you involving yourself with your patients in any way but in nursing them." She looked hard at Molly and repeated, "Do you understand?"

"Yes, Mother," Molly replied in a subdued voice. But inside she was not subdued. She had made no promises, not tied herself to what was *"comme il faut"*, she had simply said that she had understood Reverend Mother's commands. As Reverend Mother had been speaking, something had clicked in her brain, and she was suddenly clear about something that she had hardly considered before. Tom Carter. He was important to her, not as Harry's friend, not as her patient, but as Tom Carter the man, with his tired eyes and the rare smile which could illuminate his whole face. She was suddenly struck with great clarity by the knowledge that she was not prepared to stop seeing him. She found herself thanking God that Reverend Mother had only looked into her garden in time to see them leaving it, to see her with her hand on Tom's arm, but not to see the quiet peace they shared in each other's company, nor the way she had sheltered him in her arms, and most of all not the way Tom had kissed her fingers or the look they exchanged.

Afraid her face might betray her new discovery, Molly lowered her eyes, keeping them on the floor in apparently meek acceptance of the dictates of the nun, and seemingly satisfied with this, Reverend Mother told her to go and eat something before she went across to the funeral.

"I have told Padre Robert that you will be coming, so he will have someone meet you at the gate at half past three. You will take up your duties again in ward one in the morning." Thus she was dismissed.

Tom stood beside the grave as it was filled in, the damp earth falling dully in heavy clods on the wood of the coffin. The pall bearers returned to the camp, and Padre Kingston said he would be in the chapel if they wanted to speak to him before going back to the hospital.

"Don't be too long in making your farewells, Carter," he said seriously. "Being out in this damp weather will not do you any good, aren't I right, Miss Day?"

Molly agreed that he was, and the parson smiled at them before striding off to deal with the next demand upon his time.

"I've been moved to a different ward," Tom said to Molly as soon as they were alone. "Somewhere inside the main building."

"I know," Molly said. "Reverend Mother told me. It's so's I don't nurse you any more." She smiled up at him bleakly. "She saw us in her garden this morning and thinks I have become involved with my patient."

Tom reached for her hand, encased in woollen gloves against the cold November air, his eyes seeking her face. "And have you?"

"Well," Molly looked away across the rows of wooden crosses as she replied, "we are, were, both friends of Harry's."

"But that's not what she meant, is it?"

"It was the reason I gave her for being there alone with you in the garden."

"I'd like us to be friends, just for ourselves," Tom said awkwardly. "You know, not just because of Harry." His eyes searched her face and this time she did not look away. He went on, "I've never met a girl like you, Molly. You're gentle...understanding," he considered the next word, and added, "caring."

"All nurses are caring," Molly said almost defensively.

"But not like you."

"Tom, I'm not allowed to see you; not allowed to come and visit you in the restoration ward," Molly told him flatly. "If I do Reverend Mother says she will send me home."

"Then you mustn't come," Tom responded promptly. "Molly, don't worry about me, I'll be going back to the lines soon. No point in upsetting things. It don't matter if we can't be real friends."

Silence slipped between them as they stood in the chill of the late afternoon.

"We can meet over here," Molly said abruptly. "We can meet when you are in the convalescent camp, because I can come over to the chapel for services. I'm allowed to do that. Once I'm through the gate in the wall, they'll just think I'm at the service."

"They'll soon work that one out," Tom said ruefully. "They're going to be watching you. It ain't worth it."

A cold spatter of rain blew into their faces and together

they turned back towards the convent. As they reached the wall, Molly said, "The padre has an evening service on Sunday. Ask if you can go. Several do from restoration."

Molly sat through the meal that evening in the refectory, listening to the reading. She had been surprised to discover recently that as the words flowed over her she understood the gist of what she was hearing, but this evening she gave no thought to anything but the events of the day. She was glad there was no talking at meals, she wanted peace to consider the effect of what had happened. Immediately after the meal, she went up to their room. Sarah found her there half an hour later when she came up from chapel. She sat down on the edge of her bed and said, "I hear poor Harry Cook died today. Poor Molly, I'm so sorry."

Molly who was also stretched out on her bed answered quietly. "Yes, this morning. They buried him this afternoon."

"Of course you went."

"Yes, Sister Eloise sent me off at lunch time and told me not to come back until tomorrow morning."

"Lucky you," Sarah said enviously. "I wish Sister Bernadette would give me extra time off."

"It was for my cousin's funeral," Molly said flatly.

Sarah was immediately contrite. "Oh Molly, I'm sorry. Of course it was. I don't know what I'm saying. It must have been dreadful for you. You've known Harry all your life."

"He taught me to swim," Molly said, and she sounded so sad Sarah wasn't sure what to say next, so she fell back on to what was now becoming her thought much of the time.

"I'll pray for his soul."

"Better to pray for those he's left behind," Molly replied. "His ma and dad and the rest of his family, all those who'll miss him. Tom Carter."

"Tom Carter?"

"His mate that brought him in. He was at the funeral too." Her voice changed and she spoke with sudden energy. "Do you know they've moved Tom Carter out of ward one and up to restoration?"

"Well, that's good, isn't it?" Sarah sounded surprised.

"The reason they've done it isn't because he's ready to go there, he's not. Dr Gergaud hasn't signed him off. No, the reason is because he and I were becoming friends, having Harry in common, like, and I was 'becoming involved' with a patient. 'Raising his expectations!' that's what Reverend Mother said." Molly was bitter. "We shared our grief for a moment, that's all."

Sarah thought back to her run in with Sister Bernadette over her kissing Private Macdonald on the cheek. "It is one of their main worries with us I suppose," she said judiciously. "It's different for the nuns, they're protected by their cloth. I mean none of the men could even consider one of them might be 'emotionally involved' with him." She gave a little laugh. "It would be very difficult to kiss anyone wearing one of their flyaway hats."

This comment succeeded in drawing an unwilling laugh from Molly, and Sarah quickly changed the subject.

"I had a letter from Freddie this morning," she said. "Guess what? He's going on some course near here and is coming to see me. Only for an afternoon, but that's something, isn't it? I haven't told Sister Bernadette yet, or asked Mother if he may come, but she's sure to let him, isn't she? I mean he's not a gentleman caller, is he? He's my brother. And Aunt Anne will want to see him too."

"Of course they'll let him come." Molly never referred to Reverend Mother as 'Mother' unless she absolutely had to.

The idea of calling anyone other than Mam "Mother" seemed strange, especially if the person concerned were a nun. "Of course they'll let him come, they can make that day your free afternoon."

"You're right," agreed Sarah happily. "I'll go and see Mother tomorrow. It'll be wonderful to see him, I haven't seen him for months."

They got into bed. Sarah, physically exhausted from her day and happy with thoughts of Freddie's visit, fell instantly into a dreamless sleep, but Molly, emotionally exhausted from hers, lay in the darkness and thought about Tom, reliving their time in the garden and the cold dank cemetery until at last she too, drifted off into an uneasy sleep from which she was to awake unrefreshed and strangely disconsolate.

Sunday, 14th November

I went to church in the camp this evening and when I got to the gate Tom was waiting for me. I couldn't resist a glance behind me in case someone from the convent was watching. Sister M-P always seems to be around and sometimes I think she's spying on me. Perhaps Reverend Mother has told her to watch me. I don't know, anyway she wasn't there to see me go or to see who met me. Anyhow, I'd got permission from Sister Eloise to go. She thinks I'm next best thing to a heathen, so she's quite keen for me to attend service at the camp, even if it is a Protestant one. I like working for Sister Eloise. She stands no nonsense, but she's kind and generous in her outlook, and though she is often brisk with us she never is with the patients and always has them at heart. She's taught me a lot even though my French is still so bad.

Tom and I walked to the tent Mr Kingston has turned into his church. It is lovely inside, with a little altar draped in a white cloth and candles in brass sticks. I think they are his own and they go with him wherever he goes. He isn't always at the camp, he told me he sometimes goes up to the front and has even held services in a dugout. We all sit on benches and chairs he has taken from all over the camp.

After the service very few leave, we all sit around and talk. Tom and I sit together. There is so much to know about him. He hasn't had an easy life, brought up in an orphanage. He tells me about life in London, and I tell him about Charlton Ambrose. He's heard a bit about it from Harry, of course. I haven't told him about Dad, don't suppose I ever will, except he's so easy to talk to. Sometimes it feels like I've known him all my life. So, maybe, one day.

I don't think Mr Kingston has talked to Reverend Mother, or I am sure I'd be sent straight back to the camp after the service. It is wonderful to be outside the convent for a few hours each week, especially as Sarah and I haven't been to the village for some time. There are days when the walls seem to close around me, hemming me in. Now I have Sundays to look forward to.

Thirteen

On Sunday evening Molly walked through the gate towards the convalescent camp. It was already an accepted thing that she should go to the evening service there whenever her duties permitted it, and unless there was a panic on, Sister Eloise made no problem in giving her the time.

Tom was waiting for her the other side of the convent wall, and together they walked through the camp to the tent Robert Kingston had converted into his church. At first they walked in silence, an unaccustomed awkwardness between them. Both knew that something between them had changed after the moment in the garden and their exchange in the cold air of the cemetery, but neither could put into words exactly what.

Their friendship, one brought about through the chance of war, had grown with their mutual concern for Harry. It might have developed quite differently or not at all, Molly had thought as she lay in bed, her mind whirling in the darkness, if Reverend Mother hadn't issued her prohibition. She might never have thought of Tom Carter as anything more than an injured young man who needed a little comfort after the death of his friend, but because the nun had forbidden them to meet, Molly had come to realise how much she wanted the friendship to grow, to develop...into what? Tom was shy. He would never have suggested that they defy

Reverend Mother. It was not up to her, Molly knew, to take the initiative, but she was glad she had when she suggested they meet at church. After all, she told herself, it is the way we'd be allowed to meet at home.

As she came through the gate and Tom had turned and seen her, his face had broken into his rare and vivid smile, lighting his dark eyes, their usual weariness dropping away and Molly found herself matching his smile with one of her own. They greeted each other but did not touch. There was no shaking hands or taking of arms, their smiles were enough, and they turned and walked side by side to the church.

"How's your arm?" Molly said at last to break the silence. "You look better, more colour in your face."

"Much better, thank you, Nurse," Tom replied with a grin, and the ice was broken.

So it began. Each Sunday they met at the gate and strolled over to the church, and after the service when, encouraged by the padre, several of the men stayed to chat, Tom and Molly stayed as well, sitting together, talking. Robert Kingston watched their friendship growing but made no comment. Life for young men such as Tom was likely to be short, and the padre thought that there was no harm in the young couple getting to know each other, chaperoned as they were by himself and a group of others. It was all perfectly proper. If he had known of Reverend Mother's feelings on the subject he might have thought otherwise, but he did not.

When later they returned to the convent, they walked together as far as the gate in the wall, and then Molly went through and straight up to her room, Tom waiting a few moments before following her and going up to the restoration ward; both were uncomfortable with this small deceit, but neither wanted to draw attention to the their meeting at church.

Molly found herself living for Sunday evenings. She worked long, hard hours in the ward, her experience and competence growing daily, but she found that Tom was in the back of her mind all the time, and often slipped to the forefront if she were working on a routine job that did not require her full attention. She stored up small incidents, little things that might make him laugh, like Sister Marie-Paul seeing a mouse, leaping onto a chair and dropping the bed pan she was carrying, and the time when a bird flew in through the door and the nuns chased it flapping round the ward, to raucous encouragement from the men. Molly loved to hear him laugh, to see the worried look drop from his face as she told him these things in their precious time together on a Sunday evening, and the knowledge that he was thinking of her too, warmed her as she dealt with the chilly bleakness of suppurating wounds, amputations and death.

At the end of each day she went, exhausted upstairs, but before she fell into her bed, she sat down with her journal and recorded both her thoughts and the happenings of the day. Their tiny room with its stone walls was always cold, but Molly would take the blanket off the bed and drape it round her shoulders as she wrote. Even if she made only a one-sentence entry, she tried to write something every day, but more often than not she wrote several pages before she went to bed. It was a form of release to pour out her heart in her diary, for though she could talk to Sarah about their nursing cares, she could not mention Tom. For a start, Sarah would not approve of their meetings on a Sunday in direct defiance of Reverend Mother—Sarah greatly revered Reverend Mother—but apart from that, Molly's awakening feelings were too private, too precious to share with anyone else.

Sarah always came up later than Molly, as she never went to bed these days without a visit to the chapel first.

"How can you pray for half an hour?" Molly asked one evening when she came to their room even later than usual.

Sarah considered her question seriously. "It's not prayer, exactly," she said, "I do pray, of course, but mostly I just sit there and think over the events of the day and try to come to terms with some of the things that have happened. It's very peaceful in there, and when I come out I feel that I've handed my problems over to God and He knows what to do about them."

Molly still had grave reservations about God. He seemed to her to be entirely irrelevant to what was happening in the war-torn world about them, but she could see that her time in the chapel was important to Sarah, and so she said no more.

It was two Sundays later that they paused outside the gate. Tom had tucked Molly's arm through his as they walked the short distance in the dark from the camp to the convent, and Molly could feel the warmth of his body against her own in the chill of the evening. Just before they reached the gate Tom stopped and pulling Molly aside from the path turned her towards him. Her face was a pale oval in the darkness, turned up to him half-expectantly, and he slipped his good arm round her, drawing her against him. He looked down into her face and though he could not see her expression in the dark, she made no move to pull away. As his arm tightened round her, her pale face under its Sunday hat tilted towards him and he felt her arms slide up and round his neck. He lowered his head and very gently kissed first her forehead and then her lips. For a moment her lips were cool and dry against his own, then to his delight they parted and she returned his kiss. After a moment they drew apart, a little breathless.

"Molly?" Tom whispered, wonder in his voice.

"I'm here, Tom," she answered softly.

"You didn't mind?"

"No, I wanted you to." Molly stifled a laugh and added, "I shouldn't say that, should I?"

"Why not if it's true? Is it true, Molly?"

For answer Molly pulled his head down, and this time she kissed him first.

They stood together, their world contained in their embrace. Even as they stood there, each held close to the other, Molly thought, I've held him in my arms before, but it felt nothing like this.

"I've never walked out with anyone, Molly," Tom told her, "you're my first girl...if you'll be my girl?"

She smiled up at him in the darkness and whispered, "Oh yes, please, Tom."

She believed what he said. She knew he was shy, not the sort to have been consorting with girls like some of the other lads. She had never walked out with anyone either. This was the first man she had ever allowed near her except her father, and with him it wasn't a question of allowing him. She wondered again, if she could ever tell Tom about that, but doubted that she could. For the moment that didn't matter; for now it was enough to feel his arms around her, to feel protected and safe. Safe within the circle of his arms she felt she would never need to feel afraid of her father, or anyone, again, and she gave herself over to the new and wonderful sensations that were sweeping through her body as he kissed her hard and long.

This time when they drew apart he said, "I love you, Molly Day."

Molly didn't answer, simply laid her head on his chest,

nestling against him like a child, not wanting the moment to end. The wonderful moment was short-lived; from the other side of the wall there was noise, raised voices, and the spell was broken. Reluctantly Tom released her and Molly said urgently, "We must go back. Something's happening."

She hurried to the gate and saw at once that more wounded were arriving. Men were being led round from the front of the building and brought into the wards at the back.

"Looks like I'm needed," she said briefly over her shoulder and without a backward glance headed directly to ward one, where Sister Eloise handed her an apron to cover her church clothes and a clean cap to replace her hat and the work began.

Molly was up most of the night helping with the influx of men. "How will we fit all these in?" she asked Sister Marie-Paul as they tried to sort the waiting men out.

"Those go up to restoration," Sister Marie-Paul nodded over Molly's shoulder. Molly glanced round and saw six of their patients, almost all of those who were able to move, collecting their few possessions and leaving the ward. Two novices were hard at work stripping and making up the beds with fresh sheets.

Used to be my job, Molly thought, but she knew that Sister Eloise needed her for the nursing side of things now, and she turned back to look at their next patient. As she helped strip and wash the man Pierre had lifted up on to the examination table, peeling away the filthy bandage that covered a jagged wound in his shoulder, her thoughts were concentrated on the job in hand and it was only later when she and Sarah were once more creeping into their beds for a few hours' sleep, that she thought what the consequences of clearing the ward might be for Tom. They would need space for the men who had moved into restoration. Almost certainly Tom would have been sent to the convalescent camp. She felt suddenly cold. Once he was in the camp it would not be long before he was sent back to his regiment. Everyone knew of the huge losses suffered during the fighting at Loos in September, and though the onset of winter had halted any major confrontation with the Germans and there was a dreadful stalemate in the trenches, it was also common knowledge that the British army was desperate to bring its number up to strength. Private Thomas Carter of the 1st Belshires would be sent back to the lines the moment he was considered fit for duty.

The time he spent in the restoration ward had worked wonders. Tom's gaunt face had filled out a little, his skin no longer stretched, a pale shade of parchment over his cheek bones, but had regained its normal, healthy colour. His arm had regained much of its movement and the film of constant pain no longer covered his eyes. He would probably spend only a comparatively short time in the camp.

Molly knew it had to come. They had talked of it, but only as a distant prospect. Now, she felt, it was about to become a reality.

This very evening, Molly thought, Tom had told her he loved her. She had not responded, not in words at least. She had not reassured him with a declaration of her own. Why not, she wondered? She had never been in love before, had no experience with men at all, but as the prospect of losing Tom back to the trenches stared her in the face she finally accepted what she had known for some time, that she loved him and couldn't bear the thought of losing him. How she wished now that she had told him so. He had been braver than she, telling her of his love without being sure she returned it.

She lay in bed in an agony of despair. She wouldn't be able to see him again until Sunday, but suppose they had moved him on before then? Suppose they decided that he was fit to go and she never saw him again? He might be killed and she would never know.

I must see him, she thought. I'll go over to the camp. We've done it before.

So they had, but always she and Sarah together and not recently. She would not be permitted to go on her own, and what reason could she give for wanting to? If she asked permission it was unlikely to be granted as Mother would know that Tom was now in the camp, and if she risked going without asking she might find she was banned from going on a Sunday. Since she had begun her meetings with Tom, she'd had the feeling she was being watched by the nuns. Was it her imagination, or was Sister Marie-Paul whispering about her to Sister Eloise, or worse still Reverend Mother? Result of an uneasy conscience, Molly told herself firmly. After all, she had no evidence that they were keeping watch on her, but what little time off duty she had enjoyed before had been cut to a minimum. Necessity, Sister Eloise called it when she regretted on several occasions, that Molly and Sarah would not be able to have their free time to go to the village. How could she get a message to him? Molly drifted off to sleep at last and when she awoke the answer seemed obvious. Perfectly simple. She would write to him and post the letter to the camp. Soldiers received mail all the time; it was important for morale and the service was good. Yet even as this solution came to her she had to reject it. First, because mail for the troops had to be sent to a special address and she didn't know what it was, and, second, there was no way for her to get the letter posted. Molly had not been in the habit of writing letters, but Sarah posted hers when they went down to the village. As they hadn't been able to go recently Molly knew Sarah's letters had been entrusted to one of the lay workers who came in every day, but Molly knew she couldn't entrust her with a letter addressed to a soldier, it might go straight back to Reverend Mother. She'd have to wait until Sunday, six whole days of not knowing.

Pale with dark smudges under her eyes from lack of sleep, Molly prepared for another day. The creeping grey dawn was cold, as she and Sarah dressed quickly, neither wanting to linger over their chilly ablutions.

"Do you think they sent everyone from restoration over to the camp last night?" Molly, who was brushing her hair, tried to make her question sound casual.

Sarah looked at her quizzically. "Most of them I should think, why?"

"I was just wondering," Molly sounded unconvincing even to her own ears. She watched Sarah in the mirror, whilst steadily brushing her hair. "We sent six up to restoration from our ward, and other wards must have had to do the same."

"We sent three," Sarah said. "I suppose they'd have to send some across anyway." She looked across at Molly and said, "Anyone in particular?"

"Anyone in particular what?"

"Molly, you've been miles away the past couple of weeks. I haven't been able to get near you, and," she added with a sudden smile, "so much church on a Sunday evening? What's going on?"

"Nothing." Molly's answer came a little too quickly. Sarah noticed the colour creeping into her friend's face, but she didn't push her. She was sure that Molly had somehow got herself involved with one of the patients, one who must have already moved on from her ward, so she simply said, "I'll try and find out how many were sent across...but a name would help."

There was a pause, and then Molly said softly "Tom Carter, Harry Cook's friend."

"Can't you ask yourself?" suggested Sarah. "Sister Marie-Paul knows most things." It was from Sister Marie-Paul that Sarah had already had a hint about Molly and a patient.

"She is your friend," Sister Marie-Paul's little eyes had lit up with the whiff of scandal. "I thought you should know. To be interested in a patient is not *comme il faut*." Unknowingly, she echoed the words of Reverend Mother, and Sister Bernadette. Nothing between patient and nurse was *comme il faut* Sarah thought wryly, yet surely something warmer than a brisk and clinical relationship which the nuns seemed to advocate must help with the healing. All she had said was, "You clearly know more than I do, Sister."

A little disappointed, Sister Marie-Paul had gone on her way. Remembering this incident, Sarah said now, "No, on second thoughts, better not. I think you should watch what you say to Sister Marie-Paul. She's, well, I'm not sure I trust her."

"Nor do I," Molly admitted. "I always feel she is watching me. It's probably my imagination, but I certainly don't want to give her ideas."

"Don't worry," Sarah said, "I'll do my best to find out from someone, but it may not be today." She suddenly broke into a huge beam. "Freddie's coming today."

"Oh, Sarah," Molly was conscience stricken. She had been so tied up with her own thoughts and problems, she had entirely forgotten that Sarah's brother was coming to visit her that day. "I'd forgotten it was today. You must be so excited. How awful I forgot!"

"Don't be silly," Sarah said cheerfully. "But I am excited. I haven't seen him since February. Reverend Mother has said he can take me out for lunch." She gave Molly a quick hug and said, "I can't *wait* to see him."

The two girls were in very different moods as they set to work that morning. Sarah was excited and light-hearted as she went about the tasks. Nothing seemed too mundane today as she scrubbed bed pans, made beds and cleaned up the ward.

"You're in a good mood, today, Nurse," said Corporal Evans as she moved him into a chair so that she could make his bed.

"My brother's coming to see me," she told him. "He's coming down from the front. I haven't seen him since February. I've been given the afternoon off. We're going out to lunch."

"No time for chatter, Nurse," Sister Bernadette said as she passed along the ward, "especially as you have the afternoon off."

"Silly cow," remarked Corporal Evans conversationally. He hadn't understood the French, but he'd understood the tone of voice. When Sarah said, "Hush, Corporal, you mustn't call her that," he gave Sarah a broad wink. "Hope you enjoy yourself, miss," he said as she moved to the next bed.

Sarah treated him to a dazzling smile and said, "Don't worry, I will!"

Molly went about her work like an automaton, her mind whirling with thoughts of Tom, and it wasn't until one of her patients, a cheerful cockney lad whose foot had been amputated, called to her, "Cheer up, Nurse, you look like a wet weekend," that she pulled herself together and began to concentrate on what she was doing. She longed to ask about the men in the restoration ward, but she knew it would be better to leave it to Sarah, even if it meant not knowing where he was until the next day.

Though she was busy, the morning crawled for Sarah, but just before twelve o'clock Sister Bernadette came and found her putting dirty linen into the laundry baskets.

"It is time you went," she said, not unkindly. "Your brother will be here soon. You'll want to change."

Sarah was surprised that the nun, whom she always felt despised her for some reason, had taken the trouble to send her off. She smiled at her and said, "Thank you, Sister."

Sister Bernadette did not quite return the smile, but said gruffly, "I hope you enjoy your afternoon."

It was a wonderful afternoon. Freddie had driven up to the convent in a battered old car and was waiting in the bleak little parlour where Sarah and Molly had first met Sister St Bruno. He turned as Sarah opened the door and she flung herself into his arms.

"Oh Freddie," she cried as she hugged him, "it's so good to see you! Let me look at you. You're looking well, very well." Indeed he was, tall and broad shouldered, with his fair hair neatly cut, his uniform clean and well-fitting. His open face with its mobile mouth and determined chin, was strong and good looking, and his deep-set eyes were alight with happiness at seeing her. She hugged him again. "You look very smart."

"So do you, sis," he replied. "But I thought you'd be in uniform. You know, apron with big red cross."

"Not quite," Sarah explained. "I just wear a cap and apron

over a grey skirt and white blouse, but I've been allowed to change in your honour." She twirled round in clothes she hadn't worn since she had arrived in France, and suddenly felt like her old self again, free from the smell of disinfectant which she felt clung to her all the time these days, or odours even worse.

"Aunt Anne wants to see you before we go out. She'll be here in a minute. Oh Freddie, I've so much to tell you, and I can't wait to hear all your news. Are you still definitely going home for Christmas? Father will be delighted."

"He'd be even more delighted if you were coming too, sis," Freddie began, but before he could say more, to her relief, Sarah heard the door open and their Aunt Anne came in.

For the next ten minutes or so they chatted together, during which Freddie listened dutifully as Sister St Bruno told him what sterling work Sarah was doing. All the time Sarah was itching to go, to get right away from the convent so that she and Freddie could really talk.

At last Aunt Anne said, "Well, I must let you two go out for your lunch. It has been a pleasure to meet you again, Frederick. You are always in my prayers. When do you return to the front?"

"Tomorrow," Freddie replied. "I've been on a gunnery course for a couple of weeks, now it's back to the regiment."

They climbed into the car and set off down the drive. The car had a hood, but the windows would not shut and the cold air rushed in as they bumped their way down to the village, and Sarah was glad of her winter coat and hat.

"Where on earth did you get this car?" she shouted above the sound of the wind and the engine.

"Lent it for the day," Freddie called back. "Chap with a posting at HQ in Albert. Shall we go to Albert for lunch?"

"If we don't, it'll have to be Madame Juliette's," Sarah said.

"Sounds like a house of ill repute," laughed Freddie.

"No, it isn't," said Sarah. "Well, at least I don't think it is. I go there with Molly when we have any free time. We walk down to St Croix and have gateaux and tea there. It's perfectly respectable." She laughed and added as an afterthought, "But we don't mention it to the nuns!"

"I should think not indeed."

Half an hour later, when they were sitting in a snug little restaurant in the centre of Albert, he asked, "How is little Molly, anyway? How did you persuade her to come with you on this mad escapade?"

Sarah looked at him sharply. "It's not an escapade any more than you being in the army is. We're here because we're needed, and that's the end of it. You're as bad as Father, Freddie. You think girls should sit at home and sew a fine seam. Well I tell you this, that is not for me. I can't fight in the trenches, but I can look after those who do."

"Hey, hey, whoa there," Freddie cried, putting up his hands as if to fend her off. "Keep you hair on, old girl. I only asked how Molly was doing."

"Better than I am, if the truth were known," Sarah admitted as she studied the menu. "She is far more use than I am. Sister Eloise says she is a born nurse, and though she has to do most of the things that I have to, cleaning bedpans..."

"Hey, steady on, old girl, I'm about to have my lunch," protested Freddie.

"She is far more involved with the actual nursing of the men. Sister Bernadette hardly lets me near a patient, 'specially since I kissed one of them!"

"Kissed one! Sarah, I don't believe you."

As they ate their meal, the best Sarah had had since she

left London, Sarah told Freddie all about Private Iain Macdonald, and then other stories and incidents which had occurred over the time they had been there.

"Another sad thing, especially for Molly was when Harry Cook from home was brought in. Do you remember Harry, lived at High Meadow Farm?"

Freddie nodded. "Of course I do, he's in my company, or was before he was wounded. Is he here?"

"No, I'm afraid he died. They had to amputate his leg, but it was too late. Poor Molly, she was with him when he died. He was her cousin you know and it sounds as if they were fairly close as children. It was very difficult for her." Sarah looked across at him in surprise. "Didn't they tell you he had died?"

"Hasn't come through to me yet," Freddie said, "but I haven't been there for a while, off on this course."

"If he was in your company, then we've got another of your men here," Sarah said, the glimmer of an idea coming into her head. "Harry was brought in by his friend, Tom Carter, who was wounded as well."

"Yes, I know Carter," Freddie said. "He and Cook were always good mates. You say he's here at St Croix?"

"He's probably been moved to the convalescent camp," Sarah said and she explained about the arrival of more wounded the previous night. "I expect they had to move him across to make room." She looked across at Freddie and said, "Perhaps you should go and see him while you're here. He was pretty cut up when Harry Cook died."

"Yes, that's a good idea. I will when we get back. I can pass on news of him to the other men. They will have heard about Cook by now, I'm sure. His brother's in my company too. He'll have been notified, I expect."

"What's it like?" Sarah asked him as they sat over their coffee. The rain was beating on the windows of the restaurant, but they were sitting cocooned in its warmth, safe from the elements outside and Sarah felt suddenly very close to her brother. She hadn't asked him very much when he was in England, but now where they were both so much closer, more involved in what was going on, she felt she needed to know.

"What's it like in the trenches? You'd never say much when you came home last time, but you looked awful."

"I felt awful," Freddie said. "Exhausted." He stared out at the rain falling steadily from a leaden sky, his eyes distant for a moment before he turned them back on his sister. "It's the futility of it all, Sarah, more than the physical miseries, the damp, and the cold and the mud and the lice and all that. I can put up with that if I have to, if it is serving some purpose."

"And isn't it?" Sarah prompted as he lapsed into silence.

"We sit in our trenches and Jerry sits in his. We bombard them with heavy artillery, they bombard us. We raid their lines to take prisoners and destroy their trenches, they raid ours. We send miners down to burrow their way under no-man's-land, they do the same. And all the time men are dying and neither side gains an inch of ground."

"But surely there are big battles," said Sarah.

"Yes, sometimes we are thrown in to attack, and we lose yet more lives, thousands of men to move forward a few hundred yards. We take over enemy trenches, only to be thrown out of them in our turn." Freddie's earlier cheerfulness had vanished and he seemed to Sarah to have aged several years in the time it took to tell her these things. "Of course, I can't say any of this to anyone else," he went on. "Be bad for morale among the men, though the Lord knows most of them realise it for themselves. They're not stupid, but many of them think the officers are. You can't blame them. Seasoned soldiers find themselves being led by boys straight out of school with no experience beyond minimal basic training. They must wonder if this bloody war will ever end; if they'll ever get out of the stinking muddy holes they have to live in and get back to living like human beings again."

"Does Father know how you feel?" Sarah wondered.

"Hope not," Freddie replied. "He wouldn't understand and think it the most cowardly, defeatist talk. No one who hasn't lived in the conditions most of the men have to cope with day in and day out, and that includes some of the top brass, have any idea of how soul-destroying it is. Don't get me wrong, Sarah, I know this war has got to be fought, but the cost in lives and human misery...unimaginable. I couldn't say this to anyone else, sis, only to you, and you mustn't repeat it. I'm not being defeatist, just realistic. People like Harry Cook, dying of wounds, blasted to death, or machine gunned down, they have no future, they've given it up. We can only pray the one we have fought for is worth the cost of their lives."

Their happy outing together had taken on such a sombre mood, that Sarah shivered. Freddie put his hand over hers.

"Come on," he said, "don't let's spoil our day. We're going shopping so that I can buy you a Christmas present, and then," he added as he helped her back into her coat, "we'll go to that camp of yours and see how Carter is doing."

They spent the afternoon in the shops where Freddie bought Sarah a pendant on a silver chain, and Sarah bought a fountain pen for her father, which Freddie would take home with him and a propelling pencil for Freddie, which he chose himself.

"Better than a pen up at the front," he said, "so don't be surprised if my letters are written in pencil from now on."

They drove back to St Croix as the evening was drawing in. The rain had eased somewhat, but the sky was an unrelentingly grey. Sarah pointed out the lane that led round the exterior wall of the convent to the main entrance of the camp.

"We could go through from the convent garden," she said, "but I think it would be better for you to arrive at the front gate."

There was a sentry on the gate, but he was one of her ex-patients, and recognising Sarah, waved them through. "We'd better find Mr Kingston, the padre," she said to Freddie. "He'll know if Tom Carter has been sent across, and if so where he is."

They found the padre just finishing a confirmation class for a small group of men, and as they waited at the back of the church tent, Freddie watched him speaking to each man as he left. When he saw Sarah and Freddie, Robert Kingston came over. Sarah, who had only met him once or twice, reminded him who she was and introduced her brother. The two men shook hands.

"I was wondering if one of my men has come across to the camp today, from the convent," Freddie said. "Private Thomas Carter, 1st Belshires."

"Yes, he did. Last night actually. He was moved out to make way for more men coming in, I believe."

"Well, when Sarah told me he was here, I thought I should visit him and see how he is. I understand his mate, Harry Cook died recently." For a moment his eyes flicked to the graveyard beyond the fence.

"Yes, I'm sorry to say he did," Kingston said. "Did you want to see Carter? I'll send someone to fetch him. You can meet him in here if you like, I've finished for the moment."

He sent the last man, just leaving, to find Tom Carter, and then left them himself, saying, "I'm sure he won't be long."

Tom Carter was lying on a cot staring up at the roof of the tent when he got the message. He was feeling very down. Being moved into the camp brought the prospect of being sent back to the front very much closer. He wanted to talk to Molly, but he didn't even know if she knew he had been moved. Their moments together the evening before had filled him with a joy he had never before felt. Molly had not said she loved him, but her response to his kisses assured him that she did. In all his rather disjointed life, Tom had never had anyone to love, and the discovery of it filled him with wonder.

"Waiting for you in the chapel, an officer and a lady," the man said, "I'd look sharp if I was you."

Tom walked across to the church wondering who could want him. An officer and... surely not Molly. He quickened his step and was astonished to find his company commander waiting for him, with the other English nurse, the one who Molly was maid to.

"Captain Hurst, sir," he said coming awkwardly to attention.

"At ease, Carter," Freddie said. "Just come in to see how you're getting on. Hope the arm's better. We need you back, you know." He tried to sound jovial and bracing, but he could see the resignation in the man's eyes. "My sister," Freddie indicated Sarah standing behind him, "my sister tells me that Cook died of his wounds. She says he wouldn't have made it this far if it hadn't been for you. Well done, Carter. I shan't forget."

"No sir, thank you, sir," Tom mumbled.

"Seen the MO, have you?" Freddie asked. "How's the arm?"

"Getting better sir, most of the movement back, though it still hurts if I move quickly, like. Saw the doc this morning, sir. Said it'll be another couple of weeks and then I should be ready for light duties, sir."

"Well done, Carter, that's good news. We'll look forward to having you back after Christmas." Freddie nodded again and began to turn away when Sarah spoke.

"Good to see you making such progress, Tom," she said. "You were in Molly's ward, weren't you? I'll be sure to tell her how well you're doing. She's always interested in how her patients are getting on."

Tom stared at her for a moment dumbstruck. Though he knew who Sarah was, he'd never spoken to her. Then he gathered his wits about him and said, "Yes, miss, thank you, miss." There was no message he could send to Molly with Captain Hurst standing there, and he wasn't even sure if Sarah's remark meant she knew about him and Molly or if she had spoken out of simple kindness. He thought hard about that after they'd gone. It seemed unlikely Molly would have told Sarah about him, but they were friends after all, so maybe she had. At least Sarah would tell Molly where he was, and for how long. There was little chance they would meet before, so they would just have to wait for Sunday.

Freddie and Sarah returned to the convent, where Freddie hugged his sister and left her at the door.

"Look after yourself, sis," he said. "I'll give your love to the governor and pass on your present." He held her away from him for a moment, looking at her with pride and then said, "And I'll tell him what you're up to here. He ought to be as proud of you as I am."

Sarah's eyes filled with tears. "It's been wonderful to see you, Freddie," she said. "Thank you for today, it was lovely."

She smiled up at him through her tears and said, "I'll pray for you, Freddie, every day."

Freddie looked faintly embarrassed by this. He didn't mind the thought of her praying for him, he even did a bit of praying himself from time to time, but he wasn't sure it was the sort of thing a girl said to her brother. "Thanks," he said awkwardly. "Thanks, old girl. Yes, well, I must go. Got to get this old banger back to Horton before he thinks I've bent it round a tree." He swung the handle on the car and as its engine coughed into life, scrambled aboard.

"Don't forget to write," Sarah called as he put it into gear.

"I won't," Freddie promised and waved as the car gathered speed and disappeared round a bend.

Tuesday, 21st December

Christmas is coming close and we are trying to make the wards bright and cheerful. Sarah and I went out to collect holly and ivy today. It was very cold and the sky was very low as if it was going to snow, but it was lovely to be out in the country. I don't realise how shut in I feel in the convent until I am outside the walls again.

Some of the men have received parcels from home, which is lovely for them, but we have been trying to find some sort of present for Christmas morning for everyone. Sister Magdalene got some Red Cross parcels the other day, and it was decided that they should be opened and the things sorted out for Christmas Day.

I wonder if Mam and Dad will miss me this Christmas. I have to be at the Manor for Christmas Day, but I usually see them in church and I go home for Boxing Day. I will go to the Christmas evening service at the camp. At least I can wish Tom Happy Christmas if nothing more. I've no present to give him. How I wish I had.

Fourteen

Sarah stood looking at the empty road for a few moments. She dashed the tears from her cheeks and turned resolutely into the convent, wondering as Freddie headed back to his regiment at the front, if she would ever see him again.

She spent the half hour before the evening meal in the chapel, and, much comforted, was able to face the refectory feeling a little less lonely. She was further cheered by the way Molly received the news that though Tom was now in the convalescent camp, he was not likely to be sent back to the front until the early New Year.

"Did you have a lovely time with your brother?" Molly had asked. She could call Sarah by her Christian name quite easily now, but she couldn't do the same for Freddie.

"Yes, really lovely," Sarah sighed. "I couldn't believe he was really here, and the time just flew." She told Molly about their lunch and the Christmas shopping and then said, "I bet you can't guess where else we went."

"No, where?"

"When I was talking to Freddie, I told him about Harry Cook, because of him coming from home and being your cousin and things." She paused.

"And?"

"And, he said he knew Harry had been wounded because

they are in the same company. Freddie is Harry's company commander!"

Molly still didn't guess what was coming. She looked puzzled and said, "So, you told him Harry had died."

"I did, but I also told him there was another man from his company here, Tom Carter, and I suggested he should visit him in the convalescent camp while he was here...so that's what we did."

At last there was animation in Molly's face. "You went to the camp?"

"Yes, and Tom was there. The padre had him brought to the chapel, and we talked with him for several minutes."

"But what did Mr Freddie think of you wanting to see Tom? Didn't he think it strange?"

"Not at all, because he didn't know *I* wanted to see Tom, he thought *he* did. He asked how Tom was getting on and what the MO had said to him about rejoining the company."

"And what did Tom say?"

Molly sounded fearful and Sarah said reassuringly, "Don't worry, he's been told he'll be fit for light duties in two weeks' time, so that doesn't even mean he'll go back to the front. It also means he'll be here for Christmas. Didn't I hear they have special Christmas dinner in the camp? A bit of a party?"

Molly stared at her and repeated slowly, "He'll be here on Sunday."

"He'll be here for at least two more weeks, so you'll see him before he goes." She saw Molly's face light up and added, "But do be careful, Molly. Don't get too involved. You'll only get hurt."

Christmas crept upon them. Released from their duties one crisp December afternoon, Molly and Sarah went out together to gather holly and ivy from the wood on the hill above the village. They returned with armfuls and all the wards were decorated. One of the men in Sarah's ward had received a parcel from home, which included a paper chain made by his little sister. With great care Sarah draped it above the man's bed. Another had some tiny silver bells on a string, and these were hung near the stove so that the rising heat made them twist and chime. The nuns were determined to make the wards as festive as possible, and each sister in charge was given a large candle to place among the greenery, to light on Christmas Day.

The day itself began much as any other for Molly and Sarah. Up at six, they started duty well before breakfast. Each man found a present at the end of his bed, a few cigarettes, a pair of socks or mittens, a note book and pencil, a bar of chocolate. The Red Cross parcels which had arrived earlier had yielded something for every man.

"Special dinner today as well," Molly told them as she admired the presents they had received. "Sister Evangeline in the kitchen has been saving ingredients for ages. It won't be turkey and plum pudding, but it will be special."

Father Gaston came round the wards bringing communion to any men that wanted it, followed an hour later by Robert Kingston from the camp. He visited each man, offering him communion if he wanted it, and when he came to leave the ward he drew Molly aside.

"There is a concert party arranged for the men in the camp this evening," he told her. "After evening service. If you and your friend would like to come, I will ask Reverend Mother if you can be spared."

Molly stared at him incredulously. "Do you think she will let us?" she asked.

He grinned, suddenly boyish, "I can only ask," he said. "Would you like me to?"

"Oh yes, please," cried Molly in delight. "I've leave from Sister Eloise to come to the evening service, but if Sarah and I could come together and stay for the show..." Words deserted her.

"I'll ask," he promised, and moved on to the next ward.

Late in the afternoon, as the dusk fell across the courtyard, a small company of the sisters came into each ward to sing carols. They sang in French, but many of the tunes were familiar, and their voices were joined with an occasional tenor and baritone. It was an emotional time. The men thought of their families in England and longed to be there. Some remembered the short unofficial Christmas truce that had occurred spontaneously in some parts of the line the previous year.

"Really strange it was," Private Button told Sarah. "The Jerries was singing in their trenches, 'Silent Night' it was, and someone joined in, in ours. One of my mates went over the top and wandered out into no-man's-land. Crazy, we thought he was, thought he'd get blown away, no, but, lo and behold, out came Jerry as well. One of them gave my mate some chocolate, and then more blokes came out from either side. Weird it was, I can tell you. We'd been hammering them to blazes, pardon me, miss, and then there we all was walking about sharing cigarettes. Ordinary blokes they was. Next thing we know it's back to bombarding them again."

There'd be no such truce this year, Sarah knew. Freddie had told her the order had gone out there was to be no fraternising with the enemy this Christmas. She didn't say so to Private Button; it was too dreadful to think of men killing each other on Christmas Day; she simply admired the balaclava his young daughter had knitted and sent him for Christmas.

Sarah, too, had been thinking about home and trying not to feel too lonely. She could picture Freddie and her father dozing by the fire in the drawing room after their Christmas dinner, the dogs asleep at their feet. Freddie would have been out with them earlier, striding across the fields and up into the woods that covered the shoulder of hill above the village. It was their traditional Christmas walk taken between church and lunch. She had taken it on her own last year, when Freddie had already gone to the war. Now it was his turn to walk it alone. A wave of homesickness threatened to engulf her, and she made herself look forward to the coming evening.

When the girls had met for their midday meal, Molly told Sarah what Robert Kingston had said. "Do you think they'll let us go?" she asked. "I'm allowed to go to the service, but if you came too… It would be such a lovely way to spend Christmas, make it really special."

Sarah could see how much Molly wanted to go, and she knew why. She herself had been to Mass in the convent chapel, and didn't know if she'd be spared from the ward again, but she smiled and said, "Of course I'll come, if they say we may. When will we hear, do you think?"

They heard almost immediately. At the end of the meal they were summoned to Reverend Mother's room.

"The padre from the camp has invited you to the concert party to be held over there this evening. It is Christmas. I have told him you may go. It is after his evening service. You will be met at the gate and escorted. You will stay together at all times, is that understood?"

"Yes, Mother," they chorused.

"And Sarah, I'm afraid you must go to the service too. You must stay together."

"Yes, Mother."

Molly returned to the ward her step light, her heart lighter. She had a wonderful evening to look forward to. Sarah was also looking forward to the concert party, but she couldn't help worrying about Molly. This thing with Tom Carter, a man she knew little about, was getting too serious. In some ways Sarah regretted her visit to the camp with Freddie, but at the time it had seemed such a little thing to do to cheer Molly up. Now she felt she had colluded in something that she shouldn't have. By doing so, she had given tacit approval to what was going on, and she didn't approve of it at all. She disliked the clandestine nature of the affair, and she longed for Tom to be sent back to his regiment. She wished him no harm of course, but she was gradually coming round to Reverend Mother's view, it was not *comme il faut*.

The service was lovely, with all the traditional carols and readings. A time of peace and goodwill, the padre reminded them, and Molly and Sarah raised their voices with those of the men, in singing the Christmas hymns.

Molly saw Tom in the congregation, saw his smile as she caught his eye, and a bubble of happiness grew within her.

After the service they were led across to the huge tent, which acted as mess hall for the men. It had now been converted into a theatre, with a makeshift stage across one end. The benches and chairs were almost full and there was a great buzz of talk and laughter.

The show was a great success, with songs and sketches got up by the men themselves. The audience received them all with roars of appreciation and rounds of applause. Molly and Sarah, sitting with Robert Kingston, laughed and applauded with everyone else, and as the show ended with the singing of the national anthem, they all stood to attention and for a moment the mood was more serious. The seriousness was short-lived, however, as the men began to leave and head back to their bunks. Robert Kingston spoke to many of them as they left. He was clearly a popular officer and had made himself accessible to anyone who might need him. Sarah found herself wished Merry Christmas by several of the men who had passed through her ward, and she chatted with them easily enough as she heard how they were doing, and how soon they were to go back. Several had been told it would be early in the New Year. And Tom will go too, thought Sarah, with guilty relief.

As soon as the show was over, Tom had found his way to Molly's side. Still chaperoned by Sarah and the padre they spoke softly to each other.

"Can we talk alone for a few minutes?" Tom asked her softly.

Molly looked across at Sarah. "It won't be easy, both Sarah and the padre have promised Reverend Mother we will stay together. Perhaps if we just step aside..."

Sarah, seeing them in conversation, came over to join them.

"We should go," she said. "Perhaps you'd escort us through the camp, Private Carter." Surely that could do no harm, she thought. I'll be with them all the time.

They said goodnight to the padre and thanked him for the invitation. He smiled at them. "I'm glad you could come," he said simply. "You both deserve a treat." He glanced at Tom and said, "Carter, please see the ladies back to the convent gate."

"Yes, sir." Tom couldn't have received a more welcome order.

The moon came out as they walked across the camp, gleaming silver on the frosted grass, shining coldly on the grey stone of the convent buildings. Just before they reached the gate, Molly turned to Sarah and said, "Sarah, would you mind if Tom and I had a private word? It won't be long,

I promise," and, seeing Sarah was about to protest, added, "We won't go out of sight, honestly."

Sarah knew she should say no, they must go in, but the look on Molly's face was such that she said instead, "Only a minute, Molly. It's freezing out here." She moved closer to the gate, turning away from them and hugging herself into her winter coat, but she did not go through.

At once Tom produced a small parcel from his pocket. "Happy Christmas, Molly," he said handing it to her.

"Oh Tom," her eyes filled with tears, "oh Tom, I've nothing for you."

Tom took both her hands and said, "That doesn't matter, Molly. You're here, that's what matters. That's all that matters. Go on, open it."

Molly unwrapped the little parcel and found, wrapped carefully in tissue paper, a silver bracelet, plain silver links held together by a clasp in the shape of a heart. She held it up so that it caught the light and then looked up at Tom with shining eyes.

"Oh Tom," she breathed, "it's beautiful. Oh, thank you, thank you. Where did you get it?" She held out her wrist to him and he slipped it on, clicking the clasp shut with a snap.

"Bought it off a bloke," he replied. "But it's not what I wanted to give you," he went on, still holding her hand in his.

"Isn't it?" She glance up at him enquiringly. "I think it's beautiful."

He possessed himself of both her hands and drew her towards him, looking down into her upturned face. "No," he replied. "I wanted to give you a ring. Molly, my darling girl, I've been called up for a medical board." He placed a finger on her lips as she cried out in dismay. "It's on the 2nd January. If they pass me as fit, and I'm sure they will, I'll have to leave a few days after. Before I go—" He hesitated uncertainly again. "You know I love you, Molly, don't you?" Molly nodded and he went on, "I wanted to ask you, please, Molly, my darling, darling girl, will you marry me when this..." he bit off the vicious words he might have used, and simply said, "...when this war is over?"

Molly's face suffused with such joy that Tom's heart jolted within him and he caught her to him, hearing her say as he did so, "Not after the war, Tom, now. I'll marry you tomorrow."

Sarah, waiting close by but out of earshot saw the embrace and her heart was troubled. She knew she should not be countenancing this clandestine meeting between Molly and Tom. If Reverend Mother knew...and what would happen to Molly? Tom must be recalled at any time now. But when she saw Molly's radiant face as she rejoined her by the convent gate, she swallowed the comment she had been about to make and only said, "Come on, Molly, we must get back inside."

Upstairs in the safety of their room, Molly, still glowing with happiness showed Sarah the little silver bracelet and told her that she and Tom were to be married.

Despite her growing reservations and misgivings, Sarah hugged her and said, "I'm very happy for you, Molly." She listened as Molly poured out her happiness, and Sarah's only caution was to say nothing of it to anyone in the convent.

"I think Reverend Mother wouldn't approve," she warned, "and if you say anything to anyone else it will surely get back to her."

Molly, who didn't care if Reverend Mother approved or not, agreed cheerfully. "The only problem is that Tom's been called up for a medical board. If they pass him fit he'll leave the next week. I want us to get married before he goes."

"Molly, dear, Molly," Sarah sighed, "I doubt if that is possible."

It wasn't. On the next Sunday evening, their last together before Tom had to leave, they sought Robert Kingston out after the service.

"We want to get married," Molly told him. Tom, less forthright, said, "I've asked Molly to marry me, and she's said yes."

The padre smiled, but worry lurked in his eyes. This was his fault, he realised. He had allowed them to meet in his presence, and now with the pressure of the war they were trying to rush into marriage when, he felt, neither knew the other at all.

"Congratulations, Tom," he said, shaking his hand. "You're a lucky man." Turning to Molly he said, "I hope you will be very happy."

Molly had wanted to get married straightaway, but Tom was against it. "What would happen if I got wounded?" he said. "You might be tied to a blind man or a cripple for the rest of your life."

"I wouldn't mind if it was you," avowed Molly.

"My darling, I know you think you wouldn't," Tom replied gently, "but you might come to mind, and I couldn't bear that, for either of us. We should wait till the war is over."

"The war will never be over," Molly said petulantly.

"It will one day. Molly, I want us to be together, to be married with a home and a family. I've never had a family and I want us to be one more than anything in the world."

"I want that too," Molly cried. "Oh Tom, I want that so much."

"I might be killed and you'd be left. I don't want you to be a widow, Moll."

"If you're being that morbid," Molly said quickly, "if you're going to think like that, you might be killed anyway, and then we'd never be married at all. We have to live for now, Tom. There may not be a tomorrow." At last she had persuaded him at least to speak to the padre, but now Molly could see that, despite his congratulations, Robert Kingston was not happy with what had happened.

"I'm afraid I can't marry you, just like that," he said quietly. "You need a licence, and there's no time for that. But that is not the only issue here. You've known each other a very short while..."

"Long enough," Molly interrupted him abruptly.

"How old are you, Molly?" the padre asked, ignoring her rudeness.

Molly looked surprised. "Twenty," she said. "Old enough to know my own mind, padre."

"Perhaps," he conceded, "but not old enough, legally, to get married without your father's consent."

"I'm sure he'd give it," lied Molly.

"Well, I suggest you get it, in writing, and then perhaps you could be married when Tom next has some leave. Though it isn't encouraged, you know."

Molly had been very disappointed at the padre's words, and she said to him defiantly, "I'm twenty-one in May, then we can get married without my father's consent."

Tom had felt a certain measure of relief. It wasn't that he didn't want to get married, when he'd said to Molly that having a family was his dearest wish, he had not been exaggerating, but he also had no illusions as to his possible fate; he knew what he was returning to, and had a very real fear that Molly would be left a widow, or worse, landed with a cripple.

"I'm putting you as my next of kin," he told her. "That

way if anything happens to me, you'll be the first person they tell." He gave her the address she should write to and promised to write to her in return.

On Wednesday, 5th January 1916, Tom Carter marched out of the camp among a squad of thirty others, all returning to their various regiments. Molly stood at the convent gate and watched them go. They were singing as they marched and Molly's tears were not only for Tom and herself, but for all the men who were marching so bravely back into hell.

2001

Fifteen

R achel arrived at the offices of the *Belcaster Chronicle*
next morning and made straight for Drew Scott's office.
Cherry said, "He's very busy, Rachel. Is it important?"

"It is to me," Rachel said and with a sigh Cherry let her by.
"I've a load of stuff for you this morning," she warned her.
"Don't forget to pick it up on the way out."

Rachel promised, and went in to tackle Drew. He looked
up and smiled.

"Rachel, what gives?"

Rachel took a deep breath. "Drew," she said, "I'm on to
something that will make an amazing feature article, even a
series maybe, and I want to follow it up." Briefly she outlined
what she had discovered.

The evening before she had read Molly Day's diary long
into the night. When she came to its end she was still curled
into her chair, but was stiff and cold. She stretched her aching
limbs, and peering at the clock, she saw that it was past one
in the morning. She crawled from the chair and, with another
stretch, put the notebook diary onto her desk. The diary of
Molly Day, her great-grandmother.

What an amazing story, Rachel thought as she considered
what she had read. What an incredibly courageous thing for
two women to do, to set off into a foreign country where war

was raging, not as part of any recognised organisation, but on their own, to work in a convent hospital. As the diary unfolded their story, Rachel had read avidly, almost as if it were a novel unfolding a fascinating plot. She was longing to know what happened next. But the end was disappointing, indeed there was no proper ending. The diary stopped at the beginning of January 1916. So far Rachel didn't know why it had come to such an abrupt end, all she knew was that the man whom Molly Day had loved had marched back to the front, and Molly had stopped recording her thoughts.

Rachel looked at the packets of letters still lying in the biscuit tin. Maybe they would carry on the story. She didn't know, but she couldn't read them now, she was too tired. She would read them tomorrow...today it was already. She put the diary back into the tin and putting the tin into her desk drawer, went to bed. There was surely a story here, much more complex than that of two women setting off bravely to nurse in France.

So far the diary had posed more questions than it had answered, and though she had decided she could read nothing more tonight and her head ached with tiredness, the things she had been reading in the diary spun round in her brain, keeping sleep at bay. She was fascinated by her great-grandmother, by how much she had changed and matured even during the short time in France which the diary chronicled; leaving behind the insecure and submissive housemaid of only elementary education and growing into the determined and efficient nurse, expressing herself ever more fluently. Faced with the rigours and stress of nursing badly wounded men, with the pain of watching some die, Molly must have drawn on a strength she hadn't known she'd had. Gone was the wide-eyed girl who had been surprised to find there were trees in London, and in her place was the strong young woman who had stood and watched the man she had come to love, march back to the horrors of the front. Taken out of her natural environment, and treated with friendship and respect, faced with responsibility, Molly had overcome her uncertainty and grasped her own life with both hands.

There was Sarah Hurst, too. Sarah seemed far more at home with the nuns than Molly would ever be, mostly because she shared their brand of Christianity, but also because she accepted the hierarchy of the convent more readily. Rachel was intrigued by how well Sarah fitted into the community, despite her occasional run-in with authority. Clearly she had a mind of her own—she was, after all, the instigator of their trip to France. Molly would never have dreamed of it. It was Sarah who had been determined to go and "do her bit", and Molly was towed along in her wake. Sarah had appeared to change over the weeks covered by the diary too. She had taken the unusual step of treating her maid as an equal, not just suggesting it, but carrying it through, so that she and Molly had become true friends. In many ways this was more difficult for her than Molly. Sarah, however graciously, had been giving Molly orders for years, and to change their relationship so suddenly could not have been easy. Perhaps the sharing of the room, the rigours of the work and each being the only link with home for the other, may have contributed to their real and growing friendship, but Rachel couldn't help wondering if it would withstand real difficulties, or a return to the rigid social strata at home. Then she remembered that, according to Cecily, Sarah had never come home; their friendship had never been put to the test.

As sleep continued to elude her, Rachel had made a mental list of things she wanted to do, there seemed so many leads to follow up from what she had learned. She slept at last, but when she awoke to the buzzing of her alarm next morning, she felt as if she had only just dozed off. A quick shower, followed by a banana and a cup of strong black coffee, revived her and sent her on her way to speak to Drew. She had come to a decision even as she slept, and when she awoke this decision was firmly established in her mind.

When Drew had heard her out he said, "I can't give you time to research this. Delve into its past if you like, Rachel, but in your own time. If you produce a good feature with an interesting angle, I'll look at printing it in early January. Things will be slower after Christmas. Sorry."

Rachel took her courage in both hands and said, "I understand, Drew, but in that case I'd like to take some holiday."

"Holiday!" Drew stared at her. "In the run-up to Christmas? You have to be joking! Have you seen the list of stuff Cherry has for you today?"

"No, not yet," Rachel replied evenly, "and I won't leave you in the lurch, Drew. I'll cover today's work and tomorrow's, but after that I want time off. I am entitled, you know."

Drew glowered at her. "We have to get this Christmas edition out."

"I know," Rachel broke in, "but if you're honest, Drew, most of it is done already."

"I need you to follow up what is happening in Charlton Ambrose at present, not in the past."

"And I will," soothed Rachel. "I promise, but after tomorrow there won't be much, and next week's paper is mainly small-time local stuff, it always is the week after Christmas." She grinned at him impishly, "Let's face it, Drew, even if a big story breaks it won't be me who's sent to cover it, will it!"

This sally drew a reluctant laugh, and he said, "OK, I give in. From Wednesday. Two weeks, and this article had better be bloody good!" He waved aside her thanks and snapped, "In the meantime, get on to the planning office today about the Brigstock Jones thing. When does Mike Bradley meet with the planning office?"

"Tomorrow, I think."

"Right, back on to him tomorrow after they've met to write a short update and then we'll probably have to wait until after the New Year for anything further from them. Remember that the whole building trade will close down from Monday for two weeks over Christmas. That should also give you a chance to contact the various families concerned with these memorial trees before they do. I doubt if they'll have anyone working on that over the Christmas period." He gave her a wry smile, adding, "I assume that they feature in your research anyway." When Rachel said that they certainly did, he wished her good luck and a happy Christmas. "But I'll see you on Thursday at the bash in the Royal. You're coming to that, aren't you?"

"Yes, I'll be there," Rachel said.

When Rachel left his office Drew looked at the closing door and thought: That girl does have the makings of a really good reporter. She has the nose for a good story and is prepared to back herself.

He could manage without her for a couple of weeks, and he let her go in the expectation that she would get her story and that it would be worth waiting for.

Back at her desk, Rachel rang the planning office and was told that the next meeting of the planners to consider applications wasn't until the end of January.

"Our planning meeting is the last Friday in the month," an impersonal voice informed her, "so there will be no December meeting."

David Andrews was unavailable and Rachel had been put through to someone else who did not give his name.

"But what about the planning application put in by Brigstock Jones for their development in Charlton Ambrose? I understood there was a meeting between them and Mr Andrews tomorrow."

"I'm sorry," said the voice on the end of the phone, "we can't possibly comment on individual applications. Mr Andrews is out of the office for the rest of the week, but the plans are on display in the council offices if you wish to inspect them, madam."

Realising she was going to get no further in this direction, Rachel thanked him and rang off. There was nothing to be learned from them until after Christmas, which meant the pressure was off. She rang Brigstock Jones, but neither Mike Bradley nor Tim Cartwright was available to take her call. There really wasn't going to be a great deal of follow-up to the Charlton Ambrose story in the immediate future, except from her own point of view, but Rachel wrote a short piece saying that the question of the Ashgrove was still being considered and inviting anyone who had any information about the trees or those they commemorated, to contact the *Chronicle*. That should be enough to keep the story in the public eye until she could discover more.

Before she left the *Chronicle*'s office, she took Henry Smalley's history of St Peter's Church from her bag and made photocopies of the pages which referred to the Ashgrove and its planting. With these pages safely copied, she could return the book to the rector. She wanted to go out to Charlton Ambrose again anyway. She looked at the list of things that Cherry had given her to cover and sighed—all very routine stuff, and she was dying to get on with her own research.

She was just leaving the office for the magistrates' court when her mobile buzzed, warning her that a text message had arrived and she paused to read it. She flicked to received messages and saw it was from Nick Potter. She remembered then his message from last night. She hadn't answered it. This one said,

Do U fancy pub supper 1 night? Thursday?

Rachel considered. She did quite fancy having supper with him, but not on Thursday. That was the paper's Christmas party. She tapped a return message. *Not Thursday. Wednesday?* The reply was immediate. *OK. Suggest where?*

Rachel named The Castle in Belcaster. It was near her flat and she wanted to be able to walk. The reply buzzed into her phone. *C U there 7.30.*

She smiled, pleased to have something to look forward to, and, had she known it, Nick was smiling too.

When the court rose at the end of the morning session, Rachel decided to surprise her grandmother and scrounge some lunch.

"Rachel, darling, what a lovely surprise." Rose Carson had been about to go and have lunch in the communal dining room, but when Rachel arrived she changed her mind. "I'd much rather stay here and chat to you. I've soup, and bread and there's cheese in the fridge. I'm glad you've come, I've got something to show you."

"What's that, Gran?" Rachel asked as she laid the food out on the table.

"I'll show you after lunch," replied Rose.

As they sat eating, Rachel talked about the diary. "Did you read it all, Gran?" she asked.

"Do you know, my dear, I can't honestly remember. I certainly read bits of it. Have you read it all? You must have been up all night!"

"Yes, I read it right through when I got home." Rachel looked across at her grandmother. "It really is the most interesting thing," she said. "It is a piece of social history. It gives a very clear picture of what went on in the convent and its hospital. The trouble is, it just stops. The last entry is 5th January 1916." Rachel looked across at her grandmother. "It's fascinating. Do you know, it mentions the death of one of the men who are commemorated in the Ashgrove? Harry Cook. Molly says he was her cousin. He died there, in the hospital. Cecily Strong told me that Mary Bryson was a Cook. She still lives in Belmouth. Her granddaughter runs the post office in Charlton Ambrose. That makes her some sort of cousin of ours, doesn't it, Gran? If he was Molly's cousin and Molly was your mother?" Rachel's eyes were alight with pleasure. "I've no relations, other than you, Gran. Now I might find several, even if they are distant."

Her grandmother smiled at her, "So you might," she said. "What else did you discover?"

"I found out more about Sarah Hurst," replied Rachel. "I still don't know what happened to her. As far as Cecily Strong knows, Sarah never came home. She said she thought Sarah was killed when the hospital was shelled, but there is no mention of her as being among those who died for their country. As it was her father who put up the memorial, you'd have thought he would have included her too, wouldn't you?"

"Not necessarily," said Rose. "It wasn't usual to put women on to the war memorials, you know."

"But that's appalling," cried Rachel. "If she was killed by German shellfire while nursing in a hospital, she died for her country as much as any of the men did. You know what I think? I think the ninth tree is for her. I reckon her father had it planted afterwards, and then he and the rector pretended not to know anything about it, but dedicated it anyway. What do you think?"

The old lady looked doubtful. "I wouldn't have thought so," she said. "I think if Sir George had been going to commemorate his daughter at all, he would have done it properly. Are you sure she died? Who told you she did?"

"Cecily Strong, the old lady who set the cat among the pigeons at the meeting. She said that she was sure Sarah didn't come back from France, but the bit about her being killed might be wrong, I suppose."

"Well, if she wasn't killed she certainly wouldn't have been included in the memorial," said Gran. "There could be another reason why she didn't come home. Perhaps she married someone out in France and stayed on when the war was over. One of her patients perhaps."

Rachel nodded doubtfully. "Perhaps," she conceded, "but if that was the case surely she and the new husband would have come home at the end of the war. People in the village would remember that."

"Maybe Sir George didn't approve," suggested Gran.

Rachel got up and clearing the plates into the sink, began to wash up. Gran wheeled herself over and picked up a tea towel to dry. "What you have to remember," she said, "is that attitudes were entirely different in those days. Girls didn't marry without their fathers' consent, or if they did they were often cast off from the family for such lack of respect. The father's word was virtually law within the family."

"Yes, I agree, but Sarah had already managed to get her own way about going to France in the first place. She seems to have known how to handle her father."

"To a certain extent perhaps," agreed Gran, "but suppose

she fell for a man from the ranks, not an officer, her father certainly wouldn't have countenanced that."

"I doubt if she did that," Rachel said. "Despite her treatment of Molly once they were in France, it is clear she was class-conscious before that."

"Maybe France changed her."

"Maybe," Rachel agreed, "but I don't think so. Somehow it doesn't fit." She emptied the sink and said, "I must go, Gran. I shouldn't be here really, I'm supposed to be at St Joseph's Day Centre Christmas party this afternoon." She dropped a kiss on her grandmother's forehead. "I'll ring you in a day or two," she said, "and I'll be here on Christmas Eve. I'll bring the diary and the letters with me and tell you how I'm getting on."

"Before you go, I've got something for you." Her grandmother reached into her bag and pulled out a tired-looking envelope. "I suddenly remembered it after you'd gone yesterday."

Rachel took the envelope and pulled out a small photo. It was a sepia picture of a young girl standing by a gate. She had dark hair pulled up off her face and was wearing a summer dress with a flowery pattern on it. Beside her was a dog, and she was reaching down to it with one hand while smiling up at the camera. Behind her was the door of a house and what looked like a yard. Rachel stared at it for a long moment and then looked at her grandmother.

Rose smiled and nodded. "Yes," she said, "that's my mother. That's Molly Day."

"Where was it taken?"

"At her parents' farm. That's Valley Farm just outside Charlton Ambrose. It must have been taken before the war, I think. She only looks about seventeen, doesn't she?"

"Molly Day," Rachel said. "Your mother. Have you got any other pictures, Gran?"

Rose Carson shook her head. "Afraid not. I'd forgotten that one. I found it in a book belonging to my grandmother when I cleared out her place after she died and put it away in my desk. I only know it's Molly for certain because it's written on the back."

Rachel turned the photo over and there, sure enough, written in pencil in a spidery hand were the words, *Molly, May 17th 1912.*

"Can I take this with me, Gran?" asked Rachel. "I'll take great care of it."

"You can keep it, darling," Gran replied a little sadly. "I don't want it any more."

Rachel went to her assignment at the day centre and joined the elderly who met there for their Christmas party, talking to them and the volunteers who kept the place afloat. There was an appeal being launched to mend the roof of the hall where they met, and Rachel's brief was to raise the profile of the centre for the appeal. Several cups of tea and a piece of Christmas cake later, she had plenty of material for an interesting piece to increase public awareness of the centre and the work it did. Jon turned up to take some photographs, and then they both left to visit a couple who were celebrating their diamond wedding anniversary.

Rachel spent the first part of the evening conscientiously writing up her stories from the day, and as always she enjoyed writing them. She e-mailed her work into the office, and then turned her attention to her own interests.

First, she scanned the picture of Molly into her computer and having enlarged it printed it out on photographic paper. She propped the picture up in front of her and studied it. There was Molly, long before she had gone off to France. A young girl petting her dog and smiling up at the camera, untroubled and entirely unaware of what lay in her future. She looked thin, her features small in her narrow face, but her smile lit her eyes and Rachel could see what had attracted Tom Carter.

Though she was longing to read the letters waiting in the biscuit tin, Rachel made a conscious decision to leave them for a couple of days. She had to finish her work for the *Chronicle* tomorrow, and then she could devote herself to her own researches. In the meantime she knew her brain would still be processing all she had learned so far. Let all the information soak in gradually, she had once been told, and you'll find it has a way of sorting itself out.

Wednesday evening found Rachel going into The Castle, and there sitting at the bar waiting for her, was Nick Potter. He bought her the gin and tonic she asked for, and then picking up his pint, they moved to a table near the fire. Each of them felt an unaccustomed reticence in the company of the other, so they spent time studying the menu and deciding what they were going to eat.

"Gran sends her love," Rachel said, once they had chosen.

"So you gave her my message," he said with a laugh.

"She said she'll take any love on offer."

"Good for her!"

"Sorry I didn't reply to your message on Sunday night," Rachel said, "but something had come up."

"You replied to the important one," Nick answered, taking a pull at his beer. "So, what came up? A good story?"

"Yes," said Rachel thoughtfully. "Yes, I think it is."

"Can you tell me?" Nick's eyes rested on her and Rachel, who seldom discussed her stories with anyone but Gran or Drew, returned his look and suddenly felt that she could. "It goes back a long way," she said. "Do you know what I've just discovered? That I am related, distantly, to one of the men who the Charlton Ambrose trees are for."

"The Ashgrove?" Nick was instantly interested. "Really? Who?"

"I found out that my great-grandmother was a cousin of Harry Cook's. He died in France of wounds in 1915. I think that makes me his first cousin three times removed."

"I never quite understand removes," Nick admitted.

"Same relationship, just down three generations," Rachel explained. "Anyway, I found out that I might be, so I spent a bit of time in the record office today, checking the Charlton Ambrose parish registers."

"And you found out for sure?"

"Yes, my great-grandmother's mother and Harry Cook's father were brother and sister. So, apart from anything else, I've found myself some new relations."

"Do you want any?" enquired Nick with a grin.

"There's only me and Gran," Rachel said and found herself telling Nick how Gran had brought her up when her parents had been killed.

Their food came and as they ate Nick asked, "So is this story to do with the Ashgrove? How did you discover that you might be related to this Harry Cook?"

When Rachel didn't answer immediately he glanced over at her and said, "Sorry, you may not want to say anything about it yet. Don't tell me if you don't want to."

Rachel reached into her handbag and pulled out the old photo her grandmother had given her. She held it out to Nick, who peered at it and then producing a pair of glasses, looked at it again. He turned it over and looked at the back. "Your great-grandmother?" he asked.

Rachel nodded. "Gran found it and gave it to me. It's her mother, and the only picture she has. Her mother died when she was quite young and Gran hardly remembers her. They used to live in Charlton Ambrose. I think this picture was taken outside the farm where they lived. I'm going to walk up there soon, if the weather's anything like, and have a look. Take some photos of what it is like now."

"Do you know where it is?" asked Nick. "What's the farm called?"

"It was called Valley Farm," replied Rachel, "I don't know if it is now, or even if it's still there."

"I think I know where it is," Nick said. "I walk a lot, have to exercise my dog, Wombat.

"Wombat!" laughed Rachel. "Why's he called that?"

"Another long story," grinned Nick. "Let's finish yours first. I'll get us a coffee." He came back from the bar with two cups of coffee and two brandies and set them down on the table.

"Well..." Rachel decided to take the plunge. She had watched Nick as he stood at the bar, and there was something reassuring about him, something quiet and steady, and yet when he smiled at her she knew a quickening of her pulse rate which she found disconcerting, and she didn't want any man to disconcert her. He was an attractive man, anyone could see that, but there was something about him that made her trust him. He would be a good person to go to if one were in trouble, she thought, and then laughed at herself for being fanciful. How could she possibly know that on such a short acquaintance?

Let's face it, she thought, I hardly know the man. But, she realised, she wanted to know him better, her earlier reticence was gone, and she found she actually wanted to tell Nick all about the diary. She needed to discuss it with an entirely disinterested person.

She picked up the brandy glass and took a sip. Then looking at him over the rim she began, "Well, when I went to lunch with Gran last Sunday…"

Nick listened without interruption, drinking his coffee and sipping his brandy as he did so. As she told him about Molly and Sarah, Rachel found that the story had indeed become clearer in her own mind. She knew now where she would go from here.

"There are so many things I want to check up on," she said. "I want to go to Charlton Ambrose and find Molly's grave. I want to find out what happened to Sarah. I want to find out what happened to Tom Carter. I want to know who the ninth tree in the Ashgrove was planted for. I'm sure it ties into this story somehow."

"Where will you start?" asked Nick.

"Charlton Ambrose, tomorrow," answered Rachel. "I've got to return the history of the parish the Rector lent me, and I want to look at the graveyard and see who is buried there, and I'm hoping to find Valley Farm."

"Aren't you working tomorrow?" asked Nick.

"No, as of today I'm on holiday. I took time off to follow this up. That's how I was able to spend all today in the record office, looking up Cooks."

"When will you read the letters?" Nick asked. "Or won't you?"

"Oh, I'll read them all right," Rachel said. "I know Gran felt she couldn't. She was afraid they were love letters and didn't want to intrude on her mother's privacy. I understand that, but I have to know what happened to these people. They have become very real to me, they're part of my history." She looked at Nick earnestly and said, "We don't even know for certain that Tom Carter is my grandmother's father. I can't

think that it can be anyone else, but until I read those letters…
Do you think I'm wrong to read them?"

Nick considered for a moment and then said, "No, I don't
think so. Especially if your grandmother doesn't mind."

They changed the subject after that, and Nick told Rachel
about his move out of London and how his firm, a partner-
ship of architects, was establishing itself in Belcaster, and they
talked about the city and what it had to offer.

When they left the pub Nick took Rachel's arm as they
walked briskly back to her flat. The night air was very cold
and the feel of his arm through hers warmed Rachel. When
they reached the house she thanked him for the meal, and he
kissed her lightly on the forehead.

"I enjoyed it too," he said. "Good luck with your research.
I'll give you a ring after Christmas."

"Thanks, that would be lovely," Rachel said. "Happy
Christmas."

"Happy Christmas," said Nick and, with a quick smile,
turned and strode off into the night.

Rachel lit the gas fire and flopped into a chair. Part of her
wished she had invited Nick in for another coffee, but before
she had left home to meet him, she'd already decided that she
would not. It might send out the wrong signals and she was
determined not to get involved with anyone in the near future.
It made life too complicated.

She reached over for the large print of Molly still propped
up on her desk and studied it. Her great-grandmother.
Tomorrow she would go to Charlton Ambrose and, when she
had done all the research she could on the diary, she would
turn her attention to the letters.

Sixteen

Thursday morning dawned bright and cold. The sun streamed down on the frosted ground, striking sparkling fire from hedgerows laced with spiders' webs, and etching the bare branches of the trees against the palest of blue skies. Rachel drove the country lanes to Charlton Ambrose, marvelling at the winter beauty around her. As the road threaded its way through high winter hedges and Rachel met no other cars, she thought that things must look much the same as they had when Molly had lived here.

Her first port of call was the rectory. Adam Skinner was just going out but he greeted her cheerfully as he put a box of papers into his car.

"I'm sorry," he said, "but I'm literally on the doorstep as you see."

"Don't worry about it," Rachel replied. "I only wanted to return your booklet on the history of the parish. It was fascinating, particularly the part about the Ashgrove."

"I'm glad you found it useful." The rector put it inside the front door and then pulled the door closed behind him. "Any news on the trees yet?"

Rachel shook her head. "I don't think there'll be any more on those until well after Christmas," she said. "Things move very slowly at County Hall, and the building trade closes down for two weeks over the holiday period."

"Well, good luck with it. Sorry to dash, but I'm late... as always."

Rachel spent much of the morning in the churchyard. She had a list of names for whom she was hoping to find gravestones. The Hursts were easy enough, theirs was the large sarcophagus tomb beside the path leading to the church door. Protected by the church from the worst of the elements, the inscriptions were still easily legible. Sir George Hurst was the last, born 25th June 1860, died 6th September 1921. His beloved wife, Charlotte, who had died in childbirth in 1900, was also buried there, with their son, James, who died with her moments after his birth. No mention of Freddie, of course, who was buried somewhere in France... if he actually has a grave, Rachel thought. She made a note to look him up on the war graves' website, and then wondered with amazement why she hadn't thought of this before; she could look up Tom Carter as well. No mention of Sarah.

She moved slowly round the churchyard, peering at the stones and reading their inscriptions. In a quiet corner, well away from the church itself, she found the grave of Edwin and Jane Day. The stone simply gave Edwin's name and dates, followed by *and of his wife Jane* with her dates and the text:

COME UNTO ME ALL WHO TRAVAIL AND ARE HEAVY LADEN

Had Gran chosen those words? Rachel wondered. Poor Jane, she certainly travailed. What a bleak life she must have led, living with a man like Edwin.

Rachel continued to search that area, but it was some time before she finally found what she was looking for, Molly's grave. She had been beginning to wonder if Molly's parents

hadn't bother to erect a stone for the daughter they thought
had disgraced them, when she came across a small stone cross
at the end of the graveyard, tilted tipsily and almost covered
with brambles. It was on the very edge of hallowed ground,
as if those who had buried her thought she should not be there
at all. Inscribed on the bar of the cross were the name
and date:

EMILY DAY

1895–1924

It had to be her, Rachel decided, though she had not thought
of Molly as a diminutive for Emily before. Poor Molly, Rachel
thought as she looked down at the stone memorial, that was
no memorial at all. There was no 'loving memory' or 'beloved
daughter'. Disgraced and unloved, Molly lay forgotten in an
overgrown corner of her village churchyard.

Rachel took photographs of each of the graves she had
found and then continued her search. Nearer to the church she
found several Cook graves, one of them Anthony Cook, born
1888, died 1957. That was Tony, Harry's elder brother. Rachel
had assumed that he had survived the war as he was not
named in the memorial, and had found him during her search
at the record office yesterday. With him lay his wife, Sandra.

Rachel found she was getting cold and she decided that she
had seen all she wanted to here. She found no Chapmans,
Hapgoods or Winters. Her next stop was the post office. Gail
was behind the counter, and recognised Rachel when she
came in. Her smile was perfunctory.

"I've spoken to my dad," she said. "He doesn't want
my gran bothered by the papers. Says he'll tell her about
the trees."

"That's good," Rachel was conciliatory. "It's much better that she hears it from him."

"Not that she'll take it in much," sighed Gail. "She's not really with it these days, well, it's not surprising her being ninety-six, is it?"

Rachel agreed it wasn't. "Did her brother, Tony, have any children?" she asked.

"No. He and Auntie Sandra got married late. Too late probably for her. Anyway, they didn't have any kids." Gail looked at her suspiciously. "What do you want to know for, anyway?"

"Gail," Rachel took a deep breath, "Gail, I discovered something yesterday."

"Oh yes," Gail didn't sound particularly interested, but her eyes were sharp. "And what was that then?"

"My great-grandmother and your grandmother were first cousins. That makes us related."

"Suppose it does," Gail conceded with a shrug. "Not close, though, eh?"

"No, something like third cousins, I should think," said Rachel, disappointed with this reaction. "I just thought you might be interested. Well, anyway, I came in to ask where your grandmother lives, but if your father doesn't want her worried with this, perhaps I could talk to him instead."

"He won't want to talk to you either," Gail said sharply, "not even if you are some sort of cousin. We don't want to get involved in this tree business, right? So, leave us alone. My Great-uncle Harry's long gone. He doesn't care if there's a tree or not. We have to think of the living now." She placed her hands on the counter and looked across at Rachel. "Now, did you want to buy something?"

Gail's attitude towards her had so changed since Saturday, that Rachel left the shop knowing that Gail and her family had discussed the situation over the weekend, and some sort of decision had been taken. Gail and her husband wanted the building to go ahead for the growth in their business that it might provide; Granny was too old and gaga to be consulted, they could all use a little extra cash, and so they had decided to take whatever compensation was going and shut up about the trees.

Oh well, that'll please Mike Bradley, Rachel thought.

The sun was still shining when Rachel had finished a quick snack in the pub and she decided to make the most of the afternoon and walk across the hill to see if she could find Valley Farm. She had provided herself with an ordnance survey map, and found Valley Farm still marked on it. A path led from the village starting at a stile in Church Lane, and seemed to lead straight up over the hill and down into the next valley where the farm lay. She went back to the car and put on her walking boots and her fleece and set off with the map in her pocket. As she walked along the lane she saw some large stone gateposts, in need of repair, and swathed with ivy. Attached to one was an estate agent's sign offering "The Manor" for sale. Period Georgian House, it declared, with two acres, in need of renovation. Across the board was another smaller one saying "Sale Agreed".

The Manor. Rachel stared at the sign. How could she have forgotten such a thing? It was still there, of course it was, the family home of the Hursts for so long. But who lived in it now, she wondered? Did anybody? By the look of the gateposts and the drive, which Rachel could see was overhung with bushes and overgrown with weeds, it didn't look occupied; it certainly hadn't been well looked after. She glanced at her watch and wondered if she had time to go in and take a quick look at the house now. She decided not. She didn't know how long it would take her to find Valley Farm, but she wanted to be safely back in the village before it got dark. She would go to the estate agent in the morning and get a copy of the particulars, and then come back and explore it properly; take some photos for her file.

She walked on and came to the stile. Molly must have walked this way every time she went home, Rachel mused. It was the quickest way to the farm from this end of the village, unless you had a vehicle of some sort and had to go round by the road. Rachel could have driven and found the track or lane that led there, she supposed, but she was looking forward to the walk, and it pleased her to be following in Molly's footsteps.

As she headed on up the hill towards the hedge at the top, a small furry creature exploded from the woodland that edged the field and rushed towards her. It was a dog of extremely mixed origins with a woolly coat, long floppy ears and an extravagantly waving tail. It pranced round her barking with delight at having found someone who might throw a stick.

"Down dog, down," she shouted as the creature began to do vertical leaps in its efforts to please her.

"Wombat! Come here. Come here at once." Nick Potter emerged from the copse and on hearing his master's voice the dog turned his attentions to him. As he leapt within reach, Nick made a grab for his collar and snapped on the lead.

"Sorry," he began and then on recognising Rachel grinned at her and said, "Rachel, it's you. Sorry about that. He thinks everyone in the world loves him. We haven't quite got the bit about coming when called sorted out yet."

"So this is Wombat," Rachel said looking down at the still gyrating dog. "He doesn't look like one."

"What does one look like?" asked Nick, amused.

Rachel shrugged, "I don't know," she admitted with a grin.

"No, nor did I, I just thought one was a small woolly animal, so that's what I called him. You're right of course, I've since looked one up and he doesn't look anything like one."

"What are you doing up here?" asked Rachel.

"Walking him," Nick replied innocently. "Wombat has to be walked every day."

"Are you on holiday too, then?" Rachel asked suspiciously. "You didn't say."

"Not much happening in the office at this time of year," Nick said casually. "Where are you off to?"

Rachel fixed him with a beady eye. "You know very well where I'm going," she said.

"Valley Farm?" suggested Nick with a look of polite enquiry. "Want any company? Wombat's finished looking for rabbits here."

Rachel said that she'd love company, and together they went on across the field to the next stile, with Wombat, released from his lead, dashing on ahead of them and then tearing back to make sure they were still coming.

"He does ten times the mileage I do," remarked Nick.

They finally came to the top of a rise and looked down into the valley below. There was an old farmhouse on its far side, crouching into the hillside that protected it from the worst of the weather. Behind it were farm buildings of much more modern construction, dwarfing the original house, and standing out harshly against the hill.

"That's Valley Farm," Nick said pointing. "I often walk that way home from here."

Rachel looked down on the house that had been the childhood home of both her grandmother and great-grandmother.

There was nothing warm or welcoming about the long, grey house and she shivered.

The sun disappeared behind a bank of rolling cloud now and the wind swept across the open hillside, biting through her fleece.

"It looks a pretty bleak place even now," she said, pulling her jacket more closely round her. "Imagine what it was like eighty years ago."

"A hard place to make a living," agreed Nick. "Do you want to go down?"

"Yes, I want to see if I can pinpoint where Molly's picture was taken; and I want to take some photos of how it is today. I'll take one from up here." She took her camera out of her pocket and took her picture, then suddenly swung it round on Nick who was sitting on the stile laughing at Wombat's antics and took another.

Nick laughed. "That won't come out," he said. "Wombat was moving."

They followed the path down the hill and on to the track that led to the farm gate. The gate, which stood open, was a modern galvanised one, with the name Valley Farm propped up beside it. There was a muddy Land Rover parked in the yard, and on the far side was a modern milking parlour. There was the sound of the milking machines and they could see the cows still waiting to be milked in an enclosure beyond the yard. Clearly the farm was still a working farm. Rachel snapped off a couple of pictures and then Nick took the camera from her and said, "Stand by the gate there, and I'll take one of you."

Rachel stood in the almost identical place to Molly, and as he looked at her through the view finder, Nick wondered if he were being fanciful when he thought he caught an echo of Molly's face in Rachel's.

"Do you want to go in?" Nick asked as he handed her back the camera.

Rachel looked at the old house and shivered again. "No," she said, "No, I don't think so."

"Well then, I think we should be making tracks," Nick said. "We're going to get wet."

Rachel looked up and saw that he was right. The sky had darkened and she could feel the spatter of rain on her face.

"Come on," he said. "I'll take us the quickest way." He started off down the lane, Wombat prancing at his heels, and Rachel followed him, wishing she had worn her parka and not her fleece. Halfway down the lane they reached a stile and Nick led the way over into the field beyond. It was raining hard now, and the wind was driving the freezing drops against them so that they had to keep their heads down as they walked into it. Another stile, another field and then a track and Rachel found they were on the road leading into the village. Houses stood on the left and it was in through the gate of one of these that Nick took her now.

"Come in and get dry," he said, "it's another half mile to your car, I'll drive you there in a minute." He opened the front door and Wombat dived between his feet into the warmth of the house. Nick stood aside to let Rachel in, and drenched as she was she was pleased to get indoors.

"Take your fleece off," Nick said as he closed the door behind him, "and I'll hang it by the boiler. Want a cup of tea?" He reappeared from the kitchen and handed Rachel a towel. "Here," he said, "dry your hair."

Rachel glanced in the small round mirror that hung on the wall and saw that she looked like a drowned rat, her dark curls clung damply to her head and she could feel the water dripping down her neck. She took the towel and rubbed her hair.

"Thanks," she said. She plucked at her clammy shirt collar and Nick grinned at her.

"You're soaked," he said. "Go upstairs and have a shower. I'll put a dry shirt and sweater out for you to go home in." When Rachel hesitated he gave her a little push and said, "Go on. First on the right upstairs. I'll make the tea while you're up there." When she still hesitated he grinned and adding, "I won't come and ravish you, promise!" he pointed to the staircase and said, "Go!"

It was a long time since Rachel had been given such a direct order, but she slung the towel round her neck and climbed the stairs. When she stepped out of the shower elegantly attired in the towel, she peeped out on to the landing. There in a neat pile were a shirt, a sweatshirt and some tracksuit bottoms. She pulled them into the bathroom and moments later went downstairs with Nick's clothes hanging off her, but warm and dry.

Nick looked up as she appeared in the kitchen and laughed. "Oh, very fetching," he said as he handed her a mug of steaming tea. "Here come inside, I've lit the fire."

He led the way into his sitting room, and gestured to an armchair at the fireside. "Get yourself warm," he said, and flung himself down into the chair on the other side of the hearth.

"Thanks for the loan of the clothes," Rachel said, "and for the tea. How do you know my car is parked half a mile away?" she suddenly shot at him, and he laughed at the abruptness of the question.

"Saw you leaving it there this morning," he said.

Rachel looked at him across the rim of her mug. "So our meeting on the hill wasn't as accidental as it seemed," she said lightly.

"No, well, I just thought you might like the company on your walk." Nick seemed entirely unfazed by the question: "And anyway, Wombat said he wanted to go."

"I see, so it's all your fault, is it, dog?" Rachel said prodding the recumbent animal blissfully asleep on the hearthrug. "What a coward your master is to blame you for his decisions!"

"Oh no," said Nick cheerfully, "I'd already made my decision, he just encouraged me in it." He paused and, looking at the girl dressed in his clothes, curled up in a chair by his fire, asked, "Do you mind?"

Rachel appeared to consider for a moment before answering, "No," she said, "I was very happy to have Wombat's company." She finished her tea and stood up. "I must go, it's the office Christmas drinks tonight." She looked out across the rain-swept garden to the winter dreariness of the allotments beyond. "I see you look out on the famous allotment patch," she remarked as she realised what she was seeing. "Those new houses will be looking straight over your wall."

"So they will," Nick agreed mildly, "but I hope to have moved from here before they're built."

He drove her to where she had parked her car and she switched cars clutching a carrier bag with her wet clothes in it.

"I must return yours to you," she said.

"I'll come and collect them after Christmas," Nick replied. "I'm off tomorrow, to spend Christmas with my mother."

When she got home there was a text message on the mobile.

Happy Christmas, Rachel. Keep in touch.
Wish there had been a bit of mistletoe in my house.

Rachel smiled at this, and on impulse zapped him a return message, *So do I.*

It was the day after Boxing Day before Rachel finally settled down to look at the letters in the biscuit tin. She had spent Christmas with her grandmother as she always did and they had passed a quiet three days together, eating their Christmas dinner, going down to walk along the front at Belmouth, watching television and talking. Rachel heard a little more of Gran's childhood, her heart aching for the motherless girl. She told Gran about finding the graves in the churchyard, and Rose said she too had found them when her grandmother finally died. She had added Jane Day's name and the text.

"I didn't love her," she said, "but I knew she'd have been a different woman but for my grandfather."

"And Molly? Your mother?"

"I let her rest in peace. My life had moved on."

The three days were also punctuated by text messages from Nick.

Force fed turkey ... it was stuffed ... so am I
Mistletoe here. Wish you were!
Wombat pining for a decent walk. Sends licks!
If I c another mince pie will burst
Play station good fun, pity not mine!
Drink Thursday? Castle?
How did you get into my brain like this?

Rachel sent flippant replies to all but the last. That one she couldn't answer, either flippantly or seriously. Indeed, she could have asked him the same question. Nick had been resting in the back of her mind ever since she had left him in Charlton Ambrose on Thursday, a comfortable presence, undemanding, but there. She had been wondering why he had texted her, rather than rung her, but with the arrival of the last message she realised it was easier to drop throw-away lines like that into a text message. There was no pressure to answer them, they could be answered or ignored without awkwardness on either side. For the present she ignored it, and Nick receded to his position on the perimeter of her mind.

When she got home on Wednesday afternoon, Rachel lit the fire, drew the curtains against the early evening dark and at last settled down to read the letters in the tin. She opened both packets and discovered that not all of the letters to Molly were written by Tom. There were several addressed in different handwritings. She laid them out on the table by date from the postmarks, taking letters from both piles, so that she would read them in the right order and the correspondence would flow.

She wondered how Molly had possession of the letters she herself had written to Tom. Had they been returned to her when he had been killed? She had looked up both Freddie and Tom on the war graves' website and so knew what was officially known about their deaths.

Freddie had died on the first day of the Battle of the Somme. According to the website, Captain Frederick George Hurst 1st Battalion Belshire Regiment (Light Infantry) killed in action on 1st July 1916 aged twenty-four.

Captain Hurst was the husband of Heather Mary Hurst of The Manor, Charlton Ambrose, Belshire. He is commemorated on the Thiepval Memorial, Somme.

Private 8523241 Thomas Carter 1st Battalion Belshire Regiment (Light Infantry) died on 1st August 1916 aged twenty-three.

Buried at Thiepval Memorial, Somme.

There was a picture of his gravestone with his name, regiment and date of death. No other details. No mention of family. No mention of Molly.

So Rachel had discovered when each man had died, but she also knew that most of the men commemorated on the Thiepval Memorial had no known grave. Had Freddie simply been obliterated, buried in the mud of no-man's-land? Clearly he had been killed in the bloodbath that was the first day of the Battle of the Somme, when sixty thousand men had been wiped out in one day. Had Tom been in that battle, too? Rachel wondered. It was likely as they were the same company, but it was possible that he wasn't there for some reason. Obviously he had survived the carnage of the day and had died of wounds or been killed at some later stage in the battle which had dragged on for three weary months into October. Whatever had happened to him, the letters he had received from Molly had been sent back to her, and were there for Rachel to read.

Having sorted the letters into chronological order, Rachel opened the first, addressed in black ink in a strong and spiky hand. It was postmarked October 1915. It was from Sir George, sent after he had discovered Molly had left home without permission.

Sunday, 31st October

Dear Molly Day,

I was most displeased to discover that you went to France with Miss Sarah without your father's knowledge or permission. That was an extremely wrong thing to do, and I am as angry as he.

I have had a letter from the Reverend Mother about you. She says you are making yourself useful out there and that she needs you to stay. My daughter also says that she needs you, so, I won't insist that you come home. Whilst you are there I will be paying your wages to your father.

If you need money in France you may apply to my daughter and she will consider what is necessary.

Yours truly George Hurst Bt.

Rachel read this through and wondered if Molly had replied to it. What would she have thought of her entire wage being paid to her father? She looked back to the relevant part of the diary, but found no reference to the matter. Having made her decision not to go home, Molly seemed to have put family matters out of her mind.

The second letter was dated 20th November 1915 and came from Harry's mother. It was the reply to the one Molly had written to her aunt when Harry died, the *"most difficult letter I've ever had to write"*. It was the letter of a simple country woman who had lost her son and it brought tears to Rachel's eyes.

20th November 1915

Dear Molly,

Thank you for your letter telling me about Harry. We had the telegram from the king of course, but he did not tell us all the details. I am so glad Harry was brought to your hospital. Did they know where you were? Thank you for his last message, it was a comfort to know he was thinking of us. I told your mam and dad that God must have put you there to be with my poor boy when he was dying. Your mam has been very kind. It must be very strange working in a hospital where no one speaks the King's English, I think you are a good girl to go, even if not everyone round here thinks so. We are looking forward to you coming home to us.

Your Uncle Charlie sends his best and so do I.

Your loving Auntie Vi

Rachel slipped the letter back into its envelope and took the next. This was the first from Tom, written in pencil on a piece of lined paper that looked as if it had been torn from a notebook.

Friday, 7th January

My dear Molly,

I can't believe it is only two days since we left the hospital. We have returned by bus and are in billets at present. Not sure when we shall be going back to our company.

I have put your name on my pay book as next of kin, which I can do now we are going to be married.

I hope you are keeping well and not working too hard at the hospital. My arm is getting better all the time, not much pain now, and I shall soon be back to normal.

I am not very good at writing letters, my dear Molly, as I have never written one before. I can't tell you much anyway or the censor will cross it all out. But I can tell you that I have never met a girl like you before and that I love and miss you very much. It makes all this war business bearable to know you will be waiting for me at the end of it.

Think of me my dearest girl as I think of you, all the time.

Your loving Tom.

The next letter chronologically was Molly's first letter, her reply.

Monday, 10th January

My dear Tom,

I got your letter safely and am glad to know your arm is going along all right. Things are just the same here. Sister Eloise has been ill, so we have had Sister Bernice trying to run our ward. She is not very good at it, but Sister Bernadette comes in sometimes and then things start to jump, I can tell you.

Here's some strange news which you won't believe. Sarah has had a letter from her brother Freddie, you know, the Captain who you saw. He was in England on leave for Christmas and New Year and he came back married. He stayed with another officer in London and has married his sister. They had met before and been writing letters ever since, and when he got home this time her asked her and she said yes. Of course because he is an officer there was no problem with them getting married in a hurry, not like us. Sarah was very disappointed that she wasn't at the wedding, but it doesn't sound as if anyone was much. She says it was only Sir George who travelled up to London specially, and the girl's parents. Her name is Heather. Sarah says that Freddie went home just for Christmas Day to break the news to his pa, and then went back and spent the rest of his leave in London. Not the usual Christmas at the manor. I wonder if he is back with you again now.

Tom, dearest, I think of you every day and hope you are keeping well and safe. I go to the usual Sunday service at the camp, but it isn't the same without your dear face in the congregation. Mr Kingston asked if I had heard from you and I told him you were all right. Nothing from Mam or Dad about us getting married.

I hope this letter reaches you all right and that you will answer it soon. I will write again soon.

Love from your Molly.

Well, this letter has something new in it, thought Rachel. Freddie's marriage.

Rachel had been wondering when Freddie had got married. Clearly he wasn't when he had visited Sarah at the convent, but why hadn't he told Sarah about Heather while he was there? Maybe he'd been afraid that Heather would refuse him. Well, she hadn't and he was not only married, but an expectant father at the time he was killed. This whirlwind wedding on his Christmas leave explained that. Poor Heather, two or three days of wedded bliss before Freddie returned to the front, and she probably never saw him again. It was unlikely he had more leave before July. He must have known he was to be a father, but her child couldn't have been born before September. There was a touch of bitterness, Rachel thought, in Molly's comment about his rushed marriage, no problem because he was an officer. It also sounded as if she had written to her parents saying she wanted to get married, but had received no reply. Did her parents stand out against it? Rachel wondered. She moved on to the next letter.

17th January

Dear Molly,

Thank you for your letter which came today. We have moved now and are living in the usual way. I am back with the lads who I was with before. Harry's brother is here and could not believe it when I told him who had been nursing Harry. He said, "What does my little cousin know about nursing?" and I said, "A great deal, she's very good at it!" That shut him up for a bit, but he was sad that Harry had died.

It is very cold and wet here and there is shelling most of the time. Don't worry about me, dear Molly, as I shall keep my head down. Sarah's brother is back here too. He saw me just before we came up here and was pleased that my arm was quite better. I didn't say anything about him getting married, it wasn't my place, but we have to wish them well. Don't worry, my dearest girl, we will be married as soon as may be. You will be 21 in May so your dad won't matter then.

I cannot tell you what we are doing, but we are kept busy and it helps to pass the time. If you are able to send some cigarettes they would be most welcome as there are never enough here. I've never had a parcel from home so have had to rely on the kindness of the blokes who do get them. They always share, so I'd like to share something of mine with them. It is wonderful to hear my name called when the post comes up the lines. Look after yourself, my little girl. I can't believe you really are my girl yet, I have to keep telling myself.

Your loving Tom

Rachel read slowly through the letters, learning snippets about life both in the trenches and behind the lines in the billets where the men stayed when they were relieved at the front. Occasionally things which Tom had written were blacked out by the censor, leaving Rachel to guess at what he might have said that was so sensitive, but as the correspondence unfolded, she watched Molly and Tom learning more and more about each other.

In one letter Tom told something of his childhood.

5th March

My Dearest Girl,

I write this in truth for you really are my dearest girl. I told you I have never had a girl before and that was true. I also told you I have no family and was an orphanage boy. That is also true. I was found in a cardboard box wrapped in newspaper on a doorstep near University College Hospital in London. The man who found me was a carter. He took me into the hospital and they looked after me until I was strong enough to go to the orphanage. In the box was a piece of paper which said, "Look after my Tom for me". So, they called me Tom Carter. Tom for myself and Carter for the man who found me.

So, my Molly, when we get married you will have to share my borrowed name. Will you mind that? I've never lived in a house with a family, but we will. The Carter family will have a home and all their children will be wanted and loved. No doorsteps for our babies. I used to wonder who my mum was and why she dumped me. I suppose I'll never know the answer to the first and the answer to the second is obvious.

Thank you for your parcel with the cigarettes, the tinned jam and the chocolate. Very popular bloke I am at tea time! I love to get your letters, Molly, they keep me going so keep them coming!

Your loving orphan, Tom

In another letter from Molly it became clear that she and her parents were still not on good terms as she wrote,

12th March

Dearest Tom,

I have at last had word from my father. He is still very angry that I am here at all, and says he has no intention of letting his daughter marry some street urchin from a gutter in London! It has nothing to do with who you are or where you come from. My father and me have always been difficult together. I haven't told this before because it is very difficult for me, but my father wants more from me than a daughter should give. I got away from him when I was fourteen by going into service at the Manor. Mam knew, but she would never hear a word against my father, and accused me of lying when I tried to tell her. I should have told you all this when we were together, but it never seemed the right moment. Our time was too precious to waste talking about my dad, but I realise now I should have told you as I am sort of damaged goods and maybe you will change your mind about me. He used to say I mustn't tell, that it was "our secret", but I can't have secrets from you, Tom. He never did me any real harm, but he might have if I hadn't got away. I wish I'd told you before, but it is very hard even to tell you now. Anyway he will never say we can be married, so we'll have to wait till I'm 21 before we can.

I am sorry to tell you all this in a letter and not to your head as I should have done. I hope you will understand.

I will always be your loving girl, Molly

Rachel looked through the letters again to see if she had missed the letter Molly had received from her parents, but there was no sign of it. Probably she had torn it up or burned it, Rachel thought. I would have done.

Tom was very quick in his reply.

17th March

My darling girl,

What a goose you are to think that anything could change how I feel about you. It changes how I feel about your father. I don't think you'd better let us meet in the near future, Molly, or I might do something I'd be sorry for. Still little chance of that at present, him being safely in England and me being stuck here. Don't ever mention damaged goods again, to me you are my lovely Molly who will one day be my wife whether her dad likes it or not!

No time for more now, work to be done, but remember how much I love you.

Tom

1916

21st March

Molly, my darling girl,

Such wonderful news! We have been given 72 hours local leave.
I will be coming to town by train and will then come out to see
you. I don't suppose you will be able to come to the town, can't
see that Rev. Mother of yours letting you go, so I will come to
the village and see you there.

We leave here in three days time and then have two days in
billets before the leave. I should be with you about the 26th.
I will have two nights in the village before I have to set off back
again.

I can't wait to see you, my dearest. It is your face I have kept
in my mind all the time I've been here.

I will write again, but if you don't get my letter you will get
me instead. As I arrive on Sunday I will go to the camp for the
evening service, perhaps you can too!

My love to you, little darling

Tom

Seventeen

Since the beginning of the year, though there was still a steady stream of men being brought to the hospital, it had been possible to keep pace with them. There had not been the sudden influxes of wounded like those which had come during the autumn, bringing the wards chaos and upheaval, and one ward was now devoted to the medical cases which arrived. Life settled to a slightly easier pace, though the hours were still long and the sisters still exacting. Sister Eloise had recovered from the bronchitis that had taken her off duty, and the ward was running much more smoothly since she came back.

Sarah and Molly had had their off-duty hour on occasional afternoons restored to them. Winter was beginning to lose its grip on the world, though the nights were still very chilly and the stoves in the wards had to be kept alight night and day. On their free afternoon, they still went to the village and ate cake at Madame Juliette's, and the sight of a gentle greening in the trees and hedgerows lifted their spirits after the long dark cold of the winter. Wild daffodils struck bravely through the cold earth and there was the faintest heat in the spring sunshine.

Molly still went across to the convalescent camp for the Sunday evening service, and she saw the men that she had helped to nurse pass their medical board and pronounced fit for duty. Sent off to the station in Albert, they would march away from the camp in groups, heads high, uniforms clean, boots polished. Molly watched each detachment leave and wondered how many of them would see the end of this war, which seemed to be dragging on into eternity.

Sarah watched them go, and her heart wept within her, but she never shed an open tear. Over the months at the hospital she had toughened in many ways. She was no longer upset when taken to task for some failure by Sister Bernadette, she simply sighed and put right her mistake. Gradually she learned how to perform the tasks necessary in the day-to-day nursing of the men. She was not a natural nurse as Molly had turned out to be, but she drove herself hard and learned to cope stoically with the daily round in the ward; the pain of the men, both mental and physical, and her inability to alleviate it. She felt just as deeply about the men in her care, but she no longer took each death in the ward as some sort of personal failure. She drew strength from being part of the community, and though she still enjoyed leaving the convent for an afternoon, she found the routine that she now lived out strangely comforting. She and Molly still shared their room, and their friendship continued to grow. They were comfortable together, knowing each other so well. Like sisters? Neither of them had ever had a sister, so she didn't know, but they were close, drawing strength from one another.

When the post came, Molly saved her letters from Tom to open in private. She never rushed to open his letters, she needed to be alone, so that she could conjure up his face and hear his voice in the words he had written. She would put the letter in her skirt pocket and keep touching it in delicious anticipation during the day as she went about her work in the ward, only slitting the envelope later in the privacy of their room.

When Sarah came up from the chapel this particular evening, she found Molly sitting on her bed writing her nightly letter to Tom, radiant with happiness. She positively glowed with it so that the moment Sarah walked in through the door she knew something had happened.

"Molly?"

"He's coming to see me," Molly cried to her in delight. "He's got a seventy-two hour local leave pass."

"Tom?"

"Oh Sarah! Who else? Of course Tom."

"But where will you meet him?" asked Sarah foreseeing all the pitfalls in this that Molly was blithely ignoring. "Surely he won't come here, to the convent? They won't let him in. It's not like when Freddie came. He was my brother."

"I know all that," Molly said cheerfully, "but we can meet in the village, or at the camp. He'll go and see the padre, and so can I."

"In the village?"

"When we go, you and I. It'll be perfectly proper if you're there too. We'll just have tea and cakes at Madame Juliette's like always."

Sarah looked dubious. "I don't know, Molly," she began, "Reverend Mother…"

"Doesn't need to know," broke in Molly. "Sarah, we are talking about the man I am going to marry. He's my fiancé." Molly was pleased to use the word. "My fiancé. If we were at home now and he came to call for me on my day off, it would be perfectly proper for me to walk out with him. Why not here?"

"It's different here," Sarah said. "We have to live by the rules of the convent, we agreed to do that when we first came."

"Well I didn't have a fiancé when we first came," said

Molly obstinately. "Sarah," she pleaded, "I have to meet him one way or another. We'll have so little time together."

Sarah sat down beside Molly and gave her a hug. "Don't worry," she said, "we'll think of something. Perhaps I could explain to Aunt Anne that you are going to be married and she could speak to Mother."

"I don't want Mother knowing anything about it," Molly said firmly. "She as good as told me that she'd send me away if I saw him again. If he turns up now she'll know I disobeyed her and she may well send me away anyway."

When the light was out, each girl lay in her cocoon of darkness considering what to do. Molly was planning ways she could slip away from the convent to meet Tom in the precious few hours they would have. She thought about the gate in the convent wall, leading to the camp outside. As far as she knew it was never locked as the padre and the doctors used it whenever they came over to visit the wards. When she came off duty, it would be easy enough to slip through the gate instead of going up to their room. If she chose her moment no one would see her, and no one, except perhaps Sarah, would miss her, and there Tom would be, waiting for her. She only had to persuade Sarah to cover for her if necessary.

Sarah was wondering what she ought to do in the situation. Should she allow herself to be drawn into this deceit? To be used as an illicit chaperone by Molly and encourage her to flout the convent rules, or should she stand back and let Molly get on with this on her own? If she did that there was almost no doubt that Molly and Tom would be caught out, yet if she connived at their meeting, she might be making everything worse for Molly in the long run. She was seriously concerned with how things stood between Molly and her Tom. The letters had come thick and fast, and Sarah knew that there was a new dimension to their relationship since Tom had left. She felt in her heart she shouldn't be doing anything to encourage Molly in her infatuation with this man, but she could see how happy it made Molly and she couldn't bring herself to destroy that happiness either.

"When does he arrive?" she asked Molly as they were getting dressed the next morning.

"He says the 26th," answered Molly casually. "That's Sunday."

"And will you be going to the service at the camp as usual?" Sarah asked innocently.

"I always go to the service when I can be spared," replied Molly with equal innocence.

"Let's hope Sister Eloise can spare you then," teased Sarah.

Molly stared at her dumbstruck. " Oh Sarah, you don't think that this Sunday, of all Sundays…"

"No, Of course I don't, silly! I was only teasing you." Sarah had decided that Molly going to church in the camp was the very best way of her meeting with Tom. The Reverend Kingston would be there, and so would a host of other people; it would be perfectly proper, and, more to the point, she, Sarah, would not be compromised in any way.

Molly waltzed through the next few days, her eyes shining. She wrote to Tom saying she would be at the evening service and would see him there. No other letter came from him and occasionally she was attacked by doubts. Perhaps something had gone wrong. Perhaps the leave had been cancelled. Perhaps they hadn't been relieved at the front. Perhaps he'd been… She forced aside such thoughts and imagined him, waiting at the gate to meet her when she crossed through, perfectly properly, for Sunday evening service.

Sunday finally arrived and for Molly every minute was an

hour. She woke early; the day had finally come. She had been terrified that they would have an unexpected arrival of wounded so that she couldn't be spared from the ward, but as the hours crawled by, this became less and less likely, and eventually Sister Eloise said, "You may go to your church now, Molly," and with demure thanks, Molly slipped out of the ward to take off her apron and fetch her coat and hat.

The day had been a fine one, and as Molly crossed the courtyard, the sun was beginning to paint evening into the sky above the high, grey walls. She paused with her hand on the gate and looked behind her. There was no one in the courtyard, the ward doors were now closed against the creeping chill of the March evening, and the windows that overlooked the yard were dark and empty. There was no one to see her leave, or to see who was waiting as she closed the gate behind her.

He was there, looking as handsome in his uniform as she had ever seen him. For a moment they simply looked at each other. Each had been afraid that this magical thing that had grown and flowered between them might have mysteriously perished; that things would not be the same when they saw each other again. Would they find the person they thought they knew, or someone different; someone whom they had known once and remembered only hazily, or worse still had never known at all?

Would Tom still be the brave yet sensitive man Molly had nursed and comforted, or would he have changed, over the intervening months back in the trenches, become a stranger hardened by war? Would Molly still be the same beautiful young woman, that Tom remembered, her face eager and bright, her eyes lit with inner determination and strength?

Each searched the face of the other. Tom spoke first, his

face breaking into a smile; he held out both hands to grasp hers. "Molly! Is it really you, my darling girl?"

His smile, lighting his face, drew an answering one and Molly gripped his hands tightly for a moment before she whispered, "Tom! It's really you." She slipped into his arms like a bird coming home to roost, and he folded them round her in an embrace that crushed the breath out of her.

She looked up at him as she had before. "I can't breathe," she murmured, and as he relaxed his hold a fraction, she slid her arms up round his neck and held up her face to be kissed. Some men passed them on their way to the chapel tent, but glanced away from a couple clearly lost in each other. Each man could imagine his own sweetheart in his arms, and walked on to the service his heart filled with envy at the lucky bloke who seemed to have his girl right here in France.

"We must go to the chapel," Molly said at last, straightening her hat. "We can talk afterwards." They walked through the camp, Tom tall and straight beside her, Molly's hand on his arm. Molly knew an exhilaration she had never known before. Gone were all her doubts about how she would feel about this man once she saw him again. She looked up at him with pride in her eyes, a pride that was reflected in his, as he looked down.

At the service they sang the familiar hymns, joined in the Lord's prayer and listened to the padre's sermon, but neither had thought for anything or anyone but the other. They sat on opposite sides of the tent, as they always had, Tom among the men and Molly with the officers and nurses from the camp, but each felt as close to the other as if they were hand in hand, arm in arm. At the end of the service when the congregation mingled, Robert Kingston came over and said to Molly, "Well, Miss Day, I see you have your beau back from the front."

"Yes, padre," Molly replied.

"Good to see you looking so well, Carter," he said, nodding to Tom before moving on.

As people stayed chatting, Tom and Molly withdrew to a corner. At first things seemed stiff between them, their conversation stilted and awkward, there was so much to say it was hard to begin, but when Tom said, "Oh Molly, it is so good to see you. I can't believe I'm really here," Molly felt tears in her eyes.

"I can't believe it either," she whispered. "I was so afraid that something awful would stop you coming, that you would be wounded or killed in those days after you wrote. I couldn't have borne that, Tom."

"Well I wasn't, see, so don't you waste tears on what hasn't happened."

They talked for a while, but the tent began to empty and they couldn't stay there any longer. Robert Kingston was watching them, and so they went up to him before they left.

"Goodnight, Mr Kingston," Molly said. "I'm going back now. I'll see you next Sunday."

"Goodnight, Miss Day," replied the padre. He nodded to Tom. "Carter." Then he asked, "Where are you staying, Carter? In the village?"

"Yes, sir," replied Tom. "I got a room down there."

"Well, goodnight to you." Then he added with a wry smile, "I've no doubt you'll escort Miss Day through the camp to the convent gate."

"Yes, sir. Certainly, sir."

They spent their last few moments together planning how to meet again the next day, Tom's only full day.

"I'll come out as soon as I get off duty tomorrow," Molly promised. "Sarah and I sometimes get a couple of hours off in the afternoon so that we're in the wards when the sisters want to go to chapel later in the day. Any time after noon. I'll meet you on the track leading to the camp."

"Will they let you out alone?" asked Tom, surprised.

Molly shook her head. "No, but Sarah will come, I know she will, and if she doesn't, well, I'll slip out through the side gate anyway."

She carried away all his arguments and objections, saying at last, "Tom, we only have tomorrow. If we don't see each other then, it won't be for months." He allowed himself to be persuaded and they held each other close as they kissed with a passion neither had experienced before.

"Now I'm definitely coming," Molly said a little shakily.

Next day things did not go as Molly had hoped. Sister Eloise announced that there was a hospital inspection in the next few days, so she would need Molly all day to prepare. Molly stared at her dumbfounded for a moment and then just nodded and said, "Yes, Sister." She started her work in the ward kitchen, but her mind wasn't on what she was doing, it was racing furiously, hatching and discarding schemes that would allow her to meet Tom as they had planned. She had no way of getting a message to him, to warn him of a change of plan, but she was determined to see him once more before he had to go back.

Eventually she fell back on the simplest of her ideas. She would tell Sister Eloise that she was ill and have herself sent to her room. From there she would slip downstairs and away. Sarah would be the only person who would know she was not in her room, unwell, and surely Sarah wouldn't say anything? All morning she worked with a distracted air, causing comment from Sister Marie-Paul, and eventually Sister Eloise said, "Molly, is something wrong?"

Molly produced a brave smile and said, "No, not really Sister, I..." she hesitated as if not liking to mention such things and then said softly, "I have my monthly, and this time the pain is bad."

Sister Eloise was surprised at this confession, but as she had no reason to doubt what Molly told her, she asked, "Can you still work?"

Molly managed another brave smile, "Of course, Sister, but I will lie down for a while at midday."

"You will not come for your meal?" asked Sister Eloise.

"No, I couldn't eat, Sister, I would be sick. If I lie down for a little I will be better." Molly surprised herself with how easily the lies came.

"Go now," said the nun, "it is almost midday and I will send Sarah to you with a little food." She handed Molly some aspirin. "These will help," she said. "Tomorrow you will be quite recovered, hein? Stay in your bed. I will see you tomorrow."

After that it had been remarkably easy. Molly went up to her room and got her hat and coat. She scribbled a note for Sarah, hoping that it would indeed be Sarah who came to see how she was. That's a risk I've got to take, she thought as she left it propped on Sarah's pillow.

Dear Sarah,

I have to see Tom once again. I told Sister E. that I wasn't well with my monthly. Not due back in the ward until tomorrow. Please cover for me. I will be back before it gets dark. This is the only time we have.

Molly

The Angelus was ringing as she crept down the stairs, after which the nuns would be eating. With all the sisters in the

313

refectory, Molly risked using the front door. It was safer, she decided than crossing the courtyard where she might be seen from one of the wards. She closed the heavy door behind her and cut round outside the convent walls. Tom was sitting patiently on a fallen tree beside the track and he leapt to his feet as he saw her.

"Molly!" he exclaimed. "I didn't expect you yet."

"Quickly, Tom. Let's get out of sight." She took his hand and hurried him down the hill and into a copse of trees that would hide them from any watching eyes at the convent windows. Once safely screened, they paused and Tom gathered her into his arms. "How did you get out?" he asked when he had kissed her. "Where's Sarah?"

"No off duty today," Molly explained. "I pleaded sick and am supposed to be in our room, lying down."

"But you'll be missed."

"Only by Sarah, with any luck," replied Molly. Going on bravely, she added, "and if I am, I am. It'll be too late. We shouldn't go to the village though."

"We can't stay here either," Tom said. "Blokes from the camp often walk down through here on their way to the village."

Molly thought for a moment and then said, "We'll go along the river. There probably won't be anyone down there."

She led the way across the fields, skirting the village and ending up on the path that she and Sarah had walked so often in their early days at the convent.

The sun had been shining all morning, but now clouds were building in the sky, and a rising breeze fluttered and whipped the strands of the leaning willows and drew darting cats' paws on the smooth-flowing water of the river. Tom and Molly noticed none of it. They sat in the shelter of one of the trees and shared the bread and cheese Tom had bought in the village, and talked. Not of the war at first, but of themselves and the future they planned together; the home they would make, the children they would have, their life as a real family. The perfect world, after the war, when the pain was over and the killing had stopped. The thought of this time, somewhere beyond their lives in the hospital and the trenches, brought them inevitably back to the present.

"There's a big push coming," Tom told her. "Everyone's talking about it, there's definitely something in the wind. They say it's the push that's going to end the war. Sweep the Germans out of the trenches and right back into Germany."

"When?" cried Molly. "When's this big push?"

Tom shrugged. "Don't know. No one does, but it's coming all right. We've had no rest even when we've been relieved at the front. We've been marching, carrying stores, digging trenches and training, training all the time we've been in billets, as well as the usual chores."

"Training? What sort of training?" asked Molly.

"Some of our company have been trained with Lewis guns," Tom replied. "Special courses teaching them to maintain and clean them. Fix them when they jam. They're light, those Lewises, a bloke can carry and fire one on his own if he has to. We've all had rifle and bayonet practice. Men are moving everywhere, new trenches are being dug, sunken roads built to move stuff up the line out of sight. And all the time the old ones have to be repaired. It's what we do most of the time when we're up in the front line. Jerry shells us all day, then at night we have to repair the damage. Some of the older trenches cave right in." Tom paused for a moment, thinking of the three stinking corpses that had been unearthed from the collapsed wall of the last trench he and his mates had been repairing.

"Christ!" Tony Cook had yelled leaping backwards as what looked like a stinking bag of rubbish fell out at his feet. It was only a decomposing arm with its hand still hanging off, sticking out from the stinking bundle that had told them what they had found. As they had mended the wall of the trench they had re-interred that body and the other two that were with it.

No need to tell Molly about that, he thought, and jerked himself away from the vision of the black-fleshed arm which had slid into his mind. "The wire in front has to be re-laid as well," he told her. "Has to be fixed up so that the Jerries can't come through on a raiding party. We go out after dark looking for holes and mending them."

"And the Germans just let you?" asked Molly.

Tom shook his head. "Nope. But they're doing exactly the same," he said, "trying to mend what our gunners have flattened. Flare goes up, everyone freezes, snipers try and pick off a few and then as it gets dark again everyone gets back to work."

"All for this 'big push'?" asked Molly faintly.

"Definitely coming," said Tom. "There's men coming in from everywhere."

An angry flurry of rain brought them back to the present and Tom looked up at the sky, lowering grey, filled with rain. "We're going to get drenched," he said. "We'll have to go back, or at least find somewhere to shelter."

"I know just the place," Molly cried. She was determined that she wasn't going back to the confines of the convent yet, for as she listened to Tom's rumour of the big push and the carnage that must accompany it, Molly had come to a decision. Pulling Tom to his feet, she led him along the path. With their heads down against the wind and the driving rain, they battled their way to the old stone barn where she and Sarah had sat in the autumn to eat their picnics. Laughing, they ducked inside and collapsed amongst the last of the hay that was still stored there. Molly took off her coat and laid it down on the hay, and then Tom pulled her into his arms and they lay together, their bodies close, intensely aware of each other. As he kissed her and Molly returned those kisses, Tom tweaked off her hat and pulled the pins from her hair. It fell round her shoulders, framing her face, and he came up on his elbow to look down at her, his Molly with the shining eyes and the gentle, loving mouth. Even as he looked, she reached for him again, pulling him down so that her mouth could claim his, and he felt her hands pushing at his jacket, sliding in under his shirt to touch his skin.

"Molly!" His voice was ragged and he twisted away. Molly sat up and very deliberately began to unbutton her blouse. He watched as her fingers undid each small white button, as she slipped her shoulders free and shrugged her arms out of the sleeves. He made no move to touch her, but he ached in every inch of his body.

"Molly!" he groaned again, but Molly laid a finger to her lips and unhooked the waistband of her skirt. Without getting to her feet, she slid it deftly down her legs and kicked it free, away over the hay. Dressed only in her chemise she reached out and began the same deft work on his tunic and then the shirt underneath. As she slid the shirt from his shoulders, her fingers ran cool and softly down his arms and then across the skin of his chest. It was, at last, too much and he pushed her back on to the hay, his body hard against hers as he stroked the bare flesh above her chemise, as he pulled the white cotton away, up over her hips, over her shoulders, over her head, leaving her breasts naked and beautiful. He raised his head to look at her, and Molly put her arms up above her head, stretching like a cat, the skin smooth and taut across her breasts and belly. Tom put his finger on her cheek and from there traced a wondering line, circling each breast, touching each eager nipple before moving slowly down her body. The touch of his exploring finger made her quiver. In that moment she heard her father's gruff voice saying, "Lovely little bubbies you've got, Moll," and she stiffened. Tom looked sharply into her face, but when she saw the anxiety in his eyes she smiled up at him and relaxed again. The memory vanished and she closed her eyes, arching her body towards him. He knelt beside her, his hands wandering lingeringly over her skin until he came to the drawers that still covered her. His fingers came to rest on their waistband and Molly murmured huskily, "Tom. Don't stop!" Her eyes flew open and he looked into them anxiously.

"We shouldn't be doing this, Molly," he said. "Not till we're married. Not till you're really my wife."

Molly slid her hands down his body and played with the fly of his trousers. "We may never be married, Tom," she said softly. "We have to face reality. You go back tomorrow and I may never see you again. You say there's a big push coming. You may be killed and we'd never have known what it was to love each other properly, completely. If we never spend another hour together at least we'll have had this. We'll have shared our bodies as well as our hearts." Her fingers, stroking him, aroused him almost beyond endurance. "I want you to make love to me, Tom, so that I can hold this moment to me on the bleak and lonely nights when you're not there. If you love me, Tom, please make love to me now."

"I love you, Molly, too much to be doing this to you, but I can't help myself." He lowered his head and as they kissed the last of their restraint faded away.

Later, as they lay side by side in the hay listening to the rain still pattering on the roof, Molly curled herself against him and sighed. "I love you, Tom," she said. "I'll always love you."

The wind dashed a flurry of rain in through the open doorway and Molly shivered. Tom said, "You're cold. You must get dressed. Look at the time, Molly, you'll be missed."

"I don't care," Molly insisted, but she took her chemise when he handed it to her and put her clothes back on. Tom helped her pin her hair back up with the few hairpins they could salvage from the hay, and then she set her hat on her head. Looking at his watch, she saw that the hours had fled and it was half past six. They stepped out into the rain and hurried back towards the convent. The heavy blanket of grey cloud made the evening dreary, and the wind was cold. They didn't speak, just huddled together as they walked. When they reached the copse at the end of the track they kissed again.

"I'll go in through the courtyard door," Molly said. "It should be open. With luck nearly everyone will be at supper and I won't be seen."

"Will you be all right?" Tom asked. "You know I have to leave here at first light."

"Yes, I know." Molly was fighting to keep back tears. "I'll never forget this afternoon," she said.

"No more will I," Tom said. "Look after yourself, my darling girl."

Molly nodded and whispered, "You too."

They walked quickly up the track to the gate in the convent wall, and with the touch of her hand on his, Molly went through without a backward glance. The courtyard was empty, the ward doors all shut against the cold wet evening.

She pulled the gate closed behind her and was just starting across the yard for the door when the door to ward one opened and Sister Marie-Paul emerged carrying a bucket. She looked at Molly in surprise and said, "I thought you were ill."

"I was, earlier," Molly replied, "but I felt better and I thought a breath of fresh air would do me good, so I came down into the courtyard."

"You don't look ill," remarked Sister Marie-Paul suspiciously. She had been annoyed when Sister Eloise had sent Molly to rest just because it was the time of the month. Didn't they all have to contend with that? No one would have dreamed of even mentioning such a thing, let alone going to bed with it. She'd had to work an extra hour because Molly was sick.

"As I said, I feel much better now. Sister Eloise gave me some aspirin. They must have done the trick."

Sister Marie-Paul sniffed and turned away to empty her bucket in an outside drain and Molly took the chance to scamper inside. Thank goodness Sister Marie-Paul hadn't come out thirty seconds earlier and caught her actually coming in through the gate.

She gained the safety of their room without meeting anyone else, and with a fast-beating heart she threw herself down on the bed. The note she had left for Sarah had gone, so she must have read it.

Sarah had indeed read the note. When Sister Eloise told her, whilst she was having her midday break, that Molly wasn't well, Sarah went straight upstairs to find out what was wrong. All she found was an empty room and the note. She read it through incredulously and then a second time with mounting anger. How could Molly do something so deceitful, so stupid and then worse still expect her, Sarah, to cover her tracks?

When she came up to the room at the end of the day she found Molly in bed. "How dare you!" she exploded. "How dare you, Molly Day? You break all the rules we've been asked to keep, you creep out in an underhand manner to have a clandestine meeting with a soldier you hardly know, and you expect me to cover it up for you. You expect me to lie for you. 'No, Sister, she isn't very well, but I'm sure she'll be fine tomorrow. No, Sister, she doesn't want anything to eat just now, I'll take her a tray up at supper time. Yes, Sister she has been looking a bit peaky. Yes, Sister, I'm sure you are right, sleep is what she needs. Yes, Sister, she was fast asleep when I came down. Please don't trouble yourself, Sister, I can look after her, you've enough on your hands.' How dare you involve me in your tawdry little affair!" Sarah's eyes blazed with anger as she stood looking down at Molly. "What have you got to say for yourself, you little slut? What have you to say to me?"

Molly felt the words hit her, battering her like hailstones, so that she almost put up her hands to ward them off.

"I'm sorry, Sarah," she began, "but I had to go. There's a big push coming, he may be killed..."

Her voice trailed away as Sarah interrupted. "Sorry isn't good enough, Molly. I expected more of you than running out to a man like a kitchen maid..." She, too, broke off as she realised what she'd said.

"I am a kitchen maid, Miss Sarah," Molly pointed out softly. "But that don't make me a slut. I went to say goodbye to the man I'm going to marry. A man fighting for his king and country, for you and me. A man that's maybe going to die."

"Oh, Molly, I'm sorry, I shouldn't have said that," cried

Sarah dropping down on to her own bed. "But you shouldn't have gone, really you shouldn't. What Reverend Mother would say…"

"She isn't going to know, Sarah…unless you tell her."

"Why would I tell her now?" asked Sarah resignedly. "I've been lying for you all afternoon. I certainly shan't be telling her now. Oh Molly, I've been so worried about you. Where've you been? Surely not to the village? Not to Madame Juliette's."

"No, we walked by the river and then when it rained we sheltered in the old stone barn, you know where we used to picnic?"

"Oh, Molly," Sarah said, not knowing what else to say.

"Thank you, Sarah, for standing by me."

Molly held out her hand and Sarah took it with a reluctant grin. "Don't ever put me in that position again, Molly," she said. "Has he gone back now?"

Molly nodded. Sarah's burst of anger had at least served to deflect her thoughts for a moment or two, now she felt the tears pricking the backs of her eyes. "Yes, he leaves at first light. But next time we meet I'll be of age and we'll be able to get married."

"What's this 'big push'?" asked Sarah and Molly told her what Tom had said.

"So I suppose Freddie will be in it too."

"I suppose so," Molly said uncertainly. "Well they're in the same company, aren't they? So he must be in it too. Tom says there are men being brought in from everywhere. A load arrived from Egypt the other day. I bet they notice the difference in heat."

"I had a letter from Freddie, today," Sarah said. "Heather, his wife, is going to have a baby. It's due in September." She looked bleakly at Molly. "He may never see it."

"Now, come on, Sarah, this big push is going to end the war. Our boys are going to shove them Germans right back into Germany where they belong."

"Those Germans," Sarah corrected her absently.

"Yes, well those an' all!"

They both laughed at that and when at last they put out the light and lay as always with their thoughts, it wasn't very long before both had drifted off into sleep.

15th June

Dearest Tom,

I got your last letter and am glad you're safely back in billets, though it sounds as if you are very busy. I know you can't tell me much because of the censor, but it is nice to know that you are safe. Thank you for the snap, you look very spruce!

I have some news for you, Tom, which I hope will please you, but may cause us a problem as well. It is difficult to explain how I feel so I'd better just tell you straight. You are going to be a father. I am going to have a baby. I know we planned to have children, but it will be difficult over here. I will have to go home, dear Tom and have our baby there. No one else knows yet, not even Sarah, as nothing shows and I am keeping well, thank goodness. I am sure that they are not handing out leave at present, but if you could manage to get 48 hours I could meet you somewhere and we could get married. I know you will stick by me, dear Tom, whatever happens, but I would like the baby to have your name, and this may be the last time we could get married for a while. Now I am 21 my father has no say.

Eighteen

Tom came in filthy from the digging he and his mates had been doing all day. As they reached the barn that served as their billet Sergeant Turner bellowed the order to fall in. There were moans and groans from all of them.

"What the hell do they want us for now?"

"Christ, is there no rest?"

"Not another bleeding route march!"

Then someone mentioned the words scrub down, and with great alacrity they did as they were ordered and had soon marched to the other end of the village. There amongst the trees was an old barn, its grey stone walls thick and sturdy, its roof patched and repaired. It was the billet bath house. Inside was a huge vat of hot water, a great tin bath big enough to hold anything up to thirty men.

"All right, ten minutes," bellowed Corporal Johns and the whole company stripped off their filthy clothes and plunged into the already murky water for a ten-minute wallow and scrub. Relishing the warmth of the water and ignoring its colour, they scrubbed and scraped at their lousy bodies, knowing this would be their last chance to feel clean for some time. Water at the front had to be carried up in cans and was strictly rationed, both for drinking and washing. Now they could wallow in it, sluice it over their heads, washing the accumulated mud and filth from every inch of their bodies. No soap, but nobody cared, the water was enough. Their lice-ridden underclothes, beyond redemption, were unceremoniously burned.

Tom and his mates emerged from the bath, the water now the colour of brown Windsor soup, and rejoiced in the feel of clean underclothes and socks before they put back their uniforms.

"'Ere Cookie, didn't know you was a carrot top!" shouted Jack Hughes as he watched Tony Cook towelling his head.

"Watch your lip, Jacko," Tony retorted, flicking the wet towel at him. "Better'an having no 'air at all!"

"Christ! You look almost human, Carter!"

"You never will!"

"Get your togs on," snapped Corporal Johns. They scuffled for their uniforms, with more good-natured backchat.

"That's my shirt!"

"Have it, mate, don't want to be hatching your chats!"

"These boots've shrunk an' all!"

"Try putting your own on and give me mine!"

Despite the uniforms, it was wonderful to feel their skins were their own for while. It would be a feeling short-lived, but it was a warm June evening, and though there was the ever-present background music of the artillery, distant on the evening air, it was a rare time of peace and well-being and each man revelled in it.

Back at the barn they were about to eat when the cry, "Mail's in!" echoed round the yard. Men tumbled out of the outbuildings and scrambled to the door of the farmhouse from where the mail would be distributed. Post was a marvellous boost; as the letters, packages and parcels were handed out, the men listened avidly for their names.

"Farmer, Short, Tamper, Jones M J, Hooper, Dalton, Carter, Cook."

Each man carried his post off in triumph as his name was called and those who received nothing tried to think it didn't matter, that they'd had letters last time. As always, Tom's letter was from Molly. She was the only person in the world to write to him. Until he'd met her there had been no letters for him at any mail call, but now there was almost always a letter and often a small package too, with cigarettes and chocolate she'd bought in the village that he could share with his mates. Once she had even sent him some gateau from Madame Juliette's. It had been packed in a box and had arrived completely crushed, but it had been scoffed down with as much enjoyment as if it were still in perfect shape.

Tom took his letter away into the barn and dropping down on the blanket on the hay that constituted his bed, he pulled it open. What he read made his heart stand still. He read it again and then again, trying to take in what she was telling him, what she was asking him to do.

15th June

Tom,

I got your last letter and am glad you're safely back in billets, though it sounds as if you are very busy. I know you can't tell me much because of the censor, but it is nice to know that you are safe. Thank you for the snap, you look very spruce!

I have some news for you, Tom, which I hope will please you, but may cause us a problem as well. It is difficult to explain how I feel so I'd better just tell you straight. You are going to be a father. I think I am having a baby. I know we planned to have children, but it will be difficult over here. I will have to go home, dear Tom and have our baby there. No one else knows yet, not even Sarah, as nothing shows and I am keeping well, thank goodness. I am sure that they are not handing out leave at present, but if you could manage to get 48 hours I could meet you somewhere and we could get married. I know you will stick by me, dear Tom, whatever happens, but I would like the baby to have your name, and this may be the last time we could get married for a while. Now I am 21 my father has no say.

A father. A father. The word hit him like a cudgel. How could he be a father? He had no idea what a father did. Molly thought she was having a baby, his baby; he was going to be a father. In almost any other circumstances the news would have delighted him, exhilarated him, so that he'd have run from friend to friend telling the great news, but now? Now it had to be a secret, something to be hidden; something shameful. He thought back, as he had a hundred times, to the afternoon he and Molly had spent in the stone barn, that wonderful afternoon when each had belonged entirely to the other. How could they have allowed themselves to be so carried away? But how could they not? And now there was a baby on the way, and Molly would have to go home to England. If they were not married before she went, she would have to face shame and humiliation of giving birth to an illegitimate baby, a bastard. Tom had been called that often enough in his life to be certain that no child of his should have to face such abuse. Part of him rejoiced in the fact that he was going to be a father, to start a family with the girl he loved to distraction, but that rejoicing was soon submerged and drowned by the dreadful position in which Molly now found herself, and he unable to go to her aid.

Every day for weeks now they had been rehearsing for the big push, manoeuvres, training, working with other platoons and companies as they gathered, making up the miles of front line that would move forward together when the day came, driving the Germans before them, bringing the war to a speedy end. Every man was needed, not one could be spared. How could he ask for leave, even for so short a time, when the great preparations were in such an advanced stage? No one knew when the attack was to come, but that it was imminent was beyond doubt.

Molly had finished her letter with brave words, telling him,

> I regret nothing, Tom. That I promise you, and if we cannot be married before the child is born, then we will be married after. I consider myself your wife already. I became that on our last afternoon. I think of you as my husband and shall do, whatever happens to either of us. My darling Tom, I know in my heart that you will come home safely to me, but, if I am wrong, at least I will have some part of you with me for the rest of my life.
>
> I love you and am proud to be your wife.
>
> Molly

Tom looked blankly at the words, not knowing what to do. His darling Molly was being so brave about it all. But in the eyes of the world, she was not his wife. She was the one who would suffer the shame if he didn't get to Albert and marry her before she went home. She, and the baby. Poor little mite, it would have the stigma he'd had to live with all his life. He felt a surge of protective anger rise up in him, no child of his was going to be branded a bastard. He wished he had someone with whom he could discuss it. If Harry had been alive... but there was no one now. Tony? Tony was a good enough mate, but they weren't close, not like he and Harry had been. He couldn't discuss this with Tony. Anyway, Molly was his cousin. Tony might not take too well to Tom's having put her in the family way.

That night as he lay in the barn surrounded by snoring, grunting men, tossing and turning in their sleep, Tom hardly slept. His mind churned as he thought about the various possibilities of what they might do. He thought of Molly lying alone in the dark worrying about herself and the baby, for, despite her fine, brave words, she must be very scared. It would not be long before she had to tell someone, if only Sarah, so that plans could be made for her to go home. Tom hated the idea of that too. He had a pretty fair idea of what Molly's home life had been, and there was no way he wanted her to return to her father's house; but if she had to, and it looked as if she did, whatever happened, Tom wanted her to go there clad in respectability, a married woman, having her baby alone because her husband was at the front. From what he had heard of Molly's bullying father, he had no doubt of how she would be received and used if she went home carrying a bastard child. Her mother loved her, Molly had said, but she had never protected her before, so was unlikely to now.

At last, through sheer exhaustion, he fell into a fitful sleep, but when reveille sounded, he felt as if he had not slept at all. He awoke to a feeling of foreboding and then it all flooded back into his mind, and he realised with a jolt that Molly must be waking to this feeling every day. He managed to scrawl a note to her that day. It was couched in careful language so that the censor would not understand what he was saying, nor feel the need to blank any of it out.

Dearest Molly,

I got your letter and am delighted with your news, but are you sure? As things are at present it will be quite difficult to do as you ask, but I will make every effort to do so if you are really sure. It is not as we planned, but have <u>no doubt</u> you will always be my darling girl.

Tom

He posted it and hoped that it would reach her before very long, so that she could take comfort from his support.

For the next few days, as he was carrying stores to the supply dumps, manhandling sacks and boxes along the network of communication trenches behind the lines but not out of range of the German artillery, his mind was on Molly and what he must do. If she was certain she was expecting, there seemed to be no alternative but to go to Captain Hurst and explain the situation and ask for forty-eight hours leave. Like an automaton, he hefted the crates of stores on to the flat trucks of the light railway, which took them to yet other dumps, further up the line, always part of the same working party, yet apart from it.

"Hey, Carter, you look like a wet weekend," Joe Farmer said to him when they paused for a break one day. "What's up, mate?"

"Nothing," replied Tom shortly.

"Girl dumped you, did she?" enquired Sam Hughes amiably.

The look on Tom's face at this remark, made everyone draw back, and Sam Hughes, feeling he must have hit the mark mumbled, "Sorry, mate. No offence."

Tom moved away, but he heard Cookie mutter, "He had a letter."

Yes, he'd had a letter, but now he was waiting for another one. He didn't have long to wait. Molly's reply to his note was swift in coming.

Dear Tom,

I'm as sure as I can be. I have missed twice now and, though I have no sickness like some, I cannot eat a piece of cheese at present! Makes life difficult here, but so far no one has commented. I know it will be difficult for you, but please try for our baby's sake.

With our love,

Molly

Tom read the note again. Our love. Love from herself as always, but from the baby too. Our love. His mind was made up.

That evening when the work party returned to the farm and collapsed with fatigue in the barn, Tom went out to the pump in the yard and washed his hands and face. He combed his hair and brushed at some of the drier mud on his uniform. Then he went over to the old farmhouse which served as officer accommodation.

Sergeant Turner was coming out and when he saw Tom, he stopped him and said, "Where're you off to, Carter?"

"Have to see Captain Hurst, Sarge."

"Oh, do you now? And why's that, then?"

"Private business, Sarge."

The older man looked at him. He liked Carter, a reliable man, and never afraid of hard work. He remembered Tom carrying the wounded Harry back to the lines from no-man's-land; you didn't forget a thing like that. He eyed Tom now, speculatively. "Anything I can help with?" he asked.

"No thanks, Sarge. Just a bit of personal business that I need to talk to Captain Hurst about."

Sergeant Turner nodded and watched him go to the farmhouse door, then he crossed the farmyard to where the rest of

Tom's mates were billeted and asked, "Anyone know what's the matter with Carter?"

Tony Cook looked up and answered, "Nope." Then he added, "But he had a letter the other day."

The sergeant nodded. Men were always getting bad news from home, but he wondered what Carter thought Captain Freddie Hurst could do about it.

Captain Freddie Hurst could do nothing about it. When Tom came in to see him he listened to what he had to say and then said, "Let me get this straight, Carter, you've got some poor girl into trouble and now you want to dash off at a moment's notice to marry her?"

"I suppose that's it," Tom agreed miserably.

"You must be mad to ask," the Captain said. "You know the state of things at the moment. You know that within days every single man will be needed, and you ask me if you can push off to Albert for a couple of days just to make an honest woman of some girl you've put up the spout."

Tom felt the anger rise in him as he heard the casual phrases the officer used. "She's not 'some girl' she's my fiancée," he replied sharply. "We were getting married as soon as we could anyway."

"But you jumped the gun." Captain Hurst's face softened a little and he went on. "Look, can't say I blame you for that, Carter, but it still doesn't mean you can walk out on the army to get married. Heavens, man, there are hundreds of men here who'd love to do the same thing. There're girls all over England waiting for their men to come home and marry them, but they have to go on waiting, and I'm afraid your girl will have to wait too."

"But my girl is here in France, sir. Two days is all I need, then she and the baby will both have my name, she will be an army wife and be looked after if...well, you know sir, looked after."

"Sorry, Carter." Captain Hurst spoke sharply. "Out of the question." Seeing the man's stricken face he added, "Ask me again in another few months. We should be able to spare you then if all goes to plan."

Another few months would be far too late and they both knew it, but they also both knew that Tom would get no leave just now.

That evening when the others went off to the estaminet in the village for a few beers, Tom stayed behind and settled down to write a proper letter to Molly. He knew it would be read by an officer somewhere, maybe even Captain Hurst, but he had to forget that, forget that his most private thoughts would be scrutinised. The officers weren't interested in declarations of love or marital problems, there were those in most of the letters they had to censor; all they had to do was to check that no information about places, dates and exercises had crept in as well, in case they were captured somewhere along the way.

My darling Molly,

I have been to see Sarah's brother and explained our situation, though I didn't say it was you. He turned down my request flat, as I'd been afraid he would do. You know the reasons from when I saw you. I can understand why, but it is a bad blow. He said to ask again in a couple of months, but by then I expect you will have to have gone back. I suppose you will have to go back to your father's house and stay there until I can come for you. Surely your mother will help you with the baby. As soon as I can, I'll come and take you away, and we'll make a home for ourselves. This bloody war can't last for ever.

My darling girl, I think you should confide in Sarah now

and begin to make arrangements for your journey home. It's not what I want, but I am sure in the long run it is best for you. I wish I could come to you straight away and hold you in my arms and tell you everything is going to be all right, but I can't. Remember that I love you more than life itself.

Look after yourself and our little one. I send my love to you both,

Tom

When he had sent the letter Tom tried to settle to the routine around him. His company was sent up to the front again, and spent four days in the front-line trenches. Most of the time their day was reversed. At dawn and dusk there was stand-to, when every man took his place on the fire step, rifle levelled to watch for signs of a German attack. These early mornings, with grey light filtering in from the east, and mist rising from the damp of no-man's-land, were the perfect time to attack, the sun creeping over the horizon, low in the sky, shining into the eyes of the rows of watchful men; and the evenings as the twilight drew the colour from the world, left a landscape of shifting shapes and shadows from which an enemy might suddenly emerge. The real work began after dark with the repairing of trenches, laying of wire, and digging of saps and tunnels. Tom's company was not involved in this last, it was left to specialist troops, but there was always something and they worked all through the night, catching up on what sleep they could in the day. Shelling from both sides meant that they lived in a cacophony, a steady barrage of sound, with the occasional whine of a sniper's bullet to remind them to keep their heads down. Tin hats had been issued several weeks earlier, and the men had got used to their tin lids, but even so an unwary head above the parapet could prove fatal.

At the end of their four days, they had lost Dick Tamper, killed as he helped lay wire in front of the trench, and Mick Jones had been sent back down the lines with a shoulder wound. The rest of the platoon were relieved and edged their way back down the communication trenches and returned to their billets in the farmhouse outside Mesnil. Exhausted, they fell into the hay and slept, but when they awoke, there was no rest. Everywhere there were more and more men, guns being moved, sinking into the quagmire that so many roads had become. The preparations were fast and furious now, and the men had no time to think about anything as they practised their attack, not as they had attacked before in a rush of men, but in lines across at walking pace. They trained with other companies learning their combined attack formations, practised clearing enemy trenches with bombs and grenades, and always the normal fatigues, parades and duties.

When they had been back for three days, Tom was called up the farmhouse.

"Freddie Hurst wants to see you," Tony Cook told him when he'd found him in the barn reading his latest letter from Molly.

"What does he want, Cookie?"

Cookie shrugged. "Don't know mate," he replied. "Just said to find you and send you over. Wasn't full of sweetness and light. What you been up to then?"

"Don't know. Better go and find out."

Tom went across to the farmhouse and reported to Captain Hurst. The officer looked angry and said without preamble, "I've had a letter, Carter, from my sister. Do you know who my sister is?"

"Yes, sir."

"And where she is?"

"Yes, sir."

"She says it's her maid, Molly Day whom you've made pregnant. Is that right?"

"Yes, sir."

"And it was Molly Day who you wanted to go and marry when you spoke to me before?"

"Yes, sir."

"My sister is sending Molly home," Freddie Hurst said. "How could you get yourself and her into this mess, Carter?" Freddie spoke with angry frustration. "For God's sake, man, why couldn't you have kept your hands off her? It's a disgrace for her and for my sister. She brought her here to live in the convent where my aunt is a nun, a nun for God's sake, Carter, and you, having been nursed back to health in that very hospital, pay them back by putting one of their nurses in the family way. What the hell have you got to say for yourself, man?"

"I met Molly when I was in the hospital. We fell in love and wanted to get married, only Molly was under-age, see, so the padre said no. When I had three days' leave in March I went back to St Croix and we spent the afternoon together."

"And this baby is the result."

It was a statement, not a question and Tom nodded. "Yes, sir."

"My sister wants me to give you your two days, so that Molly can go home a respectable woman," Freddie said. "She's going to write to my father and explain the situation to him."

"Does she have to do that, sir?" asked Tom. "It'll make things very difficult for Molly."

"The idea is that it makes things easier," Freddie said coldly. "My sister will do what she thinks is best for Molly. She's very fond of the girl. She'll be left on her own at the convent now. She's determined to stay even when Molly has gone. However," he looked hard at Tom, "that decision has nothing to do with you. You realise, Carter, that I can't do what she asks, don't you? I can't give you a leave pass with the push about to start, whatever my sister insists." He managed a rueful smile. "What I will do is give you compassionate leave to go the moment this picnic is over. After the attack there will be supply units going back and forth. I will give you a permit to go back with one of them. Sarah will bring Molly to Albert on her way home. You'll have to meet there and find a padre who'll marry you. Maybe the one who's at the convalescent hospital, what was he called?"

"Mr Kingston."

"Yes, Kingston. Well, Carter, I'll write to Sarah and tell her what I've said," Freddie Hurst said, "but you'll report back to me within three days, understand."

"Yes, sir. Thank you, sir."

"Don't thank me, I think you're a damn fool. Thank my sister if you must, she seems to think well of Molly despite everything."

"Surely you know her as well, sir," ventured Tom.

"I do," agreed Freddie. "She's a maid in my home, but that's not why I'm letting you go."

He pulled a paper towards him and filled in the details of Tom's pass. "I don't know the date of the attack," he said. "Could be any day now. I've dated this for 8th July. Something should have happened by then, but if we haven't attacked by then, you can't go, understand?"

Tom said, "Yes, sir," and Freddie looked hard at him.

"You will tell no one about this, Carter. I don't want trouble with the other men. I'm giving you this much against my better judgement."

When Carter had left the room, Freddie Hurst sighed. He still knew he should not have issued a pass, but it was the thought of his own darling Heather, and their baby due in a couple of months which had persuaded him. Fear stabbed him, not for himself that he should be killed in the imminent offensive, but for Heather, a widow, his child left fatherless.

Threat of imminent death changes one's perspectives and priorities, Freddie thought. He knew why he had issued the pass, but even with that knowledge, he also knew it was a mistake.

Tom returned to the barn with the pass safely in his breast pocket. He was glad Cookie wasn't there to ask what Hurst had wanted. As it was, events overtook them so fast, that Tony Cook never gave Tom's summons another thought. They'd had their evening meal when they were told to fall in with all their kit. Tom had hoped to write to Molly telling her that he would be coming very soon, but instead he found himself marching with the rest of the platoon, heading back to the front line. The roads were clogged with troops, all moving up to the front, and the murmur throughout was that this was it. The big push. At last they were going to attack the German lines.

Monday, 26th June

My darling Molly,

As you will see I think it would be better for you to keep all the letters you have sent me so far. I would hate them to be lost and there is nowhere here I can keep them safe. So here they are, all except the last one which I will keep with me. I am sorry I will not see you for a while, but you will know that I think of you and our child all the time. You are my family. We are in our usual billets at present. Your cousin Tony is here and we are all in good heart.

Have you told Sarah yet? If you haven't, I think you should. She will be a good friend to you and see that you get home safely...

Nineteen

Molly knew that she would have to tell Sarah about the baby very soon. It would not be easy to travel home on her own. She needed to make proper arrangements and she knew she could not leave it much longer. Very soon her condition would start to show. She already felt that Sister Marie-Paul was assessing her with suspicious eyes.

She can't know anything yet, Molly told herself firmly, there is nothing to see.

Molly was right, there was nothing outwardly to show she was expecting. She had had to let her skirt out a couple of inches, and her breasts were fuller, but both these things were concealed by her voluminous apron. She was tired though. As she went about the ward she found herself longing to sit down, and if she did in the ward kitchen or the warmth of the linen cupboard, she dozed off at once, only to wake with a jolt and wonder how long she had been asleep and if anyone had noticed. Sister Marie-Paul would soon, unless she were very careful.

She decided not to tell Sarah until she heard from Tom. If he got the precious leave, then all would be well and it would only be a question of sorting out where they could be married. Each morning she prayed to a God she didn't really believe in, asking that Tom should be allowed to come to her, and

341

each day that no letter arrived she prayed again. When at last Tom's letter did come, saying that he had been refused any sort of leave for months to come, Molly had cried for the first time. She read the letter sitting on the lavatory, where she knew she would not be disturbed by anyone, not even Sarah. Tom had done his best, but now he could only offer her his advice.

> My darling girl, I think you should confide in Sarah now and begin to make arrangements for your journey home. It's not what I want, but I am sure in the long run it is best for you. I wish I could come to you straight away and hold you in my arms and tell you everything is going to be all right, but I can't. Remember that I love you more than life itself.
>
> Look after yourself and our little one. I send my love to you both,
>
> Tom

Molly sat staring at the letter, the words becoming blurred as the tears coursed unchecked down her cheeks. She was on her own. She told herself she regretted nothing, but the idea of returning home an expectant mother and unmarried, terrified her. The thought of her parents' home, bleak and cold in the valley, without the warmth of love to temper its coldness, filled her with dread. She knew Tom was right, but she kept putting off the day when she would have to admit to Sarah what had actually happened on the afternoon she had slipped away and Sarah had lied for her. Sarah would be so disappointed in her, and that mattered to Molly. She had always had great respect for Sarah when their relationship had been one of mistress and maid, but over their months together in France, as friends, she had come to love her.

Finally she braced herself and two evenings later she said, as casually as she could, "Sarah, I've got something to tell you."

After her first exclamation of horror, Sarah listened without interruption as Molly poured out what had happened.

"I know he'd come if he could," Molly repeated weakly as she finished. "He isn't deserting me, it's just that he can't."

"No," said Sarah coolly, "I don't suppose he can. So," she looked across at Molly, "what are you going to do?"

"I'd like to stay here, if I thought they'd let me," Molly said.

"Well, they won't," Sarah said flatly. "Apart from the fact of your disgrace, you'd be a liability. You wouldn't be able to help with the nursing. They can't spare anyone else to look after you and a baby."

"I'd look after the baby," Molly said stoutly.

"Of course you would. Even so, I'm sure you'll have to go home. It would be far better for you both if you go home." Sarah heaved a sigh and went on, "Oh Molly, how have you come to get into such a scrape? What on earth were you thinking of?"

"I love him," Molly replied.

"That's no answer," snapped Sarah.

"It is to me," Molly said simply. They fell silent for a while and then Molly said, "I know you don't understand, Sarah. I can't explain it to you. All I can tell you is that I don't regret it for minute. Not the love, not the baby. I am sorry it will be born without its father's name, but that can't be helped now. If we'd been able to get married before Tom went back everything would have been different."

"You couldn't, Molly. You know you couldn't. Even now you hardly know him, just through letters."

"It was all right for your brother to get married quickly when he was on leave, he's an officer." There was no mistaking the bitterness in Molly's tone. "He didn't have to wait. His wife is expecting too. That's all right, *he's* an officer. *She's* an officer's wife."

"Oh, come on, Molly," Sarah said impatiently. "Being an officer has nothing to do with it. You know that. They were on leave. They were both over twenty-one, the circumstances were not the same."

"So his baby is welcomed and mine is not."

"Molly, it's different..." began Sarah.

"Yes," agreed Molly wearily. "Isn't it always?"

"Look," said Sarah, "this isn't getting us anywhere. What we have to decide now is what we do next. Did Tom say why he was refused leave? I mean, they do give compassionate leave. Why not now?"

"I told you," Molly said, "there's going to be a big push any day now. They need every man there is. Hasn't Mr Freddie told you?"

"They can't say that sort of thing in letters," Sarah said. "I know almost nothing of what is going on."

"Well, from what Tom told me when he was here, and from what he's hinted at since, it's that they are going to attack the Germans very soon. A huge attack all the way along the front line. Until that is over and the Germans have been pushed back a long way they need every man they've got."

"When?" asked Sarah, her thoughts immediately with Freddie.

Molly shrugged. "Don't know," she said, "I don't think anyone knows, but it's soon. I told you what Tom had said at the time, remember?"

"I know, but that was weeks ago." She thought for a moment and then said, "Who did Tom go to? To ask for leave I mean?"

"Didn't I say? He went to Mr Freddie. He's his company commander. He told Tom that he couldn't possibly have leave now."

"Perhaps if I wrote to him," suggested Sarah, "explained how important it was he might change his mind. What do you think?"

"Oh, Sarah, would you? He'd listen to you. You could tell him we only need Tom for a day. I would go to Albert and meet him and then we'd get married and Tom would go back."

"It might make a difference," Sarah said, "but it might not. I'll write to him tonight, but you mustn't get your hopes up, Molly. He may not be able to do anything."

Molly grasped her hand. "Oh Sarah, I knew I could count on you. Tom told me to tell you, but I kept putting it off. I thought you'd be so angry with me."

"Well I am," said Sarah. "I'm condoning nothing that you and Tom have done, but I can't leave you to sort it out on your own." She gave Molly a fleeting smile. "I know if I were in any sort of trouble you'd help me. So, I'll write tonight, but I think we may have to tell Reverend Mother in the end. We have to explain why you are going home."

Before they put the light out the letter was written and in its envelope, waiting to be posted.

22nd June

Dearest Freddie,

I am writing to you about Molly Day and one of your soldiers. His name is Tom Carter, he's the private in your company whom you met when you were here. Molly and he met here in the hospital, fell in love and decided to get married. It wasn't possible before he had to return to the front and so they jumped the gun. Now Molly is expecting and though the man says he will stand by her, he can't get here to do the decent thing and she will have to go back to England to have the baby without benefit of clergy! Is there any possible way you can give him a 48-hour pass so that he can come down to Albert and we can get them married there. I think the padre here, Robert Kingston would marry them in the circumstances, both are of age now. Anyway, dear Freddie, please see what you can do. We understand the position at present, but surely one man for 48 hours wouldn't be too much to ask. I know you will say it is their own stupid fault that they are in this mess, and I agree, but Molly has been with us a long time and perhaps we owe her our help now. It would be a dreadful thing for her to go back home as an unmarried mother. She has been truly wonderful in our work here at the convent and certainly "done her bit". Also, they weren't lucky, like you, able to get married when they wanted to and I know their baby is just as important to them as yours is to you, and they so want it to have its father's name!

I know you will do what you can, and look forward to hearing from you soon. Take care, brother mine, especially over the next few days, your wife and baby need you as well…not to mention me!

Your loving sister, Sarah

It was sometime before Molly and Sarah had any more news from the front, and when it came it came in two pieces of mail; a trench postcard from Tom to Molly, telling her exactly nothing, and a scrawled note to Sarah from Freddie.

Wednesday, 28th June

Dear Sarah,

I've done the best I can. TC may be able to come to the town in a few days' time, but don't bank on it. If he's not there by the 15th July, send the silly girl home. She won't be the only one in her predicament while this war is on! Pray for me and for success in the coming weeks.

I have written to the governor and Heather. I send my love to you all.

Freddie

"He's done the best he can," Sarah told Molly, "but it doesn't sound very hopeful. His letter was dated 28th, something must have happened by now."

Four days later news began to filter back from the front of the grand offensive which had finally been launched. The sound of the artillery had rumbled round them for days, and continued an ever-present though remote thunder, and then the convoys of wounded began to arrive. Sister Magdalene went to Albert to meet the ambulances and the hospital trains, telling the medical staff who arrived there with their loads of wounded just how many they could accommodate at St Croix. She took Sarah with her to translate, and when they returned to the convent, they were both pale and shaken by what they had witnessed. Thousands of wounded were pouring in from every front, many simply to be transferred to trains and taken to the waiting hospital ships that plied non-stop across the channel with their broken cargoes.

The news that arrived with the wounded was very mixed. Some said that the push had been a great disaster. Others that the allies had broken through the German lines and though there were heavy casualties they had achieved their objectives; yet others that the battle was still raging with trenches changing hands and Germans launching a counter-attack. Most were only aware of what had happened to them and their mates, and for many who had survived the fateful attack on 1st July, the memories of it were haunting and terrifying. The wounds to their bodies were many and terrible, the wounds to their minds could not be reckoned.

All thoughts of tiredness gone, Molly and Sarah worked flat out in their wards trying to keep up with the injured men flooding in. The two medical officers from the convalescent camp spent their days in the convent hospital along with the overworked Dr Gergaud. Hours were spent in the operating theatre, and hours more in the wards with treatment and aftercare. The regular duty hours were gone as the nuns and the two girls snatched sleep as and when they could. Molly was no longer the only one with a tendency to fall asleep almost without warning, exhaustion caught up with all of them, and still the wounded flooded in.

Nothing was heard from Tom or Freddie. The chaotic state of affairs at the front persisted, with a handful of brave and exhausted men hanging on to their trenches in the face of a powerful enemy. Molly thought of Tom and could only pray that he had survived the carnage of the attack. If he had, he must be among the survivors who had been thrown back into the allied trenches to hold them against the expected German counter-attack. There were no men from the Belshires in the wounded that arrived at the convent, but several of the men that she and Sarah questioned said that the Belshires had been in the thick of it near Beaumont Hamel. There was no news of Freddie either, and Sarah found herself praying, a mantra in the back of her mind as she worked,

"Please God, let Freddie be safe. Please God, let Freddie be safe."

The 15th July came and went, but neither of them gave any thought to Molly going home now. She could not be spared, and if her condition became apparent to all, well, she told Sarah, she would deal with that when it happened.

June 30th

Dear Molly

    I am well. ~~I have been unwell.~~
    I received your letter
    ~~I received your parcel~~
    I will write again soon.

    I send my love, Tom

Twenty

The artillery barrage had been thundering round them for six days. Six days of unrelieved blasting from the great guns set two miles back from the front line. The men of the 1st Belshires arrived from their billets in the early morning, having trudged all night through the maze of communication trenches, bringing more supplies up to the front line with them. Their section of the front trenches ran through the last shattered trees of a copse, zigzagged and narrow, with little room for movement. Artillery had flattened almost every tree, leaving only occasional stumps pointing like accusing fingers to the sky. It lay in a small defile, so the ground gently sloped up and away from them towards the German lines less than a mile away at Beaumont Hamel. Wreaths of early mist twirled and drifted like smoke, hiding and exposing no-man's-land as it moved on the breeze. The men they relieved hurried thankfully back down the lines and the Belshires dug themselves in and waited. The pounding of the artillery continued non-stop, unending, head-banging thunder, crash and boom.

"If the bloody Hun don't know something's up by now," remarked Tony Cook gloomily as they stood to next morning, peering into the early morning mist, "they must be thicker than trench mud. When they finally decide to send us over, it's 'ardly going to come as a surprise now, is it?"

Young Davy Short, newly arrived in the platoon, in the front-line trench for the first time, looked across at him. "But surely, Cookie, no one could have survived that barrage, could they? I mean, it's been days now them guns 'ave been pounding 'em. Their trenches must have been all but flattened."

"Maybe." Tony Cook looked at the fresh face of the man, no, not a man, a mere boy. He couldn't be a day over seventeen, Tony thought, bitterly. They're sending us babies to fight now. He glanced across at Tom Carter. He and Tom had been together from the start. He and Harry and Tom had joined up together. They had trained with Hugh Broadbent, Charlie Fox, Jim Hawkes, Bill Jarvis, Peter Durrant, little Andy Nugent, and now there was only him and Tom left. Harry, Davy Potts, Will Strong, all gone, buried in a front-line grave or the mud of no-man's-land.

Tony Cook shifted his feet on the fire step and peered cautiously over the parapet. "What do you think, Tom?" he murmured, "Must be soon, eh?"

Tom nodded. With his leave pass tucked safely in his tunic pocket, he couldn't wait for the order to come. All this waiting was giving him too much time to think and his thoughts of Molly were driving him mad.

All day they were kept busy checking equipment, despite the fact that they'd had almost no sleep the night before, and when they finally stood down in the early evening and were eating a scratch meal, Captain Hurst came round with Sergeant Turner and the rum ration. As the sergeant dished out a double tot to each man, Captain Hurst spoke to them all.

"It's set for tomorrow," he told them quietly. "You know the drill. The barrage will continue, and there'll be smoke. The artillery will have destroyed the wire so there'll be no problem there. We move at a steady pace across no-man's-land to take the enemy trenches just as we've been practising. The artillery will have destroyed their machine gun positions, so once we're on the move we'll have very little opposition from the Hun. With no covering fire they'll have to evacuate their trenches, if there's anyone left alive to evacuate them."

So said Captain Hurst, but Tom wasn't sure he believed him any more than any of the others who had survived previous attacks; but for the new boys, the raw recruits brought up to the front-line trenches for the first time, like Davy Short, it was a rallying call, and the shuddering fear which had built up over the last dragging hours receded a little. Now the battle was upon them they could face the enemy with a certain courage; hearing that the way had been cleared before them and resistance would be non-existent, boosted their morale, so that when Captain Hurst finally blew his whistle they would scramble out of the trench and cross the desolation of no-man's-land with courageous and steady tread.

Before Hurst and the sergeant moved on along the trench, they handed trench postcards to the men, telling them that these were the only communication they would be allowed to send that day. Tom took his and with a stub of pencil crossed out the irrelevant lines so that his postcard to Molly simply read, "I am well. I will write again soon. I send my love," and he signed it, Tom. The postcards and other letters, letters of farewell written on the eve of this great battle to be sent only if the writer did not survive, were then collected up by Corporal Johns and passed back down the lines with other personal belongings screwed up into sandbags...to be returned later...or not.

The battalion padre came along the trench, speaking quietly to the waiting men. At the corner of a bay he met

Freddie Hurst, who clapped him on the back and said, "Smalley, you shouldn't be up here."

"I certainly should," the padre disagreed cheerfully. "Tomorrow I'll be at the dressing station, but tonight I wanted to come up here, just in case, well in case anyone wanted to talk to me before he goes over, you know?"

"Yes, I know," replied Captain Hurst. The two men shook hands, and the padre continued his round through the trench in one direction while Captain Hurst continued his in the other, each speaking softly, encouragingly, to the waiting men.

None of them got much sleep that night, as the barrage pounded on throughout the night. Each man checked again what was in the pack he must carry, shirt and socks, two days' iron rations, a bandage wrapped round a bottle of iodine, a bottle of water, a rolled groundsheet and a gas helmet. They were heavy packs and cumbersome, but they were only part of the load. As well as their packs, their rifles and entrenching tools, they carried a small haversack of grenades, ready to hurl into the German trenches as they reached them, to clear out any final pockets of resistance that there might be. Some carried rolls of barbed wire for fortifying captured trenches, others were laden with picks or shovels, wire cutters and empty sandbags. Extra ammunition had been issued, the bandoleers slung across shoulders and selected men carried Lewis guns to set up in the enemy trenches. Laden as they were, bayonets fixed, they would cross no-man's-land at no more than a steady walk, following the barrage of the artillery which would clear their way, pulverising the first then the second lines of enemy trenches, pushing the Germans before them.

Tom and Tony warmed their hands round a mug of tea heavily laced with rum as they waited in the grey dawn for the call to stand to.

"Should be a piece of cake," Tony said, "young Short is right. No one could have survived that barrage, what d'you bet we find the Huns all dead or better still gone?"

"Pray God we do," Tom said sincerely, "because if we don't..." his voice trailed away and he and Tony both thought about Harry and the others who had disappeared into the mists of earlier assaults and raids and had not survived.

They were gathered ready to move, hundreds of men crammed into the narrow front-line trenches, pushing up from the support trenches behind. As they shifted uneasily, waiting in the press of men for the signal to go, they were glad to be moving at last. Tony and Tom waited with the rest of the platoon on the fire step. Ahead of them another unit had crawled out over the parapet under the shelter of darkness and were even now lying concealed in no-man's-land ready, at the signal, to rise up and begin the attack. Behind, others waited to move forward as the second and third waves.

With ten minutes still to go before the attack was due to start the guns fell silent. So accustomed were they all to the constant boom and whistle of shells, the thud and crump of explosions all around them, that for an instant Tom wondered if he'd suddenly gone deaf. Silence rolled over the trenches like the smoke, which even then began to billow out from behind the lines in eerie spirals, seeping between the tree-stumps, enfolding them like a thick and heavy blanket. Tom glanced across at Tony who shrugged a shoulder, and then the air was shaken by a huge explosion; not the usual rumble or crump of an exploding shell, or the pounding crash of a heavy artillery gun, but an earth-shaking, sky-shattering bang, rolling on and on like an extended clap of thunder with echoing aftershocks.

"Christ!" exclaimed Tom almost falling backward with the sudden unexpectedness of it. "What the hell was that?"

Tony, equally stunned by the deafening boom, shouted over the dying echoes, "Sappers, I suppose. Must have blown a mine."

As the sound died away, the expectation reached fever pitch in the waiting trench. Smoke wreathed round them, wafting out through the little copse; it rolled out over no-man's-land, blanketing the bleak and barren land that lay before them, hiding the shell-holes, and smothering the barbed wire.

"For Christ's, let's get on with it," came a muttered cry, and this was echoed up and down the lines. It was time to attack, so why weren't they bloody attacking?

"They must know we are coming now," growled Tony, "What the hell are we waiting for?"

Beside him Hughes and Farmer, who were to carry the Lewis gun with them, heaved the gun up onto Farmer's shoulder, ready to haul it out as soon as Hughes was over the parapet. Hughes glanced across at Tony.

"You stick right with us, Cookie," he said nervously. "We need that ammo."

Tony, with two bandoleers of ammunition draped across his shoulders managed a grin. "Just don't you get lost in that smoke, mate," he retorted, "or I'll be hefting this lot for nothing!"

At last, just when it seemed that the order to attack would never come, Captain Hurst pushed his way through the crush of men to the bottom of a scaling ladder.

"It's over to you now, lads. This will be a glorious day, this first of July, and we'll make it ours." With that he blew a loud and long blast on his whistle, which in the instant was echoed all down the lines. The artillery barrage began again and, to the accompaniment of whistling shells and mortar fire, the Belshires rose up from their trench and, with a ragged cheer, followed Hurst up the scaling ladders and scrambled over the top.

Tony Cook turned back to help Hughes haul the Lewis gun from Farmer and then to heave him up over the edge. Tom was up beside them, scrambling to his feet and heading into the smokescreen, and then all hell was let loose as machine gun bullets ripped into the smoke and men began to fall. Tom pressed doggedly forward, aware of a man on either side of him. A savage rattle of machine-gun fire removed Davy Short from his left-hand side, bowling him over so that he disappeared into the smoke. Ignore the wounded, they had been told, and another man moved up beside Tom and they plodded onwards, rifles held in front of them, into the wall of sound and bullets. There was a crump behind him and Tom was pitched forward into a shell hole, while earth and metal rained down around him. He lay, his face pressed into the foul-smelling earth, his chest heaving as he tried to regain his breath and fought against the singing in his ears. How long he lay there he didn't know, probably only minutes, but it felt like eternity. At last he raised his head cautiously over the edge of the hole to look out on the battle raging around him.

The coils of wire had not been cut, the six-day barrage had done little to flatten it; the promised gaps for easy passage were not there, and as Tom peered out from the shelter of his hole, he could see men in their hundreds, stranded. The few carrying wire cutters struggled with the vicious wire, trying to force a way through, while the German machine gunners, from the undestroyed positions, trained their guns on the few gaps there were. Men crowded to push through, and the gunners continued to cut them to ribbons with sustained and rapid fire. Piles of bodies grew round the gaps; many hung like limp laundry on a line, wounded and dead together, easy target practice for the enemy gunners, their bodies ripped, fragments of flesh flying, combining with the ooze about them. Some men howled as they died slowly, the blood pumping from their bodies from severed arteries and gaping holes in head and chest; limbs were blown away as they called for aid, called for mothers and lovers, called on God or screamed pain-induced abuse. Others never knew the burst of bullets that ripped through them, they simply crumpled or pitched forward on to the ground in a heap; yet others were thrown on the wire, their bodies jerking and twirling on that grisly washing line.

Even as Tom watched, another wave of men came from behind at a steady walk and threw themselves into the supposed breaches in the wire, only to be mown down, falling as hay before the scythe, their bodies covering those already fallen, the wounded among the dying, the living among the dead. Still they came, pouring up out of the trenches as the shells whistled and thudded from behind the German lines, and the steady rattle of machine guns poured the scything bullets from the entrenched nests of German gunners set up along the line of battle, still concentrating their vicious fire upon the few gaps in the protecting wire.

The shriek of a shell made Tom dive down into the safety of his shell hole, and the explosion only yards away half buried him in flying muck and mud. Amid the din of the battle, he heard a new and closer sound, a man crying out for help, a man close at hand, his voice rising to a shriek. Once again, Tom risked his head above ground level, and saw that, where there had been rough ground, a low wall and a stunted tree, there was now nothing but a huge hole where the shell had landed. The cries were coming from there. Grasping his rifle again, Tom crawled from the relative security of his own hole, and, keeping his head as low as possible, scurried across the few yards of open ground and then flung himself over the edge of the next hole, landing heavily on two rag-doll bodies which lay in the bottom. They were both dead, one with half his head shot away, the other staring open-eyed at the sky as if watching for further shells. A third was cowering against the side of the hole, one leg severed at the knee, his foot in its boot lying in the dirt several feet away as if cast aside, the blood pumping out of the wound in steady, rhythmic jets. He held both hands across the stump of his leg as if trying to keep the blood inside and to stem the flow, and his hands and arms were bathed in his own, ever-flowing, blood. It was his cries that Tom had heard, the screams of a terrified boy, dying alone.

Tom ripped off his pack and webbing and grabbing the field dressing from the pack, tried to hold it in place over the stump.

"Hold this, hold this," he screamed at the man, as he wound a piece of bandage round the leg and tried to twist it into a tourniquet, twisting and twisting again to cut off the blood, and the life, flowing from the boy. For a moment it seemed that nothing would work

It's got to be tighter! thought Tom in panic. He grabbed the wooden handle of his entrenching tool from his webbing and forced it through the bandage, twisting viciously, so that his makeshift tourniquet finally tightened enough to do its job, and Tom saw the flow ease and stop. The boy fainted, his hands fell away from the blood-soaked dressing he'd been trying to hold, and Tom could see the ragged end of the leg, cut through above the knee, white bone projecting, jagged, through the mangled flesh. He turned away and was sick, throwing up the contents of his stomach into the glutinous mud in which he sat. Then he heard a moan and realised that the wounded boy was beginning to come round. The remains of the lad's pack was underneath him. Swiftly Tom pulled it free and took out the field dressing it contained, bandaging it as securely as he could over the exposed stump. He knew he must keep the wound covered if they were to try to get back to their own trenches and find help. His ministrations made the boy pass out again, and Tom was glad, for he knew the pain must be unbearable.

There was nothing else he could do for him here, and there was little possibility of moving him back behind the lines until darkness fell and stretcher parties came out into no-man's-land to drag the wounded back to safety...if stretcher parties did come. He looked more carefully at the man and saw that he was indeed a lad of about seventeen; his face, now deathly pale, had the unformed lines of youth about the chin and mouth. His ears stood out like jug handles, all the more prominent because his hair was plastered to his head with mud. Most of his uniform was gone, ripped away by the blast, and his shirt hung in shreds about his scrawny shoulders. The sun was up now, a blazing disc in a clear blue sky, burning off the coolness of the early morning mist. Tom knew the temperature would rise steadily and with no shelter from its pitiless heat at midday, any wounded would stand little chance without water and care. Tom looked at the youth and was suddenly determined to keep him alive. If the bleeding had really stopped, there was still a chance he might be saved. Tom peered at his makeshift bandage, and saw that it still seemed to be in place, and was not completely saturated with blood, so presumably the tourniquet was doing its job, but despite the heat, the lad was shivering violently. Somehow he must be kept warm. Stripping off his own tunic, Tom wrapped it round the inert body, pushing the arms into the sleeves to help hold it in place. The boy moaned, but didn't regain consciousness. Tom looked anxiously at the tourniquet. He remembered Molly had told him that tourniquets must be loosened from time to time so that gangrene did not set in, but how often and after how long? Tom had no idea but he was afraid to release it now, terrified that the blood would start pulsing again. Rather than lose any more blood and face certain death, the boy would have to run the risk of the tourniquet. Tom propped him up as best he could, and while he was still out for the count he checked to see if there were any more injuries that needed attention. He could see none, but as he ran his hands over the boy's chest he felt the identification dog-tags hanging at his throat. He peered at them and found that he was trying to save the life of Private Sam Gordon.

"Hold on, Sam," he ordered the slumped figure. "Just you hold on and we'll get you out of here." Then he turned his attention to the two other bodies, and found their tags as well. Private John Dewar and Corporal David Shapwick. Tom looked at them. Should he take the tags with him, knowing that it was unlikely they would be recovered otherwise, or should he leave them with the bodies in the hope that they would be recovered for burial and thus identified? Tom didn't know. Their only hope would be if the attack had achieved its aims and that the battle lines were now redrawn, with their shell-hole in friendly territory. He eased his head above the edge of the hole. The smoke from the guns mingled with the smokescreen, forming a curtain across the ground. He couldn't see anything but ragged mist, forming and re-forming, giving glimpses of the wire, still festooned with bodies and parts of bodies, but for the moment no more men were appearing from behind. Perhaps the rest of the attack had been called off, or all those attacking from these forward trenches had already passed through to the German lines. It was impossible to tell.

All round him the sounds of battle still raged, the unremitting pounding of the heavy guns, the whistles and booms of the shells, the clatter of the machine guns, none of them abated; yet Tom could see nothing. He dropped back down beside the wounded boy. Sam's breathing was harsh and ragged, his face deathly, the face of an old man.

If I am going to get him back to safety it has to be now, thought Tom. I can't shift him alone, so I'll have to crawl back to the trench and bring a stretcher-bearer back with me.

He looked at the haft of the entrenching tool, twisted into the tourniquet and decided to leave it there. There was a rifle sticking out from underneath Corporal Shapwick. Tom pulled it free and tying a rag from Sam's shirt to it, left it projecting a foot from the shell hole as a marker. He wanted to be quite sure that he and the stretcher-bearer would be able to find the hole again. Then, clutching his own rifle, he scrambled up over the lip of the hole, and, in crouching run, scurried back the way he thought he had advanced that morning.

Tom heard the shell, screaming its way through the murk, and once again dived flat in an instinctive effort to save himself, and then there was the boom of impact and explosion and the world went black.

When he came round again, Tom had no idea how long he had been unconscious, but it must have been some hours as the day was fading into twilight. He lay, more than half buried, with only his head and shoulders and right arm free, a weight of earth and debris pinning his lower body and legs. It was hard to breathe, and there seemed to be no feeling in his feet. Cautiously he wriggled his shoulders and moved his arm. Some of the earth fell away, and he pulled his other arm free. The noise of battle was intermittent now, with the whistle and crash of shells, and the occasional burst from a machine gun, not the ever-present thunder of earlier, but in the swirling smoke he could see nothing and no one; he could have been alone in the world. He scrabbled at the constraining earth with his hands, gradually shifting the stones and earth that imprisoned him. It was slow work as he could only reach so far, but at last he managed to loosen himself enough to lever himself to a sitting position and then finally to ease himself free. He lay for a long moment face down on the ground, exhausted by his exertions, and completely disorientated. His feet began to tingle and then to ache as the blood was restored to them, but he welcomed the pain, he knew it meant that there was no permanent damage done.

He had a sudden vision of a severed leg, still in its boot and he remembered with a jolt, the dying Sam Gordon. Trying to orientate himself, Tom raised his head and looked round in all directions for the shell hole in which he had left the boy. He had no idea from which direction he had come. There was no sign of the rifle with its tiny flag, no sign of the shell hole. The shell that had buried Tom must have finished the work of its predecessor; Sam Gordon, David Shapwick and John Dewar had vanished, they had been completely obliterated. There would be nothing left of them to find or to bury, their burial had been completed by a German shell. Tom didn't even have their identity discs. Their names in his memory would have to be enough.

His rifle had vanished and without any weapon, his pack or his tunic and his uniform in rags, Tom decided it was better to go back rather than forward. He had seen the everlasting coils of wire still stretching out between him and the day's objective, and knew there was little likelihood of him getting through them, let alone achieving anything useful even if by some miracle he did make it. The coming dark and the mist added to his disorientation. Which way was forward? Which way was back? With the guns thundering from both sides of the line, it was impossible to tell from which direction he had come.

Still shaking from his efforts to drag himself free, Tom knew only that he had to get away from where he was. Keeping his head as low as he could, he began to crawl. Slowly he dragged himself across the uneven ground; he tried to move in a straight line back to where he thought the British lines must be. Downhill must be right, they had been moving up a slight incline this morning. There were shapes and shadows in the swirling mist, but when Tom called out to them his voice was swallowed by the thunder around him. Here were men, the remains of men, the debris of human bodies; flotsam tossed aside, grotesque in death. He could hear an occasional scream or cry, a voice begging for water, but Tom knew there was nothing he could do for the wounded man who uttered them. He had no field dressings, no water bottle, his own clothes were in rags; the shreds of his shirt wouldn't even supply a makeshift bandage. He shut his ears to their pleas, and continued to make his way tortuously across the battlefield, at times falling into shell holes as the ground gave way in front of him, at others, crawling round them, becoming muddier and more exhausted by the minute. Once he saw the sprawled figure of a man he actually recognised, Sid Jackson, a private from his own platoon. Sid's face was twisted to the sky, his eyes staring, his mouth open on a shriek of pain. Gently Tom closed the wild eyes, and crawled on, but to his horror, what felt like hours later, he found himself face to face with Sid's lifeless body again. He had been crawling round in circles.

Tom collapsed full length on the ground beside Sid, and wept. He wept for himself and for Sid and the thousands of others he knew must have died that day. He thought of the thousands at home waiting for those who would never come back and he thought of Molly, his Molly, so pretty and bright and clean. He remembered the way her eyes shone as they laughed up into his own, the shy way she had kissed him and the passion that had followed. He thought of the child, his child, that she carried, and of his promise to marry her. They would be a family, he and Molly and the baby, a real family and it would be the first he'd ever known. For Molly and the baby he had to pull himself together and get out of here. In his tunic pocket was the permit to travel back to Albert and the convent, for forty-eight hours' precious leave. Forty-eight hours in which they would marry, after which Molly would go back to England to have their baby in the safety of her parents' home. Tom knew he had to get back, behind the lines, back to the convent, back to Molly. Even as these thoughts made him raise his head, he realised with a stab of panic and despair, that his special leave pass had been left with Sam Gordon in his shell hole. Intent on keeping the wounded man warm, he had wrapped his service tunic round Sam's shoulders, and when he had been obliterated by the German shell, so the tunic and the leave permit had been obliterated with him. The precious letter of leave, Molly's last letter and her photograph; he had kept them all in the pocket over his heart and now they were gone. He gave a bellow of fury and despair. There would be no leave.

Molly. She was now his aim and his talisman. He had no idea where his unit was, if indeed there was anything left of it to be anywhere. Tom's sole intention now was to get back to safety behind his own lines. Molly needed him.

Once more he set himself to crawl back over the battlefield, and as the charcoal of early evening deepened into night, he gradually edged himself clear. The barrage seemed to have lessened, though there was still sporadic gunfire and the occasional whistle and crump of a shell.

At last he came to the edge of a trench, not a firing trench, nor living quarters, perhaps a communication trench, or a sap pushed out into no-man's-land for a listening post, or to give some sort of shelter to the sappers. It was hardly more than a slit in the ground, but Tom dived into it with relief, able to move at a crouch in its cover. He saw no one; there was no sign of life, no sign of death, indeed no sign that anyone had ever been there, except for the hardened, churned mud which lay along it. Rough going though it was, Tom made swifter progress here than he had on the ground above. He had no idea where it led, but clearly it was going somewhere, so he followed, hoping it led to safety, but before long the trench petered out, becoming shallower until he was crawling once more above the ground. The summer darkness surrounded him, but the feeble starlight showed him the emptiness of a lunar landscape. All he could see before him was a flat and blighted land, pitted with craters and broken earth. Round him were the sounds of war. Though the crashing boom of the artillery was intermittent, the darkness was still punctuated with the occasional rattle from machine guns on either side and the single, angry rifle shots of the snipers; and all the while there were the sounds of men, moans and cries, scufflings and scrabblings like the rats which scuttled about the trenches.

I must get back behind our lines, Tom thought desperately, but which way? He crept cautiously through the darkness, making very slow progress as he skirted shell holes and crawled over the wreckage of battle, edging his way towards what he thought were the British lines. Occasionally a flare exploded into the sky and hung there illuminating the earth below in horrifying detail. Each time, Tom froze, lying motionless, face down, like so many around him who would never move again, until the merciful darkness covered him once more and he could begin to crawl forward again.

Suddenly he was aware of soft voices nearby, only yards away. Once more he froze, straining to hear what language they were speaking. It was clearly a stretcher party that had crawled out into no-man's-land to search for wounded, but from which side? A sharp cry of "Oh God!" hastily stifled, told him they were British, and he edged towards them over the pockmarked ground.

"Who's that?" The challenge came sharply through the darkness. "Who's that? I can hear you. Show yourself."

Tom was about to do exactly that, when there was the whistle and crump as a shell hurtled to earth and exploded close by, blowing them flat, knocking the wind from them and setting their ears singing. As Tom shook his head, trying to clear it, he heard the same voice rasp, "Come on, mate, let's get you out of here." There was the sound of scuffling, grunting and a deep moan as the wounded man was heaved onto the stretcher, and then the whole scene was flooded with light from a bursting flare above the enemy lines. Tom saw the stretcher party grasp the handles of the stretcher and make off at a crouching lope away from him, zigzagging round the shell holes and stumbling over debris which barred their way to the safety of the British lines. Tom followed, also running at the crouch to the illusory safety of a shell hole. As he dropped into its shelter, he heard a husky voice coming from a parched throat, and, in the light of the still blossoming flare, he saw a white face, only inches away, peering at him.

"Give us a hand, chum," said the voice, calmly.

The very calmness off the voice made Tom pause. He reached out a hand and was greeted with a tired grin. "Glad you could drop in," the voice drawled. "Can't get out of this bloody hole; legs don't work." The control in the voice faltered for a moment, and the owner added, "Have you got any water?"

Tom found his voice at last. "No, sorry, no water. But I'll get you back to the dressing station. How bad is it?"

"Legs broken," came the reply, with only the slightest waver in its tight control. "Both buggered."

For a moment the vision of Sam Gordon flooded Tom's mind, the pumping blood and the severed leg, but he forced it aside. Clearly this man's wounds were different or he'd be dead already.

"Can you take any weight?" asked Tom.

"Doubt it, but I'll try."

"What's your name?" Tom asked as he knelt beside the man and prepared to lift him.

"Jimmy Cardle...at your service!" Jimmy drew a sharp breath as the movement jolted his injured legs.

"Well, Jimmy, hang on to me and I'll get you home."

Tom gathered Jimmy in his arms and heaved him up over the edge of the shell hole. There was an agonised moan and then Tom felt Jimmy go limp as he passed out.

Best thing, thought Tom as he scrambled up beside him. The darkness had reclaimed the field, but guns were never silent. Trying not to listen to the staccato fire around him, Tom heaved the unconscious man up on to his shoulder and with Jimmy draped across him, his useless legs dangling behind, Tom set off awkwardly in the direction that the stretcher party had taken moments before.

It was not easy to cover the broken terrain, Jimmy was a big man and heavy, the ground under foot was treacherous, but as his eyes had adjusted to the darkness again, Tom could make out the front line of trenches ahead. As he approached he saw another stretcher party crawling out to search for more wounded. There was the rattle of a machine gun and the zip of rifle fire and even as the men came forward, they pitched into crumpled heap and lay still. Terrified, Tom fell, tumbling to the ground with Jimmy, mercifully still unconscious, on top of him. He expected, any moment, to be ripped from behind with another burst of fire, but at that moment a burst of firing came from a position in the British trenches, and, taking advantage of the possible cover this might give him, Tom crawled backwards towards his own lines, dragging Jimmy Cardle, his broken legs bumping over the rough ground behind him, yelling as he came, "Wounded coming in! Don't shoot, wounded coming in!"

"All right, mate, bring 'em in," called back a voice, and Tom made the last few yards at the crouch, Jimmy still hoisted awkwardly over his shoulder. As he reached the trench, hands reached up to grab him and help him haul Jimmy down into the relative safety it offered.

"Well done, man," said an admiring voice as Tom collapsed on to the duckboards below the fire step. "That was a brave effort. Are you wounded too?"

Tom looked up to see a lieutenant he didn't recognise, bending over him and taking in his sorry state. "No, sir," he replied. "But this bloke is bad."

"We'll get him to the dressing station," said the lieutenant, and turning round called down the trench behind him,

"Stretcher!" He turned back to Tom and passed him a water bottle. Tom grabbed it and drank greedily. Jimmy Cardle moaned beside him and Tom reached over and dribbled some of the water between the man's lips.

"It's all right, Jimmy. You're safe now," Tom reassured him. "You're back behind the lines. We'll get you fixed up in no time."

The lieutenant looked down at the two men and called again, "Stretcher! Stretcher here, men." Still no one came, and then a small man, white-faced in the light of yet another flare, hurried up carrying a stretcher.

"Howes and Norris have gone, sir," he gasped. "They just mowed them, sir, just mowed them." His voice cracked on the words as he went on, "Them Huns must've seen they was a stretcher party going out for the wounded. Must have. Just mowed 'em down. Fuck the bloody lot of them I say! Fuck the bloody lot of them!" Tom could see the tears coursing down the little man's face, and knew tears to be rising in his own eyes, but the lieutenant said harshly, "Sharpen up, Jones; man here needs you." He glanced down at Tom and said, "You too. Name and unit?"

"Carter, sir, 1st Belshires."

"Right, Carter, you and Jones take this man back to the dressing station...and keep your heads down. Where's your helmet, man?" he added as an afterthought.

Tom waved vaguely towards no-man's-land. "Out there somewhere, sir, with the rest of my uniform." The officer disappeared into a nearby dugout and reappeared with a grubby shirt and a grubbier tunic and tossed them to Tom.

"Put these on," he said, adding as Tom shrugged himself gratefully into the clothes, "and find yourself another tin hat...first opportunity. Now off with you." He turned away and moved on up the trench, speaking to the men who were standing on the fire step trying to give some cover to the wounded crawling back to the lines and the stretcher bearers who went out to their aid.

Jones and Tom lifted Jimmy Cardle on to the stretcher, trying to arrange his legs to lie along the length of it and not stick out at the strange angles they seemed to want to choose for themselves.

"I'll take the front," Jones said. "On three, lift."

They set off through a maze of communication trenches, away from the front line, twisting their way back to the sunken road that led to the remains of a farmhouse that was being used as an advanced dressing station. Men coming the other way stood aside for the stretcher, averting their eyes from the man who lay upon it. Tom had no idea where he was, it was not the section of the line where he had been before the attack, but Jones seemed to know his way through the maze and when they reached the farm house Tom thought he remembered passing such a building on the way up to the front three days earlier. Was it only three days? It seemed like an eternity since they had threaded their way up trenches just like these to take up their positions in the front line. Where was the rest of his unit? Cookie, Hughes and Farmer with their Lewis gun? Captain Hurst, Sergeant Turner, Corporal Snotty-nosed Johns? Had they got through, or had they been blown away like poor Davy Short, dead within minutes of leaving the trench? Where should I go to find them, Tom wondered? Where do I begin to look?

When they reached the dressing station it was shambolic, as wounded streamed in from all parts of the line. Some, badly injured like Jimmy Cardle, lay on stretchers in patient agony for attention, assessment and first aid before being loaded on to ambulances for the long and bumpy journey back to the casualty clearing stations and field hospitals. Behind the farmhouse, in the shelter of a sunken road, some horse ambulances were being loaded with wounded, ready to start that dangerous journey. They were still well within range of the enemy artillery and nowhere this close to the German line was safe from shells and whizzbangs; death could still scream in from the sky.

Other men, less seriously hurt, were sitting in groups trying to keep their spirits up as they waited for their wounds to be dressed and bandaged. All were in pain, but few cried out. The occasional scream came from within the farmhouse, and those outside shuddered inwardly and thought, "Some poor bugger..."

Jones and Tom put the stretcher down with the other stretcher cases, and Tom gave Cardle's name to a harassed orderly and told him what he knew of the injuries. When he turned round Jones had disappeared into the throng.

Tom felt dog-tired, but his brain was racing as he decided what he should do next. He, too, faded into the crowd before anyone could give him anything else to do. His one object was to get back to the hospital at St Croix and find Molly. He had leave, he told himself firmly. Captain Hurst had said he could go back with a supply party once the push was over. Well, he, Tom, had made his push and been pushed back. He had brought in a wounded man from the field, and he hadn't a clue where the rest of his unit, if indeed there was any "rest", was now. He didn't even know where he was. Once again his brain played back the vision of the men caught on the wire, blown away by the interlocking fire of the enemy machine guns. He forced his mind away from them, would not allow himself to think about them, nor to listen to their cries that still rang in his ears. The sight of Sam Gordon rose unbidden to his memory, and he turned away from the sight of the wounded strewn about him outside the little farmhouse. He had done his bit, and though he was quite prepared to do more, it would not be until he had got back to St Croix and to Molly.

First stop must be Albert. He could find St Croix and the convent once he got there.

If I can just get to Albert, he thought, I can be in St Croix in a couple of hours. He thought about Jimmy Cardle and wondered if he'd make it. Surely his was a Blighty one, he'd be going home, his war over, that was if he survived the journey. Tom thought about the ambulances that would jolt off down the tracks taking the wounded out of immediate danger.

That was when the idea came to him. Though aching and exhausted, he heaved himself to his feet and made his way back to where the ambulances were being loaded. Stretcher cases were being slotted inside, and then the drivers were heading out along the sunken road to the tracks and roads that led away from the front. As he watched an ambulance began to move off. The next was still being loaded and he climbed up beside the driver who didn't seem at all surprised to see him.

"You Henderson's relief?" he asked.

"Yes, Carter," replied Tom, wondering who Henderson was and why he had been relieved, but not questioning this piece of luck.

"Right," said the driver, "I'm Gerard," and they pulled away.

"Complete shambles," remarked Gerard as they trundled down the track. "Complete cock up."

Tom nodded his agreement, but said nothing. He didn't want to get drawn into conversation with this man. Although they were moving away from the front line, they were not out of danger yet. A shell whizzed over their heads and exploded in the field beside them. The blast made the horse rear up, it heavy hooves pounding the ground as it plunged in the shafts. Gerard leapt down to quieten it, soothing it with his hands and voice, before they could continued their plodding way down to the casualty clearing station.

Here, too, all was chaos, with wounded pouring in from all fronts. The ambulances lined up to be unloaded, and as their turn came, Tom and Gerard lifted their stretchers down and carried them over to where others were already in rows on the ground, waiting. When the final stretcher was out, Gerard went round to the front and led the horse away.

"I'll give him his nose bag and a drink at the trough," Gerard said, "You go and get us some grub." He pulled a couple of mess tins from under his seat and handed them to Tom, waving his hand vaguely in the direction of a large hut. Tom headed to the hut, suddenly aware that he hadn't eaten since dawn and that he was starving. The hut was hot and crowded. Tom took the mess tins to a counter where an orderly dished out some sort of hot stew. Tom carried the tins outside where Gerard found him and together they polished off the hot food in double quick time. It was nearly sunrise again, the sky was lightening in the east and the ambulances were continuing to roll in.

"Time to go," Gerard said. "Just got to go and splash my boots." He headed off towards the latrines and Tom turned in the other direction. He headed into the mêlée of men, losing himself among the shadows, so that when Gerard returned to drive his ambulance back to the front for more wounded, Tom was nowhere to be seen. With a job to be done, Gerard shrugged and swung himself up behind the horse and headed off alone to collect more men.

From the shelter of the mess hut, Tom watched him drive away and then set off himself. He needed to be well away from the clearing station before it was full daylight. The rising sun told him which way was east and he struck out south across country towards Albert, St Croix and Molly.

10th July

My darling Molly,

I am writing to you from near the town where we were going to meet, where I am under arrest at present. Sarah's brother did give me a pass in the end, but I lost it in the battle, and so until they find out from him for sure I have to stay here. I am well treated and have exercise, but the rest of the day is a bit boring. But it won't be for long, I am sure. It does mean that I shan't be able to come to you as we'd hoped. You must go home, my darling girl, and I will come and find you as soon as I can...

Twenty-one

Tom walked steadily for nearly two hours and then knew he could go no further. He had made his way cross-country. The roads and lanes were crammed with troops and equipment moving both up to the front and away from it; a steady and rather confused traffic of marching men, limbers, double-decker buses packed with troops, ambulances, staff cars and occasional heavy artillery. Vehicles were going in both directions and it seemed to Tom far easier to stay off the roads, he could move more quickly and now the only thing his mind focused on was getting to Molly. There would be no meeting in Albert as originally planned, she would have no idea that he was coming, he must find her at the convent.

At last his legs refused to carry him further and he looked round for somewhere he could rest up for a while, just catch a couple of hours' sleep. Amid the twisted tree stumps of what had once been a copse at the edge of a field, Tom could see the remains of some sort of building. Summoning up the last of his strength he plodded over to it. It was indeed a ruin, but the gaping hole in its back wall gave access to the welcome shelter of three walls and half a roof. Tom crawled inside, and found to his amazed delight that there were some wisps of straw strewn on the floor. It was damp and smelt of mould, but never had a bed seemed so welcoming. Raking it together with his fingers, he dragged the wet and smelly strands into the corner beneath the roof, and collapsed on to it, instantly asleep.

He woke hours later with the evening sun slanting in on his face, his body stiff and cold, his teeth chattering and his head pounding. For a moment he looked blankly around him and then the previous day flooded back to him, the mud and the blood, the shattered bodies and Sam Gordon dying in a shell-hole; Jimmy Cardle on his back, the nightmare journey with the ambulance.

Exhaustion claimed him and Tom lay back on the dank straw and tried to take in his surroundings. Three walls, jagged-edged where the stones had fallen away and sloping steeply were all that had sheltered him, with the remains of a thatched roof hanging precariously from broken rafters above him. The fourth wall had collapsed into a heap of rubble, beyond which Tom could see the sky, a gleaming, polished blue shot with the crimson and flame of sunset, stretching away into the distance. Somewhere beyond the rubbled wall he could hear a trill of birdsong, a sound that seemed to the bemused Tom completely alien... how could there be birds on a battlefield? For far away still playing out their thunder, he could hear the guns, the ever-present accompaniment to his life in the past weeks. He raised his head again, heaving himself up on to his elbow, but his head reeled with the effort of it, and he dropped back again closing his eyes. He could feel the last rays of the sun on his face, but it didn't warm him, he felt chilled to the bone and his whole body seemed to be shaking, and yet he was covered in sweat.

Trying to concentrate on what he should do next, Tom realised that he was incredibly thirsty. His mouth was dry and his tongue stuck to the roof of his mouth. He tried to swallow, but had nothing to swallow with. Once he had recognised it, his thirst seemed to increase until it threatened to consume him. He had had nothing to eat or drink since dawn at the casualty station, and though he felt no hunger, his thirst dried his throat to a rasping ache. Water became his only concern, and again he made the effort to get up. He was in an animal shelter after all, maybe there was a trough somewhere, perhaps outside, or even a hollow in the rubble of stones where rain might have gathered. He dragged himself across the muddy floor towards the collapsed wall, and hauled himself up to peer over it. The country stretched away before him, flat fields, their emptiness only broken by occasional clumps of stunted trees, broken stone walls and tattered hedgerows. Beside the barn was a single tree, leafless and gnarled, and it was from the branches of this that the thrush was singing its evening song. Beneath it was a small wooden trough, its water oily-surfaced in the sun. With immense effort, Tom pulled himself to his feet and staggered across to the trough. At his movement the thrush flew away in alarm, but Tom's whole being was focused on the water. He reached the trough and kneeling beside it, scooped the brackish water into his parched mouth. It tasted foul and he almost threw up, but after a moment he forced himself to drink a little more. Then he collapsed back against the tree and, closing his eyes, sleep claimed him once again.

"Aye, aye! What have we here?"

The guttural voice jerked Tom awake and he looked up to see two military policemen standing over him, each with a rifle in his hand.

One, with sergeant's stripes on his arm asked, "What are you doing here, son?"

Tom stared up at him for a moment and then said, "I'm on my way to Albert."

"Oh you are, are you? On your feet, man. Name and number?"

"Private 8523241 Thomas Carter, 1st Battalion, Belshire Light Infantry, Sarge."

"Well, Private Carter, why are you here on your own and not with your regiment?"

"Don't know where they are, Sergeant."

The sergeant's voice hardened a little as he said, "What do you mean, Carter? Don't know where they are. You deserted, have you?"

"Course not!" Tom was stung by the suggestion. "I was sent to carry this bloke to the dressing station."

"Ain't no dressing station round here," pointed out the sergeant.

"No. I know. Then I came down with an ambulance to the casualty clearing station. I've come from there."

"Why didn't you go back up with the ambulance?"

"I had to get to Albert," said Tom. He wondered if he should say he had a leave pass. They wouldn't believe him and he couldn't produce it. It had disintegrated with Sam Gordon. Tom blinked hard to banish the vision of Sam Gordon and his leg in the shell-hole.

"Why Albert?" It was the other MP who spoke for the first time. "Why not back to the front to find your mates?"

"My mates are strung out on the wire in no-man's-land," Tom said bleakly. "My mates are blown to smithereens by Jerry shells. My mates are ripped to shreds by machine gun bullets. That's why I can't go back to my mates."

"Afraid, are you?" asked the MP.

"Course I'm afraid, we're all bloody afraid. Anyone who says he isn't is lying." He looked at the MP red caps and said, "You wouldn't know. You weren't there. There were others like you there, standing back ready to shoot any poor bloke who held back."

It was the wrong thing to say and the sergeant said abruptly, "Well, you're coming with us. You're under arrest, Carter, for desertion." He prodded Tom with his rifle barrel and said, "Start walking."

Weak though he was, Tom fell in between the two policemen and was marched down a track that ran past the far side of his barn to a road beyond. In the distance he could see the buildings of Albert, the cupola of its basilica standing defiantly against the guns, topped by the golden Madonna still leaning out at right angles above the rubbled square below.

Tom was taken to a command post where the MPs passed him over to an officer.

"Private 8523241 Thomas Carter, 1st Belshires, sir. Trying to desert," said the sergeant. "Hiding in a barn."

The nightmare began. The officer, Major Gyles of the military police, looked at Tom, standing to attention before him, dishevelled, unshaven, his uniform filthy. He took in the red-rimmed eyes and the grey pallor of his skin and knew that the man in front of him was on the point of exhaustion.

"Well, Carter," he kept his voice even, "what have you to say for yourself, man? Were you deserting your comrades?"

The major was a young man, with smooth dark hair and a neat moustache. His eyes, dark brown and deep set, probed Tom's face as he asked the question.

"No sir," Tom said. "Never, sir."

"So why were you hiding in a barn?"

"I wasn't hiding, sir," replied Tom. "I was resting up, before coming on to Albert."

"Where had you come from?" asked Major Gyles. "Where is your regiment?"

"At the front, sir. Beaumont Hamel, sir."

"So why aren't you with them, Carter?"

"We went over, sir, on the first day. Most of my lot were blown away, sir.

"But you survived." Major Gyles's voice hardened. "How was that, Carter?"

"I was blown flat by a shell, sir. When I came round, I was half buried and I had to dig myself out. By the time I'd done that there wasn't no attack any more."

"So you just scuttled on back to the safety of your own lines."

"No sir. It was getting dark by then. Stretcher bearers was coming out for the wounded. I found one bloke, Jimmy Cardle, in a shell-hole, both his legs broken. I carried him in, sir."

"Back to your own unit."

"No, sir. Everything was so confused out there, with the smoke and the shells and bodies everywhere. I didn't know which way to go at first. I must have crawled round in a circle, because I saw Sid Johnson twice."

"Sid Johnson?"

"A bloke from our unit, sir. He was dead in a hole, sir. I saw him and went on trying to get back and then I saw him again."

"So what did you do then?"

"Followed a stretcher party, sir. That's when I found Jimmy Cardle. I took him back to the trench. I kept shouting, 'Bringing in wounded,' so that they wouldn't think we was Jerries, sir."

"Who was in the trench?" asked the major. His face had relaxed a little as Tom told his story, but his gimlet eyes still bored into Tom.

"An officer, sir. A lieutenant."

"What was his name?"

"Don't know, sir.

"From your regiment?"

"No, sir, Irish I think, sir."

"What did he say to you?"

"He told me to help a stretcher-bearer called Jones take Jimmy Cardle down to the dressing station. He gave me a shirt, sir and a tunic."

"Why did he do that?"

"Mine was gone, sir, I was just in my shirt and that was in tatters."

"So he gave you the tunic you have on now?"

"Yes, sir, and told me to find myself a tin hat."

"But you didn't."

"No, sir. We took Jimmy Cardle down to the dressing post."

"Then what did you do?"

Tom thought for a moment and then said, "Jones disappeared…"

"Where did he go?"

"Don't know, sir, back to the front-line trench, I suppose."

"And why didn't you go with him?"

"I went to the ambulance line, sir."

The major looked puzzled. "Why on earth did you go there?"

"I had to get to Albert, sir. I helped take an ambulance down to the casualty clearing station."

"Why did you think you had to get to Albert, Carter?" The hardness returned to the major's voice. "Why didn't you make every effort to rejoin your unit, or what was left of it?"

"I had a pass, sir."

"A pass?"

"A compassionate leave pass, sir."

"Leave!" The major was incredulous. "Leave, in the middle of the greatest battle of the war?"

"Yes, sir."

"Who gave you this 'leave'?"

"Company commander, sir, Captain Hurst."

"I don't believe you, Carter," Major Gyles said shortly. "If you have a pass, where is it? Show it to me."

"I can't, sir."

"And why not?"

"I haven't got it any more, sir. It was blown up."

"Blown up? How very convenient." The major eyed him thoughtfully. "How was it blown up?"

"We was crossing no man's land when a shell fell behind us. I was blown flat on my face."

"I thought you said you were buried by the shell," snapped the major.

"Not the first one," Tom said.

"Oh, I see, there were *two* shells," said the major, sardonically.

"There was shells everywhere, sir," Tom said. "I dived into a shell-hole for cover and I heard someone crying out." Tom paused, but the major said nothing so he went on. "There was a lad there, had his leg blown off. His name was Sam Gordon."

"One of yours?"

"Same battalion. I did what I could for him sir, put a tourniquet to stop the bleeding. He was shivering and I put my tunic round him while I went for help."

"You left him and went for help."

"Yes sir, I couldn't do nothing more for him, sir. I left a marker so's I could find him again."

"What sort of marker?"

"There were two other blokes in the same hole, sir. They were dead. I took one of their rifles and stood it up with a piece of the lad's shirt tied to it."

"And then you went for help."

"Yes sir, I'd just crawled away, when there was another shell. That was the one that buried me, sir."

"Go on, Carter."

"When I came round again, like I said, I was half buried and I had to dig myself out. I looked back to where I thought I'd left Sam Gordon. There weren't nothing there. He'd been blown away. Probably same shell as got me."

"What has all this to do with your leave pass?" asked Major Gyles abruptly.

"It was in the pocket of my tunic, sir. I'd left that round Sam Gordon."

"So you have nothing to prove that you were given leave, in the middle of a battle, to come to Albert."

"I only had leave after the battle was over," said Tom.

"But it isn't over," the major pointed out quietly. "It's hardly begun!" he thought for a moment and then asked, "What made this Captain Hurst give you compassionate leave, Carter? And why to come to Albert?"

"He gave me forty-eight hours, sir, to get married." Even as he said it, Tom realised how thin this sounded.

"To get *married*?" The incredulity returned to Major Gyles's voice. "To get married…in the middle of the big push. Who the hell is this Captain Hurst to even dream of considering such a thing?"

"There's a girl, a nurse. We was getting married as soon as we could, only now she's expecting, so I wanted to marry her before she went home to have the baby." Tom's voice trailed away as he gave his explanation.

Major Gyles looked at Tom for a long moment before he said, "So to get here to marry this girl, you deserted your king, you deserted your mates, you simply walked away from the battlefield and left them to do the fighting."

"No, sir, it wasn't like that, sir," protested Tom. "I had a pass, sir. I had leave to come. I'd never have left otherwise."

"And this girl, this nurse, does she know you're coming?"

"I didn't have a chance to tell her, sir. Captain Hurst only changed his mind just as we went up to the front."

"Changed his mind? You mean he had refused you once?"

"Yes, sir."

"What made him change his mind?"

"Don't know, sir." Tom had never been quite sure what had made Captain Hurst change his mind, but he assumed that it was the letter from Sarah. He didn't think that would be well received as a reason now, so he simply said, "Don't know, sir."

"You don't know? You mean he just sent for you and said, 'By the way Carter, I've decided to let you go and get married after all. Hope you'll be very happy.' " Major Gyles's sarcasm was heavy. "Good God, man, you must think I came down with the fairies." He stared straight at Tom, drilling him with his eyes, as if trying to see what was written on his brain. Then he sighed. "You're under arrest, Carter, for desertion in the face of the enemy. You will be held here while we try and verify your story, and then no doubt there'll be a court martial. Take him away, Tucker."

The sergeant marched him out of the room and round to a stone shed that had two cells in it. He gestured Tom into one without a word and then snapped the door shut, shooting the huge bolts behind him.

The cell contained nothing but a camp cot and a bucket. It had one high window open to the air, but barred against escape, and the sturdy wooden door. Tom threw himself down on the cot and buried his head in despair.

Surely, surely, he thought, as he lay there in the grip of panic, they'll believe me. Surely Captain Hurst will tell them that he gave me a pass...but suppose he doesn't.

It was clear to Tom from Major Gyles's reaction that it should never have been given.

Captain Hurst'll be in deep shit for this, Tom thought, and so am I. And what about Molly? What'll happen to her now? I'll never get to see her now, let alone marry her.

Sergeant Tucker appeared some hours later with a bucket of hot water, a minuscule piece of soap and some clean kit.

"Get yourself shaved and swilled down, Carter," he said, and handed Tom a razor. He stood and watched as Tom stripped off the remains of his filthy clothes and dunked his head in the bucket. The soap was a luxury he hadn't had for some time, and ignoring the rigidly alert sergeant beside him, Tom scrubbed himself from top to bottom, finishing with his hair and then picking up the razor. At once the sergeant moved towards him, but Tom managed to produce a lather on his face with the last scrape of soap and began to shave in the dregs of the water left in the bucket. Being shaved, clean and in the luxury of clean clothes was the most wonderful boost to Tom's morale. He turned to the sergeant and asked, "What happens now, Sarge?"

"You go back in your cell, chum," came the laconic reply. "Fall in."

Tom was marched back to the cell, and the door closed with its echoing boom. It was a sound that Tom was to get used to over the next ten days. He was kept locked up almost all day, let out for exercise under guard, he was marched round and round a small courtyard for half an hour and then returned to his solitary confinement.

He had been allowed to write one letter, and in it he tried to tell Molly what had happened without alarming her. He didn't know if she knew what he knew only too well; if he were found guilty of desertion, at best he'd get penal servitude and at worst he'd be shot.

10th July

My darling Molly,

I am writing to you from near the town where we were going to meet, where I am under arrest at present. Sarah's brother did give me a pass in the end, but I lost it in the battle, and so until they find out from him for sure I have to stay here. I am well treated and have exercise, but the rest of the day is a bit boring. But it won't be for long, I am sure. It does mean that I shan't be able to come to you as we'd hoped. You must go home, my darling girl, and I will come and find you as soon as I can. Look after our baby, it will probably be more than a baby by the time I see it. What will you call it I wonder? Choose whatever name you like best. I don't know if I will get letters here, but write to me if you can and tell me what plans you have made for your journey and let me know when you are safely home.

I love you, my Molly.

Tom

Each day when Sergeant Tucker came in with his food, Tom would ask, "Any news yet?"

Tucker would shake his head. "It's chaos out there," he said once, but he wouldn't say any more.

At the end of the ten days Tucker came for him and marched him back into the house where he'd first seen Major Gyles.

The major was there again, but this time there was a colonel with him. Both men sat behind a table and Tom stood to attention in front of them. The colonel was older than the major, his hair greying at the temples, his face deeply etched with lines, but his bearing was erect and his grey eyes surveyed Tom coldly.

"Carter," he said.

"Yes, sir. Private 8523241 Thomas Carter, 1st Battalion, Belshire Light Infantry."

"I am Colonel Bridger, and I am here from Brigade. We have looked into your case, Carter and it has been decided that you shall be tried by court martial. Your story seems to me to be completely preposterous, but it will be tested by the court which will convene tomorrow at ten o'clock here."

He looked at Tom's stunned face and added, "You will be assigned a Prisoner's Friend. He will come to see you this afternoon so that you can prepare your defence...if you have one." His tone made it clear to Tom and the others in the room, that he didn't consider there was a defence. "Right, Sergeant, carry on."

Sergeant Tucker snapped out the order to move but Tom stood his ground for a moment and said, "Please sir, may I ask if there is any news from Captain Hurst?"

The colonel looked surprised at being addressed, but he said mildly, "No, Carter, nor will there be. He was killed almost immediately, leading his men over. Doing his duty to the end." He paused and then added, "But perhaps you already knew that, Carter. Perhaps you saw him fall while you were hiding in your shell-hole. You'd know it would be safe to use his name then, wouldn't you? Know that he couldn't refute your lies."

Tom started to speak again, to cry out against such a

suggestion, but the colonel snapped, "Enough, Carter. Take him away."

Tucker marched him back to the cell and then said almost sympathetically, "It doesn't do no good to argue with them, Carter. Keep that for the court. There'll be someone to see you later, I expect."

Lieutenant Hill came into the cell later that afternoon. He brought a chair with him and when he was seated, he took a notepad and pencil from his pocket.

"Now then, Carter," he began, "I've been sent to you as Prisoner's Friend. We have to make out some sort of case in court, so what's it to be?"

Tom told him as simply as he could what had happened and how he came to be in the position he was. When he'd finished Lieutenant Hill said, "And you say this Captain Hurst has since been killed and can't speak up on your behalf."

"The colonel told me so this morning," Tom said dismally.

"Who else did you tell that you'd been promised leave?" asked Lieutenant Hill.

"No one," Tom replied. "Captain Hurst said it was compassionate leave, but that no one else was to know. I gave him my word."

Tom wished now that he hadn't kept his word so rigorously to Captain Hurst. If only he had mentioned the promised leave to Cookie, he could have corroborated his story. "He said no one else was to know," Tom said again.

"I can well understand that," muttered Lieutenant Hill. "What I can't understand is him giving it to you at all. You realise the court isn't very likely to believe you? What else have you to say about it? You say no one else knew?"

"No one, sir," began Tom and then said, "except Captain Hurst did say he was going to write to his sister about it."

"His sister!" the young lieutenant was incredulous. "Why on earth would he write to his sister about it?"

"I don't know if he did," Tom said wearily. "He said he was going to, but we moved up to the front so soon after, he may not have done."

"But why would he tell his sister?" Hill asked again.

"Because she was nursing with Molly. I told you it was a nurse at the convent hospital where I was sent when I was wounded. Captain Hurst's sister is her friend."

"Let me get this straight," said Hill frowning, "this officer's sister is a friend of the girl you, Private Carter, have made pregnant."

"Of the girl I'm going to marry," Tom said steadfastly. "Molly was her maid..."

"Ah, light dawns," said Hill. "You've got the family retainer into trouble."

"You don't understand," Tom said. "At home Molly is the maid, but out here they are equals. They're doing the same job."

"Maybe you think they are, but I doubt if Hurst's sister sees this girl as her equal. That would be most unlikely." He thought for a moment and then said, "Still, that is neither here nor there. We can't involve them in this."

"Surely you can ask her if she had a letter from him?" Tom said.

"Carter," Hill said wearily, "she's not here. We can't ask her. The court martial is tomorrow. The prosecution will bring its witnesses and we have to make our defence, then it's up to the court."

"Who are their witnesses?"

"The MPs who found you hiding in the barn..."

"I was not hiding," protested Tom.

"So, you tell them that tomorrow. You tell them what you were doing when they found you. Then there will be Major Gyles, who interviewed you on the first day. He will also answer the questions about Captain Hurst. It is no good trying to drag his sister into this, it won't make any difference. The thing is, Carter, you were absent from your unit without leave, and that's desertion. All we can do is try and make them see that you thought you had good reason to go."

"But I didn't desert," cried Tom. "I was going back. I had a forty-eight hour pass, and then I was going back."

"So you say," agreed Lieutenant Hill, "but they've only your word for it, so it's up to you to try and convince them. I've asked around, and the best way seems to be to put you on oath and then let you tell your own story. They may ask you questions, but you can answer in your own words and try to make them believe you."

Tom stared at him bleakly. "Is that all?" he asked.

"I think so, yes."

"Can I ask you something, sir? Have you been a Prisoner's Friend before?" asked Tom.

Lieutenant Hill looked uncomfortable. "No, Carter, I can't say that I have. It's not a popular job, you know. No one wants to do it, but," he added in a rallying tone, "since I am doing it, I will do my very best for you." He pocketed the notebook in which he had jotted notes of what Tom had told him. "After you have spoken, I can sum up your defence, and then it'll be up to the court."

"Thank you, sir," Tom said, and then once again the boom of the heavy door cut him off from the world outside.

Tom slept hardly at all that night. His brain churned over and over what he might say to the court in the morning and how best he might say it. From what Lieutenant Hill said it appeared that his being away from his unit would be construed as desertion, whatever he told them. The fact that he had come down from the front line thinking he had permission to do so, would not be believed, or even if it were, would not count as a defence. He watched the grey fingers of dawn creep through the bars of his window, and felt grey fingers of despair creeping with them.

Sergeant Tucker brought him some breakfast, but Tom was not hungry and he ate none of it, just drank the mug of strong tea that went with it. He was given hot water to wash and shave in and then Tucker came back to fetch him.

The court martial had been convened in the main room of HQ. It was in a villa just outside the town. Lieutenant Hill was waiting as Tom was marched up between two MPs. He said hastily, "Colonel Bridger is presiding, with Captain James and Captain Howard. They're all right, but the colonel is another matter altogether." He looked Tom over and went on, "We'll be on one side of the room and the prosecutor, that's Major Pilton, will be on the other. Don't speak unless you are spoken to. Understand? Don't interrupt. Your turn to speak will come."

Together they went into the room where a table was laid out with paper and pencils, pens, ink and a blotter for each of the tribunal. There was a small table on the right hand side, and next to this sat the prosecutor, Major Pilton. Hill led Tom to the other side where there was one chair and another small table. "Stand there," he said, indicating the space behind table, and as Tom did so, Hill sat down on the chair, putting his papers on the table beside him. At the back of the room were the two military policemen who had arrested him, and Major Gyles.

The sun streamed in through the floor length windows behind the main table, and as he waited for the tribunal to make its appearance, Tom found himself watching the motes of dust dancing in the shaft of sun. Just so had they danced on summer mornings through the dining-room windows of the London orphanage. Tom found himself with a vision of that old Victorian hall, with its pitted panelling and pock-marked tables, which was so vivid that suddenly it was the small court room, painted a cold and clinical white, which seemed unreal. Only by concentrating on the frivolous dance of the dust in the sunshine did Tom keep from trying to push his way from the room to find the real world outside.

The door swung open and the officers making up the tribunal strode in and sat down behind the table, followed by two more military police, who took up their positions on either side of the door.

Colonel Bridger announced his name and then the names of the officers on either side of him. The prosecutor announced himself as Major Pilton, and then Lieutenant Hill, in a rather hesitant voice, gave his name and said that he appeared as Prisoner's Friend.

"Stand forward, prisoner, and state your name, rank and number."

Tom did so, and then the colonel turned back to Major Pilton. "Read the offences that this man is charged with," he ordered. The prosecutor stood up.

"Private 8523241 Thomas Carter of the 1st Battalion, Belshire Light Infantry is charged on two counts as follow:

1. That on the night of 1st July 1916, when on active service he did, without leave, absent himself from the front line trenches near Beaumont Hamel and remained absent until he was found outside the town of Albert on the morning of 3rd July.

2. That on the night of 1st July 1916, when on active service, he did desert His Majesty's service."

"Guilty or not guilty?" the colonel demanded, staring at Tom.

"Not guilty, sir," Tom said. He managed to keep his voice steady, but his insides were churning and he had to keep his hands rigidly at his side to stop them from shaking.

"Carry on, Major," the colonel directed.

"Private Thomas Carter was part of a unit that took part in the attack by the 29th Division on the enemy line at Beaumont Hamel on 1st July. He attacked with his unit through no-man's-land, and was seen to advance in line with the rest of his comrades. As the attacking force advanced he disappeared and was not seen again. The next time he was seen was at the forward dressing post in the support trenches when he joined Private John Gerard as an ambulance driver and took a horse ambulance back from the lines to the casualty clearing station at Hebecourt. There he had some food with Gerard and then while Gerard was at the latrines, he disappeared again. He did not ride back up to the lines with Gerard, who having searched for him before leaving and been unable to find him, returned to the forward dressing post alone.

"No officer had directed him to the ambulances, no order had been given to him to accompany Gerard to the clearing station. When he appeared beside the ambulance which was preparing to leave, Gerard says he asked if Carter was Henderson's replacement." The major glanced across at the colonel, explaining, "Henderson had been Gerard's co-driver who had been wounded in the shoulder on their last trip. The accused said that he was. Gerard accepted this and Carter joined him on the ambulance. When Gerard reported back to his own officer, Captain Hicks, he discovered no one had sent this man to be his co-driver, and subsequently he has driven with another man to replace the injured Henderson."

Lieutenant Hill got to his feet and asked tentatively, "May I ask, sir, if this Private Gerard will be appearing as a witness?"

Colonel Bridger looked annoyed at the interruption and snapped, "Your time for questions will come, Lieutenant."

However, Major Pilton said, "No, Lieutenant, he won't. He can't be spared, his work is particularly vital at this time, as you can imagine. His statement has been taken." The major looked down at his papers again. "From the time the accused left the casualty station at Hebecourt until he was found by the arresting officers, he was absent without leave, and had made no attempt to report himself for duty anywhere."

"Call your witnesses, Major," said Colonel Bridger.

The two military policemen were called, and each gave the same version of events as the other. They had been on patrol in the area outside Albert and had found Private Carter hiding in a barn.

When allowed to cross examine, Lieutenant Hill asked Sergeant Tucker, "What made you think that Private Carter was hiding?"

"Stands to reason," replied Tucker. "We see it from time to time. A bloke goes AWOL and slinks off among the farms trying to get food from the French there."

"Was Private Carter at a farm?"

"No, sir, in a derelict barn...so that he wouldn't be seen, sir."

"Seen by whom?" asked Hill, but before Tucker could answer Colonel Bridger snapped, "I think the sergeant has already answered your question, Lieutenant. He said the man was in hiding from the army."

"Excuse me sir," replied Lieutenant Hill bravely, "but I don't think he said that exactly..."

"It is what he meant," said the colonel. "Have you any other questions for this man?" His tone implied that there should not be, but Lieutenant Hill said, "Yes, sir. Thank you, sir." He turned back to Tucker. "Did the accused try to run away when he saw you?"

"No, sir. He seemed exhausted. Unsteady on his feet, like."

The next witness was Major Gyles, who briefly described the conversation he had had with Tom when he had been brought in.

"Did you believe his story?" enquired Major Pilton.

"No, not really," Gyles replied.

"So you had him locked up while you made some enquiries?"

"Yes, I did."

"And what was the result of those enquiries?" asked the prosecutor.

"He said he had been given a forty-eight-hour leave pass on compassionate grounds by his company commander, Captain Frederick Hurst."

"And does Captain Hurst confirm this?"

"No. I'm afraid Captain Hurst was killed as he led his men into the battle on 1st July."

"You found no one else who was able to confirm this...leave pass?" He spoke the last two words as if they left a nasty taste in his mouth.

"No, sir. Though it has to be said that there are very few of Captain Hurst's company left. Those that did return to the lines safely have been reassigned to other units."

"So there is no one to corroborate what the accused says?"

"No, sir."

The men at the table made copious notes; indeed Colonel Bridger seemed to be writing everything down verbatim, and kept asking Major Pilton to wait while he did so.

When at last it was Lieutenant Hill's turn to ask questions of Major Gyles he said, "Were attempts made to contact some of the survivors of Private Carter's unit?"

"It is very difficult to locate individuals in the present state of affairs," the major replied evasively.

"So there is no one to say that Captain Hurst did not give the accused a pass to return to Albert immediately after the attack."

"It is so unlikely as to be almost impossible," replied Major Gyles. "This is the biggest push of the war. No officer is going to hand out leave, compassionate or otherwise."

Lieutenant Hill knew he was going to get no further with this, and he was well aware that the colonel was eyeing him with distaste.

"The accused says that he brought in a wounded man, Jimmy Cardle, into a part of the line that he did not recognise. Have you been able to find this man Cardle?"

"He subsequently died of his wounds."

"And the officer in the trench who gave Carter a shirt and service tunic to replace the one he had left on the wounded man, Sam Gordon?"

"We have not been able to trace any officer who remembers doing this."

"It is possible," Lieutenant Hill suggested, "that he too has since been killed."

"This is pure supposition," interrupted Colonel Bridger. "Have you any other relevant questions?"

Lieutenant Hill could see that any more questioning was going to do more harm than good, so he said, "No, sir. I'd like the prisoner to give evidence on his own behalf."

Tom was sworn in and then Lieutenant Hill asked him to explain exactly what had happened in his own words. As he went through it all again, he noticed that the colonel had stopped taking notes and was sitting back in his chair staring at him with his cold grey eyes.

Major Pilton stopped him at one stage and said, casually, "You say that this pass was not with immediate effect? It did not start at once?"

"No, sir," said Tom. "Captain Hurst said that I could not go until after the attack. He said he didn't know when it would be, but very soon. He said that when it was over I could be released for forty-eight hours...to get married." It sounded weak even to his own ears, but Tom went on, "I am an orphanage boy, sir. Never knew my parents. I didn't want my child to grow up without my name to protect him. Molly and me was going to get married anyway, but I wanted us to be before Molly went home."

"So," Major Pilton ignored all that Tom had said, "so your pass was not with effect until the attack was over."

"No, sir."

"It is still not over, Carter. The attack has continued ever since the morning you went over the top."

"Lieutenant Hurst had dated it for the 8th July, sir."

"Why would he do that, I wonder?" said the prosecutor.

"Because he thought the battle would be over by then, sir. He thought we'd be through the German lines and well dug in, sir, and he would spare me for a couple of days."

Too many people had believed the same thing and been proved disastrously wrong for this to be a comfortable thought for the major, so he ignored Tom's answer and continued, "So that was the date on the pass?"

"Yes, sir. The 8th July, sir."

"According to what we've heard, you were arrested on the morning of the 3rd July." He paused and then went on softly, "Your leave, if you had leave, did not begin by your own admission until 8th July. Therefore I put it to you that you were Absent Without Leave. You had deserted your comrades, you had deserted your King whilst on Active Service." A long silence followed his words and then he sat down.

Lieutenant Hill remained seated. He knew he could do no more.

Colonel Bridger got to his feet. "The court will retire and consider its verdict." Everyone stood rigidly at attention while the tribunal left the room.

"You will wait here, Carter," ordered Major Pilton, and then having instructed the two military policemen who had remained on either side of the door to guard the prisoner, he left the room, followed by Major Gyles.

Lieutenant Hill looked at Tom. "I did my best for you, Carter, but I think you just condemned yourself."

"What happens now?" asked Tom fearfully.

"Now they decide whether you are guilty or not. If not, you will be released at once and returned to your regiment. If guilty, they'll want to know more about you and your character." He got to his feet and followed the other two officers out of the room, disliking the job he'd had to do, feeling that he hadn't done it very well and angry that he'd been asked to do it in the first place.

It was half an hour before the officers returned to the courtroom. Tom had spent the time slumped in a chair with one military policeman by the open window, the other beside the door. When the officers came back in Sergeant Tucker rasped out, "Prisoner, attention!"

Tom leapt to his feet and stood to attention as the two

majors and Lieutenant Hill took their places, followed almost immediately by the tribunal.

When everyone was in place, Colonel Bridger looked slowly round the room, before he said, "Private Carter, we have listened very carefully to all the evidence in this regrettable affair, both against you and in your defence. However, at present the court has no findings to announce." He looked across at Major Pilton. "What is known about this man, Major? Do we have anything from his commanding officer?"

"Colonel Johnson was unable to attend, sir, however he sent this statement to be read in court." The major took a sheet of paper from his table and read, "'Private Thomas Carter volunteered in October 1914 and has served with B company of this battalion since he was posted here in May 1915. He has been a trusted soldier, used on several occasions as part of a raiding party because of his courage and reliability. On one occasion he brought in a comrade who had been wounded on such a raid, when he was already wounded himself. He was not sent home, but this resulted in a stay in hospital here in France. Once he was pronounced fit for duty he returned to his battalion and continued to serve willingly. He was granted seventy-two hours' local leave in March from which he returned promptly. I have not come into personal contact with Private Carter, but this report is based on information both from his service record and from officers under whom he has served. Unfortunately nearly all the officers and NCOs by whom he was best known have recently been killed in action, and so there is no close, first-hand knowledge of him. Private Carter appears to have been a brave and loyal soldier. It is a great shock to hear of the very serious charges laid against him now.' It is signed, James Johnson, Lieutenant Colonel. 1st Belshire Light Infantry."

"No other evidence as to this man's character?" asked Colonel Bridger.

"No, sir."

"Lieutenant Hill, have you anything more to say on the prisoner's behalf?"

The young officer stood up and cleared his throat nervously, "Just to say, sir, that this evidence of good character from Colonel Johnson, seems to bear out some of the things the accused said, sir. He has been wounded himself in the service of the king, he has rescued at least one, he says two, wounded men from no-man's-land. He is not a coward, sir, he has never run away from his duty before. I suggest to you, sir that he did not do so wilfully this time, but under the misapprehension that he had leave to come to Albert for forty-eight hours, leave given even at this desperate time, compassionate leave, because it was a family matter. Private Carter had no intention of remaining at large, sir, and once he had married his fiancée, he would have returned to his unit immediately. I ask you sir, to take all this into consideration when coming to your sentence, sir." Lieutenant Hill sat down again and Colonel Bridger turned to Tom.

"Well, Carter, have you anything to say for yourself?"

Tom said, "Yes, sir, please sir." He drew a deep breath. He knew as he had not been declared Not Guilty that they had found him guilty, but he also knew he had not yet been sentenced. "Everything I have told you is true. If you must find me guilty, sir, I beg you to find me guilty of being absent without leave. I didn't desert, sir." Tom spoke earnestly, his eyes fixed on the colonel. "I wouldn't never desert my mates. I wouldn't never desert my king. I joined up as soon as I could to do my bit, like, and I wouldn't give up, sir, not till the war is over. I rescued my mate, Harry, and he died. I brought in

Jimmy Cardle and he died. If nothing else I owe them Germans for them, sir. I didn't desert."

The colonel listened impassively to Tom's outburst and then said, "The proceedings in open court are terminated."

Tom was marched back to the cell where he had been kept before, and Lieutenant Hill came to see him once more.

"I'm afraid they've found you guilty," he said. "I hope what your CO said about you will work in your favour. You'll be kept here until sentence is decided and confirmed."

Tom looked at him with wide, frightened eyes. "Are they going to shoot me?" he asked.

"I don't know, Carter," the lieutenant replied.

It was another ten days before Tom heard the sentence of the court. Those days had passed exactly as the ones before the court martial. He thought of Molly, wondering continually where she was and what had happened to her. He had not heard from her for three weeks and he was desperate for news of her. She must have gone home to England, Tom decided. His letter would be following her, forwarded by Sarah. Surely she would write as soon as she could? Each day he hoped for mail, but each day he was disappointed. He wrote again himself, but he said almost nothing about his predicament. There was no need to worry her yet, so he simply told her how much he loved her and how, when the war was over, he, she and the baby would be the most wonderful family. He had no news about the progress of the battle, still grinding on after the initial push. He could hear the guns, still pounding away at distant targets, but he knew nothing of the gains and losses sustained on the ground beneath the exploding shells and vicious shrapnel.

The military police who guarded him were taciturn and seldom answered any of his questions with more than a grunt.

Sergeant Tucker was a little more forthcoming. "It's hell out there," he said, "and we ain't getting nowhere."

At last Tucker came in one afternoon, bringing a bucket of warm water with him. He said, "Hot water, Carter, get scrubbed up. You're going to HQ."

With dread in his heart, Tom duly washed and shaved. If he was going to HQ then it must mean that his sentence was about to be promulgated. He was marched over to the villa and made to wait in the room where the court martial had been held. As before two MPs waited with him until the door opened and the adjutant, Major Rawlins, came in, followed by an RAMC captain and the young battalion chaplain, wearing a dog collar with his uniform.

Tom stood to attention and the adjutant looked him up and down. The major was a good-looking man in a craggy sort of way, though his face was pale and drawn, with wide-set eyes of a chocolate brown and framed with crisp, dark hair. The chocolate eyes surveyed Tom now.

"Private 8523241 Thomas Carter, I have to tell you that the court martial convened to hear the case of your desertion from the ranks, has after hearing all the facts, found you guilty as charged. Desertion is a despicable crime, leaving your fellows to take up your slack. It is the sentence of the court that you should be taken out before a squad of your comrades and shot. This sentence has been referred to officers at every level and has finally been confirmed by the Commander in Chief himself. Mitigating circumstances have been considered, but none have been found sufficient to commute the sentence. I speak for all the 1st Belshires when I say that we are ashamed that one of our number should have so failed his friends, his regiment and his king. The sentence will be carried out tomorrow morning at first light."

Tom felt the strength drain out of him like water through a colander. His head spun and his knees felt like jelly. He stared at the pale, craggy face and knew that all colour had drained from his own. He reached for the back of the chair beside him and, gripping it, managed to remain on his feet.

"You will remain here over night. If you require the services of a padre, Lieutenant Smalley will stay with you."

Tom found his voice and said huskily, "The Colonel wrote in his report that I was a loyal and courageous soldier, sir. Doesn't that mean anything?"

"It means that it is a great pity that you degenerated into a deserter, Carter, and left your comrades in the lurch," the adjutant replied, and after one more piercing look, he turned on his heel and left the room.

The RAMC captain said gruffly, "You'd better sit down, Carter."

Tom slumped onto the chair and buried his head in his hands. Tears started in his eyes and he gave a sob. His life, which he had risked so willingly in the front line over the months he had been there, was now to be taken from him. His death was not to be in the service of his king and country, for a just and noble cause, but an ignominious death, dealt out by his own comrades. These thoughts came to him in a jumble and confusion, forcing their way into his numbed brain, but his over-riding thoughts were for Molly. She would never marry him now. Their child would never know its father, would believe him to be a coward and deserter. He'd never had a family, and now he never would.

"Oh Molly," he moaned in his misery. "Oh Molly!"

He felt the touch of a hand on his shoulder and looked up to see the concerned face of the young padre.

"I'll leave you to it, Padre," said the MO. "I'll come back if you need me."

"There's a room for you upstairs," the padre said quietly. "Take Private Carter up," he ordered the two MPs who still stood by the door.

Tom was led upstairs to a small room which was furnished with a bed, two chairs and a table. The windows were small and looked out on to the courtyard below and then to the flat country beyond. The padre followed him inside and so did the two MPs, then the door was locked behind them. The guards stood, one at the door, one at the window as they had downstairs. Tom flung himself face down on the bed and the padre sat down on one of the chairs. There was no sound in the room except for Tom's heavy breathing as he fought to control the panic inside him. He was condemned to death. He was going to die. He was going to be led outside, blindfolded and shot. He had been paraded once, early on, for an execution. The man, only a young lad, had been half dragged, half carried from his prison and tied on a chair. The terror in the boy's eyes before they had been blindfolded was etched on Tom's mind. They had been forced to watch as the signal was given and the firing squad raised their rifles and fired. The man slumped forward and the chair had toppled over. Every man there had felt sick at the sight, standing to attention, not allowed to move until the medical officer had confirmed that the man was dead. Now this terrifying end was to be his. Another sob escaped him. A childish scream echoed through his brain. It's not fair! It's not fair!

The padre rested his hand on Tom's shoulder and said quietly, "I'm going to stay with you, Carter, you aren't alone. If you want to talk, we will, if not, it doesn't matter, I'll still be here."

Tom lay on the bed with his face pressed into the blanket. He didn't want to talk. He didn't want to think. Thoughts brought to mind images too painful to contemplate; the memory of the other execution, the thought of Molly, laughing up at him, her arms twined round his neck. A groan escaped him and his fingers tightened into fists. Abruptly he swung his feet round to the floor and immediately the two guards, who both carried rifles with bayonet fixed, took a step forward to forestall any unwise break for freedom or violence upon the padre.

Lieutenant Smalley looked up and his eyes met Tom's level gaze.

"I'm going to die tomorrow," Tom said. "Aren't I?"

"Yes," the padre agreed. "I'm afraid you are."

"Then there's things I've got to get sorted out," Tom said. "Will you help me?"

"I will do anything I can for you," Smalley replied. He looked across at the two military policemen who had relaxed again at the sound of reasonable talk.

"Will you men wait outside?" Smalley said to them, but the corporal said, "Sorry sir, orders not to leave the room, sir."

The padre sighed. "I'm afraid everything you say will be overheard," he said to Tom.

"It doesn't matter," said Tom. "Nothing matters except that I get things sorted out. It's my girl, Molly."

Slowly and in great detail, Tom told the padre about his life. He left out nothing; he wanted this man at least to understand why he had done what he had. He told him about the orphanage. "Not a bad place as they go," he said. "We was fed and clothed and sent to school. If they could they helped us find a trade, some of the lads was apprenticed, but most of us went into factories and that." He told him about meeting up with Harry Cook when working in the docks at Belmouth, and how they'd joined up together. He spoke of their life in the same platoon, of the raid when they'd been wounded, of how and where Harry had died.

"Molly was his cousin. She was there in the hospital nursing and, lo and behold, her cousin Harry turns up. He had to have his leg off and then he died." He went on to tell the padre how he and Molly became friends and then fell in love. "She's the most beautiful girl," Tom said. He was surprised that he could talk about her so easily to this man that he hardly knew, but the chaplain knew how to listen and his quiet manner encouraged Tom to trust him and speak of Molly as he would have to no other man. The guards in the room were forgotten as Tom poured out all he felt for Molly. He told of his March leave and the afternoon spent in the little stone barn.

"I know we shouldn't have," he said, "I know you'll say what we did was wrong, but it could have been our only time together." He gave a harsh laugh: "It was our only time together." He put his face in his hands again and the padre said softly, "I'm not here to judge you, Tom."

"No," Tom said bitterly. "That's been done already." Silence slipped round them and Smalley didn't break it. He wanted Tom to continue to talk, to sort things out in his mind.

"I've never had a family, and Molly and me was going to be a family. I had no name except what someone chose for me. I wanted my son, or daughter, to have a name. It was important to me." He went on talking, telling the chaplain about asking Captain Hurst for leave.

"He said no straight off, but then he had a letter from his sister, she was nursing with Molly, and asked him to do something for us if he could before Molly had to go home in disgrace."

"Wait a minute," Smalley said. "You're telling me that his sister knew about this leave pass?"

Tom shrugged. "I don't know if she knew he gave it me, but she did ask him to and he said he was going to write to her."

"Did you tell the court this?" asked Smalley. "That he might have told his sister about the pass?"

"I told Lieutenant Hill," said Tom, "but he said it wouldn't make no difference. She wasn't here to say if she knew, and anyway we didn't know that she did."

The chaplain frowned, but simply said, "Go on." So Tom went on, telling of every event until his final arrest by Sergeant Tucker in the ruined barn.

"But how were you going to let Molly know you were there?" asked the chaplain.

"I was going to go to the convent," Tom said. "It weren't any use going to Albert. But to find St Croix I had to get to Albert first."

There was a bang on the door and the corporal unlocked it to let in a soldier with a mess tin of dark tea and some bread and jam in another.

The padre said, "Do you smoke, Carter?" Tom said that he did. "So do I," said the padre. "I'll go and get us some cigarettes."

He disappeared from the room, leaving Tom to drink the tea and pick at the bread and jam. Once outside the chaplain hurried down the stairs and went looking, not for a packet of Woodbines, but for the adjutant. He finally ran Major Rawlins to earth in the mess, with a glass of whisky in his hand.

"Excuse me, sir," he said, "but I think you should postpone Carter's execution."

The major put down his glass and said, "Postpone it? Why on earth should I do that?"

"There's some new evidence, evidence that didn't come out at the trial," explained Smalley, and he told the adjutant what Tom had told him.

"That is irrelevant," snapped the major.

"I'd have thought it had great relevance, sir," Smalley said bravely. "It could prove that the man had a pass and so was not absent without leave."

"Whether the pass was issued or not is irrelevant," said the major brusquely. "The man was away from his unit when on active service. His pass, if he ever had one, was by his own admission, dated for 8th July. He was arrested on 3rd July, therefore he was absent without leave."

"But might not the existence of a pass make a difference to his sentence?" Lieutenant Smalley persisted, despite the look of anger on his senior officer's face. "It would mean he didn't intend to desert. Mightn't his sentence be commuted in such a circumstance?"

"Lieutenant Smalley, this man's sentence has been confirmed at the very highest level. The only officer who suggested that the sentence should be commuted is Colonel Johnson, who doesn't even know the man."

"He's his commanding officer," Smalley said.

"Exactly," said Rawlins. "Can't possibly know every man in the battalion. Far better to listen to those who knew him properly. Anyway, the sentence is confirmed by Haig himself, so it's too late to be trying to change it now." Seeing the look on the chaplain's face he said, "Look, Smalley, I know it's different for you, being a man of the cloth, you see things differently, but I'm just a common soldier, and this man left his mates and set off on his own, for purposes of his own, while they were still under fire. I have no time for men like that. The execution will go ahead tomorrow morning as planned."

"The woman who he was hoping to marry is at the convent hospital at St Croix," Smalley said. "I could ride over there and fetch her."

"Fetch her?" Rawlins was incredulous. "Whatever for? To watch him die?"

"No, sir. I could marry them. The prisoner would still be shot, but his wife and child would be protected by his name."

"No protection at all, I'd have thought, in the circumstances," snapped Rawlins. "Anyway the idea is preposterous. I suggest you go back to the prisoner and do what you're supposed to. And remember, the man's a deserter."

Smalley returned to the upstairs room with cigarettes and a pad and pencil. The guards had been changed, and the new men remained in silent attendance by the door and window. Tom was sitting at the table staring out of the window at the evening sky. He watched a flight of birds, homing to roost, silhouetted against the red sky, and knew with a lurch that shook him to his core, that he would never see the sun set again.

Smalley brought an oil lamp to the table and put the pencil and paper beside Tom. Then he lit a cigarette and passed the packet to Tom.

"I thought you'd want to write to Molly," he said quietly. He wanted to offer Tom some spiritual comfort, but he knew there could be none of that until the practicalities were sorted out.

Tom had dragged his eyes away from the window and lit a cigarette. "Thanks," he said and, picking up the pencil, began to write:

My darling Molly,

This will be the last letter you get from me. I was arrested and have now been court-martialled for desertion. I did not desert, Captain Hurst gave me compassionate leave to come, but he is dead and there is no one who knows I had the pass. Almost all my unit were killed. You'll have heard now about the battle. I am sure the convent has been flooded out with wounded, but I hope you aren't still there. They have now passed sentence on me and tomorrow morning I'm to be shot. My darling girl, I shall not be with you as we had planned. Our baby will not have a dad, but don't let him grow up thinking his dad was a coward who ran away from the fighting, and left his mates to do the dirty work. If I had died on the battlefield I would think my life well lost in a good cause, but to die as I will have to tomorrow breaks my heart. The battalion padre, Lieutenant Smalley, is with me and trying to be of comfort. I feel none, but at least I can trust him to send you all that I have. I have left everything to you, Molly. It is not a lot, but there should be some pay to come, and everything that was sent back from the line for safe keeping during the attack.

Remember me with love, my darling girl, but go on with your life and the life of our son...or daughter. I hope the baby is a girl and will be as beautiful as you. Kiss her for me. When I stand out there tomorrow I am supposed to commend my soul to God, but I promise you, all my thoughts will be of you.

Goodbye my dearest girl,

Tom

When he had finished the letter there were tears in Tom's eyes. He folded the letter and handed it to Smalley. "It'll have to be censored, I suppose," he said, "and I haven't got an envelope."

"Write down the address and I will make sure it and everything else is sent on to her."

Tom got out his pay book where he had written on the back long ago he left all his worldly goods and any money owed to him, to Miss Molly Day of Valley Farm, Charlton Ambrose, Belshire. He handed it to the chaplain. "I shan't be needing this any more," he said.

The night was long. Smalley suggested that they might pray together, and to please him, Tom agreed, though he said, "I don't have any faith in God, you know. If there was any sort of God, he wouldn't allow all this killing and pain. If you want to pray, pray for my Molly and the baby. She's the one that needs help now."

So the padre prayed for Molly and her unborn child, and then moved quietly on to pray for Tom as well. Tom didn't stop him, but he found little comfort in the words. Smalley got out a bible from his pocket and opened it at the psalms and read Psalm 23 aloud. Tom let the words flow over him. He was in the valley of the shadow of death all right, he thought tiredly, and tomorrow he'd be out of it, dead, gone and buried.

"Where will I be buried?" he asked suddenly, breaking in to the reading.

The padre looked startled, but then said, "In the cemetery just over the hill. You will not be alone, you will be buried among your comrades and receive a Christian burial, I promise you."

Tom nodded slowly, and as he said no more, the chaplain went on with his reading, moving on to Psalm 121. "I will lift up mine eyes unto the hills..."

The summer night was short, and just before the sun crept over the horizon, the MO came into the room with some food, hot strong tea and a large measure of rum.

Tom was lying on the bed, his hands behind his head, his eyes wide open, staring at the ceiling.

"Some food, for you, Carter," he said, "but you may prefer this." He handed Tom the rum, then he turned to the chaplain, "I'll be with them when they come. I suggest you get that down him."

Tom could see no point in eating the food that had come, bread and butter and some ham, but he tipped the rum into the tea and drank the lot straight down. He went and stood by the window and watched the colour steal back into the courtyard below. He could hear the tramp of marching feet and turned abruptly from the window. He knew only too well who was marching at this time in the morning and why. He turned to the chaplain and asked, "What date is it, today?"

Smalley replied, "1st of August."

Tom gave a harsh laugh. "It's my birthday," he said. "I'm twenty-three today."

The door opened and the adjutant came in. "It's time to go," he said.

Tom rubbed his eyes as if banishing sleep and then fell in between the two new military policemen who had come with him. Outside the Assistant Provost Marshal was waiting. With military policemen in front and behind, Tom was marched down the lane, away from HQ to a ruined house half a mile away. All round him were the sounds and scents of a summer morning. As he walked he felt more alive than he ever had before, and his eyes drank in the gleam of the sun on the grasses, the sparkle of dew on a spider's web and the piercing sound of a lark as it soared high above them, and he thought of Molly. Tom knew the padre was only a step behind and he was glad he was there; behind him were the doctor and the other officers. Their feet tramped on the stony track as the procession approached the execution ground. Ahead, Tom could see men formed up in three sides of a square. They halted a short way off, and the adjutant went forward and read out the charges against Private Thomas Carter and then the sentence. The men stood stiff and straight as they heard it. They made no sound as the lark, oblivious, trilled on above them. The doctor then stepped up to put a blindfold over Tom's eyes. The last thing Tom saw was the grey face of Tony Cook staring bleakly at him from the ranks.

He was led forward and tied to a stake on the fourth side of the square. Now the moment had come, Tom felt a strange calm come over him. It was almost as if he were watching the whole thing from outside. He felt someone pin something on to his chest and knew it was a piece of white cloth to mark his heart for the firing squad. He could hear the padre saying prayers in a soft voice close beside him, and though he could not see the signal given by the Assistant Provost Marshal, he felt the padre move aside and knew it was time. Behind the blindfold, he conjured up a vision of Molly's face, her eyes laughing into his, and the world exploded in a volley of rifle fire.

Lieutenant Smalley returned to HQ from the burial and met a harassed looking corporal. "Ah, there you are sir," said the man. "I think I ought to give this to you, sir." He looked awkwardly at an envelope in his hand. "A letter for Carter, sir."

Smalley took the letter and said, "Thank you, Corporal. I'll see it's sent home with his other things."

He took the letter and the letter which Tom had written to Molly and saddling his horse, rode the ten miles to St Croix.

2001

Rachel stared at the letter Tom had written on the eve of his execution. Tears burned the back of her eyes and there was a lump in her throat. So that was it. That was what had happened to Tom Carter, her great-grandfather. He had been branded a deserter and been shot at dawn. She read the letter again. He sounded so brave in it, trying to comfort Molly. What must Molly have thought when she got that letter? She must have been in utter despair. For a long while, Rachel couldn't go on reading. There were still several letters to go, but somehow Tom's last had brought her to a stop. She sat with the yellowed paper in her hand, its pencilled words still clear on the lined paper, and she felt empty inside. She wondered if Gran knew that her father had been shot. Had her mother told her? Almost certainly not, she'd have been far too young before her mother died. Her grandmother then? Probably not, it would have been adding yet more shame to that of her birth; and Gran's mother had been ashamed of her already. Gran said that she had not read any of the letters herself, so, she didn't know.

In need of comfort, Rachel picked up the phone and dialled Nick Potter's mobile. He answered at once.

"Are you busy?" asked Rachel.

"Nothing that can't wait," Nick replied as he caught the something in the tone of her voice.

"Can you come over?"

"I'm on my way," he said. "Are you all right?"

Rachel gave a laugh that didn't work and said, "Yes, just had some sad news, that's all. Thought you might like to cheer me up."

"I'm at my mother's," Nick said. "I'll be with you in about three-quarters of an hour."

Immeasurably cheered by this news, Rachel poured herself a drink and picked up the next letter. It was from Molly to Tom before she knew about his death.

25th July

Dear Tom,

I got your letter saying you are under arrest. Surely they must believe you about the pass.

Poor Sarah has just heard that Freddie is missing, presumed dead in the dreadful battle. She is very upset. This will mean that he can't tell them you had leave to go to Albert. What will happen to you now? I suppose you will be sent back to the front to your unit again, so I must go home. Don't worry about me. We have it all planned and Sarah has given me the money Sir George sent for me to go home last time, so it will not be difficult. It is a good thing we kept it. She was going to write to her father about me, explaining things, but I don't think she will now. They are both too upset to be thinking much about me. I wondered if she would go home now to be with her dad, but she says not yet. She says her place is here in the hospital. It has been a madhouse here. We've had men pouring in from the front. Usually we don't get many of the ones who will be sent home, but everywhere is flooded out with wounded, and lots of those who have come have been given a sort of first aid and sent home to England. I ought to be here too, but once Rev. Mother knows about me I shall be sent packing.

So, dearest Tom, don't worry about me. Keep yourself safe

and know that we shall be waiting for you. I will write again when I get home.

Love from Molly

How had this come back to Molly, Rachel wondered? Clearly it had been sent, as it was in a stamped envelope.

Rachel had been making notes in her notebook as she'd read the letters, now she noted down this query before she turned to the next envelope. This was addressed to Molly at Valley Farm in neat handwriting Rachel hadn't seen before and had a French stamp. She pulled out the letter and looked at the signature. It was from Sarah.

Convent Of Our Lady of Mercies
St Croix 1st August

Dear Molly,

I am so sorry to be the bearer of dreadful news, but I felt I must write at once. Tom's battalion chaplain, Reverend Smalley, was here today. He asked for you, and of course you had gone, but he knew about me and so asked to speak to me instead. He told me that your poor Tom had been shot this morning for desertion. He said that though Tom said he had a leave pass he was unable to prove it and was court-martialled. He had been in the battle which took my dearest Freddie, and after that tried to make his way to Albert. They say he deserted whilst on active service. I know this will come as a desperate shock to you, Molly, and the only comfort I can give you is to say that Reverend Smalley said Tom only thought of you and the baby, and when the time came he walked out steadily and died a brave man. I enclose the letter Tom wrote to you on the night before he died, and also return one that you wrote to him that arrived too late. It hasn't been opened, of course, the padre simply brought it with him. He was a very kind and gentle man and was upset at not having been able to do more for Tom. He said one of the problems was that most of the officers who knew Tom well, like Freddie, had been killed that first day, and so there was no one to speak up for him. He didn't condemn Tom for what he did, although I think he didn't approve. He wanted to tell you face to face, so that you would not simply hear through official channels. Tom made a soldier's will and left you everything, but apart from the enclosed I don't think there is much.

My dear Molly, life will be very hard for you now, particularly if this becomes known at home. I haven't told my father, he wouldn't understand, and I suggest you keep the news to yourself as well. No one need know and everyone will assume Tom died in action. The padre buried him in a cemetery behind the lines and gave him a Christian burial, so your Tom is lying among his comrades and at peace with God now.

There is something else I must tell you, dearest Molly and that is that I have decided to stay here in the convent and to become one of the sisters. Reverend Mother has accepted me as a novice and from now on I shall be known as Sister Marie-Pierre. You will probably be surprised at my decision, but you shouldn't be. You know that I have always felt myself comfortable here. I feel this is where God wants me to be and I am at peace with myself in my decision. Of course for the rest of this dreadful war I shall work as I have all the time we were together, but I am not sure I am really cut out for nursing, and will be happy to live a more contemplative life.

I have of course written to my father and told him. I know he will be disappointed in me, but I am sure I am doing the right thing. I hope to return to Charlton Ambrose to see him for a few days when I can be spared, so, I shall be able to see you and the baby when I come.

I am so sorry to have to break this awful news to you, Molly, but you know you will be in my prayers now and always.

Your loving friend Sarah

Rachel sat with the letter in her hand and tears in her eyes. What a desperately sad letter to receive, she thought. How on earth had Molly coped with it when it arrived? She must have told her parents that Tom was dead. Did she tell them the truth?

Unlikely, Rachel thought, I wouldn't have, considering the relationship she seemed to have with them. She certainly wouldn't have told her father, but perhaps she shared her grief with her mother. She certainly needed someone.

It was interesting that the chaplain was called Smalley. Was he the same as Henry Smalley who turned up at Charlton Ambrose after the war? He must be. In the article about him in the *Chronicle* archives it said he had served at the front in the Great War. Perhaps he had known Freddie and come to see his father after the war. Or was it Molly he came to see? Rachel wondered. Clearly Tom Carter's execution had greatly disturbed him. Why else would he ride over to the convent, in the hope of breaking the news to Molly himself? He knew where Molly lived from Tom's pay book; had he come especially to see how she and the baby were getting on? It was also clear that he had great sympathy for the men who had been killed in the war. It seemed to be he who had convinced Sir George to allow him to dedicate the ninth tree. Perhaps Sarah had sent him to her father. However it had happened, it appeared that the Reverend Henry Smalley came to the living of Charlton Ambrose in 1921 and had stayed until 1938. He had written a history of the parish and, Rachel was now convinced, he knew who the ninth tree was for. She thought she did, too. It was for her great-grandfather, Tom Carter.

How had Smalley convinced Sir George to allow the ninth tree to be dedicated to the unknown soldier? He must have told him the partial truth, that it was for Molly's soldier who had been lost, like Freddie, on the Somme, one of Freddie's men. Almost certainly he did not tell him the exact circumstances; as Sarah had said in her letter, her father would not have understood, but he seemed to have convinced the squire somehow that it was a simple act of charity to allow the tree to remain.

Nick Potter arrived with a bottle of wine and a bunch of flowers whose gaudy cellophane wrapping paper proclaimed that they had been bought in a motorway service area. He followed Rachel through to the kitchen and when she had put the flowers and the wine down on the counter she turned round and said, "Oh Nick, I'm so glad you came."

"So am I," said Nick and taking her in his arms he began to kiss her. For a split second she tensed and then relaxed against him, returning his kisses as naturally as if she'd always done so. After a moment he let her go and looking down into her face said, "If I'd known you were going to do that, I'd have kissed you before," and proceeded to kiss her again.

At last he said, "Now tell me, what's the problem?"

Rachel led him into the sitting room and they sat together on the sofa. "It's not a problem, exactly," she said, "just something rather sad, and I needed company."

"Tell me."

So, Rachel told him everything she had learned from the letters, and she read him the last from Tom and the letter from Sarah. As she did so her voice broke and she began to cry, tears sliding down her face as she imagined Molly's anguish when she received Sarah's letter and Tom's farewell. Nick put his arms round her and held her close. He said nothing, simply held her until she sniffed and said, "Sorry. Shouldn't be such a wimp."

He gave her his handkerchief and she blew her nose. He poured her a drink and handing her the glass said, "Does your grandmother know all this?"

"No, I don't think so. She says she never read the letters, and I shouldn't think anyone would have told her while she was a child."

"So this is your great-grandfather."

"Yes, and you know I'm sure that the ninth tree in the Ashgrove was planted for him. I think somehow Molly managed to plant it. You know they mention this chaplain, Smalley, who was with Tom at the end? Well he became the rector of Charlton Ambrose in 1921. He must be the same chap, don't you think? It would be too much of a coincidence if it was a different Henry Smalley." Rachel sipped her drink and went on, "In the paper at the time of his induction, it said that he had served at the front. I can't prove it, of course not without a lot of research, but if it was him, he could have helped Molly plant the tree, or at least known that she had. We shall never know for sure that the tree was for Tom Carter, but I'd like to think it was."

"Have you read all the letters now?" asked Nick

"Almost," Rachel replied. "There is one more envelope. It's bigger than the others and is not addressed or dated. I read the others in date order and decided to leave that one till last."

"Why not read it now?" suggested Nick. He was concerned about what it might contain and he thought he'd like to be with Rachel when she opened it.

"OK." Rachel set down her glass and reached for the last envelope. She turned it over in her hands. It was thick and brown, with nothing written on the outside, and its flap was stuck down. She fetched a knife and carefully slitting the envelope open, pulled out the contents. There was a smaller white envelope, also sealed and addressed to Rosemary Day. "I suppose that's Gran," said Rachel, but she was puzzled. She had always thought her grandmother's name was simply Rose. "That must be a letter for Gran. It's from Molly, look it's addressed in the same writing as the diary." She looked at it for a long moment and then regretfully set it aside unopened and turned her attention to the other things. There was an army pay book in the name of Thomas Carter, something wrapped in crumpled tissue paper and a black and white photograph. Rachel picked up the photo and held it to the light, and for the first time she saw Tom Carter's face. He was in uniform, his cap at a rather raffish angle. Looking straight at the camera, his expression was serious, but with slightest suspicion of a smile round his eyes. Rachel remembered the words Molly had used when she had received this photo, "very spruce". It was clearly a posed photo, taken specially to send her. His face was long and narrow, with a determined jut to the chin. His mouth, unsmiling, was straight, the lips full, and his eyes...? I know that expression, Rachel thought suddenly as she studied the picture. She put her hand over the bottom half of the face, and there were her grandmother's eyes, almost smiling at her, the faintly quizzical look Gran had when she was suspicious you were teasing her.

Rachel handed the picture to Nick. "It's him," she said. "That's Tom Carter. He's got Gran's eyes, well, or the other way around."

Nick took the picture and turned it over. On the back there was a French photographer's stamp and written in faded ink "February 1916".

"So it is," he said. "Has your grandmother ever seen one of him?"

Rachel shrugged still studying the picture. "I doubt it," she said. "I'll take it round tomorrow when I take her the letter."

She picked up the crumpled tissue paper and carefully unwrapped it. Into her hand fell a bracelet, its clasp in the shape of a heart. It was tarnished and black, but Rachel knew if she polished it up it would be silver. She held it up on her finger. "Tom gave her this for Christmas, when they got engaged," she said softly. "It was in the diary." She laid it gently back into its tissue. Everything in this last envelope belonged to Gran, and Gran had never known it was there.

Rachel sat for several moments in deep silence, her mind back in 1916, her heart aching for those who inhabited that time. In her researches they had become very real to her, and she ached for their pain and loss.

Nick watched her face and realised in that instant, just how much he loved this woman. She was unlike any woman he had ever known, some quality within her reaching out to him. She was beautiful, but it wasn't that. He'd known other beautiful women, and never had a shred of the feeling which engulfed him now. Rachel. He longed to hold her again, to make love to her, to share all that he was with her, and he longed from the inner depth of his being to protect her from the cares and dangers of the world. He thought about Tom Carter and realised he must have had just such feelings for Molly, enough to risk everything to protect her from the stigma of having a child out of wedlock. He had died because he tried to protect Molly, Nick thought. Would I do the same for Rachel? In that moment, he thought he would. Very dramatic! he told himself as he watched the firelight play on her face, but probably true.

He reached out for her hand and raised it to his lips. Rachel returned to the present and smiled at him.

"Sorry," she said, "miles away."

"Rachel," Nick said quietly, and his tone of voice caught her attention. "Rachel, have you any appendages I should know about?"

She looked at him quizzically for a moment, her expression unconsciously echoing the one in the photo. "No," she said. "Have you?"

Nick shook his head. "No," he said.

"Thank God for that," she said, and with a whoop of laughter Nick gathered her into his arms and kissed her fiercely.

Eventually she pulled away and said, a little breathlessly, "It doesn't mean I want any, though."

"Doesn't it?" smiled Nick. "I think I do."

Rachel wrinkled her nose at him. "Only think?"

"No," he said softly. "I know I do." His eyes held hers and it was she who lowered her gaze and looked away.

"I have to see an estate agent tomorrow," Nick said with an abrupt change of subject. "Shall we take your grandmother out for a pub lunch afterwards?"

Rachel smiled at him and said, "She'd love that."

"I expect you'll be going to see her in the morning," he said. "I'll pick you both up at lunch time."

Nick got to his feet and Rachel said, "Are you going?" she was surprised. She had asked him to come because she needed company, his company, and he had apparently dropped everything and driven straight over. He had kissed her to breathlessness and she had kissed him back and she had rather expected him to stay the night. She looked up at him, her face a little flushed, her eyes bright, but no longer with tears.

"Unless you ask me to stay," he replied.

Rachel suddenly knew that this was a pivotal point in her life. Independence was important to her, but now, amazingly so was this man, Nick. He knew how she valued her independence, he was giving her the choice, no, more than that, he was making her choose. It was too soon to choose, but she didn't want him to go.

"Will you stay?" she asked. "Please."

Nick's face broke into a delighted grin. "Since you ask me so nicely," he said, "I couldn't possibly refuse."

Twenty-three

Nick picked Rachel and Rose up from Cotswold Court at twelve-thirty. When the old lady was settled beside him in the front, the wheelchair in the boot and Rachel in the back, Nick said, "Well, where shall we go?"

"If you don't mind, Nick," Rose said, "I think I need to go to the King Arthur in Charlton Ambrose. After all that Rachel has told me this morning, I think I'd like to go back and see the place again."

Rachel had gone round to see Gran that morning, taking the biscuit tin and its contents with her.

"Hallo, darling, this is a nice surprise," said Gran. She busied herself in her little kitchen and made them coffee, while Rachel lit the gas fire to warm the room up.

"We're going out to lunch," Rachel called to her.

"Are we? How lovely. You'd better ring through to Mrs Drake and tell her I won't be in for lunch then."

By the time Rachel had spoken to the warden, the coffee was made and ready for her to carry into the sitting room.

"Who are we going to lunch with?" Gran asked as they settled themselves in front of the fire.

"Nick Potter."

"The one that sent his love?"

"That's the one."

"Good. I should like to have a look at him."

"Gran!" Rachel said warningly, but her grandmother just laughed.

"Don't worry," she said. "I'll be very discreet. Now then, tell me what brings you here."

Rachel pulled the biscuit tin from her bag and said, "This, Gran. I've been looking at the things that are in it, and one envelope is for you."

"For me?" Gran looked startled.

"There was one big brown envelope at the bottom," Rachel explained. "It was sealed, but it wasn't addressed to anyone, so I opened it. Inside were a few things which I'll show you in a minute, and a letter, addressed to you."

Rose Carson looked pale. "Who was it from? What did it say?"

"I haven't opened it," Rachel said, "but I think it must be from your mother. The writing on the envelope looks very like the writing in the diary." She held out the small white envelope and her grandmother took it, her hand shaking. She looked at the writing on the front, then she said, "I can't read it without my glasses, what does it say?"

"It's addressed to Rosemary Day. That's you, isn't it, Gran?"

"I haven't been Rosemary since she died," Gran said wonderingly.

"I didn't know it was your name," Rachel said.

"Rosemary for remembrance," her grandmother replied. "Open it for me, will you?"

Rachel slit the envelope open carefully and extracting the letter handed it to her. "I'll find your glasses," she said.

"No, you read it to me."

"Wouldn't you rather read to yourself first, Gran? I think you should." Rachel handed her her glasses.

"Do you know what it says?" asked Gran, taking the spectacles but not putting them on.

"Not for certain," Rachel replied, "but I think I can guess."

"Then you read it to me."

Rachel took the letter back and unfolded it. It was dated 3rd March 1924.

My dearest Rosemary,

If you are reading this then I am dead. I have no real reason to think that I am going to die, but we never know the future and I want to be sure you know the past. Your past. You know your father was killed in the war. His name was Tom Carter and he was a brave man. Don't let anyone tell you otherwise, but because he tried to come to me he was shot for desertion. He was not a deserter, he was not a coward. He fought in the first day of the Somme, which you will know by now was one of the most dreadful battles of the war. He did not run away, he rescued a wounded man from no man's land and took him to a dressing station. Then he came to look for me. He was court-martialled and shot. The padre who was there was our rector, Mr Smalley. He wasn't our rector then of course, he came here after the war. He knew Mr Freddie up at the manor, he had been at the front with him, so Squire gave him the living. He knew about me too because he had spent the last night with your father. When the troops came home at the end of the war, my cousin Tony Cook came with them. His brother Harry had been killed, he was a great friend of your father's. Tony told me he had been at Tom's shooting. He didn't know then that Tom was your father, he worked that out later from things he heard.

When the squire planted the trees for the memorial I asked Mr Smalley about planting a tree for Tom. He said no, it couldn't be done, especially as Tony knew what had happened to him and it would bring it all out into the open and everyone would know. I decided to do it anyway, and so I dug up an ash sapling from the copse above the village and we planted it with the others. You were with me, but I don't expect you remember. I put a paper in a photo frame with For the Unknown Soldier on it. When it was discovered squire wanted it dug up, but Mr Smalley knew why it was there and somehow persuaded him to leave it. Maybe he told him it was your father, I don't know, but he was allowed to dedicate it to the unknown soldier so that it became part of the memorial. So though Tom's name is not on the memorial in the church, he is not forgotten.

We left the village soon afterwards and came here to work. I couldn't stay with my parents any longer. Tony had told them what had happened and so we had to go.

If you are reading this letter I will not have had the chance to tell you all this myself. I have to wait until you are old enough to understand. The only things I have left of your father are his let-ters, the bracelet he gave me for Christmas 1915, his pay book, and the picture he had taken for me. Not much, but enough to remind me that he loved me. He was a dear brave man who'd had a hard life, and I loved him dearly. When he knew I was expecting you, he was pleased, even though we weren't married, because the one thing he wanted above all was a real family. Never doubt that he would have loved you as much as I do.

Your loving Mam

They sat in silence when Rachel stopped reading, Rachel watching her grandmother's expression, Rose Carson in a private globe of silence, pale, but dry-eyed.

"He was shot," she said at last.

"Yes," said Rachel.

"You knew?"

"Yes," said Rachel. "It was in the letters. His last letter, the one he wrote on the night before he was shot is with them. Also a letter from Sarah Hurst, breaking the news to Molly."

"How did Sarah find out?"

"She was still at the convent when it happened," explained Rachel. "The padre, this Henry Smalley, rode over to tell Molly himself, but she had already gone home."

"All these years," said Rose quietly. "All these years that

letter has been sitting there and I never knew." Silence enclosed them again for a while and then Rose said, "Do you know any more than what is in this letter?"

"I think so," Rachel said and began to tell her grand-mother the story of Molly and Tom that she had pieced together from the diary and the letters.

Their coffee grew cold, untouched in the cups as Rachel spoke, and when she had finished, both of them had tears on their cheeks. Rachel had read her grandmother Tom's last letter and the letter from Sarah, and the anguish in them had hit them both. Rose took the photograph of her father and stared at it, as if trying to commit it to memory. He stared back at her over more than eighty years, the faint smile lurking at the corner of his eyes his cap set at a jaunty angle on his short dark hair.

"You have his eyes, Gran," Rachel said softly.

"Do I?" Rose smiled sadly up at her. "I was always told I looked like my mother."

"You probably do, but he's there as well."

Rachel held out the tarnished bracelet and Rose took it, holding it to the light.

"We must clean that," Rachel said, "then you could wear it."

"No, I shan't wear it," Rose said handing it back. "I'd like you to have it."

"Are you sure?" asked Rachel. She held the bracelet against her cheek for a moment. "I'd love it, Gran, thank you."

They talked about the letters and the diary for a little while, and then Rachel said, "Would you rather not go out to lunch, Gran. I can easily put Nick off, you know."

"No, don't do that," replied Rose. "I'd like to go. I don't want to sit here brooding. Does he know about all this?"

Rachel nodded. "I phoned him last night when I had

read the letters. I needed someone to talk to. Do you mind?"

Rose shook her head. "No, I don't mind," she said, adding with a faint smile, "I'm glad you've found someone at last that you want to talk to."

Rachel felt herself blushing and said, "It's not like that, Gran."

"Isn't it?" said Gran innocently. "My mistake."

"Are you going to write about this?" Gran said after a moment. "In your Ashgrove story? You realise you have a vested interest in one of the trees now."

This thought had already occurred to Rachel, but she had set it aside as she came to terms with the events that made it so. The ninth tree belonged to Gran, and they had documentary evidence to prove it. They would have a say in whether the Ashgrove should be cut down.

"I don't know," Rachel said honestly. "It's an amazing story, the whole thing, but you may not want it to become a nine-days wonder, and I'm not sure I do either, even though it might help the campaign to save the Ashgrove."

"We don't have to decide now," Rose said. "We can take time to think about it."

Nick Potter had had a very successful morning and he was happy and excited when he arrived to pick up Rachel and her grandmother. Rachel had introduced them inside Rose's flat and each had immediately liked what they saw of the other. Rachel found herself beaming at both of them.

As they packed the wheelchair into the boot of his car he asked Rachel softly, "How did it go? Was she very shocked?"

"She was amazing," Rachel said. "She took it very well. I think it may come back to hit her later, but it doesn't matter if the subject comes up again, she knows you know, and she doesn't mind."

Nick smiled at her and said, "Good, because I've some exciting news. I'll tell you about it at lunch."

When they were comfortably settled in the bar of the Arthur and had ordered their food, Rachel turned to Nick and said, "Well what's this news then?"

"I've been busy this morning," Nick said. "I heard from my solicitor yesterday that we'd exchanged contracts on the house I wanted to buy in Charlton Ambrose."

"Nick, that's great," cried Rachel. "Which house is it?"

Nick didn't answer her but went on, "So I went to see Mike Bradley at Brigstock Jones."

"Mike Bradley? Whatever for?"

"I had a proposition to put to him."

"What sort of proposition?" asked Rachel. "Surely his office was still closed?"

"So it is," Nick said, "but I tracked him down at home. He wasn't that pleased to see me at first, but I convinced him that it was worth listening to me."

Rachel was intrigued. "And?"

"And I was right. We've the outline of a deal."

"What sort of deal?" asked Rachel the journalist.

"I think we may be able to save your Ashgrove," Nick said, "and still let the building go ahead."

Rachel stared at him, and he grinned a wolfish grin, pleased with the effect he was having.

"How?" she demanded.

"I've sold him my house."

"You've what?"

"I've sold him my house. You know where it is, its garden backs on to the allotments."

"But I still don't see..."

"Oh, Rachel," he laughed, "you disappoint me. I thought

you'd see at once. He will buy my house and knock it down, then he can put his access in through the space it creates instead of across the village green."

"You're joking!"

"No, darling girl, I'm not."

Rachel hardly noticed the endearment, but it was not lost on Rose and she smiled, sitting back watching them both and thinking Rachel had met her match in Nick.

"If Bradley buys my house for a reasonable price, and it is, let's face it, the sort of house that only commands a reasonable price, he can carry on with his development without touching either the village green or the Ashgrove."

"But even a reasonable price would put his figures out," objected Rachel the journalist.

"Not really, when he was already factoring in the cost of the compensation for the trees. This way it is a one-off payment, without the time and effort of tracing all the families. It avoids a wrangle about the amount of compensation, and actually," he added, "it will probably save him something on the cost of his access road. It'll be far shorter than the one round the village green."

"But what about the new hall?"

"Nothing changes there," said Nick. "That was part of the original deal for the land and had nothing to do with the Ashgrove."

"And he's going to do this?"

"Nothing agreed yet," Nick said. "He will have to talk to the planners and then apply for the permission, but in principle, yes, I think he will." He smiled the smile that usually made her heart beat faster and said quietly, "I think your trees are safe, Rachel."

"He may have problems with the families who think they

are in line for compensation," Rachel the journalist pointed out. "They'll think you've taken all their money."

"That is ludicrous," Nick said sharply. "I shall be selling my house anyway, it doesn't matter to me who buys it, or what they do with it when they have."

"No, I know," began Rachel doubtfully, "but I don't want you to end up the big bad wolf in all this."

"I've broad shoulders," Nick assured her, "but I really can't see that there'll be a problem."

"Well, I think it is a splendid plan," interrupted Rose. "It should satisfy everyone concerned. The memorial will remain undisturbed, the houses will be built, everyone gets what they want."

"Except those expecting a hefty compensation," repeated Rachel.

"There will be nothing to compensate them for," Nick said reasonably. "Their trees will be untouched." There was a pause and then he went on, "I thought you'd be pleased, Rachel, 'specially as you have a personal interest in one of the trees now."

"I am, of course, I am," Rachel assured him, "as a person, but as a journalist I have to look at every angle."

"I know," Nick said with a sigh. "I suppose I'll have to get used to that."

Their food arrived at that moment and when it had been served, Rose said in the hope of easing the tension that still lay in the air, "You didn't tell us, Nick, which house you have bought?"

Nick grinned at her and said, "No, I didn't, did I?"

"So, where is it?"

"I thought you might like to come and see it after lunch," he said, still not answering the question. "I picked up the keys from the estate agent this morning."

When they left the pub Rose said she would like to go over to the Ashgrove and look at it properly, so they wheeled her along the track and across the green.

It was a cold but sunny afternoon, and the bare branches stood out against the ice-blue sky. Some of the wider branches reached out to each other, their tips touching as they moved with the breeze.

"I wonder which one is Tom's," said Rachel.

"I've been trying to think back," Rose said. "I have this recollection of being here in the dark and being scared, but I've no idea which tree my mother planted."

Rachel moved to each tree, placing her hand on its trunk, feeling the roughness of the bark, wishing she could tell. Then she turned and smiled at her grandmother, "Come on, Gran, you'll get cold."

They went back to the car and Nick drove up the lane past the church slowing to turn in at the gates of the manor.

"I should have guessed," said Rachel almost to herself.

Nick laughed. "Yes, you should," he said. "I told you, a new roof and re-wiring!"

They drove up the weed-covered drive and pulled up on the turning circle outside the front door.

"I haven't been here since I was a little girl," Rose said wonderingly. "I came here once with my mother, but I don't know why. She left me in the garden while she went in. I remember the lion."

The panelled front door stood within a portico and beside the step was an old stone lion, its features weathered almost smooth, but its mane still curling round its head.

"I think I'll stay in the car, if you don't mind," Rose said. "You two go on inside."

As Nick opened the front door, Rachel went to the lion and

ran her hand over its head, realising as she did so that she must be echoing many another hand, the stone was so smooth.

The door opened into a square hall with doors opening off it and a staircase curving up to the first floor. Nick stood in the hall, looking round him and Rachel said softly, "Have you really bought this?"

Nick grinned at her, "Me and the bank," he said. "I saw it in the summer and simply fell for it, even though it needs a cartload of money spent on it."

Rachel laughed. "Have you got a cartload?" she asked.

"Not even a wheel-barrowful," said Nick cheerfully. "But it doesn't all need to be done at once. Come on, I'll show you round."

He took her hand and together they wandered round the house where Sarah and Freddie Hurst had grown up; where Molly Day had worked, cleaning and polishing. The house from which they had all three left for the war and to which none of them had returned. Rachel found herself trying to see the house as it would have been then, not the tired, dirty place it was now, just empty rooms in a once gracious home. The drawing room, high-ceilinged with its Adam fireplace, filthy but intact, looked across what had once been a lawn and the windows of what must have been the library faced west, catching the last of the sun. They went into the kitchen, which contained only an old stone sink, shelves along one wall and some hooks in the ceiling. There was nothing to heat the place, or to cook on. The windows gave onto a yard at the back and an old stable block, sometime converted into garages.

All the downstairs rooms were completely bare, their floor-length sash windows looking out over the wilderness of garden beyond.

"How long since anyone lived here?" asked Rachel with a shiver.

"Several years," replied Nick. "It was left in trust by the last owner, to someone in Canada, so all that had to be sorted before I could buy it."

Upstairs, the bedrooms were large and airy, the single bathroom cold and dark, with brown paint and ancient plumbing. One of the bedrooms had a window seat with an old padded cushion on it, and Rachel could imagine Sarah sitting there, looking out over the garden, watching the moon rise.

"Quite a bit to do, you see," said Nick cheerfully as they inspected it, "but it has great possibilities, don't you think?"

Rachel laughed. "There speaks the architect," she teased. They went up to the servants' quarters on the third floor, peering into the little rooms that had been partitioned off for servants' quarters. Rachel wondered which of them had been Molly's.

Nick took her hand again and they went back down to the car, but as they reached the hall, Nick pulled Rachel gently into his arms. "I'm buying this house, whatever," he said, "and I'm selling the other."

Rachel looked up at him and said, "I know. I shouldn't have said what I did. I'm sorry."

"Don't be," he said "It was Rachel the journalist who spoke then, and she had every right to." He kissed her then, standing in the dusty hall of the house where her great-grandmother had been a maid, before saying, "Come on, or Rose will be getting cold."

Epilogue

The wind whipped among the spiky black buds of the ash trees, but the crowd gathered round them was well wrapped up in the uncertain March weather. Even those in wheelchairs, with blankets round their knees and muffled in scarves and gloves, ignored the cold and waited expectantly.

Mary Bryson sat in her chair, surrounded by her children, grandchildren and great-grandchildren. Rose Carson had Rachel on one side and Nick Potter on the other. Peter Davies and his wife stood between the two trees on the extreme left, and Cecily Strong was with her niece, Harriet, beside the tree on the right. There was a murmur of conversation as the small groups gathered, and more people walked across the green to join the growing crowd.

Rachel had worked long and hard tracing the families of the men on the church memorial and had reasonable success. Only the family of Corporal Gerald Winters were not represented, and, try as she might, Rachel had been unable to trace them. Sergeant Hapgood's family still lived in Belcaster, and his great nephew, Paul Hapgood, had been fascinated to hear that one of the Ashgrove trees, which had caused such a stir in the paper recently, commemorated his grandfather's brother.

"*I shall certainly attend the dedication of the stones,*" he had written to Rachel in reply to her invitation.

She traced Alfred Chapman's family through the parish records, discovering that his daughter Jane had indeed married a man from Belmouth, as Cecily had thought, and, though she had died just a year ago, her three sons and one daughter were alive and well, and living in Belmouth. They would all like to be there for the service. Rachel's greatest triumph was finding the descendants of Freddie Hurst. His daughter, Adelaide, had been adopted by her stepfather and had taken his name, but his surname, Anson-Gravetty, had been unusual enough for her to pick up the trail, and Adelaide's grandson James Auckland was standing with his wife in the gathering crowd.

Under each tree was a small wedge of granite, engraved with the name and dates of the man it commemorated and hooded with a canvas cover. As part of his public relations exercise, Mike Bradley had agreed that Brigstock Jones should donate the stones and Rachel had researched them all with the War Graves Commission, to ensure each was correctly engraved. The crowd was swollen with people who had come out from Belcaster, the press, and not just the *Belcaster Chronicle*. The national press had latched on to the stories that Rachel had been telling each week in the paper and had come to see the dedication of the stones for the famous Ashgrove for themselves. Mike Bradley was there, with Tim Cartwright from Brigstock Jones, making sure any favourable publicity going came their way, and to add to the solemnity of the occasion, all the workers on the embryo building site beyond the trees ceased work and came over to watch the ceremony.

The buzz of conversation died away as the rector, Adam Skinner, came across the green, in cassock and surplice, and the service of dedication began. It was not long, there was an introductory prayer, a simple explanation of why they were there, and then he went to each stone, removed its canvas cover and read aloud the soldier's name. As he reached the tree off centre at the back, Rachel gripped her grandmother's hand. The rector drew off the cover, and there for the first time, with tears in their eyes, they saw the stone with the simple inscription,

PRIVATE THOMAS CARTER

1ST BELSHIRE LIGHT INFANTRY

1893–1916

Rachel leaned down and kissed her grandmother on the cheek and whispered, "He'll never be forgotten now."

They joined in the Lord's Prayer and then Freddie's great-grandson read the Laurence Binyon poem. As he read the final lines

"AT THE GOING DOWN OF THE SUN, AND IN THE MORNING

WE WILL REMEMBER THEM"

the crowd echoed the words "We *will remember them*", before a bugler played the Last Post, followed by two minutes' silence.

When the ceremony was over, Nick took Rose back to the manor while Rachel did her journalist bit on the village green. He had moved in three weeks before, having made the kitchen useable and two other rooms habitable, and was camping out as the necessary work on the house was done. Wombat gave them an ecstatic greeting, and jumped up on to Rose's knee, sure of his welcome. He and Rose had become old friends.

"How are you coping?" Rose asked Nick, as he brought her a cup of tea. They, too, were comfortable together, their friendship having grown over the months he and Rachel had been together.

"Not too badly," Nick said. "In some ways I'd have preferred to have got a bit more done before I moved, but Bradley needed the access to the building site. Still," he smiled, "I love the house and I'm glad to be living in it." He thought for a moment and then said, "Do you think Rachel might live in it with me, one day?" So far her independence had demanded that she keep her own flat.

Rose laughed. "Don't ask me," she said, "ask her!"

"Oh, I will," Nick assured her with a grin.

When Rachel got back to the house almost an hour later she was flushed and excited. She had spoken to all the families who were connected with a memorial tree and had arranged proper interviews with the few whom she had only met for the first time that day.

She flopped down in an armchair and said, "It went well, don't you think? The Ashgrove is a real memorial again, now." She smiled at the two favourite people in her life and went on, "And I've more news, two letters came today," she said. "Perfect timing!"

"Who from," asked Rose.

"One's from the convent at St Croix. You know I wrote to them, Gran, about Sarah? Listen I'll read it to you." Rachel extracted a letter from her bag and read,

7th March 2002

Dear Miss Elliott,

Thank you for your letter of enquiry about Sister Marie-Pierre. I am sorry to take so long to respond. She joined our Sisters in 1917. In 1938 she was elected Reverend Mother. During the Nazi occupation in the war, she sheltered many Jewish children

in the convent and in 1943 she was arrested by the Gestapo
and sent to a camp. She was never heard of again and we can
only imagine that she died continuing the Lord's work there.

Our numbers are small now, but we too continue in the
Lord's work, looking after the elderly.

With prayers and blessings

Marie-Therese
Mother Superior
Convent of Our Lady of Mercies

Rachel looked up at them, bright-eyed. "So, you see, Sarah
was an unsung heroine in both wars," she said. "She must
have been very brave don't you think? Now that I know the
end of it, I can write her story. If he knew what she had
achieved, I don't think Sir George would have been disappointed in her after all, do you?"

"No," agreed her grandmother. "I think he'd have been
proud of her." She smiled at the eager Rachel and asked,
"Who was the other letter from, then? You're obviously very
pleased with that one as well."

Rachel beamed at her and produced the other letter saying,
"This is the other one, and it affects us more. You know I told
you I wrote to the Belshires' Regimental Archivist about Tom?
Well, his reply came today as well. Listen. "

10th March 2002

Dear Miss Elliott,

Thank you for your letter of the 25th February. I was very
interested in what you had to tell us about Private 8523241
Thomas Carter of the 1st Battalion, Belshires. Of course, we
knew of his execution in 1916 from our regimental records.
In view of the move to obtain pardons for men shot for de-

sertion and cowardice during the 1914–18 war, and in line with other regiments, we have already restored his name to the Regimental Roll of Honour. We are delighted to hear that he will also be commemorated in the Charlton Ambrose War Memorial Ashgrove, and that his daughter, Mrs Rose Carson will be at that ceremony.

Yours sincerely

David Hobart
Curator of the Belshire Regimental Archives

"So," Rachel said, "all we need now is a pardon from the government." Smiling at the surprise on the faces of Nick and her grandmother, she went on, "There's a campaign already up and running, called the Shot at Dawn campaign, which is working for just that, and I'm going to join it. That's what we need, a pardon for Tom and all the others like him." And looking at the determination in her face, Nick knew she would never give up until she had got it.

THE END

To the Shot at Dawn Campaign

The Shot at Dawn Campaign

Tom Carter is fictitious, but he stands for the three hundred and six soldiers of the British Army who were shot at dawn during the First World War for alleged desertion, cowardice, or for refusing to carry out an order. Little account was taken of medical conditions such as shell shock; courts martial were brief and the executions were used as a deterrent to other would-be deserters as much as for a punishment for the alleged offence.

The Shot at Dawn Campaign for posthumous pardons for these men has been growing steadily. The government still refuses to pardon the men, many of them only boys in their teens when they were shot. It maintains you cannot rewrite history, but the campaigners are undeterred. They fight on. History, they say, is continually being rewritten as new evidence emerges. Evidence of these executions was kept secret for seventy-five years, but now it has been released action should be taken to put right an undoubted wrong.

Many of the regiments from which the men came have reinstated their names to their regimental Rolls of Honour. It is now time for a government which supported the campaign whilst in opposition to follow the government of New Zealand and grant pardons to these men. They died for their country as surely as did the men who went over the top.

Since the first edition of this book, The Shot at Dawn Campaign has achieved its aim. Due to the determination of the campaigners, led by John Hipkin, pardons have now been granted to all 306 men who were executed.

"The campaign for posthumous pardons has been rejected by the Ministry of Defence for no other reason then their belief that without the power to kill British Troops who cannot stand the strain it would not be possible to force them to kill the enemy."

Tony Benn, 2004